Time and Trouble

Also by Gillian Roberts

The Amanda Pepper series:

Gillian Roberts

Time and
Trouble

St. Martin's Press
New York

For
Alan and Barbara Greber
Joe and Nicole Greber
Deborah and John Dent
with major love

A THOMAS DUNNE BOOK.
An imprint of St. Martin's Press.

TIME AND TROUBLE. Copyright © 1998 by Judith Greber. All rights reserved. Printed in the United States of America. No part of this book
may be used or reproduced in any manner whatsoever without written
permission except in the case of brief quotations embodied in critical articles or reviews. For information, address St. Martin's Press, 175 Fifth
Avenue, New York, N.Y. 10010.

Design by Bryanna Millis

Library of Congress Cataloging-in-Publication Data

Roberts, Gillian.
    Time and trouble/Gillian Roberts.—1st ed.
        p.   cm.
    "A Thomas Dunne book."
    ISBN 0-312-18673-8
    I. Title.
    PS3557.R356T56   1998
    813'.54—dc21   98-4768
                                                                CIP

First Edition: June 1998

10   9   8   7   6   5   4   3   2   1

Acknowledgments

Many, many, thanks to these people for their patience, goodwill, and expertise: Jane Walsh for avian information; Susan Dunlap and Marilyn Wallace for the selfless act of critiquing this work-in-progess while I gallivanted; my editor, Ruth Cavin, for her enthusiastic gift of life to the book; my agent, Jean Naggar for just plain being great; Robert Greber for graciously enduring my see-saw ride and for making me laugh about it, and Kathleen Martin's entire now-graduated fifth grade class at St. Martin de Sales in Philadelphia for invoking truly great powers on my behalf!

Time and trouble will tame an advanced young woman, but an advanced old woman is uncontrollable by any earthly force.

—Dorothy Sayers

Time and Trouble

One

Emma sat with her feet on top of her desk. It made her feel taller and it eased a nagging tightness in the small of her back, so she could concentrate on the man on the other end of the line. He was infinitely annoying. He was also right.

"Of course I can deliver," she said. "You know me, Harold. You know my agency. It's not like we're the new kids on the block." He was not satisfied. His insurance clients expected a quick response, and so did he. Hadn't she said the reports would be ready? This was a competitive world, hard facts, friendship's one thing, business another. And damn but he was right, which left her with nothing but bluster. The report was late and going to be later. Dobson was supposed to have done it, but Dobson was gone, had quit her. Her agency was crumbling, losing employees like so many rotten teeth. Two this week, Dobson and the idiot receptionist–slash–office manager temp who'd replaced the last incompetent temp.

Philosophical differences, the dolt had said, packing her lifetime supply of tissue and allergy pills. As if she could spell *philosophy,* let alone have one. And Dobson, after all this time, claiming personality differences, whatever asinine inconsequential nit-picking issues he meant. He'd said she had a reputation for being impossible. Asked if she'd wondered why she couldn't keep employees. Snapped, "Hire a detective and find out why!"

"Let the delivery date be my problem," she said into the phone. Not much of an offer since it, along with everything else, already was her problem. Nobody left to share the burden, unless Atlas dropped the world and shouldered her load.

She heard a halfhearted, mousy knock. Who? Why? She leaned forward as much as she could, given the straight-out position of her legs, and pushed papers around the surface of her desk with her free hand. Where was that note from the answering service? What time was her next appointment?

The door opened a slice. A head poked around it. Emma's shoes framed a blonde. Pale. Straitlaced. Mid-twenties.

"Mrs. Howe?" The voice was timid and low, but it nonetheless sounded of training. Elocution lessons. How now, brown cow. "There's nobody in the outer office," it continued. "I waited, but then I thought—is this all right? I'm sorry—you're on the phone. Should I—Where do you want me?"

Two to one she was selling cosmetics. Had ignored the No Solicitors sign downstairs.

No. She was too fresh-scrubbed, up-with-America wholesome to be pushing makeup. Make that household—office—cleaning supplies.

Emma waved her hand in a *Scat!* motion while Harold, on the other end of the line, continued complaining. "Early next week," she promised into the phone. "You have my word." What was Harold going to do? Start all over with a new investigator? That'd set him back more than Dobson's defection had.

The head at the door stayed put. "But we— I—I was told to—"

"Busy!" Emma hissed. "Not talking to you, Harold. Somebody just popped—" She shooed the blonde with her hand. Did not need a cleanser peddler. Did not ever need that shiny species of woman.

Organized and efficient. Homework in on time, no coloring outside the lines, never a detention, the Good Citizen award at graduation. But the only things she'd know would be what she'd memorized.

Emma made further promises to Harold and hung up.

The young woman was still at the door. "Mrs. Howe," she said with more authority, "we have an appointment. I'm Billie August."

For Christ's sake. Emma pushed back in her chair and pulled her legs off the desk.

"*Billy* August," the idiot temp had written. As if that sweet-li'l-me voice wouldn't have sounded a trifle high-pitched for a Billy.

Emma cleared her throat. "Sorry. I thought— Never mind. Sit down. The receptionist's ill."

Billie settled into her chair elegantly, crossing her legs at the ankles, the way good girls should. "Mrs. Howe, I—"

"Ms. Or Emma."

"Miz Howe, I want you to understand how eager I am to—"

She wanted the job. Shiny-head wanted to be a private investigator. Of course it wouldn't work. For a million reasons, it couldn't. Although Emma Howe of all humans wasn't prejudiced against her own sex, still and all, she hadn't imagined replacing Dobson with a female. It had always been Emma, the boss, with two or three men working for her. There was a pride in that, versus something embarrassing about adding another woman. Particularly now that it would be just the two of them, at least for a while.

Emma's all-girl agency. She would die before admitting anything like that out loud, but damned if those words weren't singsonging in her mind with all the mortifying force they might have had on a third-grade playground.

And even if she did take on another woman, it wouldn't be this one with her no-risk perfection, her pale hair, straight features, and Career Dressing suit. She looked more like the next Grace Kelly than an investigator.

The woman passed her a manila envelope. "My résumé. Your receptionist said to bring it with me, since the appointment was so soon after I'd called."

Emma skimmed the page and tried not to laugh out loud. Boarding school in Connecticut. A fine-arts degree with a double major in drama and music. Of what human use was this hothouse flower?

"Is there a problem?" the young woman asked.

"Why?"

"You're shaking your head." She leaned forward, all eager Junior Leaguer. Whatever she was wearing smelled expensive. Eau de Right Side of the Tracks.

"No problem. I was reading your . . ." Might as well be honest. Or at least sound that way. "Frankly, before we get— The truth is, I was hoping for somebody with more ex—"

"Excuse me, but your ad said interest and aptitude were required, not experience. Or did I misread it?"

Spoken crisply and forcibly, like a well-bred drill sergeant who didn't need to shout. The sweet-li'l-me voice was so far gone Emma doubted that she'd ever heard it. "You read the ad correctly," she reluctantly admitted.

"Good. I assumed you'd prefer a novice. That way, you pay the minimum for six thousand hours. Win-win. I learn, and you have cheap labor for years."

Damn cocky, acting like she had the job just because she showed up. Emma's skin prickled with resentment, then she backed off and tried to understand what it was about this Billie that set her teeth on edge, made her thoughts ping every which way like angry pinballs. Her looks? She was the cultural ideal, not Emma's. Nothing about her appearance she had to compensate for, hide, or "cleverly disguise" as the magazines would have it. Two strikes against her right there, maybe?

But Emma had thought—had decided, had believed—that the gift of midlife was being through with all that. In her mid-fifties, she was no longer a contender in the sexual sweeps. No longer expending effort to meet some impossible definition of what was feminine and "right." You weren't even called "well preserved" at that age. Preserved for what? Nobody was waiting. Far as the world was concerned, you were out of the game, benched for life.

Which was fine with Emma. She never liked their game, and thoroughly enjoyed her own. She'd always felt as if she were sitting on a high tree branch, watching the prefabricated, pathetic lives of other girls. It seemed to her that at birth, girl children were set in line, in hateful competition one with the other, like racehorses, slapped on their behinds and told to get going—see who could be the best of breed, and told precisely what "best" meant.

Emma had always run the other way. She had a great time—but lost the race according to them. A tomboy, they called her. A hellion. Her hair was never sufficiently smooth, her contours never sufficiently voluptuous, her mouth and manners never sufficiently controlled.

And the freeing, secret magic of reaching her fifties was that none of it mattered anymore. She was finally well and truly her own woman, and entirely comfortable with her custom-tailored life and standards.

So what did it mean that here she was, glaring at this Billie person because she looked like everything "they" approved of, was young, smooth-skinned and fresh-faced, and didn't have creaky joints even on this rainy winter morning. Humiliating to have suffered an attack of hundred-proof competitive venom, rancor at the way nature worked. Can't have it both ways, she told herself. Can't live a long and interesting time and still be young. Your quarrel is with the facts of life, not with Billie August.

Emma was proud of her talent for objectively sizing people up, but here she'd been, jerking her knee so hard she'd nearly blinded herself with it.

"I read the feature about you and your agency in the *I.J.*," Billie was saying. "I was impressed by— I'm not trying to flatter you, just to explain why I'm here, why I was so excited when I saw your ad. I admire what you've done. Your courage and determination and smarts. Because you pioneered in this field and then started your own agency." She smiled and gesticulated, manicured nails and long fingers intimating that there were no words that could adequately express her admiration.

Emma forgave her for being young, enthusiastic and attractive, and for shamelessly flattering her. For not having arthritic twinges and for spending her college tuition on piano and acting classes. But all the same, if she was revving-up to say she needed a mentor or role model, Emma was going to terminate the interview. She needed an employee, not a groupie or fan. Touchy-feely made her gag.

"—and that you were also a single mother," Billie said.

How noble that *Independent Journal* article made her sound. How tactful and kind, if not entirely accurate, the interviewer had been. Heartstring-tearing. Bring your business to the widderwoman.

Emma had told her the truth. But the reporter hadn't chosen to mention that Emma's widowhood and sleuthing had begun simultaneously. Cause and effect.

Harry Howe's heart had not been up to the triple threat of gambling losses, a shaky employment status, and the demands of extramarital sex. When Harry keeled over, his frolicking partner—whose identity became the widow Emma's first very private investigation—chose not to call the paramedics, police, or even the occupant of the next motel room. Chose not to dress the man or pull a sheet over his sad naked bottom before she took off. Instead, when she was safely elsewhere, she phoned Emma to say, anonymously, where she could find her husband in flagrante deado.

Emma wondered how little Miss Eager across the desk would have reacted to the real story, and whether she would still have applied here, all aflutter.

"You raised your kids and ran this place and managed things I need to manage," Billie said. "I want to work with you and learn from you."

She hadn't said the word *mentor*. A technical victory, but still, Emma felt relieved. And annoyed. She'd hoped the profile would bring in clients—not job applicants.

"I think everyone needs—" Billie was interrupted by the high whine of a fire engine outside on Fourth Street.

Emma pushed back her chair and went to investigate. All she saw were umbrellas and rainhoods one story below, and a low dark sky above them. El Nino, they said, although it seemed just another damn rainy January to her. She shrugged and went back to her desk and lifted her stained coffee cup. "Can't see anything," she said. "It isn't us."

In other cities Emma had visited, sirens attracted no particular attention, but here, even across the bay from San Francisco, even in a winter downpour, there was always a second's frozen reaction to the warning of a fire, like the collective unconscious of 1906, always referred to as "The Fire of," not "The Quake of." Reinforced—in case anybody had forgotten—by the Oakland firestorm eighty-plus years later. Fire was out there, along with earthquakes, like the cry of a timber wolf in the wilderness. Everything you know could be gone in a moment.

"Want coffee?" Emma gestured at mugs hanging from the prongs of a Victorian hatstand above a coffeemaker.

Miss Prim shook her head. "Thanks anyway," she murmured.

Emma refilled her cup. "You were saying something about what a woman needs?" The girl had been on the verge of something either offensively sensitive and New Age or, God help us, stale and Freudian.

"I honestly can't remember. Forgive me."

Emma brought the coffee back to her desk, spilling some in the process. She put her stained cup down, wiped a bead of coffee from a file folder and looked at Billie's application again, although she really didn't need to. "Given your background," she said, "your education, I would think you'd want something in the arts."

"Well, something creative. But that's part of the appeal of this kind of work. It's as you said: Different challenges all the time. Not a daily routine."

She'd memorized the damn article. "But," Emma said, "skip-tracing is hardly spurred by the same impulse as, say, interpreting a sonata. Or starring in . . ." She peered at the résumé. ". . . *Uncle Vanya.*"

Billie August took a deep breath designed to be heard in the third balcony. "I included those things so you'd know I'm not afraid of talking to people or of playing a role. In fact, I'm good at both of them."

"But would you like it? Is this really what interests you?"

"With all due apologies, what interests me more than anything is how I can provide a decent life for myself and my son and not be bored silly meanwhile. Acting is about the least dependable profession I can think of. If I wanted to try, I'd have relocated, but I'm either not good enough or not driven enough. Doesn't matter which. As for teaching, school budgets for the arts are nonexistent and I don't want to be that nice neighborhood lady who gives piano lessons. Even if I could stay alive doing that."

"Let me see if I've got this. You don't want to move to L.A. or New York and wait tables and act, and you don't want to teach kids scales. And once those jobs are eliminated, investigating is left as the only option?"

Billie grinned. "I am currently working at The Final Touch—we sell scarves, belts, and earrings. Accessories. I can also type. Clean houses. Sell shoes at Nordstrom, get my broker's license or perform telephone sex. The thing is—this is what I want to do."

Emma sat back and steepled her fingers.

"I am able-bodied, intelligent, cooperative, adequately creative, and not particularly afraid," Billie said. "Did I forget anything?"

"Loyal, steadfast, never planned to overthrow the government . . ."

"And I can program my VCR."

"Mechanical aptitude duly noted."

"Miz Howe." Billie's voice pitched low, her head tilted and her eyes narrowed. "I sense reservation on your part. I trust you do not suffer from pigmentation intolerance."

"From . . . ? Not that I know——" Emma put her hand to her cheek. Was something wrong with her coloring? Was this some goddamn new politically incorrect offense? "What are you talking about? What's 'pigmentation intolerance'?"

"A critical inability to believe that blondes have brains."

Emma gave a half-nod of acknowledgement. "Touché," she said.

Billie wasn't smiling. "I do not put Wite-Out on the computer screen."

"Why is it that you never hear jokes about gray-haired women? At least not about our IQs." Emma ran her fingers through close-cropped silvery hair at the nape of her neck. "Never heard of a ditzy . . . There isn't even a word for us. Blondes, brunettes, redheads, and . . . old ladies. Not so great in the world at large, maybe, but a plus in this business. We go unnoticed. Even if we color our hair."

"But if you're thinking a young woman—— I can be invisible, too. Honestly. I'm kind of a blank without makeup. I can make myself look lots of ways, including barely noticeable."

Emma understood what the other woman meant, although she knew that no female in her twenties——no well-built, pretty blonde, no matter how much makeup she left off or put on, no matter what she did with her dress and no matter how bad a hair day she had—— could comprehend just how invisible, even fully bedecked and trying her best, a middle-aged woman could be.

Time would teach her that. Emma didn't have to. "So you think this job is creative. You think you'll be reinventing yourself a lot, wearing disguises, shooting——"

"I didn't—"

"It isn't like that. It's not like in the movies."

"I know that."

"You're mostly checking records, accessing databases, surveilling rotten husbands or crooked employees or insurance fakes, or finding the addresses of poor dummies who never heard of *The Maltese Falcon*."

Billie sat straighter. "I'd be good at that. I'm an excellent researcher. Good enough to have already read everything I could find about what it is you do. And to be computer-literate. And to have at least a rudimentary idea of accessing information online."

The sugarplum fairy had a solid core. Wonder if she would last. Wonder if the agency would last. Her research skills weren't foolproof—look, she applied for a job with a company everybody else quit. But let her find that out for herself.

"Here's something you should know," Emma said. "This may be the Bay Area and all, but what we are is hired investigators. Our job is to find information for our clients—and deciding whether clients *deserve* it is none of our business."

"Why would you—"

"Because there is a local geographical imperative to be outraged, to protest and picket and have opinions. Something in the air, maybe. But even if you're an animal rightist and we have a furrier who needs to know who's threatening him, or you're hell-bent on saving the black-antennaed slug from extinction, and a developer needs information about its breeding ground, or if we're getting information to help the defense of a sadistic child-abuser, or doing corporate investigation for a company you think is the very definition of oppressive or sexist, or—"

"I believe I catch your drift."

"Then what else?"

"Meaning?"

"What else should I know about you? Tell me about yourself."

"You have my résumé."

Emma waved the air above the application, dismissing it. "Statistics. Schools, jobs, acting roles, marital status. So you're twenty-eight, you can act, you're smart, you're divorced, and you have a son. You've lived at your current address for four years. Is that it for who you are and why I should hire you?" She raised her eyebrows. "Tell me whatever you think I should know. Bearing in mind, of course, that I am a detective."

"And you will find it out, anyway," Billie murmured.

"Whatever." There were so many damned regulations about interviews, about what you could and couldn't ask. Emma had found that if she simply did nothing, stayed unresponsive longer than was socially acceptable—too long—people felt impelled to fill the vacuum and reveal more about themselves than she could have gotten through a dozen interviews.

She folded her hands and waited.

Two

Emma Howe was a boulder. As gray as rock and just as impervious in a rough-wool sweater the color of steel, baggy dirt-colored slacks, and shoes that looked like prosthetic devices.

The woman on the other side of the desk was not what Billie had expected. The *I.J.* photographer had found so many kind angles he must have been a contortionist. Not that she was ugly—she had a good face and a strong, compact body—and not that Billie had expected a fluffy, maternal woman, but the photo had suggested a warmth and spark that turned out to be conspicuously missing. Or deliberately withheld.

Emma Howe was stony as a mean-spirited Buddha, wanting Billie to blather, to nervously provide ammunition that could be used to shoot her down.

She had to say something, but it was easier to think of what she would not tell the hummock. She wouldn't say that The Final Touch had been renamed The Final Gasp when it was locked shut this afternoon. And good riddance. Billie could not, for the life of her, generate enthusiasm for what her now-bankrupt employer called "the magic of inspired accessorizing." She had been working on an escape plan for months, but the store had staggered and died too soon. There was a sickening uncertainty as to whether her employer had

paid Unemployment Comp for her and meantime, Billie had precisely two more weeks of working capital. Enough for one mortgage,
PG&E, and telephone payment, ten days of extended nursery school,
five jumbo jars of peanut butter, and a large box of dry milk. As little as this job would pay, and as long as her apprenticeship would be,
this was nonetheless her ticket to eventual independence. To a life.
And if she didn't get it, she'd have to scramble for another dead-end
job, and with a little boy and a mortgage, she wouldn't have further
options for a dozen years.

Let Supersleuth find that out for herself.

"I grew up all over the map," Billie said. "New York, Illinois,
Georgia, Massachusetts, Texas, Arizona, and California. And for a
brief stint, Germany. My father was—still is, in fact—an executive
with what's been nicknamed the 'I've Been Moved' Corporation. We
were transferred every few years. My parents were in Santa Monica
when they divorced. I was in boarding school in Connecticut."

"Your parents still alive?"

"Yes." What did that have to do with anything?"

Emma Howe sipped greasy-looking coffee and relapsed into silence.

The rain and fog coated the window glass. Billie felt submerged
with this unyielding woman. She was tempted to lean across the
desk and poke at her. *Why should you be disappointed by me?* she'd demand. *Did you expect Sherlock Holmes to show up, eager to do scutwork for
next to nothing? This place doesn't look thriving*—and why was she supposed to believe in that suddenly ill receptionist? There wasn't a
nameplate for her, or any evidence of work left half-done on the
desk.

The boulder waited.

"There's this," Billie said. "I always did well in school. But I found
out I was smart—or I found out what smart was—when I worked
as an office temp in college; family finances took a nosedive after the
divorce. Wherever I'd go, no matter what piece of fancy electronic

equipment or word-processing program or machine they asked about, I said I knew how to use it. Once I had the job, I'd say the last fax or computer or whatever had been a little different, could somebody take a second to show me how this gizmo worked so that I didn't hurt anything? The point is that if I'd been honest, I wouldn't have gotten any of the jobs—and they wouldn't have gotten a good worker."

"This agency isn't exactly the equivalent of a copy machine," Emma said.

Bitch! Would it hurt to give a little? "I'm smart enough to think on my own and to pick up whatever's learnable. Whatever you're willing to teach me."

The boulder very slightly nodded.

"And you're probably worrying about my son," Billie added. "I know you're not allowed to ask how I'm going to work child care, but of course you'd think about it."

"Our hours do tend to be erratic," Emma said.

There was the slightest whiff of victory in the air. "That's why I was so impressed," Billie said softly. "You had two children and managed."

"They were older."

"A student at Sonoma State lives at my house rent-free in exchange for baby-sitting. Classes are scheduled for when my son's in nursery school. But in case of emergency, or conflict of any kind, two backup students with different class hours are on call. I'm covered twenty-four hours a day."

"Impressive," Emma said. "Ambitious."

Damn close to a compliment. Billie moved in for the kill. "I should mention this, too. I found my son."

"A foundling? As in Charles Dickens?"

"No. When he was two, my ex-husband disappeared with him. The police couldn't find Cameron or Mr. Macdougal. It took me seven months, but I found them."

"Excuse me, but Mr. Macdougal is your ex?"

"My ex-husband is Cameron Jay Smith. Mr. Macdougal is the name of a little man in a children's book, and what my son—whose name is Jesse—called himself when he turned two, which is right before he was taken. It was a short phase, but it lasted long enough to help me find him."

"How's that?"

Was she actually interested? Billie controlled the urge to smile. "Cameron's an artist. Makes money on the side doing house painting, carpentry, general handyman work. He has no union, no rep, no normal job, nothing constant. No trace. He could work under another name, get all-new ID. But Cameron was raised by an aunt who is his entire family and maybe the one thing in the world he'd never betray. She didn't have a lot of loves—Cameron quilting, the Evangelical Lutheran Church, and a single beer of an evening. That was about it.

"Problem was finding her. When I met her, she was already retired, driving an RV around the country, deciding where she'd settle. She loved it out here, but it was too expensive and we couldn't really help. That was the last I knew of her. Location unknown—along with whether she was still alive.

"I rented out my house and lived in the garage, and worked as a temp and searched. I found Grace Smith by gridding off the country, then checking every single Evangelical Lutheran congregation and every quilting association."

Billie was silent a moment, remembering the map on her garage wall, the big open kind kids crayon state by state in elementary school. She'd colored in her states after she'd exhausted their possibilities. Morning after California morning, she'd dialed, knowing she was insane, knowing there were faster, better methods to search if she'd had money or power, knowing she had neither and no alternative but to dial another number.

"I'd say I'd contracted for a quilt from Grace Smith, a member

16

of their congregation, and could they help me reach her so I could pay her the money I owed."

"You did this for the entire United States?"

"I would have. But Grace has arthritis. I figured—I hoped—she'd be as kind to her fingers as she could. So I started in the south and worked north, leaving cold places like New England or Minnesota for last and never did get to them. Found her in North Carolina, my eighth state, in a retirement home, and I went there. Got a job on the custodial staff and cleaned Grace's room when the quilters met, and I found it. It wasn't even hidden. Right there, in one of those little Hallmark date books by the phone. She only had about ten numbers—doctors, her pastor, the pharmacy, some woman named Milly and one for a 'C' in Arizona."

Billie was surprised that you could hide in Arizona. Its sky was too open and wide, its landscape too rugged.

Emma shook her head. In admiration, Billie hoped—if not for brains or technique, then for tenacity.

"I hired a detective. I could afford two hours of his time, max. But he had access to a reverse phone directory, and I got Cameron's address. He was calling himself Jay Cameron. I visited every day care, preschool, and nursery school around his area. Said I was moving there and needed to find a place for my little boy.

"None of them had a Smith, a Jesse, a last-name Cameron. But one had a little boy with dyed black hair and his name was Mack—short, he told me he was supposed to say, for Mackenzie, last name, Dougal." She shrugged. "So I took him home." She put her hands up and out, signifying that was the end of the tale, although for her, the story never stopped, and almost a year later, every time she picked her son up from day care, or found him safe at home with the sitter it felt like a fresh victory. Cameron had disappeared again before the police reached his apartment.

Her euphoria was always short-lived, including now, followed by the bleak heaviness of what a burden the happy unending represented. Finding her son. Keeping her son. Finding a way to keep her son. This job.

With that, Billie's cards were on the table and she had nothing left to play.

The chiseled face across from her had no expression.

Game over.

Billie tried to control disappointment so fierce she could taste it. Life would go on, she reminded herself, even if not as hoped for. She'd find something else. With less allure, maybe, no challenge except not falling asleep on the job, but she would not let herself be defeated.

It nonetheless hurt.

"Pretty creative of you." Emma nodded agreement with her own words. "But there are easier ways. Like finding out where the aunt's social-security checks were being sent. Her social-security number—the place she'd retired from would have it on record."

"I didn't know how to get it, though."

"You will." Emma's voice was flat and matter-of-fact.

It took a while for the words and their meaning to make it across the cluttered desk, then Billie, who had been trying hard to control all emotions, gave up the effort. "Really?" she said, sounding so incredulous that she was sure she'd queered the whole thing. "I have the job?"

Emma raised her eyebrows. "Long as you realize that it is not very dramatic most of the time. Doesn't generally have a payoff like yours. Most of the time you're stuck with the calling-every-Lutheran-Evangelical-church-in-the-country part, but it's for a lawyer who'll take the information and never tell you what he does with it."

"I understand."

"Good," Emma said. "Except . . ."

"Yes?"

"I think you say that to me, and you even mean it. You have a grip on reality. But somewhere in the back of your brain, a little voice is saying, 'Oh, but sometimes it must get involved and tricky like in the movies.' "

Billie looked down at her hands.

"Be honest. If we're going to be in this together, we have to learn to be honest with one another. You're thinking, 'Sometimes it must be your brain against another brain and it must get scary and set the adrenaline running till you can't believe you're involved in the whole thing. Sometimes.' Am I right?"

"Well . . . yes. You are."

Emma smiled. "Damn right I am. And damn right it does. Sometimes. Just barely often enough. Just like in the movies."

Three

Today I am Gwyneth, the girl thought. Or I can try to be.

She put her backpack on the damp earth as a cushion, then leaned against the rough comfort of a rock face as she considered how to get out of her life. Five days from turning eighteen and she felt frayed and used.

On the meadow in front of her, weekend lords and ladies re-played the Middle Ages. She'd been invited to join in, re-create and relocate herself in their world. They had even put together a makeshift costume for her, but she still felt too lost to start out in any direction. She wanted to watch for a while.

Serious rains had begun early this winter, making this clear day precious. The gold-brown meadow of summer now blazed green. She was amazed by how the earth repainted itself after the first downpour. She thought of the seeds buried below the surface, cap-sules of greenness, and envisioned them curled like fetuses through dry seasons and drought, waiting to be born and rain-baptized.

And then to dry into brown ghosts that blew and burned in the winds of summer fires.

She shook her head, physically dislodging the image and concentrating on the present, on the sunny field filled with furled banners, silvery shields, and chiffon scarves.

People called these games make-believe. The same people called what she'd left ten miles away real. By sleight of hand, "home," a rotting container tottering on barren ground—by some dark magic, that place passed as a quaint Queen Anne Victorian with shining bay windows edged with boxes of petunias, and veiled by camellias, fuchsia, and flowering plums.

Inside, her so-called family was mottled and dark, gangrenous from the pressure of secrets and rage beneath their skin.

The biggest lie was that they were a family. Not because of the *steps* and *halfs* before their relationships, but because family meant you were connected, had something in common. This group on the field had different last names and mostly lived apart one from the other. But *they* were family. The people in the house in San Rafael were boarders who swept their secrets into corners until they piled so high, they stained the walls.

Nothing was real there. Nothing was hers. Nothing was safe.

But *here,* she could become someone new. She could take a new name, become Gwyneth, leave that world and join this one. The people on the field were her kin. They, too, saw the ugliness around them and invented their own better universe, their own escape hatch. The Middle Ages as they should have been. Chivalry, courtesy, and honor. That's what bound them.

She looked beyond the jousting knights to where Luke watched from the far side of the field. He wore a thickly belted chamois vest (*kirtle!*—she had to start thinking in the right terms) and had a small falcon on his glove. She loved Luke's face, the way the muscles below his skin held his features almost regally, but kindly. Her first impression of him had been that he was astoundingly clean, even if she couldn't explain what that meant. He would have been a genuine knight, if such things still existed.

He must have felt her eyes on him, because he turned, smiled, half waved.

A breeze ruffled her hair as she returned the greeting and for once, she didn't mind. Her hair's wildness had bothered her until Luke praised it, saying her red curls—"the color and movement of firelight," his words—were like a princess's in a fairytale.

In the distance, thick-faced cows regarded the goings-on with low-grade interest. They didn't seem to care that medieval cavorting was decidedly odd in their twentieth-century pasture, or that this attempt at time-travel was, frankly, amateurish. The jousters's broadswords were rattan wrapped in duct tape, their shields, aluminum foil over cardboard. Some knights were female.

And Luke's hawk had been rehabilitated after being grazed by a semiautomatic bullet. Not a King Arthur kind of injury. Hand-raised, the kestrel couldn't be released back to the wild and wasn't much of a hunter. A few years ago, Luke had adopted her and stocked his parents' freezer with "kestrel chow"—mouse carcasses, which infuriated his mother so much she ordered her son, his bird, and his bird's mice, out of her house.

Which was fine with him. You have to know what you want, Luke said. And then, you have to know how to let go of all the rest.

Luke knew, and she would learn. He would teach her.

Tension claws ungripped, let go their hold, so that the sun finally reached and warmed her, all the way through. The field blurred in a haze of contentment, colors dancing on motes of light. Maybe she could stand the rest of her life. Maybe she could even change it, save herself and Wesley, too. Something in her chest cavity stopped clawing at her. Relaxed, expanded, gave off warmth. The future unfurled, possible.

And as if echoing the feeling, something glowed on the ground.

Treasure. Of course. Today, right now, here with all the good magic and possibilities. A sign.

When she looked again, the small flash was gone.

On hands and knees she combed the tall grass, feeling mildly foolish and getting very muddy, knowing that she'd find a fragment of a beer bottle or taillight, if anything.

Still, she wanted it. It didn't matter what it had been, it mattered that it would become her touchstone and promise, a tangible reminder of that sudden sense of a future. Something her own to hold onto.

She patted the ground with fingers held flat, searching, refusing to believe the gleam had been no more than a trick of the light.

"Lost a contact lens, mistress?"

She smiled as she continued exploring. "What happened to staying in character? Medieval contact lenses?"

Luke stood above her, tall and radiant, the kestrel riding his right forearm.

"I saw something. Now I can't find——" And then her palm grazed it and her fingers circled its cool solidity. "Look," she whispered, holding out a heart-shaped wafer. She passed it to Luke, who now kneeled beside her.

His kestrel cocked its head as if appraising the trinket's worth. "It'll be pretty when it's cleaned," Luke said. He rubbed it with his thumb. "Gold, I think, and there's a design cut into it. Like filigree, I think they call it. Pretty. You can wear it on a chain. It has the loop for it."

"You think somebody in your group dropped it?"

He shook his head. "This is the first time we've been here, and this thing's been around awhile. The design's packed with dirt. It's the rain. It pushes all kinds of things up." Besides, nobody but you's been over on this side. He stood and held the charm to the light. "Bet it's been here a long time."

Waiting for her to find it. She felt a thrill at the base of her throat, like a purr wanting to happen. "An amulet," she whispered. "A sign. I was so upset——"

"I know."

"—because of—"

"I know."

"—then I felt this hopefulness, and that very second, that's when I saw it was there for me. Like I made it happen. Do I sound—do I seem crazy?"

"Not a bit." He bowed, his hand cupping the trinket as if it were priceless treasure as he transferred it to her palm. "Your token, m'lady. Might be we're standing on a treasure trove, a pirate's booty. We aren't far from the coast, from where Sir Francis Drake himself landed. Maybe the rains split open a long-buried treasure chest of his, and there's more."

"And you accuse me of having an overactive imagination." She slipped the heart into her jeans pocket, while Luke found a digging stick. She didn't need more treasure. She had her amulet. But she didn't want to dampen Luke's pleasure in turning everything into an adventure. In the sunshine, the hair on his head and forearms became spun gold, hyper-real and fantastic at the same time. She watched him poke the ground, pull back tangled grasses with his stick, dig shallow trenches. His hopeful noises of discovery were followed by sighs and mutters.

"I was wrong," he eventually said, brushing perspiration from his forehead. "No treasure, no pieces of eight, no gold—"

"No matter." It was better that there'd been only the one special thing waiting for her.

"No trunk," Luke continued. "Got roots, but not a trunk or branches. Sorry."

"About no treasure—or about that awful pun? Botanically speaking, there couldn't be a trunk. There's only grass here. No trunk, no roots, no branches."

"Wrong, because there are roots. Look." He poked the stick vigorously, almost angrily. The kestrel raised her wings, then seemed to remember they'd been clipped and she couldn't fly.

The thin, bright sounds of madrigal singers traveled across the field as Gwyneth squinted into the shallow depression where a cluster of brown twigs splayed out of a piece of bark. "Must be left from a tree that died long ago," she said. But these weren't wispy like root ends. And their shape, so basic, so familiar . . .

"No." She straightened up and put her hands in front of her face, literally pushing back the idea blustering its way into her brain. "Oh, no."

"What?" Luke asked.

She swallowed hard and took the digging branch from him, carefully pushing earth off the spot where the twigs joined. And there five of them became one, part of a sturdier looking stick. "A hand," she whispered. "A skeleton. An arm."

"Impossible. Your imagination is so . . . They're brown, not the right size. They don't look anything like bones, they're pieces of something—"

"They've been in the ground. They're tiny. They wouldn't look like a Halloween toy or biology-class model." She pushed away more dirt, slowly following the line of bone as if deciphering a grisly map. "Maybe it's an Indian burial site. That must be what—"

"Jesus! What's *that?*" Luke shouted.

She took deep breaths and stared at the ragged-edged, discolored clot.

"It's a . . . It's clothing. For a minute I thought—there might still be . . . It's mostly clothing," Luke said softly. "Pants? Plastic pants?"

She gagged. The things babies wear over diapers. So small, no more than a toddler. And no ancient Miwok Indians wore plastic pants.

The madrigal singers' voices played vocal tag, rising, then cascading in counterpoint, crossing paths, interlocking, reversing order.

"There must be a reason," Luke finally said.

She pushed and scraped again. They both saw the hollow-socketed, earth-dyed skull. She let the stick fall.

"Maybe this was a family cemetery," Luke said. "Used to be lots of babies died, and they buried them right on the farm."

"Wouldn't there be a marker, a coffin?" In the full heat of day, she felt chilled.

"Probably once was. Things disintegrate."

"No. There was still that stuff . . . and the pants." Her mouth flooded with a sour fluid, and she had to swallow again, hard. "Pioneers didn't have plastic pants. It can't have been buried all that long ago."

The ugliness of the real world was back with a vengeance, wings beating, talons tearing at her until she covered her eyes, to block out everything. "Somebody buried a baby in an unmarked grave," she said from behind her hands. Her grief astounded her. For the baby, yes, but also for herself. Knowing this made her more dead now, too.

"We'd better tell the police," Luke said.

"Not me! No police!" She didn't want her name on anything. Besides, if she let herself see them as protection, a refuge, she'd tell them more than just about this child. She'd tell too much, because she wanted to. But she wasn't finished high school yet, she had to hang on a few more months, she couldn't endanger Wesley, she had to think it through. Her mind tilted, became hard-edged and out of alignment. "No police, Luke! Please!"

The kestrel blinked, unfazed by screams, as if its reptilian eyes had impassively watched a thousand years of human distress.

She couldn't think. Couldn't risk. Couldn't move.

Be Gwyneth. She slipped her hand into her pocket and clutched the charm and calmed at its cool pressure. She took a deep breath.

"Maybe you'd better go home, then," Luke said. "I won't do or say anything until you're gone, and I won't mention you. It's okay. Doesn't matter."

She slowly released her breath. The edge of metal pressed against her palm. "Luke?" she said, "about the charm? It's too big to have belonged to a baby, so would you not mention it? It was above the ground, separate, and it's—it's my talisman." She sounded like a baby herself, but she couldn't control a rising panic so hot and total, she was in danger of spontaneous combustion.

"Still and all," Luke said. "I'm not sure we shouldn't—"

"I *need* it!"

"Get ahold of yourself," he said. "Not everything has to do with you. You're so . . . Try not to mix things up that way."

She was listening only for his decision about the golden heart.

"What the hell," he said. "Keep it. Why not?"

She blinked hard and smiled through a haze of suppressed tears that gave him a halo, as if he were made of heat and light. He didn't know it, but he was her true talisman, her knight in shining armor. He would save her. If only she could keep him in her pocket, with her all the time.

But at least she had something now. And she could be Gwyneth when she needed to be. That was also something.

Four

I can do this, Billie told herself. I can definitely do this. Fact was, anybody could sit and stare. An autistic three-year-old could pull it off. But all the same, it felt good to be competent, even at inert passivity.

She'd bulldozed her way into this job, then had come to understand that she probably hadn't needed to. Not that Emma Howe admitted it for a minute, but you'd have to have zero powers of observation not to notice the two empty cubicles at the agency or that the office manager–receptionist's "illness" seemed permanent.

Billie tried not to imagine what had happened to the trio. A plague, a force of nature—or Emma?

Emma's ad was still running, and twice, Billie had seen men whose half-hidden air of supplication suggested they were looking to be employed by Emma, not looking to employ her. Still, the extra cubicles remained unoccupied.

Yet despite all the evidence against it, Emma still behaved as if she'd done Billie an enormous favor by giving her a chance. She narrowed her eyes suspiciously each time she looked Billie's way, as if the interloper were attempting a scam that Emma was determined to expose.

"Not yet," she'd said when asked if there was anything she could do besides read a dry tome about rules and regulations. But then, Billie heard Emma on the phone, sounding less sure of herself than was usual. She was promising someone that she'd make him, it, a priority. "No more delays, Harold, I promise you that," she'd said, and immediately stomped into Billie's cubicle, tossed a file onto her desk and said, "This'd fit you. A lifestyle verification. One Sophia Redmond slipped on the pavement on 'A' Street. Hit her head on the way down on a lamppost and claims permanent disability. Can't work, can't walk without help. Wheelchair or cane-bound from dizzy spells, loss of balance plus back and neck pain. No known medical reason ascertained for it. Insurance company wants a look-see, and they want it immediately. They've authorized two, maybe could stretch it to three days."

Her first case, albeit it of less than Sam Spade caliber. All decked out with cheap and quick business cards and a beeper. Very professional. On surveillance. She loved the sound of the word, so much better than "a look-see." Sur . . . veil . . . lance. Rolled on the tongue like a chocolate truffle.

But it boiled down to sitting in her car diagonally across the street from Sophia Redmond's house. Mostly in the passenger side of her Honda as she awaited Sophia's exit and whatever happened next.

So far, in two days, Sophia had emerged once, during a lull in the storm. A tall, sinewy woman with a frizzy halo of rusty hair, she'd leaned on a cane and a redheaded girl's shoulder as she slowly navigated the five porch steps down to the pavement, her face gray with effort and pain, until she settled into a waiting wheelchair and directed the girl's attempts to clean storm debris from around the house.

Later, with branches and twigs piled at the curb, the sullen girl reversed the process, slowly guiding the woman up the front stairs and into the house, then folding the wheelchair and dragging it up as well.

Billie was pretty well sold on the authenticity of Mrs. Redmond's woes. She filled the time by reading, with frequent eyes-to-the-white-house interruptions, three newspapers, using a flashlight when the sky darkened and heavy rain made vision difficult. She had the *San Francisco Chronicle,* the Marin-Sonoma *Independent Journal* and the *New York Times.* She read them in reverse order of circulation size, and was now up to date on Bosnia, AIDS research, a burst dam in Rwanda, the drug-related death of a TV star, current political sniping, a new play by Tom Stoppard, the estimated density of the Sierra snowpack, the All-Pro Conference in Hawaii, and the latest *Doonesbury.* That information had been acquired in fits and starts throughout the day, and now, with yet another glance toward the house, she thumbed the *I.J.,* starting from the back section with "Lifestyles," human interest stories. The section that had profiled Emma a week ago. She worked forward, tossing the sports section. Local teams' stats and scores could wait until Jesse was older and Billie presumably would be obliged to care about such things so that she didn't warp her son out of acceptable shape.

The downpour eased, but that was the only change. The white house was sealed, lights on against the dullness of the day.

Billie needed a bathroom. She had avoided all liquids even though every movie detective—male, of course—ingested countless cups of coffee. Which sounded irresistible on this wet and chilly day.

But she'd had none. She was, in fact, dehydrating while sitting in the middle of endless rain.

All the same, her bladder had hit flood level.

She had read a suggestion that a PI carry a wide-mouthed jar for such emergencies, but this did not seem applicable to those of the female persuasion, particularly when wearing slacks. Stripping and straddling a jar in the back of a Honda wasn't her idea of professionalism, but heeding the call of nature bare-assed on this quiet, privileged cul-de-sac, seemed an even worse idea.

If she had to come back tomorrow, she'd wear a skirt. Long, loose, retro Summer of Love type thing if she could find one. And carry a mixing bowl with a lid. Had Tupperware ever considered this a selling point for their burp-top containers?

The question remained. How did the penis-challenged PI pee? True equity lay in being able to unzip and relieve oneself standing up and barely revealed. Not penis envy, Sigmund. Peeing envy.

Meantime, she tried to dissociate from the discomfort. Think positively. What a good job she'd done of doing nothing. A-plus for effort, if not achievement.

Not much longer to go, in any case. Emma would observe Sophia Redmond after five, would make note of any after-dark boogying, and the insurance company had only authorized two days' worth of surveillance.

Billie reached the last of her reading material, the front page of the *I.J.* She skipped the newest commission report which—surprise, surprise—said the county needed better mass transit and moved to the description of another heist by the jogging burglar. Very Marin to have an aerobically fit thief who knew the hillsides well enough to remove jewelry from their wealthy homes and flee on his secret woodland paths so quickly that security companies answering the alarms found the valuables—and the burglar—long gone. She imagined his ad in the personals: *Self-employed professional, fit, loves nature, diamonds and starlight runs, seeks slender SWF who likes same and can keep secrets.*

She scanned the street again. The rain had become negligible, no more than driblets. She thought she saw two shadows, both of them upright and moving at the Redmond's bay window, but they were blurred by a lacy curtain so that they could have been anyone.

Tomorrow, if the insurance authorized a third day of surveillance, she'd bring her Walkman and a book on tape. She was getting whiplash from the up and down of her vigilante newspaper reading.

She folded the *I.J.* for the last bit of print left in her car, the bottom half of the front page.

POLICE RESUME SEARCH ON NICASIO FARM the headline said.

> In a windswept West Marin pasture, with only cows as observers, police resumed digging for a possible answer to the mystery of the unknown person who has come to be known as the "Meadow Child." In January, the buried remains of a child estimated to be two to three years old were found in dairy farmer Earl Blankenship's pasture by participants in a mock medieval pageant being held on the property.
>
> A preliminary forensic report hypothesized that the child had been dead for approximately five years. Stopped from search attempts for over two weeks by inclement weather followed by an injunction by Blankenship who feared disruptions of the terrain would endanger his cattle, police resumed excavations this morning in a fenced-off area.
>
> "At this time, we have no reason to suspect further burials took place at this spot, but we can't eliminate that possibility without some investigation," the Sheriff's Office said. "Meanwhile, we have no leads to the child's identity and no open cases matching this child's description. Anyone with information is encouraged to call us."
>
> Meantime, the Blankenship cows watch from behind their fence as the digging continues.

Billie read every word of the account, with the prickly sensation that she had entered an alternate dimension where there was another version of her own lost child's story.

Whose child had disappeared so silently, with so little ceremony or respect for his brief life? What possible perceived offense could provoke such violence? When Jesse was missing, no matter how often she told herself that Cameron wouldn't harm his own son, she'd at the same time known how tenuous and shallow her self-assurances were. Out of displaced rage, for a perceived desertion, for love turned inside out, people did the unimaginable.

Jesse could have disappeared as completely and irrevocably as this child had. Five years somebody had been waiting. Five years counted in minutes, seconds. The cul-de-sac suddenly grew noisy with the arrival of both a gusty cloudburst and a long yellow car. Almost a limousine, an ancient one with unfamiliar contours, but it had blind sides in back and tinted windows. An old hearse, she thought, painted the color of butter. A pet hearse.

It passed Billie, then slowly made its way down the street, as if unsure of its destination, finally braking and honking three times in front of the Redmond house. Billie dropped the *I.J.* onto the seat beside her and sat up straight. The rain was fast and sharp, beating a tattoo on the car roof, pelting the windshield.

Seeing anything except the exhaust of the waiting car was difficult.

The front door of the house opened. Billie scooted over to lower the side window for better visibility. It wouldn't budge. She'd locked those controls against car-pool explorers.

She climbed to the driver's side and opened the door, crouching halfway out of it to watch.

The redheaded girl slammed the door behind her after she dragged a suitcase free of it, then clunked down the steps, one at a time, bracing the case against her so that it didn't plummet.

When she was three stairs down, the door opened again, this time by none other than wild-haired Sophia Redmond, she who formerly could not stand upright without assistance.

Sophia's screaming ability was unimpaired, but the younger woman continued her bumpy descent. Behind the open car door, Billie patted the rear seat for her camera, cursing until she located it on the floor.

She was already half drenched. Would have worn her raincoat except that Ivan had laughed at the sight of her this A.M., when it was still dry out. "Good!" her six-foot-three Russian nanny said. "Is very Humphrey Bogart uniform but would be better with slanty hat, too. Is very subtle." The fact that he pronounced the *b* in "subtle" didn't make his barb less sharp. She'd left the raincoat home.

She pointed the video camera at the ready. So far, Sophia was inert except for her mouth.

The girl reached the sidewalk, turned back toward the house, ran up the stairs, gesticulated, then retrieved a bicycle from the porch. The hearse's driver, an agile-looking male in a hooded windbreaker, jumped out of the car to put the suitcase and bike inside. The young girl turned her back to the house and opened the passenger-side door.

Which produced a burst of movement as Sophia Redmond erupted out of her house and down the front stairs, her balance intact even in the slippery rain, her agility remarkable, particularly when she jumped the last step and raced to the street.

"Yes!" Billie softly shouted, aiming the camera. "Go for it, Sophia! Gotcha, baby!" The camera whirred. She felt like a sports narrator. "See, Emma? I've got what it takes—I got her. The blonde got her. And praise the Lord—she's totally recovered. A miracle— look at that! A leap, a levitation, for God's sake, she's Olympic gold!"

At that moment, Billie remembered that videotapes recorded sound along with image. Her cheeks heated, even in the chilly rain, and she concentrated on keeping her mouth shut while she recorded the young man shutting the trunk, the young woman slamming her car door and Sophia's race to its window, which she pounded with both fists.

But what if she were too far back for a clear picture in the downpour? That blur of wild woman could be almost anyone. Billie crouched, closed the back door, opened the front and moved forward as far as she could, resting the camera on the car's roof.

Sophia's screams were swallowed by the rain. Her blouse stuck to her back, her wild hair sagged.

The driver released the brake and was off, shooting ahead until he apparently realized he was on a dead-end street, a cul-de-sac, and with a squeal, U-turned on two wheels and sped out, veering to pass the screaming Sophia.

Billie ducked, hoping it was an illusion that he was about to plow through her, and indeed, he didn't. Not through, but into.

A yellow metallic, glassy crunch as the hearse caught her right front fender and moved on.

As Billie grabbed for the sliding video camera, the swinging driver's-side door slammed into her, knocking her down, hard, onto the curbside mud. Her proving grounds, indeed.

She clutched the still-whirring video camera, now taping a closeup of her left front tire. She took a deep breath, stood up, brushed herself off, managing only to muddy her hands and the camera which she again aimed at Sophia Redmond. The soaked woman stood still and seemed disoriented. Then, she tilted toward Billie, to push her head and neck forward, the better to see what was going on with the white Honda down her street. Billie ducked and cursed, and when she again dared to peek above the car, Sophia Redmond was hobbling toward her house, the image of a dizzy, enfeebled woman. She made her way up the stairs on her hands and knees.

Billie wasn't going to win an Oscar for this film. She muttered a prayer to the god of P.I.s that the videotape had some clear and convincing footage of Sophia's feet in action. And that it wasn't only on the part where Billie had babbled like a fool.

Now the street was empty, disrupted only by the sounds of the rain and wind until Billie, having stashed the camera in the car, felt entitled to finally inspect her fender.

"Damn it all to hell!" she screamed, kicking the tire. The car was disfigured, conspicuous and illegal with only one working headlight. Knowing squat about cars but enough about the paths her life took, she understood that the estimate for repairs would be within a few dollars of her deductible. And would be many times the amount she'd earned doing this surveillance.

She sat back down on the muddy grass curb. Last month she'd been occupied with strands of beads, with cuff links and turbans and demonstrations of special effects with multiple belts.

Now what? She had battled to be employed by a failing agency, to work for a harpy she'd mistaken for a mentor, and she'd just completed her first Very Private Investigation. And what had she gained from her glamorous new career? Stained and soaking slacks, filthy hands, one probably blurred but definitely embarrassing videotape, a still-pathetic income, and a looming car repair bill.

This was not The American Way. This was the opposite of progress.

She should have stayed where she belonged, behind a counter, demonstrating forty-three ways to tie a scarf. At least that place had rest rooms.

Five

I've adopted a pet, Emma thought. A cute but clumsy stray, a well-meaning pain in the ass.

She sat in her office, door closed, and watched the tape again, shaking her head. Shouldn't photography have been part of Billie's artsy-fartsy course work?

"It, uh, isn't too good," Billie'd said when she handed over the tape. "I hope there's a way to take off the, um—my voice. I accidentally . . . It isn't something that'll ever happen again, but I think maybe I'd have to go back, except of course this event—the running away—won't happen again, so I don't know if she'd ever be this way again and . . ."

Emma, unable to bear the stammering apologies, sure the girl was being overmodest, prepping the boss for extravagant praise, waved her out. "Give me a chance to look at it," she said.

Now she had. And she thought Billie should have entered the office on her knees, banging her head on the floor as she approached. Point and shoot, that's all it took. But in addition to pointing the wrong direction half the time, in addition to problems of dark sky and inadequate light, her focus was all wrong. The rain was clear and fierce, the human figures a background blur, fuzzed and featureless, useless for purposes of identification.

And the situation had indeed been perfect. A lucky one-time-only break. And it was recorded, more or less—as long as nobody wanted to identify the dark little figures who flickered through, always unrecognizable. One of them—obviously Sophia, but only because Emma knew the players—raced down the front steps of the Redmond house, leaping off the last one like an aging gazelle, then taking off after the car. No sign of being wheelchair-bound or suffering vertigo. Could have been good. Very good.

Then for a few seconds the tape grew focused, gained clarity so that Sophia was recognizable. Unfortunately, she was also standing still, shouting, demonstrating no mobility, except of her vocal cords. Nonetheless, the segment was entertaining for its loud voice-over. *"See, Emma? I've got what it takes—I got her. The blonde got her."*

Emma pressed her front teeth into her bottom lip, reminding her mouth that this was not funny. This was expensive and worthless. This time, she feared, Harold would be well and truly sick of her agency. Bye-bye client. The six thousand hours of training required of novice PIs were not going to be enough for this Billie girl. She'd need to repeat the course, get outside help. A brain transplant, maybe. Look what she did. Look what she did next!

Because just as the tape's clarity gave the viewer hope that this was going to work since Sophia was down there on the sidewalk and would need to get back inside on her own—at that precise moment, the lens suddenly veered up to the treetops, to the leaden sky, around into a whirlpool of blur and down. As if Billie had decided that rather than film these people she'd set a mood.

But that obviously hadn't been her intention, or why say, *"Shit!"* Why repeat it twice, just in case Harold and the entire insurance company hadn't heard it the first time.

Billie's car had been hit by the careening yellow thing. Slapstick surveillance, a new specialty of Howe Investigations.

Emma reversed the tape again. Maybe *this* time she'd see a way through the blunders to get usable, not laughing, stock. She was back again to the "blonde got her" soliloquy, finding it less amusing with each replay, when her phone rang and she lifted it to hear a wavery voice say, "Emma, there's a criminal in my neighborhood and I'm scared."

As if Billie weren't enough. "Call the police, Miriam," Emma said. "Immediately."

"He's not here now. This happened last night. In the dark."

"Did you call them then?"

"Well, by the time I realized what the noise was— I mean, I thought it was a car backfiring, if they still do that. Do they?"

"You heard a gunshot?"

"It took me awhile to realize that's what it must have been. It took me until right now, in fact. When I heard more noise, I thought it was a racoon into the garbage at first—the can was full, you see, and even though I try to have nothing attractive to raccoons in there, sometimes . . . This morning was collection day and—"

"Miriam? I'm really rushed this morning."

"—it was too late. The noise stopped. He was gone. What would I have told the police? They'd think it was a raccoon. Besides, I went and asked my neighbors if they'd heard a shot and they said no. But they listen to their TV so loudly. In the summer, you could go deaf living next door! And then I thought—maybe the noise was on their TV, but I didn't know how to ask them that."

"It probably was a raccoon and a backfire, so why are you scared?" Miriam was a relic of Emma's past, the barely remembered Emma, as out of place in her life now as a miniskirt. But the older woman was tenacious, and failing, and Emma had so far been unable to find an uncruel way to dislodge her.

They'd met when they both had children climbing all over them and they'd taken their collective offspring over the mountain to the ocean, into the city to the zoo, on easy trails, and to library story hours. They'd sat at totlots and over coffee. Emma's standards for companionship in those days were that you spoke English and didn't need your diapers changed. And back then, Miriam was well above the water line. She was older, had been a botanical researcher, and hadn't had children until her late thirties. At the time, before women's lib and delayed parenting, that made Miriam seem seriously different, a bohemian in suburbia. Miriam had been freewheeling for years, way ahead of any cultural swings or permissions. She was funny, artistic, and sufficiently quirky to be entertaining.

But as her children moved on, Miriam lost her way and her personality, growing increasingly querulous, pathetic, and tedious. And when she was widowed, three years after Emma's husband screwed himself to death, Miriam began a decline that now seemed permanent.

Somebody had once told Emma that the Sanskrit word for *widow* meant "empty." She'd been vastly annoyed by the demeaning definition. She felt filled to the brim, sometimes overflowing. So she didn't have a husband—she still had a life, a job, friends, and, in fact, a man for when she wanted him. Children, too, to the degree they wanted her. But Miriam had indeed emptied out. Her husband dead, children scattered, the once super-involved and creative woman was now devoid of resources, and she'd designated Emma as the replacement team for all that was gone. Calls such as this were commonplace.

Emma looked at the videotape, frozen now on an unintelligible shot that made more than half the screen black. The tire of Billie's car, she decided.

"There's blood."

"What? Where? Mir— Call the police!"

"Inside my garbage can. Wouldn't they laugh at me?"

"Should they? Did you toss out bloody meat? Is it really blood, or beet soup or tomato sauce?"

"How would I know? I didn't taste it! I didn't touch it! It's a garbage can! I know about AIDS and bodily fluids. Besides, beet soup would go in the compost."

"Okay, so you heard noises last night around the garbage can and you thought it was a raccoon. And one of the noises seemed like a shot—"

"Earlier. That was an earlier noise."

"Okay. An earlier noise sounded like a shot."

"Well, it did once I found the blood this morning."

Nothing quite like retroactive hearing. Besides, who inspects her trash can interiors?

"I wasn't looking for the blood, Emma," Miriam said as if she'd read her old friend's mind. Her voice was aggrieved and suddenly fully aware of and sensitive to the nuances of her surroundings and self. That happened, and made dealing with her still more difficult. "Like I said, the trash men came this morning so I was putting the can back where it belongs and I saw it."

Emma looked at her watch. First the worthless video, now Miriam with a bloody trash can. Bloody nonsense. Miriam was seventy, which seemed way too soon for sporadic senility. Emma constantly found herself doing math—if Miriam decayed at seventy, did that mean Emma had only fifteen years until her brain developed potholes?

She worried how any of the army of aging single women, including her, would know they were losing it, each of them living alone in a large or small container. How could they tell when their hardwiring went bad and they were on Disconnect with the world?

She should try to reach Miriam's kids, tell them their mother needed attention. Talk to Miriam about giving up the house, moving to a supervised facility. "Call the police, Mir," she said. "They'll be able to tell you if it's really blood."

"And where will I put my trash meantime? On the floor?"

Emma gave up. "I'm being buzzed," she lied. "A business call. Let me think about what you should do."

"I'm frightened," Miriam said before hanging up.

"You're not the only one," Emma muttered. About lots of things—business, bills, about whether we're individualists or demented, about why the only person willing to work with me is an idiot. At least Miriam's husband had left her enough money to allow her to tiptoe in and out of a fogbank.

She'd watch the video one more time. This time, she'd discover the salvageable part and the Redmond investigation would be done, the insurance company pleased and ready to hand over more work.

She reached her favorite part: *"See, Emma? . . . The blonde got her. . . ."* and repeated it three times before she moved on to Billie's exuberant *"she's Olympic gold!"* shouted so loudly it was hard to believe the Redmonds hadn't heard. They were moving toward the collision and there seemed no point in further viewing. The tape was worth zero, and Sophia Redmond was not likely to perform in that style again. The case would go to court, the insurance company would settle and decide to forget about Emma, whose bills would pile up further.

So that was it for Harold. She should have known Billie wasn't going to rescue anything.

Maybe she'd sent the girl out too soon. Maybe she should teach her something else, start her where she couldn't hurt much.

"Hey," she said after knocking on Billie's open office door. The girl looked up, startled. She'd been tidying a desk that needed no straightening, that had nothing on it except the regulatory book, opened, and a small, fabric-framed photograph of a little boy in overalls and a peaked cap. Emma never had understood the need for family photos at work, as if people were afraid they'd forget their kids between nine and five, or stop working if they didn't have those hungry-looking relatives watching them.

A radio played softly, a man's rich voice talking about Presidents' Day and U.S. patriotism.

"How about learning what's available on the databases?" Emma said. "It's the only way to go, to a point. Save you so much time, you'll do fifteen cases at once."

Billie smiled brightly and nodded, turning to snap off the small radio. Before the sound stopped, Emma heard the words "hard-working, decent—" and recognized the rich voice. "You listening to Talkman?" Her shock, hidden, she hoped, was real. Of course she believed in freedom of speech and freedom of listening, but the man was a pain-in-the-ass advocate of "moral values." He was very popular, the current number-one radio personality, but only because he played to the lowest common denominator. She'd expected Billie's taste to be on a higher plane.

"Who? What?" Billie stood up to follow Emma.

"That radio guy. The one you were listening to. Isn't that who it was?"

Billie looked at the small radio as if waiting for it to answer the question. Obviously, she'd been lost in a daze. Emma wondered where she'd been, what could have so absorbed her thoughts. Surely not memories of her excellent performance with her first assignment.

"Program must have changed," Billie said softly.

"We'll use my computer," Emma said.

"I don't particularly like him," Billie said.

"I don't get what he's doing here. This isn't back country."

"Seems to appeal to city folk as well," Billie said.

"That 'lad from Nevada' crap?" Emma said. "What's that supposed to mean? I never got it."

"I think it's supposed to make him sound folksy."

"Who needs right-wing folksy—in the Bay Area?" Once in her office, she gestured for Billie to pull up a chair and settled herself at the computer, talking all the while. "When he moved here, they made a fuss about his being the number-one radio personality in Vegas. As if that meant something. Who listens to the radio there?" She hit keys on the computer while she spoke. "I used to keep that station on all day, till they changed format when he arrived. I've waited half a decade for him to fail and go back to Nevada." She shook her head in mild disbelief as she put a CD-ROM in the computer. "So, supposing you want background on somebody," she began. "Say . . . who?"

Billie shrugged. "Is everybody in there?"

"As long as they've had some interaction with the law or the state, like getting married or divorced, being arrested, buying or selling property, taking out a license to hunt, own a business, own a gun, being drafted . . . you get the drift."

Billie nodded.

"So name somebody," Emma said. The girl wasn't going to play passive-aggressive in her office.

"Okay," Billie finally said. "Audrey Miller."

"You have a specific Audrey Miller in mind?"

Billie nodded. "This girl I knew in tenth grade. Actually, I didn't know her. There didn't seem to be anything to know. She had no personality. You forgot her the minute you met her." She looked at Emma quizzically. "Maybe not the sort anybody would ever search for. She's sort of a generic female."

Emma put her hands up, palms out. "Interesting choice. You know anything we could work with? Where was that high school?— what year would she have been born?"

Billie dithered, wasn't even sure which of her many relocations this had been. "Boston," she finally said. "Framingham, actually." She didn't know much beyond that, except to estimate that colorless Audrey would be around her own age of twenty-eight—"unless, of course, she'd been left back. Or skipped." She shook her head. "Audrey couldn't have skipped."

Emma was on to the Social Security records. "We can find out if she's dead," she said. "That would save time." No Audrey of Billie's vintage was on the list. "Let's see if she's married. Or has a license for a business."

"Under her birth name, right?" Billie asked.

"As a starter—until we find a husband's name."

They didn't. They discussed the chance that Audrey had moved away and married years earlier. "You remember her parents' names?"

Billie shrugged and shook her head. "I'm surprised I remember Audrey."

"Remember whereabouts in Framingham they lived? We could check property records. There's a chance they're still there and we'd have a contact with which to find her. There's also the high school's alumni association. The reunion committee tracks most grads down."

Audrey had apparently not married, at least not in Massachusetts. But she was, as they backtracked, registered to vote in the next town over. And, once they'd checked licensing, Audrey fleshed out into the owner and proprietor of Audrey's WeCare Pet-Care, Inc.

"I'd bet that's your girl," Emma said. "We can find out more, but the thing is—you've done it, located her. You found somebody. So maybe we should look at somebody else, start somewhere else. Suppose we didn't know the high school, or year of birth. Maybe we know something else, like what she does or where she does it. See how you can go about it differently. Give me a new nominee."

Billie looked around Emma's office, as if seeking inspiration. "Him, then," she said. "Talkman, the guy I wasn't listening to. We know his job and that he does it and lives in the Bay Area."

Emma sighed. She'd asked for it. "In Marin, actually. You'd think his views would violate zoning laws, wouldn't you? Don't get me started on what used to be a good radio station. Let's get some background. We can start with what we know—last name is Marshall and he moved here from Nevada five years ago. Trying to give you a sense of the scope of this, the possibilities. We don't really need to know about him, so I'm going to move fast. Next time, we'll take it step by step, when it's for an actual case. But let's do a search for his name and . . ."

She meandered through driving records. "They're not public records in California, but I have an account, so once you get a license number, we could find it out. In other states, there's no hassle. You pay a fee, you get your guy's name. The good news is we know he's from Nevada. The bad news is, if you were really looking for the guy, Nevada addresses wouldn't help you find him 'cause he's not there anymore. But old addresses can be a lead, or a suggestion that somebody wasn't where he says he was, for example. Or where he used to live. And see, look here—his birth date, height, weight. Who knows what could be useful?—the birth date can help get other records, sometimes."

She could feel small gusts of air when Billie remembered to exhale after a long spell of holding her breath. She felt like a performer boosted by applause and heard a new enthusiasm in her voice. "Lots of data depends on the state. For example, marriage records are not public in New York City, but here they are, and presumably in Nevada. Let's look."

Which they did, accompanied by Billie's soft puffs of breath and they found seven Marshalls, most of whom were too old, too young, or female. Harley was their man, they decided. "So you see," Emma said, "the records keep feeding into each other. Here's Harley's marriage license. Married Genia Ann Christophe. Wonder if he stayed married? Should have, he's such an advocate of the 'nu-cleer' family." She moved to divorce records, searched, shrugged. "Practices what he preaches," she said, not at all pleased at learning that.

"Or he divorced her in California," Billie softly suggested.

Emma swiveled around in her chair. She tended to forget what the girl looked like when not facing her, imagined her a faceless marshmallow. And then the girl would say something intelligent and Emma would be surprised by the precise features and the cleverness in the eyes. "Could be," she said. "Divorce records can be good— find out lots of things. Not about him, per se, but they can include things like allegations of abuse, or third parties involved, or a sense of what happened to the assets. Lots of stuff. They're filed by county."

Meanwhile, she moved through voter registration files.

"To know their politics?" Billie asked.

Emma thought she was joking, but didn't turn around to verify it. "More like addresses, Social Security number." She loved shifting around the databases. Snooping at its easiest, a boon to her aging bones. "You still have to get your ass in gear and go outside, however." She wasn't sure if she meant that remark for Billie or herself. "Amazing the things you find. People put phone numbers on pet licenses which are public records. Your friend Audrey could help you there with her client list. You can check for ownership of assets— tell you something about somebody. Automobiles, trucks, RVs, airplanes—who knows? Then there's property records, there's licensing records if the guy's, say, a carpet cleaner or a beautician. . . ." She swiveled around again and faced Billie, who seemed delighted by the potential in the box. "Let's do somebody else. He wasn't a great choice," she said.

Billie's face fell.

"Not your fault!" If she was going to have to watch every damned word . . . "He's a public figure. We should look at somebody harder to find, way less known, at least to us."

"Like who?" Billie now sounded like a student afraid she'll be called on.

Emma sat back in her chair and steepled her fingers under her chin. Then she smiled and sat up straighter. "Why—how about you?" she said and felt a thrill when Billie's neon eyes opened wide with undisguised fear. "You'll be all over the place—birth, marriage, divorce, property files, neighborhood-worth rating . . ."

"But—" Billie said. "Why? I mean, I know about me. I know all about me."

"Perhaps," Emma purred as she swiveled back to face the computer. "But I don't." She didn't turn around to delight in the younger woman's discomfort. She wasn't a sadist.

Six

She thought that maybe she hated them. All of them. She'd expected them to welcome her, make her a part of their group, so she'd have a new, better family. Instead, they looked at her as if she were an alien.

It wasn't really new or better here, except for being with Luke. They wouldn't even let her be Gwyneth, and that had been the point of it, that she could stop being Penny and become somebody new. Start over.

"Look here," Kathryn purred at Luke. Kathryn had invented that voice, probably practiced that throaty purr until it sounded sexy no matter what words floated in it. "There's more about it in the paper." She made the news sound like a secret for their ears alone.

Penny kept her back to all of them and looked out the window of the kitchen's Dutch door. She liked this part of Marin, the valley between the Bay and the ocean. You couldn't see the edges of land, the way you could in other parts of the county. She felt safe here in the soft foothills of Mount Tam. Cradled. In the distance, silhouetted against the sinking sun, a dog barked at a horse grazing on a green hillside. The way Luke's house was situated at the back of its lot, you didn't really see its neighbors. She could look out and see a barely touched slice of landscape and pretend the world was all new and she was the first person to see these soft hills, that she was nestled and protected in a green palm of land. Except that when she heard their cold voices and saw their icy eyes, she knew she wasn't safe anywhere.

Penny heard the newspaper rustle. "They've found another one," Kathryn said in a whisper, like a lover.

Penny sighed and turned, saw Luke raise his eyebrows. Kathryn, her big boobs practically on him as she leaned his way, pointed at the newspaper.

Did she think he was illiterate? It was enough to make a person gag, the way she pressed her pudgy finger on the newsprint, like it was something she'd prepared. She acted like he was a superhero for finding bones in a meadow. Which, of course, he hadn't really done. Or known he'd done. Penny was the one who'd understood what they were, but she couldn't be mad at Luke about that—he was doing as she'd asked, keeping her out of it.

Big, sloppy Kathryn drooled over him. If she knew what a fool she looked like . . . Penny had half a mind to tell her.

Half a mind. That's the kind of thing her mother said. Stupid. On the other hand, Kathryn did seem to have just half a mind.

And why did she act like Luke was up for grabs? He'd brought Penny here to live with him. Sure, the half a mind Kathryn had was stuck in the Middle Ages, but even back then, wasn't three considered a crowd?

Actually, nobody noticed her, even if the rest didn't make moony eyes at Luke. They didn't make any eyes at Penny. They pretended she wasn't there. There was Gary, the gigantic computer genius who looked like a scarecrow, and Alicia, a CPA who was too serious and acted like she was in charge, and Toto. She didn't know Toto's real name or what he did. He was cute and funny, always cracking jokes, but not with her.

Their big ideals of chivalry. And kindness. They said they tried to bring those ideals into their mundane lives, but that obviously didn't extend to *her* mundane life.

They acted like she was something ugly they should look away from, like it bothered them she was here, that she was a problem, not a person. They were too polite to say those words, but they made sure she knew it all the same.

She'd asked them to call her Gwyneth, but they refused. She hadn't researched it, they said, and before she could officially use it, she had to prove it was used in the period and place she chose, and she hadn't even picked a country or time. Besides, they didn't use those names here in the mundane world. They sounded like kindergarten teachers. The name she'd eventually take—if, indeed, Gwyneth was a European name before the seventeenth century—would be for her Medieval life, and did she understand the difference between the two? They were all members of the group—except for her, of course—and they lived together, too, because they liked each other, but this wasn't the Middle Ages. This wasn't a reenactment. This wasn't their other personae.

All as if she were retarded, or barely spoke the language.

Her so-called new life was turning out to be just as chilly and unsatisfying as the one she'd left, with the older people still dumping on the younger ones. Even Luke—except she wasn't supposed to call him that, either, or his actual other name, Lucan, the duke who'd died protecting King Arthur, even though that's who he was to her.

Look at them sitting around, drinking coffee and tea and beer, and not one person—not even Luke—saying she should join them. She didn't like the mundane world.

The house was nice enough, with rooms for everybody and an office for Alicia, and a big living room and kitchen and a sort of "whatever" feeling to where things belonged. Paint peeled on high kitchen cupboards and the dusty rugs, loose nails, creaky risers, threadworn upholstery and unmade beds that would have driven her parents insane relaxed her. Or would have, if it weren't for the people.

"Read it out loud, whatever it is, would you?" Toto said to Luke.

Luke grimaced. "Blah, blah, blah, blah . . . okay, here goes.

" 'The county sheriff's office who have once again resumed digging following the recent storms have discovered a second burial site fifteen feet from the spot where a toddler's remains were recovered last month. At this stage of the investigation, deputies said only that the newly unearthed gravesite's unidentified adult is female and appears to have suffered a fractured skull. However, they could not say whether it was the cause of death. Preliminary testing suggests both bodies have been buried for approximately the same length of time. Police in California and continuous states are checking all open missing-persons records. . . .'

"One with a skull fracture, one a baby, probably buried same length of time," Luke said. "Why not come out and say these people were murdered?"

"A mother and her baby, is what I think." Kathryn sounded as if her idea were a stroke of genius. "Right where we had the tourney." She shivered, as if she'd come close to being killed herself.

"Abducted first, probably," Gary said. "Else how'd they wind up in that field? There's nothing but cows around there."

Alicia pulled the newspaper closer to her and scanned it. "A fractured skull. If it happened before she died, wouldn't it show signs of mending? Wouldn't it look different than a new, never-healed split?"

Toto held an imaginary magnifying glass up to his face and squinted at the paper. "I thought CPAs only understood numbers. In a minute, your brilliant deductive powers will reveal the name of the killer who is right here in the kitchen with us!"

"Common sense." No one else seemed to mind Alicia's "I am so superior" voice.

"Did they question you when you reported the skeleton? Do they suspect you?" Kathryn's attention was still on Luke.

"Yes and no," he said. "They asked what I was doing there, where exactly I'd been, why I was poking at it—" He glanced at Penny then just as quickly looked away from her. "And they asked who all of you were, and the others who'd been out on the field, but they didn't suspect me. They suspected *us*. They thought the idea of restaging medieval events was seriously weird. I had to explain that twenty thousand members all over the world couldn't all be crazed killer deviants, and that we were a handful out of thousands in the Kingdom of the West alone. He still thought we were crackpots."

Alicia nodded in a tired way that suggested a whole lot of people thought they were odd, and told them so.

"Why would they suspect me?" Luke continued. "I'd have to be insane to point out a crime I'd committed years ago. A crime I'd gotten away with."

"Probably a drifter," Gary said. "They'll never find him."

"Him! Him! Always assuming everything was done by a man," Alicia said, making it clear she wasn't serious. "What if it was a woman—many women, a girl gang, female muggers? Don't make assumptions."

Toto pounded on the table for emphasis. "And I say equality for murderers!"

"Was it creepy?" Kathryn whispered in her nightclub voice. She wrote PR for a man who managed singers and considered herself in showbiz. "Finding it, I mean? Those tiny bones and all."

Luke looked at Penny as if he was waiting for something, and as if he, too, was annoyed, but why should he be pissed with her? She wasn't doing anything but standing there.

She realized she was clutching the gold chain that held her heart-amulet. Maybe that's what annoyed him—her standing there looking like a nun saying her beads. Her bead.

Luke still frowned.

She should never have come to this place, never believed she could change her life, never believed in Luke. But he'd encouraged her. It wasn't fair, wasn't fair at all.

"I mean," Kathryn went on in her sleepy, throaty voice, "most people would have left them. The bones, I mean. Not recognized them for what they were. I certainly wouldn't have!" Her tiny cute-girl laugh put Penny's teeth on edge.

They didn't want her, didn't count her as a person with a mind and opinions. She was tired of acid scalding her midsection, sick of fighting back tears.

She'd show them. "I'm the one who found the bones," she said. Luke and Kathryn looked startled, and Alicia and Toto craned their necks around to look at her. As if they'd absolutely forgotten she was there. "If you don't believe me," Penny said, glaring, "ask Luke."

Gary pursed his lips. Wrong name again, but she didn't care.

"*I* was the one who knew that was the skeleton of a hand. Luke thought the bones were the roots of something. They were very small and brown, you see, from the earth. Not all connected." She pulled out an extra chair and sat down on it and folded her arms over her chest. Now. A little respect.

Having heard this person they treated like a doorstop speak their language made them mute with shock. Even Luke. Especially Luke, who took a deep breath, tilted his chair back, stared at the kitchen ceiling, then righted himself and looked at her again and sighed.

"What?" she finally asked. "What did I do?" She regretted the question as soon as it was out her mouth—it sounded so babyish, so like Wesley.

"It appears you've changed your mind. Decided not to keep your involvement a secret anymore," Luke said.

He sounded like he was accusing her of something. "My 'involvement'?"

Maybe he was using that heavy solemn language as a joke, a

setup. Maybe he was finally about to pull her into the group. Her only involvement was him.

"Given that you've gone public," he said, waving his hands to the "public" seated at the table, "the logical next step is to go to the police about your necklace."

He'd spoken in a too-calm voice, as if dealing with a child, a wild beast, or an insane person. When he was around them, he was just like the rest of them. And he acted like he didn't remember who she was and didn't know why she couldn't do what he wanted.

"You mean the heart?" she asked, grasping it with one hand.

He nodded. "Now that they've found another body—or what's left of it. A grown-up this time. A woman. A logical person to have owned that heart. Now, I feel like . . . I feel just as much to blame—it wasn't all your fault, but we should have said something then."

Blame. Fault. Wasn't all *your fault,* like a big chunk of it—of something—definitely was. The words spun in her head. She could barely see straight. Everything was wrong and upside down. "Why?" she asked.

Toto emptied a small bag of corn chips into his hand. "That's what you're talking about? That thing on your chain?"

"Penny found it near the child's skeleton. The heart, not the chain. We were looking to see if there was more jewelry there when we found the bones," Luke said.

"Maybe a relative could identify the dead woman by that heart," Alicia said.

"Or identify the killer." Kathryn's cheeks looked like they'd been stained with beet juice. Crime turned her on. "Like Alicia said before, what if the murderer was a woman, and she lost that charm in the struggle?"

"It isn't yours to keep," Alicia said without a smile.

Penny had released the charm and now stopped her hand from automatically returning to it. Her amulet. Luke hadn't treated her this way before she moved in with him. It was because of the others, and how he wanted to look big to them. "You don't know every-thing," Penny said, clenching both hands at her side. "You don't know anything about me." She flashed a hard glance at Luke. "It's more complicated than you could possibly know," she said.

Now everybody stared at Penny like she was a convict or conta-gious. "It was there, on the grass," she said. "All by itself. It has noth-ing to do with those bodies. It was a joke, poking around for more. Looking for Drake's treasure. I wish we hadn't, but Luke kept—"

"That isn't his name," Alicia said sternly. "Not here."

Penny shrugged. "That's how we found the bones. The heart wasn't attached to anything, just sitting on the grass."

"Yeah, but it was probably near that other body," Toto said.

"No. Because where we dug was right near the baby," Penny said. Why wasn't Luke helping her?

"Skeleton," Alicia corrected her. "It sounds disgusting to call it a baby."

"All the same," Gary began. "Pushed up by the storms, the mud. It probably had migrated. Maybe."

"I need it!" It was all she had in the way of hope—didn't anybody understand that? It was an amulet, no matter what its real worth. She realized too late, saw by their annoyed expressions that she'd shout-screamed her words, her voice loud, high and sharp. Like her mother, like her mother when she was unbearably crazy.

And really, if only they'd talk to her directly, act like she had a brain, she could explain. The amulet had been found on the one pure and perfect day in a stormy season when there was magic in a cow pasture, and the found thing, full of meaning, signified possi-bility instead of a dead end. A new life, a new start.

It hadn't happened that way. This rambly house wouldn't let her be anything but herself. Only difference was that now she had no place else to run. She had nothing, except the necklace, and now they wanted that, too.

She hadn't seemed particularly childish when he met her or he never would have spent time with her. The five-year difference in their ages hadn't felt like a generation's worth. He couldn't figure what had happened since the day she'd raced out of her house and, as if he'd broken a spell she'd been under, dissolved into a pouty, irrational little girl.

And she was wreaking havoc. Nobody would be put out by his sharing his room with somebody normal. Not that he'd meant for her to live with him. He'd told her so a dozen times, but she didn't want to hear it.

All he'd done was feel sorry for her and said she could crash at his place as long as she needed, till she found out what to do next. She was so unhappy, so trapped between caring about her own life and future—and whether she was abandoning her younger brother. Probably all hyperinflated teenage junk, but he'd remembered how it felt to be an alien in your own family. She shouldn't have to make such big decisions at that age. What he was doing had seemed the right, the chivalrous thing.

A Penny saved, he'd told himself, and thought it sounded just right.

But even so, he regretted the "as long as you need," because she had deliberately misinterpreted the whole thing as an invitation to live with him. He thought she was cute, entertaining, bright, a little wild yet still vulnerable. She was good company, precocious for a high-school kid. Now she acted like such an infant he felt like he'd kidnapped her.

She expected the world to stop for her, make her the sun the planets circled. Which naturally infuriated everybody else. He felt caught between his housemates and this changeling he'd somehow adopted. He didn't want to hurt Penny. He'd thought of himself as her protector, and she needed one.

But he didn't want to lose his friends or this sanctuary. He was the newest tenant, the least tested, and, if this kept up, they were going to ask him to leave. He could feel it building to that, soon, because everything was cracking and fissuring under her pressure. And then where would he go, where he could afford the rent and they'd accept his falcon and dead mice? Where nobody shouted at him from out on the street, nobody stared into his windows, followed him, knew the address or phone number?

Introducing Penny to this house had been as deadly as introducing poison into a well.

And she'd only been there three days.

A perfect example was right now. He'd been watching the little drama with the back door. Because nobody had said, "Penny, please join us for this grubby and completely informal moment around the kitchen table," she sulked and acted as if they'd banished her to a foreign land.

And she was insanely, irrationally jealous, acting as if he were cheating on her—as if Kathryn and he were having a secret tryst.

As if Penny and he were. Although he dreaded the tantrum he was sure it would provoke, he was also going to have to tell her that so that she finally heard. What he felt—or *had* felt—was more affection than sex. A few kisses and hugs. A closeness, a caring, that was all. They'd talked so much about everything; she'd seemed older than her years then, before she moved in.

A kiss or two would have been as far as it went if she hadn't— He'd thought she would sleep on the sofa downstairs, but she hadn't. She wouldn't, so there'd been that time, the first night, when she came into his bed. His fault, too, sure, but afterward he'd said it had to stop, couldn't happen again. They weren't to be that way. He'd been kind about it, but the more he said, the more she cried and the more determined she became to make them be the way she'd decided they were.

He hadn't meant to be cruel. He'd wanted to help her out of a jam, offer her friendship. He wanted to honor his own ideals, not to make this girl his life partner, or whatever she imagined.

He realized that since her outburst, nobody had said anything. Alicia was pushing chip crumbs around the table, forming them into little o's and lines. Gary had gone back to reading his book, and Toto looked ceilingward, whistling "Somewhere Over the Rainbow," a nervous habit that had given him his nickname. Kathryn had gotten up to turn on lights. It had grown dark without their noticing it. But what they were all saying, silently and in their way, was that he'd better do something about the situation.

The silence was broken by Penny, who leaned forward, reached out and put her hand on his arm. "Listen," she said. "I'm sorry. The thing is, there's no point acting like this heart was something special, except to me—like it's an object that could identify somebody. The police would laugh at us."

He pulled his arm away from her "us." He didn't want people to think of them as a couple.

"There are a zillion charms like this. It's not even solid gold, it's plate. You can see where some is worn off, see?" She pulled the chain and charm off her neck and offered it out. Kathryn was the first to accept it.

"I mean girls got them as favors at dances, as bridesmaids, or as Sweet Sixteen gifts."

"How do you know all this?" he asked. Where had this fund of knowledge come from?

"One—no, two—women I baby-sit told me. They both said they once had things that were just like it. When they were younger. We aren't talking Cartier's. Or original crafted jewelry. We're talking teen-aged souvenirs." She suddenly looked uncomfortable, embarrassed. "They were love tokens. That's what the woman—those women—told me. Somebody gave you his heart. Or maybe just your parents, you know? It was just . . . a thing. You couldn't track ownership or sales records, if that's what you're thinking."

"Well, who knows?" Luke asked. "Maybe your baby-sitting clients would remember where they got them. Maybe it'd be significant. You could at least ask."

"One's my neighbor, she'd know me, my voice. They are so Brady-bunch they'd get hung up on why I'm not home, why I left. They'd trace the call or get me to say something I didn't mean to. No."

She folded her arms across her breast like an angry teacher, and the hope that had surfaced in him took a nosedive.

What he couldn't stand was her bullheaded stubborn streak. She was like that about everything. No logic, just stubbornness. "How about the other one?" he asked patiently. "Would the other one be safe to talk to?"

She looked at him blankly.

"The other person you baby-sit for who had one of those hearts. You said there were two."

"Oh. Right." Her gaze fluttered up the wall, and she puckered her mouth. "I think . . . I think she said she got it as a 'secret Santa' gift at her office. And it doesn't matter, see? All I'm saying is that this kind of heart was as common as houseflies. You couldn't identify a skeleton through it. It would be like, like trying to trace the baby through its diapers, or a plastic rattle if they'd found one." She looked down at the amulet. "It has *symbolic* value. To me. Why can't you understand?"

"It looks like the design—it looks like a word," Toto said. "See? VUX." He passed it around and everyone nodded and Luke, who'd only glanced at the cleaned heart once or twice, realized that the delicate tracings did seem to spell those letters. "But what could VUX mean?" he asked. "It sounds like a detergent. Or a vacuum cleaner."

"It isn't Vux! There's no such word, and it just looks *almost* like that," Penny said. "It's just a design, that's all."

"Vux," Gary said. "Vux." He shook his head. "Doesn't sound like anything—not even like a foreign language. Vux. Uh-uh."

"I hope that means you understand, now," Penny said.

Luke took two deep breaths. "It could be the name of an organization," he said. "Something that could help the police. The 'X' could be for ten. The Tenth Anniversary or something. Bet if you looked on the net under Vux there'd be something—we don't know all the possible—"

Penny grabbed the chain and charm from his hand. Her skin, always fair, looked drained. "Listen," she said, her voice rough. "I'm sick of having my things taken away for no good reason. I'm sick of—there is no reason for me to turn this over to the cops. They'll keep it forever, don't you understand? And nothing will come of it, nothing can. Get real—think about it. Two bodies are found five years after they're buried. Nobody saw a car there back then, nobody filed a missing persons report back then, nobody's been hunting for them since then. So why, suddenly, could they be identified?

"What happened? A woman decides to pick up a hitchhiker, or her car breaks down in West Marin where there's nothing except grazing land for miles and some stranger decides to kill her and the baby and take the car. I'm sure it was something insane like that. No reason, no clues. No family waiting, missing her. The two of them are just gone. And the killer—what would he do? Hang around for five years? He's gone, too. Way gone and there isn't a single clue or a chance in hell—"

"But that charm, the Vux—"

Penny put the necklace back on and shook her head. "You just want to do something—anything—especially if it's about something of mine. How are they going to find somebody that nobody thinks is lost? Where would they even start? And meanwhile, they'll go to my parents and—" She shook her head again. "Remember the end of *Raiders of the Lost Ark*? That enormous, enormous storage room where things disappear forever? That's what will come of it. They'll stick it away and forget it." She sighed. "You do understand now, don't you?"

Nobody said anything. Penny smiled expectantly at him, at the others at the table. She was so relaxed all of a sudden, so comfortable, that the tension level dropped by a thousand percent. He thought his roomies had almost accepted her, forgiven him his trespasser, but on the other hand, they weren't saying a thing. Waiting for him, for the next move.

And much as he hated to mess with the calm that now reigned, something was still out of kilter. "I see your point," he said, "and I'm sure you're right, but all the same, that's for the police to decide. We're talking a probable double homicide, a serious thing. No matter how cheap or common the heart might be, the cops won't laugh at you—they'll call you a good citizen, commend you, even."

Her mouth dropped open and the goodwill that had been softening her face dried up and disappeared.

"It's about honesty," he said. "It's the most basic ideal any of us have, to live honestly, be honest. That matters maybe more than anything."

Kathryn and Gary nodded in his direction, as if he'd passed a test. Then they looked back at Penny.

"Don't you see?" he asked. "It isn't about a little gold—"

"Gold plated."

"—heart. It's about doing the right thing, so you can sleep easy."

She stood up so abruptly her chair wobbled, and would have fallen to the floor had not Gary reached out a long arm and steadied it. The sunshine in her was so completely gone that her skin seemed darker.

Maybe she was mentally ill. He'd never considered that before, but it wouldn't be the first time he had been naive or stupid and willfully manipulated by a crazy girl. "What?" he asked.

"I can't go to the police." Her voice was so low and strained her neck grew hollow-centered and veins stood out on it. "And I won't. For starters, I'm a runaway."

"Shit, man!" Gary said. "You brought a runaway here? Somebody the police want?"

His housemates glared as if he'd deceived them, put them in jeopardy.

"She's eighteen," he said. "She left home. Nothing illegal about it." He didn't want to explain his loose relationship with her, the rescuer fantasies that had gotten him into this mess. Not with her right here, ready to become hysterical if he implied she was less than everything to him.

"Besides," she said, breathing hard as if she'd been running, and facing him, eyes riveted on him. "You saw my mother run after the car. She's pretending to be crippled, committing fraud. I can't involve the police in my life. They'll arrest her, and then what? What happens to Wesley?"

He shouldn't even have tried. Surely shouldn't have mentioned honesty. Penny didn't understand it. All she understood, or thought she did, was that if her mother the insurance-scammer went to jail, then nobody would take care of Wesley. Not her father, who, she was positive, was already living a double life. And that left only Penny, and how could she make a living, do any of it? And if she couldn't, Wesley would be sent to foster care. He knew the drill and its circular form by heart, she'd said it so often. She'd built herself a trap and nailed boards over its exit.

The housemates looked at each other silently, but he heard their unarticulated questions, objections, fears in four parts as clearly as if they'd been singing a madrigal.

He tried to think his way out of this. "Let me get through this," he said. "It isn't the idea of telling the cops that worries you, it's *your* telling them, right?"

She frowned, took a deep breath, shrugged, then nodded. He didn't think she meant it, but it would have to do.

"Then don't take it in. Mail it with a letter explaining what happened. A computer-written and printed letter they can't trace."

"What if they come here, man, and pull the file out of the computer?" Gary asked. "Even if you erase it, it's there, you know, and if they bring good-enough technicians——"

He was going to punch Gary out, stitch shut his mouth. "Right," he said. "Like they'd want to, or care, or know which machine she——" He shook his head and took a breath. The girl was paranoid. Why give her extra ammunition? "Okay, we'll rent time at Kinko's, use their machine, okay? Then I'll mail it from the other end of the county." Jesus, this was stupid, kids playing spies. "And I'll write out a script, word by word, of what you could say on the phone to your next-door neighbor."

"Don't forget the one who got hers at a Christmas party," Alicia said. Penny flashed her a furious look. He didn't try to figure it out. He merely nodded.

Penny still glared at Alicia. She hated anybody he liked, and he'd liked Alicia—as a friend, mostly—since the eighth grade. "Pen?" he prompted.

She looked at him from behind a volcanic mountain. "Oh," she said, "you mean Mrs. . . . . Mrs. . . . ." her eyes darted from one to the other of the housemate and he couldn't help but see that each in turn dropped their glance to their hands, or the table. He wondered if they, like he was, were suspicious about this, thought she might be lying. "Mrs. . . . . Matterson. Sure. Same script."

"Fine. So you won't say a single thing about what's on the script, and you'll see if they can help the police find out anything about the hearts. Maybe they were only made in one place, even if a lot of them were made. Maybe that limits something. Or they have a cheap alloy that was only made for a year. I don't know—but it's wrong not to try and find out if you can. It's not like you were a witness to a crime and you'd be afraid the killer would come after you. You found a trinket near where people were secretly buried and you're providing help. And after you mail the earring and make the calls—you're done. When it's all settled out, you'll even get your amulet back."

He'd presented a good case. Maybe he should have been a lawyer after all, made himself miserable, his parents happier about him. He watched her face, could almost see the stages of thought pass over her features. Hmm. Yes? No. Okay. Maybe. But . . . What stupid, immature counterargument would she find? How long would the rest of the household put up with this crap?

After what felt like too long, Penny's muscles unclenched, her shoulders lowered, her hands loosened out of the fists by her side, and she smiled so that he could remember why he used to find her appealing.

"Good plan," she said with a nod. "We'll do it first thing in the morning."

His housemates applauded and Penny made a mock bow and beamed at them, looking like a happy child. He himself felt a rush of joy and ease. They were not going to blow each other up and away this particular evening. He was not imminently homeless.

Although . . . They didn't know her. They couldn't see that there was something wrong with that smiling girl at the table. The Penny that had come home with him was filled to the brim with fears, both semi–sane and irrational, with erratic moods, rock-hard stubbornness, an ability to always choose the dramatic but destructive option. . . . She did not change her mind, did not give in.

This sudden, sunny and complete capitulation did not compute. But peace and Penny coexisted in his home for the first time, so he'd be damned if he'd question it. Instead, he smiled back, poured himself a beer and forced himself to believe for as long as he could that all was well and going to get better still.

Seven

Emma heard the outside office bell ring and went out to play receptionist yet again. It was time to put pressure on Zack—either he was able to come back, or he was not. She had cut him more than enough slack but she had a business to run, and enough was enough of trying to make do. "I'm sorry," she said as she entered the outer office, "our receptionist is on sick leave and . . ."

A man who looked polished for an event more ornate than a visit to her office stood with one manicured hand on the shoulder of a woman in a wheelchair.

She knew that frizzy hair, or a picture of it, the one clear part of the tape. She'd seen that face over and over, screaming.

Sophia Redmond, suffering a relapse of insurance-scam paralysis, looked at a newspaper she held, then at Emma, and seemed to find the match satisfactory. "You're Emma Howe," she said.

Emma nodded agreement.

"You own this agency, don't you?"

Emma was sure she was about to be slapped with something. Billie had done her in, screwed up so badly that now they were being sued. She nodded again.

"Good," Sophia said. "I want to hire you. I read about you in the *I.J.* and that gave me the idea to hire somebody like you—to hire *you.* I knew you were the right person—and right here, in San Rafael!" She waved her copy of the article, as if it were proof of something.

The power of PR, Emma thought. A human interest story can spark a little human interest. Even in the burbs where there wasn't a P.I. on every corner, it didn't hurt to get your name out, generate business.

"I like that you're a woman detective. I think that matters," Sophia said. She swivelled her neck to watch her husband as she spoke the words with an air of defiance.

He shrugged and yawned, barely bothering to cover his mouth. "I figure a woman's just as good," he finally said. "For snooping, that is."

Emma said nothing. They were not announcing or threatening a lawsuit.

"We're here about a missing person. A kidnapping," Sophia said.

So much for new business. They shouldn't have come to her at all. "Missing or kidnapped, either way, that's a police matter," Emma said. First Miriam, then the Redmonds bypassing free and available public servants. People were nuts.

"The girl ran away," Mr. Redmond said.

"She was kidnapped—taken by a cult!" Sophia said.

The man waved his hand dismissively. "She cut out, is all," he said. "She's on drugs. Or knocked-up."

"The thing is, even though she's a senior at San Rafael High, she's a little older than some, eighteen, because we moved a lot when she was a child and also her birthday comes so late in the year, the kindergarten teacher thought—"

"Sophia," the man said.

Sophia closed her eyes. Time out. Then she opened them and continued. "I don't want you to think she's stupid because she's older. She's not. And not even that much older. There are other eighteen-year—"

"Sophia." He didn't raise his voice, but the tension in his throat as he said her name was audible.

"But even though she's still in school, her age makes her legally an 'emancipated adult.' Which means she can leave home if she wants to, so it wouldn't be a police matter, especially the way my husband puts it. As if she just plain ran away and wasn't brainwashed first."

"Sophia."

It was interesting, Emma thought, how easy it was to ignore somebody in a wheelchair. They were literally below notice, with all the unconscious contempt the expression implies. This man—the father and husband?—hadn't acknowledged a word Sophia said, not to refute or confirm it except to squelch her. All without looking her way. Not that the woman didn't need levees for her word flow, but if she'd been standing next to him, would he have treated her more like his equal?

Emma beckoned them into her office, then excused herself to knock on and open Billie's office door.

The younger woman looked like a child being summoned to the principal's office. Emma took a grim satisfaction in it. "Something you should sit in on," she said. "Ask questions if you have them. Follow my lead." She waited a beat. "And don't faint."

Billie's skin and features seemed wired to her central emotional core as if there were nothing in between. She wore a gauge on her face as easily viewed as her straight nose. Now, it registered clumsy, forgiven-puppy delight. She wasn't being punished for the mess she'd made and she seemed to want to run in circles, wagging her tail. And then as Emma's final phrase made it through the relief zone, her face-ometer changed, and registered anxiety.

Billie grabbed a notepad off her desk and followed Emma into the larger office. Despite her normally transparent emotions, when Billie saw Sophia Redmond there was a sliver of a second—imperceptible to anyone not waiting and watching for it—less than an eye-blink of recognition, confusion, and fear, and then it was gone, so quickly it hadn't happened, replaced by a blandly professional mask. She must have been a good actress, Emma thought as Billie nodded to the couple with no sign of recognition and took a discreetly placed seat to the side and slightly behind Sophia. Not obtrusive, but not out of the loop.

"This is my"—Emma tossed her a cheap thrill—"associate, Billie August. I want her involved in this."

"Does that mean we have to pay double?" the man asked.

"You're hiring our firm," Emma said. "All our resources are available to you. You're billed as we use them, and we'll surely consult you on that." All our resources, she thought, and they're right here in this room. One rapidly aging and short-tempered woman and her idiot hire, and a computer, the only resource that functions properly. "And you are . . ."

"Arthur Redmond."

"And Sophia Redmond," the woman added in a rush.

The man sighed before he spoke. He had a thin, thirties-style moustache that echoed the pout of his mouth. "We're here because our daughter—"

"She's my daughter, actually. She's from my first marriage, although Arthur here has been as good as any natural father would be to her, and she was seized by a cult. Brainwashed. She has to be saved."

"Ran away," Arthur said.

"I was there," Sophia said. "I know what I saw."

"If your daughter was kidnapped, no matter her age, the police should be informed. Kidnapping is a crime," Emma said. "A federal offense. And it's best if it gets immediate attention. When did this happen? Do you have the ransom note? Was there forced entry? Abduction? Did you see something?"

"I saw enough," Sophia said.

"But not those things, is that it?"

"There's no note," Sophia whispered. "No forced entry."

"When did this happen?"

"Three days ago. In broad daylight. Well, it was a dark day, rainy, but it was in the afternoon."

"And you waited till now because . . . ?"

Sophia Redmond twisted a button on the cuff of her blazer. "We weren't sure what was happening. Or that she was really gone. I mean she could have . . . I mean . . ."

"What are we hemming and hawing about? Do you find people or not?" Arthur Redmond asked.

"My husband's busy." Sophia was seemingly talking to her own lap. "He had to take the day off. . . . I would have come alone except I can't do much of anything because I have this weakness and back pain and these terrible dizzy spells from a fall that hurt my head and ripped muscles and my equilibrium—my head's all   "

"The detectives don't want to know that," Arthur said. "Get on with what you have to say."

Emma considered his attitude. His natural arrogance seemed intensified by his wife's being wheelchair bound. But given that her condition was a fraud, he didn't seem her partner or cohort in it. He seemed to believe she was actually, and annoyingly, disabled. This was interesting. Who was Sophia Redmond scamming?

Sophia pressed her hand against her temple, as if locating a headache. "Maybe kidnapping isn't the exactly right word. Maybe there's no word that fits the situation exactly. She's under the influence of an unstable man. Preys on the young. He's part of a group of weird people, a cult. She's lost the ability to think for herself."

"You know the young man's name, or the name of the group or their whereabouts? Or what the cult is?"

"If we knew those things, would we need you?" Arthur asked.

"Not even the name of the man?"

"We never saw him. She never met him at our house, the way a proper date would do. Always somewhere else. She didn't talk about him directly, either, but she mentioned his friends, this group that believes they can travel back into the past. They live together, too. Bunches of them." Sophia straightened in her wheelchair. "Does that sound sane to you? They're sick, all of them, and my daughter's in their grip now!"

Emma calmed the woman down, pondering the ethical issues here. The surveillance was a bust, all over but the death rattle. Client vamoose. So given that was finito, a declared failure, was there a reason she couldn't accept this completely different case and different issue? She surely didn't feel a conflict of interest and she did feel the cold breath of overdue bills. Insurance cheat or not, Sophia Redmond had the right to look for a daughter she considered in danger. "Let's get some facts down, then, all right?" Emma asked. Ethical questions sufficiently addressed.

"Then you'll help?" Sophia Redmond looked tearfully relieved. Arthur glanced over at Billie. "Which of you is going to do it?" he asked.

"We both will," Emma said. "Plus other associates." Not exactly a lie. If other associates should magically appear, they'd work on it, too. "As I explained."

"Does she have any experience? She's pretty young, isn't she?" Arthur jerked his head in Billie's direction.

Emma could feel the irritated vibrations coming off Billie, who was being discussed as if she weren't sentient. But what was she going to say? Billie had experience, yes—one—and she'd botched it all to hell. "Her youthful appearance is the main reason I'd like Ms. August on this case," Emma said. "If we're searching for a missing teenager, there will be situations where she'd obviously be much better than I would at . . ."

Billie, combed and tucked and carefully made-up, sat, her eyebrows lifted, her expression amused but intent as she focused on Emma, waiting. At what was she better?

". . . looking young. Fitting in. Less obtrusive. She is not underage, I assure you."

Billie returned her attention to the Redmonds.

Arthur Redmond grunted. Emma assumed that indicated assent.

They made note of the few statistics that Penelope Susan Redmond had managed to accumulate in eighteen years. Grades that depended on her level of interest, a level that had bottomed out of late. College plans lost in a fog. Increasingly withdrawn, sullen, vague, and nobody could think of a reason.

One sibling, Wesley, ten years younger. Mrs. Redmond rushed to overexplain the reproduction gap. "Like I said, Penelope is from my first marriage. I was young, like her. Stupid, like her, and then I was single for many years before I married Arthur. We had Wesley."

Penelope had a standard teenage résumé. Nothing exceptional or idiosyncratic that might provide leads to special-interest groups. Emma detested searching for runaway teens. They were larval creatures with no form or parts to grab. Not humans yet. Billie would do this one.

Penelope baby-sat a lot all year, and in the summer, she added working in fast-food places. "A nice, average girl," Sophia repeated several times. "A good girl."

Arthur Redmond snorted.

"And since I've been . . . incapacitated, she's been extra good. Drives me to the appointments and every single day to United Market. The one right off the freeway? I like fresh vegetables, you see, and they—"

"For God's sake, Sophia!"

"She told you about his cult?" Billie asked. "What did she say?"

Sophia shook her frizzy hair. "She didn't. Wesley, my son, told me. She told him about the time-travel. That she'd met her knight in shining armor. Her rescuer. They're very close, Penny and Wesley. Ten years apart and only half related by blood, but they're like *that*." She held two fingers together. Her other hand still clutched the *I.J.* article about Emma.

Arthur said, "Sophia!"

"She didn't tell Wesley his name?" Emma asked.

Another head-shake. "I've told you everything we know."

"This young man took her away without ever calling or visiting her?" Billie asked. Emma approved of both the question and its timing. "Where did they meet, make contact? Did he go to her school?"

"She never said . . ." Sophia stopped and reconsidered. "I don't think he could have. I mean he could have graduated a while back, but I don't think she would know him from school. He's older. He has a car. He pays rent. So he must have a job. Must be older than she is. Or a dropout with some criminal way of making his money."

"What kind of car did he drive?" Billie asked.

"Yellow."

"What kind of answer is that?" her husband asked, still not looking at her.

"I don't know cars. It's silly, big, and it looked yellow in the rain. Not a normal car color, either, not even taxicab yellow, more like—"

"Sophia!"

"No," Emma said, "this could be important. Not taxi yellow, so what kind of yellow did it seem?"

"Butter," Sophia said. "Something between a lemon and butter. Maybe margarine."

"Sophia!"

"It was raining and that's all I know."

"Her Social Security number?" Emma asked.

"Why?" Arthur Redmond this time. "She's not applying for a pension."

"If she looks for work, even under an assumed name . . ." Emma kept her voice flat.

"I don't . . . I'm sorry. I must have it at home," Sophia said. "I'll look."

"A photo?" Billie asked.

In their own way, Emma thought—possibly the way of a blind youngster and his seeing-eye dog—they were working in sync. So far.

"Uh—not with me," Sophia said. Arthur's expression made it clear that was a ridiculous question to ask him.

Billie nodded. "I'll come pick one up, then," she said. "You do have one at home, don't you?"

"Of course," Sophia said. "Her graduation photos just arrived, in fact. Not that she's going to graduate if she doesn't get back to school soon."

"Did she have money with her?" Emma asked.

The Redmonds looked at each other this time, but both shook their heads. "Just what she's saved from the sitting and summer job," Arthur finally said. "But baby-sitting doesn't exactly set you up for the long-term, and neither can we. We aren't rich. Which reminds me. About your fee?"

The Redmonds were gone and Billie was in a state of panic. "Listen," she said, "about being part of this—I mean, finding somebody. I don't know how. She's a teenager. I don't know what you'd do in that—"

"Aren't you the one who found your son?"

She was a snot, that Emma Howe. Billie'd bet the woman had thrown her kids, screaming, into pools, saying that would make them learn to swim. If they drowned instead, that was their choice. On the other hand, she was giving Billie more work, not firing her, despite the rotten video. "But you said—"

"—that there were easier ways than calling every Baptist church in the U.S.A. So you're learning them. That's what we were doing at the computer. But mostly, it's common sense, it's paying attention, it's figuring out the logic of the girl. Think of yourself as an archaeologist—looking not for a lost civilization, but for a lost girl. Reconstruct her and you'll find her."

It was a setup. It was strike two, baby. Throw you to the wolves. "The computer—"

"—isn't going to be an enormous help in this case. She doesn't have a job. If she has to pay for her bed and board wherever this house is, she isn't doing it directly to a landlord. She isn't married, doesn't have kids. You'll have to find her through him."

"The nameless one? The addressless one?"

Emma shrugged. "The one with the big yellow car that Sophia Redmond couldn't ID."

"It's an old hearse." Billie knew that Emma had watched the tape enough times to draw the hearse in minute detail. She'd heard her own voice come through the thin wall over and over and over again. Was Emma actually being discreet in not saying so? Kind? "But the DMV won't give out information."

Emma shrugged again. "To most people. I have an account. But I'd need a license number. Something. And if we had it, that'd be too easy, anyway. Where would the sport be?"

"Will you really be working on it as well?" Billie didn't know why she asked. No matter what Emma said—or even might, momentarily, mean—she would sure as hell be elsewhere when needed.

"Think of me as a consultant," Emma said, "or a coach. In close contact and as needed. The truth is, the girl has to resurface, hopefully not on the streets of San Francisco. I don't know which'll run out on her first—her funds or her boyfriend. Besides, the theory behind having both of us on the payroll is that the company could handle more work than I could all alone."

Sarcasm was uncalled-for. Was Billie supposed to feel guilty for having expected actual training? Something more than a boring rule book and a so-called one-hour introductory blitz to the computer? The good news had been that Emma had been interrupted by a phone call shortly after beginning her unsettling voyage through Billie's life. The bad news was that she'd never finished whatever it was she thought she'd taught Billie.

"Any ideas?" Emma asked.

Tips on tracking people not likely to be in the computer's databases would be a kindness, but Emma did not specialize in sensitivity. Finding a teenage stranger was nothing like finding a son her ex husband had taken. Penny Redmond could be anywhere in the country three days after she'd zoomed off with a young man whose name wasn't even known. Why would Billie have ideas on finding the girl? Why had Mrs. Redmond read the damn article and come here? "There's a chance the hearse's license plate is visible on the video. But I guess the tape's already gone," she said.

"Hmm," was all Emma said.

"Then I should . . ." Billie murmured, waiting for divine intervention, or at least a cue from Emma.

"Yes," Emma said. "What precisely are your plans?"

Plans? The ones she'd gleaned from the other successful searches she had done for missing teenagers?

"How do you plan to find her?"

And she was going to pay Billie next to nothing while she billed her services out as if an experienced, knowledgeable PI was on the job. Instead, the client had got an indentured servant who literally didn't have a clue. "I think . . ." She had lost the ability to think. Sterile sand filled her skull. A desert without so much as a mirage.

Well, not quite. This open-ended questioning, this noninstruction *was* Emma's method of instruction, and the lesson was that it was up to Billie, and nobody else, to produce a theory, a plan of attack.

Okay, who'd know about a boyfriend? "Her girlfriends at school. The counselor, if she'll talk to me. The people she baby-sat for. I'll get their names when I pick up the photo." She looked at Emma. Would it kill her to crack a smile, nod approval?

"The hearse, too," she added. "It's unusual. Maybe there's an interest group on the Internet, maybe he's part of it." She felt down-right inspired now. The possibilities were endless. "Maybe——"

"Wesley," Emma interrupted. "Little brothers know a whole lot more than anybody wants them to. Maybe more than Mom heard or was told. Penny supposedly confided in him. Bet that means he keeps secrets well."

Billie cursed herself for mentally dismissing Wesley as soon as she heard of him—the way one was supposed to, the way she once dismissed her own younger brother. According to him, she still did. "And Wesley," she said. "Sure."

"Write everything down or tape-record it for your report," Emma said. "Stay in touch. Where you are. Keep me up-to-date."

Billie nodded, resenting the way Emma, when actually offering practical advice, adopted a patronizing tone. *Take good notes.* Wow. Maybe that was Billie's delayed punishment for shooting off her mouth at her interview, about how intelligent she was, how she could tell what was important from what was not.

"And another thing," Emma said. "Clients lie."

"People who hire us?"

"Always. Ah, they don't necessarily do it on purpose and some-times they even think it's the truth, but it isn't. They want us to love them, to think they're the goodies. It would make our job easier if they'd tell the truth, but they don't."

"Like about her being crippled," Billie said. "Is that what you mean?"

"Well, that one isn't exactly subtle. But in general, about any-thing. There's undoubtedly more. Always think about what they didn't say, see what other possibilities there are."

Great. This was less patronizing, but unhelpful and downright confusing. It was enough to think about what had been said, but of what *hadn't* been?

"That about it for ideas?" Emma asked.

It shouldn't be, Billie was sure. Other diabolically ingenious approaches should be springing from her lips and brain—but guess what?

Emma nodded. "All right, then," she said. "There's hope for you yet."

Eight

The Redmonds' house looked a lot more inviting than it had on the rainy day. Today, encapsulated in scrubbed air that had the texture and shine of a bubble, everything about the Victorian pulled the viewer close: its flowering shrubs, the green-and-white pillows on the white wicker porch furniture, the white clapboard, the shutters and trim painted two shades of gray. As much as wood and pigment could sparkle, they did.

Until you were inside, Billie thought. There, despite the chintz and crisscross curtains, despite the sun reflecting on waxed oak floors and area rugs, tension leached the color. Everything was too perfect and set in place. In a room trying for hominess, nothing was personal, mussed, tossed, casual, or used-looking. A home for show, not for use.

She and Arthur Redmond had passed through a narrow center hall with its obligatory gilt-edged mirror over a small table where mail would be thrown. Or, more fittingly, carefully placed. Into the living room, where Sophia sat on a cushioned chair next to a table set out with cups and saucers. Her folded wheelchair leaned against the wall behind her.

Billie had checked the hallway staircase en route. No lift. No bed visible in the living room. How and where did poor, incapacitated

Sophia catch her *z*'s? If, as Emma suspected, she was scamming her husband, too, what did she do? Crawl up the stairs? Sleep on the dining-room table? Sit upright all night long, martyr to a false insurance claim?

"Coffee?" Sophia asked as soon as Billie was halfway into the room. "Or tea? We can make either. No problem. I can get into the wheelchair with just the littlest bit of help and make my way around the kitchen. You adapt, you know. I've been practicing short distances with a four-legged cane. Exhausting. Very hard."

"Stop babbling," Arthur grumbled. "She does that all the time. Stick to the point. She's here about Penelope." He was presumably addressing first his wife, then Billie, then his wife again, but he never tried for eye contact with either of them.

Nonetheless, his rebuke found its mark on Sophia who went blank at the moment of impact. Then she regathered her forces and plugged on. "Thank you for being so prompt. To drop everything and start on this the very same day, that's quite impressive, isn't it, Arthur?"

Arthur sighed. With no more going for him than being tidy-looking, employed, and male, he assumed the role of emperor.

"Important to get on a case right away," Billie said. "Don't want the trail to get too cold." Thank God for TV and radio dramas. Generations spouting dialogue like that had given it the gloss of authenticity.

The Redmonds nodded agreement with her sentiments. Or somebody's.

"Did Penelope drive?" Billie asked.

"Knew how. But she didn't have her own car. We aren't made of money. Rode her bike a lot."

"She was a great help to me since the accident, since I couldn't drive. She drove me around. Although I'm trying to do it myself again, now that I'm working with the cane, you see."

"Sophie!"

"Were you able to find Penelope's Social Security number?" Billie asked.

Sophia pushed a piece of paper toward Billie, who seated herself on the sofa.

"And a photo I could use?"

Sophia nodded again, but this time, her lips were pursed. "Showing a photo of my daughter to people . . . That makes me feel so . . . That 'Do you know this person? Have you seen her anywhere?' thing. It's so . . ."

"Yes, of course, I understand." It was unsettling, suggesting that Penelope Redmond had not simply gone off for a long joyride with the object of her raging hormones but had, indeed, disappeared. Possibly permanently. She thought of the skeletons in the meadow, of somebody, somewhere, going door-to-door with their photos years ago.

"I have her high-school graduation photo. The one that will be in the yearbook," Sophia said. "She had so many copies made. Here. She looks too serious, though, and she has such a nice smile."

Billie picked up the photo. Baby-faced, people used to call that look. She bet it annoyed the hell out of Penelope Redmond, and no amount of older people telling her to enjoy it would change her mind. It was the portrait of a girl who was hell-bent on becoming someone else. She had refused to smile for the camera. Her cheeks were sucked in and her eyes focused on a grand horizon far beyond San Rafael High.

Billie recognized herself in the photo. The fantasies she'd had at that point. The expectations. To be Somebody or die. "She's quite pretty," she said. A mane of curls spiked the air around Penny's face and tumbled onto her shoulders. "Her hair is lovely. Is it brown?"

"It photographed dark. It's more red," her mother said. "But there's also lots of blonde highlights, more in the summertime, and all of them natural, may I add. But she won't do a thing about those curls. Won't cut them or use a straightener or pull them back or anything."

Arthur grunted. Billie couldn't tell if he resented the idea of doing anything to Penelope's curls, or that Sophia was veering off-course again. Or perhaps he had indigestion.

"Her eyes are hazel," Sophia said. "And she's five foot six and a half. Slender. A decent student. Until this year." She pursed her lips and retreated somewhere inside herself.

Billie felt much more urgency than the girl's mother seemed to. "It would save time if you could give me the names of her friends at school and of the people she baby-sat for."

Sophia came out of her twilight sleep and nodded. "Friends," she echoed. "Well, there's— Oh, look at me! I'm so embarrassed! I asked what you wanted and never did another thing about it! Coffee or tea, Miss August? They're both easy, one or the other, so don't be bashful. Arthur will help, won't you, Arthur? And I have a little tray of cookies—store-bought, I'm afraid, and not even from the good bakery, but it is hard reaching everything while I'm in this—"

"Tea, please," Billie said. Maybe with Arthur out of the room, Sophia would speak less and say more. "And those names?"

But first, Sophia had to give excessive directions about water temperatures and the box of teabags and the small jar of sugar—or would Billie prefer honey?—or maybe lemon?—to Arthur, who was, according to her, a man who actually, literally, couldn't boil water until this accident turned them all upside down, could Billie believe that? She was so grateful to him, so impressed at how quickly he'd stepped in to help. . . .

And with a glare and a grunt, he escaped from the room.

"Now let's see," Sophia said. "There are so many friends. She attracted people. Some folks have that gift, and she was one. But their names have just—I'm in such a dither these days between my accident and then this, I can't seem to concentrate on anything. Even the names of my daughter's friends. You must think I'm a—"

"Don't worry, it'll come to you." What came to Billie was that perhaps this woman didn't know her daughter at all. Zilch.

But a name and then another slowly emerged. "I don't want you to think I'd ever let her sit for anybody unless I know their name and the hours and their phone numbers," Sophia said. "She knew that, and she was good about it. She tried, you know? She isn't a bad girl, whatever you might think, given this . . . situation. I think if she hadn't met this man . . ." She shook her head. "Anyway, there's a blackboard in our kitchen for writing things like the name of the people she'll be sitting for, and she never once to my knowledge went out on a job without writing all that information on the board."

Except. Billie heard that word waiting to be said, to negate the promising sentence.

"Except that of course, every time she'd come home from a job, she'd erase the blackboard." Sophia smiled wanly. "Who could have known it might be of any relevance? Is it?"

"I don't know yet." Billie leaned forward and patted Sophia Redmond's subtly patterned floral skirt. "Doesn't matter," she said. "It might just speed up things. Incidentally, could I speak with your son, too?"

Sophia looked terribly sorry. "He's not home from school yet. But don't worry about that. Wesley's only eight—a baby. An innocent. What would he know about things like cults and kidnapping and boy-girl things? Except the little we've already told you. He doesn't know where she is—we asked, of course. And the kidnapper never came here socially, so he couldn't have met him."

Billie nodded acknowledgment and tried to get Sophia back on track. "The people she sat for." They would know. Or the girlfriends would. She had to meet him somewhere, didn't she? It might be after school or after a baby-sitting job.

"I know a few. The regulars," Sophia said. "The Feldspars, of course. Mimi and Joe. She's worked there off and on since their older child was born. And Sally O'Neall. She's divorced now, a working mother with three children, and her ex-husband is no help at all. It's so hard in that situation."

Billie felt a flash of resentment. As if she needed Sophia Redmond in her poufed-up house to remind her of what it was like to be set adrift with a child in an expensive world.

"I was like that," Sophia said, her voice lost in the past. "Such a bitter struggle to keep Penelope and myself alive. That's why—Arthur might be a little . . . but he saved me." She nodded emphasis for her words. "I don't know what would have become of us, otherwise. I don't know whether you're married or not or have a child or not, but if you were and then you weren't, and you were left with a child to raise—it would be easier for you. You have a trade, a profession. You have special knowledge and skills. I don't."

Billie tried to look neither startled nor amused. Special knowledge, indeed. She cleared her throat. "About the baby-sitting . . ." she prompted.

Sophia nodded and glanced fearfully toward the kitchen, toward the thought of Arthur, who'd saved her, whom she was attempting to delude along with the insurance company—Arthur, who owned her poor, unskilled self. "Penelope's done more than her usual sitting this year. She was saving toward college. At least until she met him." She frowned. "Unless she wasn't baby-sitting at all. Unless that was a lie so that she could meet him." Her indignation was short-lived. She sagged and sighed.

Arthur, having presumably finally learned how to boil water, reappeared carrying a tray laden with a carafe, a box, and a small ceramic bowl.

Billie watched the Redmond's interaction, or noninteraction, with the fascination she might give the stylized motions of Kabuki theater. Husband and wife seldom looked at each other or directly responded, unless Arthur's growls counted. Now, while Arthur made much fuss over his tea ceremony, clattering cups onto the tray, twisting the carafe top, and asking Billie what flavor she wanted, Sophia, without acknowledging his arrival, continued to look skyward and mull over baby-sitting clients.

"She made up this box of different kinds," Arthur said, holding out a calico-covered box with neat rows of packaged teabags. "Any kind you can think of. Peppermint, chamomile, raspberry-lemon . . ."

"Lemon, please." Billie didn't want tea. Didn't want to stay long enough to drink it. But going along with the Redmonds' sense of timing, not interrupting their performance piece, promised to be more rewarding than forcing them into her mold.

"Oh," Sophia said, "of course! How silly of me—our next-door neighbors! Don't know how I forgot! Lord, Sunny uses her all the time, what with those three boys of hers."

Billie nodded encouragement. "Good."

"Sugar or sweetener?" Arthur asked.

"Nothing, thanks." Billie's house was chaotic and a mess, but there was a sense to the interruptions and detours. A three-year-old lived there. A Russian immigrant. And a crazed single mother. Theirs was an intricate and jaggedy dance, but it was with each other, and in the end, or at least so far, it worked. But living here in this tidy, controlled unhappiness would drive her mad. She wondered if perhaps Penny was. "If you have those addresses, or phone numbers," she told Sophia Redmond, "I'd appreciate them, and if you think of any more people, let me know."

"All nonsense," Arthur grumbled. "The kids she baby-sits didn't take her away. Neither did their folks."

Sophia said nothing.

"It's possible that the young man in question spent time with her while she baby-sat," Billie said.

"That's against the rules," Sophia said firmly.

So was running away. And so was faking an injury. "Perhaps he picked her up, gave her a ride home. Or she mentioned him by name to a client." Billie felt less and less sure of the worth of these names as she spoke, but Arthur was such a pain in the ass, she wasn't going to give him the satisfaction of agreeing with him. Besides, if she didn't gather names and a list of places to go and people to see— what would she do? "It's a start," she added. "Could I see her room before I leave?"

"Her room?" Sophia looked on the verge of panic.

Because she can't go up with me? Billie wondered. Can't monitor me, or mist the air with her babble? What is she hiding? "A girl's room has a lot of clues as to her interests, friends, maybe even this mysterious young man," she said. "Or his address."

"It must be filthy! I've been sleeping down here on a roll-away and I haven't had a chance to dust or tidy, and she isn't the neatest girl. A teenager, you understand, we've all been there, maybe you even have children of your own, you'd understand, but even so, I'm so ashamed—"

"Sophia!" Arthur uttered his rebuke/command/reflex without looking up from his teacup.

Billie took the combination of Sophia's flutters and Arthur's bark as permission. She stood up. "I'll only be a moment." She waited half a second, watching both their expressions, but their eyes still didn't meet, and she didn't think they were hiding anything. Not collectively, at least.

Sophia's voice gave instructions and running commentary the entire time Billie was en route to Penny's room. "The room at the back," she said. "When you're up the stairs, go straight back. It's all pink, you'll recognize it. I tried to make a nice place for her, but nothing was ever enough. But I'm sure that kidnapper didn't buy eyelet dust ruffles for her."

"Sophia!" Arthur's voice seemed far away as Billie entered a room so pink, she felt in utero. She wondered whose doings it was— Sophia for the girly-girly bedspread and curtains, the ruffled and useless pink desk lamp and Penelope, perhaps, counteracting by painting her walls such a hot purply-pink they were reason enough to flee?

No photos of friends. No rock- or movie-star posters. No address book or diary in dresser drawers or desk. No schoolbooks. Nothing in the wastepaper basket except a crumpled flyer about specials at Thrifty. A whole lot of clothing gone; the pieces that were left the sort that would be worn by the lampshade-bedspread girl. Penny was leaving behind the girl her mother wanted her to be.

That one, the one she'd left as a souvenir for her family, was without character or definition, and certainly mean-spirited about dropping clues to her whereabouts.

It didn't feel like a teenager's room. Particularly one who'd rushed off impetuously. She felt sure that somebody had been up here cleaning and possibly removing and Billie didn't think it had been Arthur or Wesley. That's what Sophia's protests were about— fear that Billie would know she was agile enough to climb the stairs.

Billie made her farewells, promised to keep the Redmonds informed, and left, carrying the photo and list of names. Then she drove her car half a block and sat waiting, feeling like the infamous dirty old man parents warned against.

The schoolbus discharged three children, two girls who headed around the corner and one scrawny boy. He looked even younger than eight, his head too big for his neck, his back slightly bent under the burden of an overstuffed pack. What on earth could he be carrying in it? Were the schools that rigorous about homework in third grade? She watched him until she was sure he had to be Wesley and then walked toward him.

His eyes widened.

Don't talk to strangers. How many times must Sophia have repeated that to him? And she was right, and Billie was asking the kid to break a promise, do something potentially dangerous. "Wesley?" Billie the stranger asked.

He walked more quickly.

"I know you aren't supposed to talk to strangers, but I'm not really one, and I'll only take a minute. Maybe less. Can I walk you home?"

He looked suspicious, confused and frightened. She felt a maternal pang, transposing her own son to this boy's place. Last thing on earth she wanted to do was scare a kid. "My name's Billie August and I was just at your house talking to your mom and dad. I'm trying to help them find Penny."

He stopped and narrowed his eyes still more. She wondered whether there was any basis to squinting. Did reducing vision really sharpen it? What was the boy looking for?

Wesley resumed his trudge, but less vigorously. Besides, they were near enough home for him to bolt to safety if needed.

"Could I ask you a few questions? It's okay if you don't know the answers, but if you did, it would help a lot."

"Do you know where Penny is?" His little-boy voice made his question a hopeful passage played by a flute.

"Not yet. First, we have to find out the name of the fellow she went away with, then there's a really good chance we'll find her."

"She said she'd call me, but she didn't." He shrugged skinny shoulders under an all-weather jacket. "I don't know where she is, lady."

"You must miss her a lot. Sounds like you're her special friend."

He darted a suspicious look at Billie.

"Because she told you she was going to leave, but she didn't tell anybody else. In the whole world." The white porch was close ahead. "Can we sit on your steps?"

"I don't know where she is," he repeated, but he put his backpack on the bottom riser.

"Did she talk to you about this boy?"

"He isn't a boy. He's a man. Penny said that. He was a man, not immature like everybody else. Her knight in shiny armor."

Behind her, Billie could swear someone had pulled a curtain back and was watching.

"He went to college," Wesley said.

"Now? You mean he's in college now?"

He looked unsure, then shook his head. "He *went*. Not anymore. He can go back in time, too. But like a game."

Billie nodded. "Did you ever meet him?"

He shook his head.

"Did Penny say his name?" she asked casually. "Do you remember?"

He flicked a glance toward his house, then looked at Billie. "She said it was our secret. But I think maybe he's a bad person. I think he took her away, kidnapped her—know why?"

Billie shook her head no.

"Because she wouldn't *leave*. He was gonna rescue *us*. But then he took her away and left me. Or maybe soon they'll come get me, too, and that's why she told me she'd call. She wouldn't leave." He shook his head, confirming his words. "She wouldn't leave me." He blinked quickly. "Not ever. She said."

Billie sighed, not feigning the sympathy she felt for him. And for Penelope Redmond, who had surely meant those words, before life intervened. "Well, then," she said softly, "we probably should do whatever we can to find her, correct?"

He looked at her gravely. "His name is Stewart. I wasn't supposed to tell, but if he took her away, if he's bad . . . 'My Stewart,' she said. 'The Stewart.' But I don't know where he took her. I hate him! I hope you arrest him!"

And then, before Billie could say any of the platitudes adults offer as a smokescreen against the naked pain of children, he turned, and blinking hard again, grabbed his backpack and ran up the front steps.

Nine

Arthur Redmond watched Wesley skitter double-time toward the stairs.

"Hold it right there!" Arthur boomed. The kid was his flesh and blood, no denying it. He looked like snaps of Arthur at his age, but the resemblance was skin-deep. He disliked the very thought that some of his DNA had turned into Wesley. The kid was more rabbit than boy, jumpy over the ghosts and ghoulies he saw everywhere. Including, apparently, in the face of his own father. "Where you running to?"

Wesley silently turned and walked back to the living room. Bump, slide—the bookbag behind him.

"Don't drag that thing on my floors!" Sophia called out.

Arthur winced. The sound of her was an icepick through his ear into his brain.

Wesley, minus bookbag, came in and waited.

That's how it was with both of them. They waited. Arthur felt like he had to act, do things, say things, or they'd pounce. Except for Penny, who liked to pounce first, who wasn't afraid. They'd better find her, and fast.

The kid's eyes were red-rimmed. Rabbity. Why didn't he ever smile? Why didn't he bring anybody home? Play ball after school? Ride his bike with somebody, not by himself? What was wrong with him?

"Weren't you even going to say hello to me?" Sophia's voice was almost coy, full of mellowness now that her floors were no longer in jeopardy.

Her floors. Her curtains. Her sofa. He couldn't stand how she labeled the things she took care of as "hers." "Don't put your dirty hands on my cabinets," she'd say.

If Sophia passed a dustrag over it, it became hers. What was Arthur's, then, besides the mortgage? "She make you cry?" he asked his son.

Wesley looked as if he might cry again. "Nobody made me cry. I wasn't crying!"

"Then you'd better have your doctor take a look, because you have pink-eye." Arthur could feel Sophia shoot him a glance, but the boy needed toughening. Who'd he think he was fooling? A crybaby. He needed to know he couldn't get away with lying to his own father. "What did she want?" he asked.

Wesley looked at the floor. At her floor. Her fake Aubusson or whatever it was. Supposed to make her house look homey. "Who?" he squeaked out.

"You think I'm suddenly blind or stupid?" Arthur said. "That woman you were talking to on the front steps. One minute ago."

"She said she talked to you first," Wesley said.

"I'm not saying you shouldn't have—I'm asking what she wanted!"

"Arthur." Sophia sounded like she had a whole lot on her mind, but was too tired to get out more than his name.

"Are you going to answer me? What's wrong with you?"

"She—she—she wanted to know about Penny. If I knew where she was."

"Did you?" God knows, he and Penny were always whispering, giving each other meaningful looks, laughing until their father walked into the room, although what a teenaged girl, nearly a woman, had to tell a twerp, he'd never know. It was close to sick, their relationship, like she was his second mother. Only because his first mother was so useless. "Did you maybe remember something new?"

Wesley shook his head.

"He's tired," Sophia said. "All that school and the ride home. Let him have a snack, rest—"

"He isn't a baby! We're talking! So what did you tell her?"

"Nothing."

"I saw you yakking! I saw you opening and shutting your mouth—what was that? Air coming out?"

Wesley blinked. Sometimes Arthur was convinced the boy was honestly mutating into a rabbit. The resemblance was astounding. "I told her to arrest whoever took Penny away, and I hope she does! Can I go now?"

Arthur felt the muscles of his arms clench. No, he wanted to say. No. You can't. Because I say so. He couldn't even think why he'd want to keep him here, his scrawny neck bowed, eyes on the floor—her goddamned floor—except that he couldn't stand this fearful, cowardly creature scurrying away from him. Always away. He was hers, like the floors, the dining-room table. Everything. Nothing was his. No gratitude in this house.

"Have a snack before you go upstairs," Sophia said. "The apples are delicious, and there's lots of . . ." But Wesley was long gone.

"You could get him one," Arthur said. "They're so good and healthy for him, why don't you behave like a mother? Maybe if you did, your daughter wouldn't have run off."

"I can't walk right. . . . I—"

"The cane's right there. You're supposed to try it, aren't you? You could make it into the kitchen, for God's sake."

She sat where she was, a lump. He was beginning to think she was faking the injury. Only reason it'd taken him so long to figure it out, was he couldn't understand why she'd want to. And lie to *him*, too. She didn't need money. He worked like a pig so that he could pay for everything. Just look at her list of possessions to prove that. Not like she had a real job with real working hours. She did the books for him, a few odd jobs, and the rest of her time was spent dusting and watching the tube. What more did she want?

Then it dawned on him. She wanted to avoid him. To do nothing for him. Wanted all the benefits he provided but no physical contact even if it meant sleeping on a roll-away. Which was increasingly fine with him. Let her be an invalid.

"You're wrong," Sophia said.

Of course. He always was to her. Wrong in every way. Too mean to her baby boy. Too strict with her daughter, the girl he'd taken in and raised as his own. Too cheap with the household money. Too everything. Big news.

"About her."

Her? Wrong about her? Who? "You mean that snotty kid detective you hired? I'm not wrong—she's a waste of money. Get your ass out of that chair and you could ask the same questions she's going to. You're the one had to provide all the information as it is."

"It isn't my fault."

"And when you decide to hire somebody, you use an article in the paper—a puff-piece—as a guide. And then, you didn't even *get* the goddamned owner, the one the story's about. You got a *kid*. You're crazy, you know that?"

"We got them both. And that doesn't change the fact that she knows."

"The detective? Which one? Who are you talking about?" He looked at the room. The teacups and paraphernalia were still on the table, where they'd stay till the house collapsed if Sophia kept playing cripple. Until he left. Then she cleaned up, because she could not stand clutter or mess. As if he wouldn't notice, put two and two together. "Who knows what?" He could have been questioning the ceiling, the cold tea the August woman had left. "What the hell are you talking about?"

He swore—if she didn't get her act together soon, start talking like a human being, acting like one, shape up that twerp son of hers, find her goddamned lying and dangerous slut of a daughter—he didn't know what he'd do.

Sophia peered at her hands like she'd never noticed them before, like she was so involved with examining them she hadn't heard him.

"Who knows what?"

Now she lifted her eyes, shocked that he'd raised his voice, then lowered them as she looked down at the arm of her easy chair. At the big rose flower print with the green leaves. It had taken her a whole year to find what she wanted, and when she had, it was as ordinary as mud, far as he could see.

She knew the silent treatment drove him up the wall. She used it like torturers used the rack. God knows she babbled if anybody else was around. Couldn't stop talking, except when they were alone, which she made sure happened as little as possible.

"Goddamn it," he said, "I asked you a question. What's wrong with you? Are you mute now, too?"

"She didn't leave for the reasons you said. Not because I nagged. Not because I got hurt and made her work more here, didn't have snacks in the house, like you said." Sophia kept her head down, muttering her words to her armchair.

"That's what you're making a federal case out of?" She sounded insane. He would have her committed after they found Penny, an even looser cannon. *"Who cares about snacks?* It was something I said, that's all—conversation."

She looked into middle space. Nowhere.

"Making conversation, you know what that is? God knows, you don't try, you act like a stone statue. You could get off your ass and feed your son, is all I meant. And what do you know, anyway? You don't know shit—not even about your own daughter. Not like a normal mother should. I heard you—couldn't remember her friends' goddamned names, like you were senile or something!"

Except he knew she was right. Penny knew. Said she'd *seen* him, said she knew about the houseboat, then wouldn't say any more, but that was enough, like being lobbed with a grenade was enough. He just hadn't known that Sophia knew about Penny's knowing. That was the only reason he let Sophia hire that detective. Because Penny knew, not because he thought she'd been kidnapped. She knew and ran away with the knowledge, taking it God-knows-where.

"That's why she left." Sophia sucked everything but the words out of her madwoman's voice. She wasn't there for him. Except to be the voice of doom, his judge while the walls moved closer in like in a horror story and the ceiling lowered onto his head. "Why do you really want to find her? To hurt her? To shut her up? What do you want with her?"

And the flowers under Sophia's arm and behind her neck spread and filled the lenses of his eyes until he couldn't see anything except the blob that was his wife and the bed of roses around her and his sweat that had gotten it, and red—just red.

"Don't stand over me," she said. "Leave me alone. It's your fault."

He swung his hand across her face and back. Across and back.

She screamed. No more flat voice. No more faraway. She was there, right there, and she screamed.

And he swung his hand again. Make her do something. Anything.

And back. Until—he couldn't believe it—the twerp, screaming, "Stop!" all the way down from his room. "Stop that!" And throwing something hard from the doorway—an apple, for God's sake, his snack his weapon—then tackling him. Spindle-legs and flimsy arms grabbing, kicking, pulling him away from Sophia, who stood up, forgetting she was crippled.

And Wesley, beating still, fists against his leg, his hip, kick-boxing as much as he could.

Arthur released him. Stood back and studied his son. And laughed. "Chip off the old block," he said. "You got balls, after all. I like that."

Ten

"What do you want me to say? She was my baby-sitter. I really never wanted to know much about her." Diana Golden continued to fold laundry while she spoke to Billie. "She was hard to get. Nice with the kids, trustworthy, didn't have boys over. She sat for a lot of people. And that's about it. I mean, I appreciate what you're trying to do, and how her parents must feel and all, and I wish I knew things about her—anything, really, but I don't. Here, have more coffee. Help yourself. . . . You really don't have to do that."

Billie smiled and folded a diaper. "It's second nature," she said. "It's even making me nostalgic."

"Oh, well, have another kid. That'll cure you." Diana Golden gestured toward the pot and cup, then smoothed a diaper. "I cannot help destroy the universe for the sake of convenience," she'd said when Billie commented on the cloth diapers.

Diana Golden seemed well-meaning with a vengeance. Her house was earthy. Real, she'd probably have said. A mess, but a well-meaning one, with magazines devoted to worthy causes facedown and open on the natural-fiber furniture, and everywhere else, dishes on the floor for several animals, and toys of the higher sort—easels and paints, major-but-abandoned construction projects, kiddie art papering the kitchen walls, a large bowl of flour—the bag said it was organically grown stone-ground whole wheat—and a bowl with yeast proofing on the counter next to a pile of flyers urging people to attend a zoning hearing. Diana folded diapers quickly, while the younger child slept and the elder was at playschool.

Billie's attempt to form a kinship with the woman wasn't working as well as she'd hoped. Diaper-folding was fine, but the woman was interested in issues of global survival, not those of a part-time sitter. "Did you ever have a chance to talk with her? About her plans, or her social life?"

Diana shook her head. "To tell the truth, when she'd get here, the last thing I wanted to do was sit around and chat. I know she was good about feeding the boys and cleaning up afterward. And she didn't eat me out of house and home, or smoke—but I don't suppose that's the sort of thing that's particularly helpful to you."

"Was she always available, say, on Saturday nights? Or did you get the feeling she had her own social life?"

Diana stopped folding diapers and frowned. "We only used her Thursdays, and only for about two hours. We never called her for a weekend night. If we go out, we take the boys. It's important at this stage of their life to feel safe, connected."

Then why Thursday for two hours? What was sufficiently off-limits to risk letting the kidlets feel unsafe, unconnected? Couples therapy. Bingo.

"Look, I wish I'd paid more attention—but honestly, do you? I mean to a sitter?"

Billie thought of Ivan, the nanny, whose myriad adjustment problems to the U.S., to English, to American girls, to his classes, were over-familiar. Perhaps it was his Slavic drama that made him share so much. Or her own nosiness. Or simple proximity—he lived in her house, after all, and she'd much rather sit over a cup of coffee and let the talk flow than hand out flyers. "One last thing," she said. "Did you drive her home at night? Or was she picked up by someone?"

Diana shook her head. Her hair was short and straight. Brown.

Sincere hair, Billie thought, like the rest of her. Then she wondered at the flash of resentment she felt. Or was it envy? Was this woman, so totally immersed in what she considered important—the world and her boys—was she the woman Billie had intended to be?

"Once or twice, in summertime when it was still light out, she rode her bike. And Joe—my husband—drove her home a few times. I don't think I ever did. Why?"

"Nothing. I meant . . . Well, nothing, I suppose." Diana would have noticed the yellow hearse—she would have raged against its fossil-fuel consumption. In a way, it was a comfort to know such women had outlasted the sixties. But Penny Redmond wasn't on her list of concerns.

Neither had Penny been high on the list of the woman who'd preceded Diana, a vivacious creature in tights, a long sweatshirt, and frosted hair. Her children were at school, her house was being cleaned by a tiny smiling woman and she seemed eager to talk. Unfortunately, she had nothing to talk about. Unlike Diana Golden, that woman, Char, had indeed noticed and formed opinions about Penny, but only about her hair, which had possibilities but was too long, causing it to lose body, and in need of a good, layered cut, and about Penny's underutilization of cosmetics. "That dreadful natural look they're using," she said. "I mean, they're all peaches-and-cream and they can get away with it at their age, but that girl has potential. She'd be striking if she'd pay a little attention to herself, put on some color."

By the time Billie left, she had no information about the boy with the yellow hearse, but she had a strong and shameful desire to have Char make her over or at least tell her whether or not she had "potential," and if so, what to do with it. By the time she left Diana Golden's, she was thoroughly ashamed of having had such petty, self-obsessed, superficial desires.

In any case, it was time to switch gears. The school day was about to end, so she'd troll for friends, not employers.

She drove down San Pedro, overaware of the odd configuration of the roadbed—the hillside homes, upscale markets, and school on her left; the Bay, like a poking finger, appearing erratically on her right. And each time it pushed in toward the road, business—yacht berths, boat repair shops, or upscale bayside housing developments—took advantage of it.

In front of San Rafael High, she decided that the third try would be the charm. She should have felt kinship with the mothers in need of sitters and company, but instead she felt a rush at the sight of the nondescript tan building, the comfort of familiarity, although she'd never visited it and had barely noticed it. It wasn't her alma mater, nor did it look like any school she'd attended, but all high schools were kin in primitive, compelling ways. Inside, they'd have the smell of gym lockers, lunch-room economies, and teen hormones. Hallways would sound the same no matter the words, the air filled with eyes, laughs, and exaggerated motions.

It wasn't as if she was unaware of the decade-plus since high school, or that each piece of her hard-won and not-always-welcome postgraduate learning, in and out of academia, had altered her perspective. But it hadn't altered her, except to fill in the blanks, make her more so. And the sight of the school triggered buried adolescent longings for a sheltering place of her own.

The bell rang and Billie felt the end-of-the-day panic that had once been a constant. Back then, she'd flood with apprehension about whether she had enough activities stacked up to delay going home as long as possible. Maybe that's where and how she'd learned to organize her time and plan ahead. To act, be duplicitous. Pretend. Her mother had inadvertently given her great skills.

Sophia Redmond had known the last names of Penny's babysitting clients, even if she hadn't known where they lived. It was easy enough searching the phone book and making calls. But of all Penny's friends, only one, Rebecca Dobbin, was given a full name. "Penny's best friend," Sophia had said. She hadn't had the number.

The rest of the girls she mentioned were on a first-name-only basis, and the task of determining which Heather or Chelsea was the right one felt daunting.

Even if Emma would have been willing to spend a moment demonstrating how to find juveniles who didn't yet appear in the computer files, she was up in Sacramento on a background check. Billie was on her own with next-to-nothing to go on. "Penny didn't keep a diary," Sophia said. "Penny took her address book with her." After much prodding, Sophia remembered that Rebecca lived in Peacock Gap. Either Mrs. Redmond's real-estate sense, or her basic knowledge of her daughter's life, was out of kilter. Assuming the Dobbins listed their phone number, which was a shaky assumption in Marin, there were few Dobbins in San Rafael, none down near San Pablo Bay, and none that said *Rebecca* or *R.* or *Dobbins children*. So, with the help of a detailed street map, Billie went through all the listings and called the one closest to the neighborhood, wondering what she'd do with it or the address if she knew it. Lurk outside waiting? She was reluctant to leave a message and give the teen time to consult with Penny, alert others, or construct a new story. Face-to-face would be better, but how?

And if she couldn't find Rebecca this way, how would she? Surely not through the school. If they'd blithely point out a student to a complete stranger who asked for that information, Billie would have to make a citizen's arrest on the basis of child endangerment. Besides, how could she identify herself, produce credentials? She worked for Emma, was only in training, a novice, and wouldn't have certification for six thousand hours—five thousand eight hundred and fifty-some now—if she survived. Maybe Billie didn't have enough basic imagination to investigate anything.

The voice that answered the phone was too resonant and sure of itself to be a teen. The mother, Billie assumed. "May I speak to Rebecca? This is Billie August."

"Can't talk to her here, Billie honey. Not just now," the other end of the receiver said, as if they were buddies. "School's in session for an hour more. And shouldn't you be there, too?"

"I graduated last year. I haven't seen her in a while." Billie stood in the phone kiosk and crossed her fingers against any major changes in group psychology and high-school sociology since she'd graduated. Let there still be enormous status gaps between juniors and seniors, so that Mama wouldn't be overly familiar with the last crop of grads.

"So you're in college now?" Mama asked.

"U.C.," Billie murmured, to ensure her credentials as a diligent, smart, and possibly inspirational old pal of her daughter's.

"Good for you!" Rebecca's mother sounded truly delighted by Billie's academic fortunes. "But as for Becca . . ." She sighed. "Lord knows where she'll be after school, what with all she does. I surely never know." Pride, not irritation filled her voice. Amazing. The woman liked her daughter. It could be that way, then, even during the teens. "I use the beeper to reach her, and thank the Lord for it. You want the number? It won't beep in class, so don't worry. Against school rules. All the kids keep them on vibrate. Bec tries to return all calls on her cellular between classes."

Billie entertained herself until the return call by envisioning a roomful of vibrating beepers, wondering where Rebecca wore hers and whether such implements were a new and additional reason for teenage girls to be addicted to phone calls.

"This is Rebecca Dobbin, returning your call."

"My name is Billie August and I'm helping investigate the whereabouts of Penelope Redmond—"

"Shit!" It was whispered, but powerful and straight from her center. "Oh, damn. Sorry. I thought . . . I didn't recognize the number, and I thought maybe my mom was out somewhere and had heard—"

"I'm sorry to disappoint you," Billie said.

The girl laughed. "No matter. Waiting to hear about schools is making me crazy. I really am sorry. Let's start over. Who'd you say you were?"

Billie explained again, asked if they could meet for a few minutes after school. She didn't want to say any more on the phone. She wanted the easy flow of a conversation and she wanted to see Rebecca. Her years of drama classes and performances might be of practical use in interpreting body language, deciding what role the girl was or wasn't playing in her friend's disappearance.

"Penny," Rebecca said with one-millionth the emotion she'd demonstrated about school. "Okay. And I'll tell you what—I'll bring a few other girls who knew her, too. *Know* her! Didn't mean to sound like she's dead!" Her laugh sounded nervous. "Maybe somebody else was closer to her, knows more than I do."

Which did not sound like a "best friend" speaking. How far removed from the reality of her daughter's life was Sophia Redmond?

So now Billie waited outside the school, enjoying the afternoon sunshine, and then the chorus of teenaged voices as the doors opened and school let out. She played a game of whether she could identify a "Rebecca" before the girl herself spoke up. "I'll be in the parking lot and I drive a white Honda Civic," Billie had said, and that had seemed enough for the high-school girl.

She saw now that it would be hard distinguishing which Honda was hers. Half the student body drove them, although blue was a much-favored color. She surveyed the cars, and approved of their middle-aged American makes and models. This wasn't a flaunting kind of parking lot. Wasn't overly Marin, where B.M.W. was said to stand for Basic Marin Wheels. Even the one Mercedes was acceptable, as it was twenty-five years old and in desperate need of wax.

An undersized boy with an open backpack walked toward Billie, waving, then abruptly stopped. "Sorry!" he said. "Jeez. I thought you were my . . . ride. Sorry." He shuffled off, head down, puzzling her by the visible and excessive humiliation this mistaken identity seemed to have caused him. Adolescence was a bitch, but maybe she'd forgotten just how much of one it was.

Then she saw him raise his arm again. *"Smoking?* But you *said,* Mom! You promised." Billie watched a woman stub out a cigarette, wave away the smoke she exhaled then frown as her son continued to chastise her.

Mom, he'd said. Mom. He'd mistaken Billie for his mother. She, who'd been blissfully identifying with the students, sure she hadn't changed in any significant way. She looked around and noticed other women looking bored at the doors of their cars. Their children didn't drive yet. They looked a lot like her.

The patina of shared youth she thought she'd been wearing like makeup cracked and she saw herself as the oafish wanna-be she was. Time might indeed have filled in the empty spots—but in so doing, had coated the rest of her, like a pristine building dulled with soot. She needed to be sandblasted.

No wonder Becca had been sure she'd find her. Too polite to simply say, "You'll be the old one." By the time she rounded up Penny's friends, the other carpool mamas would be gone, and Billie would stand out as if outlined in neon.

This was what it was going to be like, wasn't it? Little by little, whole populations and age groups would look at her and see only "the other." Worse—the "has-been but who cares?" The way she secretly regarded Emma. Emma might be smart and experienced and have a lot to share, if ever she would, but Emma was old, past it, whatever "it" was. Younger was better. In the cosmic scheme of splendid blazing life, Emma didn't count quite as much as Billie.

She didn't approve of such thoughts and hadn't realized she had them until she saw them reflected in the faces and eyes of the pack of girls approaching her. She wondered if Emma felt as surprised by the implicit gulf as Billie just had. If Emma felt as unchanged and fully alive inside as Billie did.

She waved and nodded, and they came toward her, five of them, looking assembled by a politically-correct casting director. One freckled carrot-top with a crew cut, one Scandinavian blonde with a French braid, one Asian—Billie thought Vietnamese—with black hair in a Joan of Arc bob, one with cornrows and tawny port skin, and one who might be Hispanic with a lush mass of brown-black waves. Nothing extreme about them except geographical ancestry. None visibly pierced or tattooed. Every one wore gauzy patterned skirts, oversized sweaters, blousey jackets, and heavy lace-up boots.

Pretty, but not drop-dead. Not weird, not nervous, as they approached her. No eyes averted, no hunched posture or awkward giggles. Too self-confident to have been cast as pariahs or losers, but probably not the reigning queens of their class, either. The great bulge in the bell curve of adolescent possibilities. Which suggested that Penny Redmond was also nice-normal. Except nice-normal didn't include running away the second semester of senior year.

She picked out the French braid as Rebecca and allowed herself a flash of smugness when that girl moved forward, taking leadership. The flash ended when the girl spoke. "Becca says you're looking for Penny, right?"

So much for Billie's ESP. The tawny-port girl nodded, setting her cornrows jiggling, and tilted her head, waiting. Billie smiled greetings to Becca and nodded at the girl who'd spoken. "I was hoping you'd be able to give me information about her. I figured you guys would know what was really going on in her life."

They wrinkled brows and looked at each other. "You police?" the French braid asked. "Could I see identification?"

"I'm not the police. I'm an investigator. A private investigator."

"A PI," French Braid said. "Cool."

Billie couldn't tell if that was praise or a put-down. "This isn't a criminal matter. Penny's eighteen. She can move out, quit school, whatever. But that doesn't mean her parents aren't worried about what's happened to her."

"Her parents," Becca said. "Worried." Words delivered in the teenage flat tone that implied complete, stunned disbelief.

"No?" Billie noticed the girl with the Joan of Arc hair shivering. "Listen, it's cold. Is there somewhere we could go to get a soda, talk more comfortably?"

Becca shook her head. Billie wondered if she'd picked the hairdo because it reacted so nicely to her tendency to move her head, or if she'd developed the emphatic head-shaking to draw attention to the braids. "I have to get back. We're rehearsing. Missy has to get back, too."

"And me," Joan of Arc said. "I'm stage manager."

Billie wanted them to know that she'd been an actress, she'd been there, knew how wonderful-awful the rehearsal process was. Wanted to see a flash of recognition, of kinship, but instead, she said, "My car's right here. It'd be warmer. I can turn on the heater."

They nodded and filed in, four in the back, giggling over the squeeze, the partial overlaps, the girl with the bob up front with Billie, who swiveled to face Rebecca. At Billie's request, they identified themselves. Dru in red hair, Becca in cornrows, Missy in French braid, Cara in the dark waves, and Anne as Joan of Arc.

"I wondered if you could tell me about her. What kind of person she was. Interests. Things like that."

Almost as one, they shrugged and looked to each other for inspiration.

"She wanted to be an actress," the girl with the black hair said. "To be famous. I know you have to have a passion to be a success in the arts and all, but she kind of overdid it for a long time. And then, boom, she didn't even go out for this play, so I don't know what she meant. She said she was coming to tryouts, but she didn't."

"I liked her better last year," Becca said, "but it wasn't like we were close or anything, even then. Not that we were enemies, but I was wondering why Mrs. Redmond gave you my number. I didn't think she approved of Penny hanging with me, my being a dark-skinned girl and all." She laughed as she drawled out her last few words.

"Then with whom was she close? Whom might she have confided in?"

Becca shook her head. "Like I said, she was real private this year."

"A snob is more like it," Dru said. "Called everything 'babyish.' She meant us, too."

"Private," Becca repeated. "Way more than she used to be."

"Like nobody here was really, really interesting enough to pay attention to." Dru was not about to give up her take on the missing girl. Nor was she or anyone providing any help in finding her.

"Do you think it might have been because she was involved with this guy?" Billie asked.

"What guy?"

"I was hoping you knew. She went off with a guy in a yellow hearse. Strike any bells? Did you see that car around?"

"There really was a guy?" Dru said. "We thought . . ."

"To tell the truth," Becca said, "I don't think Penny ever would have met him here—if she met him anywhere—where everybody could see."

"Whyn't you admit it?" Cara said. "If she did tell you something, you couldn't count on its being the truth."

"She . . . exaggerated?" Billie suggested.

"You could call it that."

"Or lying."

"Harsh," Becca said.

Cara shrugged. "Why'd he have to be a secret, then? I mean, like from us? Why should any of us believe her—this time? Her true love. Really!"

"Her parents," Becca said. "Really strict on her. She was probably afraid they'd find out."

"Did she ever say a name?" Billie asked, but without consulting each other, they all shook their heads. "Does the name Stewart mean anything?"

This time they did check each other out before shaking their heads, then they muttered about a long list of boys named Stewart who were, however, the same age or younger than the missing girl. Plus, nothing mysterious. Plus, "in relationships anyway," or "just too geeky to be a possibility," or "maybe gay."

And within minutes, they reminded Billie that they had to get back to play rehearsal. She wrote down their names and phone numbers, gave them her number and asked them to please call if they heard from Penny or remembered anything that might be at all helpful.

She thought she saw one of the girls flip the business card she'd handed her into the first refuse basket she passed. But maybe that was a trick of the light.

She shouldn't be depressed or feel defeated. Even Emma had talked about slogging around, getting no results for a long time. But she'd been so set for a quick breakthrough. Her First Case, after all. Or second, if she had to count the surveillance, which she chose to think of as a warm-up exercise that didn't count. But this was for real and with her first day gone, all she'd learned was that the missing girl needed a good haircut and was a liar.

On the other hand, maybe she should be depressed.

Eleven

People were incredibly stupid, Emma thought. Which was good news for her. She'd never entirely lack for business because human beings would inevitably, irresistibly screw up, lie, cheat, pose, and, in general, wreak havoc. And at some point during that process, someone who still believed life could be brought into alignment would want help from a person like Emma.

She drove along Route 80 from Sacramento, past stretches of tract homes that looked dropped from above, possibly onto the cows that till recently had been the only inhabitants, toward the East Bay urban sprawl. The latter mess was appealing because it meant home was over the bridge a few miles ahead. Her back ached for her chair—"nothing more than an impression of your butt with ugly up-holstery," her daughter had said three years ago, the last time she'd deigned to visit. Emma found the insult apt and endearing, and now she thought with yearning of the butt-chair and a cold beer, feet up while she wrote her report on the laptop. And then *if* she could find one, her favorite lullaby, a subtitled foreign film on TV.

Meanwhile, she worked on getting over personal disappoint-ment about Glenda Walker, self-declared candidate for change, pop-ularly known as Glenda the Good. Glenda was the advocate of everything compassionate. Perfect for her North Bay electorate. And furthermore, she was a newcomer to politics—a citizen-candidate with no prior elected office. She was what everyone wanted—a politician who wasn't one. Luckily, in addition to intriguing ideas, she also had a husband who'd made millions in software and who doted on and bankrolled her, so she was not accepting any special-interest money. She was even photogenic and had photogenic kids. A pure-gold candidate, Emma would have said.

Except that, having been hired to check up on her, Emma now knew that the woman was either overly sure or pathetically unsure of herself. One or the other impulse had prompted her to invent a past. To lie about items so easily checked, they weren't worth the effort of fabrication.

Touching Glenda's dossier was like grabbing an overripe peach. Emma's fingers slipped straight through its rottenness.

Glenda was not the Phi Beta Kappa grad of U.C.-Davis her press releases and shiny-paper pamphlets claimed. She was an idiot. Why lie about that when university records showed that Glenda Arnold had never completed her degree, let alone been honored for scholastic excellence?

And, of course, this revelation prompted Emma's employers, the gleefully disloyal opposition, to request further examination of her résumé and past life. Past *lives* had turned out to be more like it. Nothing criminal, but one more marriage and child than she'd chosen to mention and two fewer positions than she'd claimed to hold. She had indeed worked at those agencies, but as an office temp, not exactly the policy-making position she'd presented on her résumé. Automatic upgrades via frequent-liar coupons, as Emma put it. At one point, her excellence at word-processing won the heart of her employer, Mason Walker.

Unfortunately, in order to acquire Mason, Glenda had had to shed an inconvenient pre-existing husband who was delighted to talk to Emma and the world about Glenda. And to detail why he'd been granted sole custody of their child (that person being another omission on her curriculum vitae).

Emma had a sick sense that Mr. Walker knew nothing about either his predecessor or his wife's first child, and that all this news was going to result in something much more than an aborted run for state office.

The damnedest part of it was that if Glenda Walker really believed what she preached, she'd have made a great candidate and nobody would have cared about a missing Phi Beta Kappa key. Nobody had to be as smart as she'd pretended to be.

But neither did anybody—not even a senator—have to be that stupid. California didn't need another double-talking, truth-twisting dummy lawmaker.

In any case, while Emma had lost a candidate, she'd gained a loyal client for a job well done.

She reached the span, paid, and waited to see if this toll-taker would break the San Rafael–Richmond Bridge's code by uttering a civility. Not that she was hoping for the Golden Gate's toll-taker effervescence. After all, in the waterbound, bridge-rich Bay Area, this was the stepbridge, the unremarked joining of two outposts of The City. No postcards showing refineries on one side, San Quentin on the other. No songs about this bridge. The desperate were never so overwrought as to commit suicide off it, make it the last thing they saw and touched. No wonder the toll-takers took a vow of silence.

As had this one, who took the bills as if they were tainted. Emma wondered whether these workers were recruited for their sourness, indifference, and lack of curiosity. Or maybe they were all burned-out former PIs who'd examined and questioned too much. Matter of fact, the more she thought about it, the more appealing the taciturn toll-taker's life seemed. No office to maintain, no overhead. No bumbling hires. On a clear day, they even had a view across the Bay to the soft contours of Marin.

She, on the other hand, felt dizzy with problems. Wherever she pointed on her personal horizon, she saw something askew and worrisome.

Like Billie. Bright and eager, but, bottom line, she'd totally botched her first job. Beginner's luck was supposed to be good, so what did that presage except even worse performances?

That job was over, but tonight she'd give it one last shot, write the company, find an excuse for her office's incompetence, try to hang on awhile longer. Maybe she could say the video camera jammed, the investigator got sick, or . . .

Toll-taking looked better and better.

She reached the end of the span and approached San Quentin, the biggest waste of real estate in the universe. Why reward hardcore prisoners with a view across the Bay to San Francisco's lights and towers? They could relocate the inmates, put ranges and hot tubs in the cells and sell them for millions.

Who had Saint Quentin been, anyway, and what had he done wrong to have his name used this way?

And then the saint was forgotten as she approached the futuristic ferry landing under its canopy of struts and skylights awaiting the return of waterbound commuters. A better way to get places than the road, for certain, as witness the bottleneck directly ahead.

When she crept forward a hundred feet or so, she saw the reason. A dead deer halfway across the freeway entrance, its neck twisted out of all its living elegance. Poor stupid beast. Nearly a century to grasp the concept of motor vehicles, but the lesson wasn't taking.

George, her companion, her lover, her whatever, thought cars and deer represented the new Darwinism. "What else kills them, anymore?" George asked. "The mountain lions' comeback is too little, too late." It was illegal to harm a deer, except in the brief hunting season—although hunting wasn't allowed anywhere locally she knew of. Deer were reviled and protected. In fact, Meatloaf, a neighbor's Golden Retriever, had bitten a deer that later died, and although any idiot could see that Meatloaf had not brought down the animal—that it must have been ill and near death before encountering the old, bandanna-wearing dog—despite that, Meatloaf was on probation as a deerkiller. One more injured or maimed animal near his mouth, its owners were told—one more set of matching tooth prints—and Meatloaf would be history.

Meanwhile, the deer, the PLO of Marin, insisted that they'd never relinquished their ancestral lands. Which didn't make the sight of the startled, stiff and still-beautiful carcasses less upsetting.

She finally made her way around the dead deer and onto the freeway, and once again returned to eager anticipation of home and ease. Her chair, her beer . . .

Which was when she clearly remembered drinking the last beer in the house the night before. She was too tired even to feel as annoyed as she wanted to. Just get thee to a market. The nearest one. United. Right off the freeway. Ah, yes. Sophia Redmond's daily stop for veggies. That woman was a tedious pain in the butt.

She backed into a parking slot and tried to remember what else her pantry lacked. Bacon, she decided. For the hell of it. Her cholesterol was low, her weight satisfactory, but George's wasn't. Even at this age, level of mutual tolerance, and nonexistent legal bonds, even with all that going for them, coexistence with the opposite sex remained complicated. While she pondered the ethical ramifications of George's blood chemistry versus her taste buds, the door of the car in the handicapped space against the curb opened and a cane emerged, followed slowly and heavily by none other than Sophia Redmond, grimacing and moving with a stiff-backed, glacial pace. A martyr to the need for fresh vegetables.

Her performance deserved an Oscar. Emma's pulse accelerated. She waited until Sophia stiffly inched her way into the store before she herself bolted out of her car, opened its trunk and retrieved the always-present video camera. Then she rummaged through her briefcase until she found an unused piece of yellow lined paper and her pen. SORRY ABOUT THE DENT! she wrote in block letters. GOOD THING IT DOESN'T LOOK TOO HARD TO FIX. OR TOO EXPENSIVE. I DON'T THINK THE THING HANGING DOWN IS AN IMPORTANT PART, AND I'M SURE THEY CAN MATCH THE PAINT. IF I HAD A JOB I WOULD PAY YOU, I SWEAR, BUT TIMES ARE TOUGH. GOD WILL PROVIDE AND BLESS YOU AND FORGIVE ME. End of message.

She smiled at her prose as she walked to Sophia's car and put the note under a windshield wiper. Then she postponed buying the beer and lolled in her car, hands folded across her chest, fighting the urge to doze in the late-afternoon sunshine. She imagined Sophia slogging through the aisles, asking everyone for help. *I'm hurt and deserted by my daughter. Could you get that can of soda off the top shelf for me?*

Finally, there she was again, using the shopping cart as a walker, her cane protruding from between two paper bags. Emma sighed with gratification, slid lower in her seat so that the video-cam rested on the dashboard and was barely visible, and watched.

Sophia wheeled her cart to the car, then, seeing the note under the wiper, stopped, took the cane out of the cart and slowly made her way to where she could retrieve the paper. She read it, frowned, glanced at the driver's-side door, near where she stood, then looked left and right. Then she read the note again, her expression darkening. Once more, she looked around, this time, not at her car, but at the parking lot, searching for the dent-maker.

Emma started the videotape as Sophia examined her front bumper, bending low to one side, and then the other. She made her way around to the back of the car where, standing tall, she looked down at the trunk and twisted to see the bumper. After another quick look at the parking lot, she was miraculously and totally healed so that she was able to do a deep knee bend, straighten up, bend from the waist, then lean over and crane her body left and right. She could have led a yoga class. Having thoroughly searched for the dent and found none, she stood up, brushed off the knees of her slacks, and briskly repeated the drill on the other side.

Emma controlled the urge to laugh out loud. She didn't want to contaminate her tape with the same childish behavior Billie had shown. Sophia was demonstrating enough flexibility and balance for a career in ballet.

Finally, confused and enraged, Sophia ignored her cane altogether and without so much as a grimace, hoisted the two bags of food. Holding one in each arm, she walked to the trunk, put one bag on the ground, unlocked the trunk, bent over it when it was opened, and put her groceries away.

People were indeed incurably weird. All you had to do was figure out who they were versus what they wanted, and you had it made. Glenda Walker and Sophia Redmond. Two in one day, and, still better, she could bill both clients.

Emma had saved herself a client. Plus she'd saved Billie's ass.

This one time. She didn't intend to make a habit of it.

Or ever to tell her.

Twelve

Penny sat quietly on the back steps in the early-morning stillness and watched Mr. Oliver next door examine a plant. He half stooped, a coffee cup in one hand, the puzzling leaf in the other, engrossed and completely unaware of her. His posture, his caring, reminded her of long ago when she was little and feeling sick. Something about the unsaid words that filled the space between her mother and herself then, Mr. Oliver and his plants now.

But that was then. Her mother—that mother—had disappeared. Arthur had put a spell on her eyes and ears while he hit and shouted at her.

Mr. Oliver sighed so loudly she heard it on her side of the fence. "Time to go to work, good friends," he said. Once she would have laughed at a man talking to leaves. Now she didn't think it was so funny. He loved them. They were his first concern in the morning and his last at night.

Maybe everybody had things that filled their heads as soon as their dreams were over. She surely did. Mr. Oliver's were nice, and the worry and care made them grow. Hers were not nice, not to be fed and let to flower. But even as she thought this, another part of her brain replayed the pictures she didn't want to see, replayed the day the ice-thin image of her family had shattered once and for all.

Almost two months ago, she'd been out on her bike on a Thursday given over to teacher's meetings at her school, but not at Wesley's. She'd had no responsibilities, no guilt, and she set out with no known destination or purpose except to work herself and move. She headed south, toward the Golden Gate and Sausalito, where she wanted to sit in the little park and watch the City across the Bay.

It had been a good plan, except that as she pedaled down Bridgeway toward the park, she felt hungry and decided to buy a bagel at Molly Stone's. And parked in front of the market, she saw a dark blue, waxed and shining Lexus with the license plate JUS KIDN. Arthur's true love, pampered and adored, always garaged and even dusted, for God's sake. He said he kept it in perfect shape and Penny couldn't borrow it because it was a mobile ad for Just Kidding, the children's-wear "outlet" store, final resting place of the samples and stock of the lines Arthur represented.

But the store was in Novato, the other end of the county, as was their house in San Rafael and Arthur's office in Terra Linda for his repping. He literally had no business in southern Marin. Besides, this morning, after criticizing everybody else, he'd said he was "off to the salt mines." He said that every day, as if it were witty or ever had been. Then he added that he'd be in Novato, getting a special sale ready.

She stared at the license plate, as if it might rearrange itself into something less familiar and troubling. And then at the supermarket.

Her stepfather *never* did the food-shopping. Never even helped. She'd had to drive her mother every single day to her big adventure—food-buying. Arthur wouldn't pick up a loaf of bread on his way home. Even if he'd had an impulse to suddenly buy a treat for himself, why detour to Sausalito for it? Besides, he was so miserly, he'd never enter an upscale market like this. Arthur had told Penny she'd better find a way to put herself through college because she and her mother spent so much money, he couldn't afford one more expense. Something smoky and caustic filled the pit of her stomach.

This wasn't where he should be or what he should be doing. This wasn't anything like his so-called "normal" behavior and it was therefore frightening.

She squelched an impulse to clamp down her mind, to stop knowing anything more, the way her mother did. Pretend it's okay, that it makes sense, that there's a good reason for it, even if you can't think of one.

Arthur had a secret. She was sure it was another woman. She *wanted* it to be, wanted her mother to feel as miserable and hate Arthur as much as Penny did.

What if she was wrong? After all, this was only a market. Maybe Arthur had suddenly discovered a kind and charitable impulse, making history, and he was saving a starving family.

In Sausalito. Right. In which of the picturesque million dollar hillside homes?

The fierce, hot pressure she felt gave way to a sense of peace. *Good.* Something real, finally. This would force her mother to notice. Provoke a break. She'd have grounds, even if this was a no-fault state. She'd have reason—as if she didn't already with his foul treatment of his stepdaughter and natural son.

"How could I leave him?" she'd said too many times. "I don't have money or skills, and I do have two children—one not his—and I don't even know if the law would make him provide for you." Her mother always told her both more and less than she wanted to know.

Penny had said that as soon as she graduated, she'd get a job, help out—that away from Arthur, Wesley wouldn't cringe and try to disappear all the time and her mother wouldn't be weepy and crippled. Would stop playing helpless and waiting to die.

The words blew through the house and were dusted away by her mother. No job Penny could get would make enough money. Then maybe this sighting would do the trick, much as Penny didn't want to know this, not really. She detested him, but the idea of the delicacies he was probably buying, or how much he'd pay for sex on the side, made her literally ache with rage.

The smart thing would be to leave now and have the pleasurable day she'd envisioned. Contemplate the sailboats on the bay and drink a latte. She walked her bike to the end of the lot, and waited, not sure what she was going to do next.

There were no questions, however, when she saw him emerge from the store, a shopping bag in his arms, the tops of two champagne bottles visible. She was galvanized by her fury. When his car pulled off the lot, she followed without thinking it through. Odds were, she was on a futile trip and wouldn't be able to stay with him for long. He could be on the freeway in seconds, or heading away from the water up toward the hills where her pedaling power had no chance against his horsepower.

She was in luck. He stayed on the flats, turning right on Bridgeway, then right again, into the marina and the houseboats.

She wouldn't have thought of an assignation in a village of beached boats in Richardson Bay. She had always thought the Sausalito colonies were romantic, but not for Arthur! It made him still more disgusting.

She followed at a distance, watched him park, then walked her bike as he and his groceries progressed past the recycling hut to the entrance to the boats and then, onto the walkway between the two lanes of them. At least he couldn't lose her there. There were no side "streets" or off-roads. She stayed well behind him, somewhat hidden, if he turned, by the dock's angles and the potted foliage that lined both sides.

Still, she felt foolish, a kid playing detective games. Nervous, too. But more than any of that, she felt compelled to find out and expose his secret.

They passed houseboats with spiral staircases, roof gardens, fantastic towers with stained-glass windows, but the one he finally entered was a small, stubby thing, more boat than house, more box than boat. The sort you'd pass right by.

She waited to move closer when it felt safe, but he came out again within minutes and without his groceries, heading back toward the parking lot—and her. There was no place to hide, only the walkway with short-planked entries like side roads into each boat, so she turned and hurried off, waiting behind a car in the parking lot in a state of confusion. Was it really possible he had been dropping off groceries on a mission of mercy?

She felt foolish until she wondered what variety of mercy required two bottles of champagne.

Then it appeared he wasn't leaving. He leaned into the backseat and brought out an undersized violin case, one a circus midget might use. Then he extracted a silvery tube—a music stand, she thought, the kind an orchestra used.

He wasn't musical in the least—didn't even like listening to it. Would never have provided such luxuries for Wesley.

He checked that his car doors were locked, and headed back to the dock.

She waited, then edged all the way back out to the house. But she couldn't see anything because the drapes were drawn over the small front windows. She couldn't remember if they'd been that way earlier.

Couldn't hear anybody playing the tiny violin, either. Maybe the child for whom it was intended was in school now, didn't have a teacher's workshop. Maybe Arthur was using the instrument as a bribe, a gift to the child via the mother, when it was the mother he wanted.

She couldn't tell anything about the inhabitant from the blandness of the exterior. One semi-alive plant slumped over in a clay pot on the step at the front door. The most a person could say was that this place was easily forgettable. She made a point of memorizing its number.

Finally, she rode off, leaving him to his mistress. Or, for all she knew, his entire other family including the musical midget. On the way off the dock, she tried the mailbox for that number. It, like all its unidentified neighbor boxes, was anonymous and locked.

That night, she asked him about his day, giving him a chance to come up with an alibi, a chance to make her suspicions foolish hallucinations.

"What's to say? Same as always, too much work." He dunked a piece of sourdough into the chicken gravy. "Why do you suddenly care? What do you want?" He didn't even glance at her. Her spying had gone unnoticed.

So she repeated the act three more Thursdays, cutting school to make a circuit to the houseboat parking lot at about the same time of day. Once nobody was there, but both other times, her stepfather's car was parked in the lot.

On one of those days, while she paced at the beginning of the dock, two men carrying a green velvet sofa came through the narrow opening to the dock. " 'Scuse us," one of them said, and she pressed herself and her bike against the wall of mailboxes.

She watched them progress down the dock to, surprisingly, the mistress's house. He was buying the bitch a sofa the day after he'd told Penny that if she went out for the play and had to rehearse at night instead of baby-sitting, he would not make up the difference, and she could forget about going to her own senior prom.

She watched them maneuver the green sofa into the house, and even though it hadn't touched her, she felt its velvet against her skin—against the Mistress's skin until she thought she'd be sick.

Leaving the dock, she passed a parked van that read, Rooms to Rent: The Comforts of Home in an Hour. She didn't connect the sofa with the van until she was on the road home, but there hadn't been any other commercial vehicle in the place. Maybe he wasn't counting on this affair's lasting too long and he only loaned his woman things. That would be like him.

From then on, when her stepfather punched or slapped her mother, blamed business reversals on his wife, treated Wesley as if he were a failure at age eight, called Penny a slut—the heat of her knowledge worked its way from behind her ears up into the top of her forehead until her brain was on fire with it. He called Penny a slut while he drank champagne with his whore and furnished their love nest.

"Mom," she said one afternoon when they were alone. "I have something to tell you." She spoke as gently as she could, hating herself for deliberately hurting a woman who already looked down for the count, and she didn't mean the wheelchair business.

"I have bad news, but I'm sure you'd rather hear the truth than have me lie to you."

Her mother put down the calculator, deep worry-lines between her eyebrows. "Are you in trouble?"

"No. Well, maybe we all are. I saw Arthur—"

Her mother winced. She hated that Penny called him by his given name, but damned if she'd call him "Dad" the way her mother wanted, and "Stepfather" sounded too weird, especially for this conversation.

"I think—I'm sure—Arthur is having an affair."

Her mother's mouth dropped open. "Why would you say such a thing? And how would you possibly know if it was true, which I can't believe." A sudden single tear hovered on the lower lashes of her mother's right eye. "He wouldn't," she said, and the tear dislodged and made its way down her cheek.

"I saw him. Three times."

"With . . . with somebody?" Her mother looked pitiable. Penny wondered if she should hold her hand during the telling, or pat her head, but it all seemed so sordid and topsy-turvy, she stayed where she was.

"Not exactly."

"Well, then, how dare you say such an ugly—"

"First time was by accident. I saw him where he didn't belong. Carrying champagne. And food."

Her mother shook her head; she all but clapped her hands over her ears. She looked old, and like a loser.

But the way she looked and the things she did weren't to be trusted and surely not to be pitied. Penny had seen her mother get out of the wheelchair when she thought none of them could see. She'd seen her walk normally to go have a cigarette—also a secret, and denied—outside the back door. She thought she understood why her mother chose to live like an invalid, why she wanted the disability money. She also understood that she couldn't trust her mother.

"Arthur promised me he would never—" her mother said. "I was so shaken by your father when he turned out to be such a . . ."

Her real father, whose mention was always followed by "bastard" or "liar" or "cheat." Sometimes "whoremonger." Sometimes all four of them in a string. Penny hadn't seen or heard from him—although she'd certainly heard enough about him—since she was five, two years after he dumped her mother. But because he'd been so bad and had made her mother's life so hard, she was never, ever, to say a word against his successor.

" . . . I couldn't stand it if it happened again and in my condition!"

"He brings her gifts. Champagne. Food. He brought a violin one time—a really little one. And a *sofa* next time, and you know how cheap he is with us."

Her mother's mouth dropped open a little. "A violin?"

Penny nodded. "She probably has a child. A musical child."

"Where?" Her mother leaned forward in the wheelchair. "Where were you? How could you see this?"

She was paying attention at last. "A houseboat. In Sausalito."

Her mother relaxed back to her normal slump.

"Do you know her, then?" Penny demanded. "You look like

you know who it is." Her mother's focus had moved to the far wall. "Mom?"

"What? Oh . . . no. I don't know anybody in a houseboat, but you're all wrong. Besides, it's wrong to sneak around after Dad that way."

"He's not my dad! He's a man who treats you like shit while he brings champagne and gifts to somebody else. Why don't you care?"

"There's an explanation."

"Name one—besides what I said."

Her mother shrugged. "It's not important. Don't worry about it anymore."

"Fine. I'll ask him myself at dinner."

"Don't. You'll only—"

"Are you telling me you knew about this?"

Sophia looked blank, momentarily confused. "It's business, not that I know every single promotion and detail. There are home demonstrations, fashion shows as school fund-raisers."

"Twice in the same tiny home? Come on, Mom—there was no sign of people and the drapes were closed. And why deliver a sofa? That's crap and you know it."

"It's business. But the manufacturer doesn't like spending the money, so it's kind of . . . siphoned-off, then put back. You wouldn't understand. Arthur has his faults, but what you said isn't one of them. Besides, even if it was, it's not your marriage, it's mine. When it's your turn, you do better. You find the perfect man, all right?"

"I'm trying to help and you're treating me like—"

"This is the last I want to hear about you sneaking around and slandering him. You look for reasons not to like him, you make up stories about him, and I won't stand for it anymore. Who provides you with a roof over your head? With a beautiful house? Who puts food on your table? Do you understand?"

She didn't and she couldn't. What she understood was that her mother was determined to stay as crippled in her mind as she pretended to be in her body.

What she understood was that she couldn't live in that place anymore, to pretend that it was a home or shelter of any kind.

In that moment, she knew she had to move past or over or through her mother in order to knock down Arthur and change things. To get the chance to breathe. She couldn't spell out what she meant except that action was required. She had to escape, because if not, she'd die.

That was when she slammed out of the house and headed for Fourth Street where she saw a yellow hearse parked outside the yogurt store. When she met her rescuer, knew that he was the way out, the one who would save her. And now, two months after that first Thursday sighting of the houseboat, a month after the scene with her mother and her first meeting with Luke, she was here, on the back stairs of a house in San Geronimo.

And nothing had been resolved or gotten better.

She stood and dusted herself off. Listened. Silence inside. Not even the sound of cups lowered onto the table. No talk. He was still asleep, then, and most or all of the others were gone.

An opportunity. Too much was still unfinished. This was as good a time as any to begin to finish it.

Thirteen

Emma had referred to the nonexistent receptionist/office manager often enough, waving imperiously at the tiny outer area as if its desk would be reoccupied any instant. Privately, Billie had assumed the missing person was a figment of Emma's imagination, born of her need to appear more successful than she was.

Nonetheless, the day before, day one of Billie's search for Penny Redmond, a tall and handsome Amerasian named Zachary Park had appeared. Korean, Billie thought, because of his last name. Half, at least. Plus something or several somethings else. He was all cheekbones, dark hair, gold skin, and grace.

Stern Emma was on the verge of tears—although, of course, the verge was as far as she let herself go. Nonetheless, she barely masked her emotions with gruff mutterings and throat clearings before presenting him as the much-missed receptionist/manager.

His long absence wasn't explained. That omission, plus Emma's relief and pride at his return and Zack's own earnest intensity suggested to Billie that he was in recovery from something major, but whatever it was remained unmentioned. He was a model of efficiency at this, his day job, and from the moment he sat down at his desk with a happy sigh, he answered calls efficiently, relayed messages, did the billing, and fielded calls Emma didn't want to handle, all while appearing a good-enough sort. No wonder he'd been missed. Like barely audible background music, he established a base level of sanity and coherence the office had painfully lacked. Plus, he didn't seem to have hangups about working for and with two women.

"Gorgeous day," he said when Billie entered in the late afternoon.

"Hmm?" She was appalled by the non-information she'd amassed in two days. Take good notes, Emma had said, and she had. Except there was nothing to note. What could she report about her interview with Penny's school counselor, in an ambience of barely controlled chaos—piles of papers on the desk and floor, weighted with her pocketbook, a phone which rang incessantly, a giant-size bottle of aspirin and a doorstop shaped like a dalmatian. Her "client list" was massive, her days too short, and she had nothing to add to the existing fund of knowledge about Penelope Redmond. "Her grades were falling," she said. "I tried to get her to talk about the skid she was on, but she was clamped-up, silent, seemed increasingly isolated—I'd see her walking to class alone. Didn't used to be like that, but she wouldn't tell me a thing except that it was her life and she'd handle it."

She'd waved at the stacks of papers. "I wish I could have followed up, seen about counseling. I tried once, called the house, spoke to her father, who told me to butt out. I should have persisted, and in a perfect world I would have, but I'm also involved in their college application process which is overwhelming. Besides, it isn't as if I could force families to do anything. . . ." She let go of the sentence and sighed.

Billie's attempts to plow for information had yielded a pathetic harvest. Famine time.

"Not a nice day for you, then?" Zachary asked.

His initial pleasantry belatedly reached her consciousness and she realized that it was indeed a very nice day, with winter-crisp sunshine and no wind at all. "You're right," she said. "And I hadn't noticed, so thanks."

"Good going, Sherlock." His fingers still poised over the computer keys, he studied her. "Truth is, you don't look like you're having a great day. Something wrong?"

She made a small *tsk* of impatience with herself. "I thought . . . I had fantasies about investigation. What it would be like questioning people, finding things out and putting two and two together. Now, I've talked to her parents, two of her babysitting clients and four of her so-called friends, plus her high-school counselor, and you'd think—at least I thought—but not one knew—or at least said—a single tangible thing about her. No one knew her, and that's sad enough, but it's sadder still that I'm right where I was when I began. The single thing I had to go on was a boyfriend who apparently doesn't exist. It isn't supposed to be like this. Or else I'm just so bad at interviewing I should quit right now."

"Have a panacea." Zack held up a dish filled with Tootsie Rolls. "Have several."

"Do you always do this?" she murmured, unwrapping one. "Why aren't you fat?" The prodigal son had returned bearing M&M's the first day. The menu would vary, he promised, but the concept would not. He was convinced that chocolate was the antidote to all life's woes. Popping a Tootsie Roll in her mouth, she decided he might be right.

She went into her cubicle and called home, where all was apparently well. "I'll be awhile," she told Ivan, and, more gently, her son. "I need to see a few people who weren't around earlier." She wasn't going to end the day with zero to show for it. Other days, maybe, when she was secure enough to understand that such things happened. But not yet.

"I'll be home to"—she glanced at her watch—"tuck you in,

maybe even before, to give you your bath." Certainly, now that she thought of it. Because the baby-sitting clients, if home, would have tucking-in duties of their own and not want to talk with an investigator at that hour. "I'll read you a story, sweet Jess. Pick out a book."

She suddenly missed him acutely. Wished she could be enjoying him in person. Saw him growing, stretching, changing contours until he was Wesley Redmond with his skinny neck and his enormous backpack, and she felt panic, the danger of missing her son's intervening years while she searched for other people's kids.

Wesley lingered in her mind, dragging his load both literally and figuratively, missing his sister, his ally. He didn't think of Penny as a cipher the way everybody else appeared to.

The way she had been doing. She'd discounted Penelope Redmond the same dismissive way the girl's so-called friends, her oblivious employers, and even her parents, seemed to. Penelope had changed, her friends and counselor agreed. Aloof, a snob, slipping grades. Put that together with a deliberate disappearance, an escape from her life, and it had to mean trouble. Her father had mentioned drugs, a pregnancy, but her mother didn't seem to think so. Either way, a crisis. Either the kind she herself had created or one she was trying to avoid. Whichever one, she'd been lost long before she ran away.

Billie knew almost nothing about the pleasant-faced girl who'd been a name, a challenge, a problem: Missing Girl—one half-step up from the "Have You Seen Me?" kids on milk cartons. But neither did anyone else know her, and the sadness of the situation was a spur. It became imperative to find her, and not only for the sake of Billie's job security.

She was searching the phone book for the rest of Penelope Redmond's baby-sitter clients when Zack appeared at her door. "Could you take this?" he asked. "Weepy woman wants Emma, but Emma's still digging through records in Sacramento. I tried to patch in this call and couldn't. She said she already talked with Emma, so I thought you might know about it. I don't want to screw up something the boss is working on."

"Sure. Let *me* be the one to do that," Billie said. She lifted the receiver. "This is Billie August, an associate of Emma's. Can I help?"

"No," the woman said. "Okay, yes. This is Miriam again."

"Yes, I'm sure, but perhaps your last name?"

"She knows me! Tell her I was putting the trash can back—not till late this afternoon because I forgot about it and my arthritis was killing me, but when I did, I remembered. And I thought to tell my next-door neighbor. After all, they could be in danger, too. Except they weren't home."

"Yes," Billie prompted. "And?" Agreeing to take this call hadn't been one of her better ideas.

"I thought they might be out back and there, on their pool well, really next to the pool. The cement, what do you call it?"

"Deck?"

"Stains. Dark ones. Something had been there. Blood. Don't try to tell me that one was beet stains!"

Billie stared at the "While You Were Out" pad on which she'd written *Miriam* and *bloodstains on neighbor's pool deck.* She added, in quotation marks, *"Not beet stains."* Was this perhaps Emma herself playing a practical joke? "Did you call the police?" Billie asked.

"I don't want a lot of men milling around, asking questions and I already explained that to Emma, and why hasn't she gotten back to me?"

"It's been really hectic here—"

"But this is *urgent,* can't you see? Tell her *Miriam!*"

"I surely will, the second she comes in. You want to give me your phone number?"

"She *knows* it!"

She had let Zack's woeful expression and their shared fear of Emma con her into taking a crank call. "To save her time looking it up, could you please give me your phone number?"

"You don't think I actually know Emma Howe, do you? Old people are crazy, that's what you think!" She slammed down the phone.

Billie resumed her search for the addresses of people Penny Redmond baby-sat for, then dropped Miriam's message, for what it was, on Zack's desk. "You've worked for Emma awhile, right?"

"Two years," he said. "Two years and seven weeks. Not counting time out for bad behavior."

"You saw a lot of my predecessors come and go, I'll bet." She had her jacket on and came into the outer office.

"A few."

"Short-timers, right?"

He nodded in a sad, slow way.

"Now I understand the amazing attrition rate. You asked each one of them to handle Emma's crank calls—maybe the same woman does it for you each time—until they get canned for incompetence. Was that a setup?"

"The call was that bad? Sorry."

"Something about blood, not beet juice, on a deck. I'm tempted to rip up the message and save my job."

He shook his head and put his hand out for it.

"You take the crazy call-ins," she told Zack. "I think that's under your job description, anyway, not mine. Besides, you apparently have tenure. I don't."

"Have another Tootsie Roll."

Chewing one, she was off to San Anselmo, to question another of Penny Redmond's employers. This batch had to yield something.

And yet, for all their late-night talks, what sort of things did she know about her own baby-sitter? If Ivan disappeared, what could she tell an investigator? That he'd been born near Moscow, that his father was dead, his mother Tatiana, was a dressmaker in Eureka. She knew what courses he was taking, that he was attractive, soft-spoken, and addicted to TV because he said it helped his English. She knew he was good in the sciences, agonized over every paper he had to write in his new language, that his mother didn't speak much English, had iffy health, something about the lungs, lived with a cousin, and wouldn't or couldn't relocate closer to Ivan. And that was it, except for the names of girls who floated or stormed through his nights off.

She knew more real things about Ivan's mother than about him.

She hoped fervently that this new batch of Penny's employers were more observant and inquisitive than she was. If they were as vague and unhelpful as the earlier interviews, she had no idea where to turn next. Another failure on the résumé, and Penny among the missing.

She drove through downtown San Rafael until the street broadened and the solid blocks of California-retro buildings were replaced by more randomly placed strip malls and fast-food stops. She checked the address and made a right turn that changed the landscape to homes that climbed the street up into the hills. Number twenty-seven turned out to be a modest, wood-shingled cottage with a fenced-in, shallow front yard.

"Hi," she said when the doorbell produced a pleasantly rumpled man in a plaid flannel shirt, jeans, and socks. He held a drink—scotch on the rocks, she thought—in one hand and had a small and silent blonde girl attached to his right leg. "Mr. DeLuna?"

He nodded, and waited while she explained her mission. "So," she concluded, "if Mrs. DeLuna's around, she could—"

"Carole? Carole won't be home for hours." The little girl looked up at him as he spoke, then stared at Billie.

"Then perhaps tomorrow would be a better time to talk with her? Or tonight, if you'll tell me a—"

"Why ask Carole about Penny? She didn't know her."

Nobody had known Penny. Nobody. She might as well question

the silent clinging child. How had Penny passed through so many households without touching a single one? What had happened to community?

"I'd be the one," he continued. "Not that I know much. But feel free to come in and ask away."

Billie felt herself balk, do the automatic calculations self-preservation required. Going into a strange man's house. Safe? Did the existence of a child, attached to him like a wart, confirm his sanity and acceptability? How did her new job mesh with her old cautions?

"Listen," he said. "Maybe the situation isn't clear. I'm the one hires the sitters, changes the diapers, does the carpooling. Don't look shocked. Such things happen." His smile took the slight abrasive edge off his words. Even in Marin, househusbanding must not be the easiest role. "If you need to know something about the daily care and maintenance of our kids, Carole is not the one to talk to. On the other hand, if the kids assault you and you need a crackerjack lawyer, then it's smart to talk to Carole." He grinned and ran a hand through his already mussed and thinning blond hair. "I'm Russ," he said. He stood back from the door, dragging the leg with the girlchild attached, allowing Billie passage if she wanted it.

I'm a goddamned PI, she reminded herself as she briskly entered. I go where I want to. Need to.

The DeLuna house was rustic, with wood-paneled walls and not quite enough light for Billie's taste. But comfortable and comforting. Bookshelves lining one entire wall. A playpen full of toys and a dozing infant in stretch pajamas to one side. All surfaces appeared to have been cleared of breakables.

She liked to think she was beyond sexist prejudice, but she was surprised by how well he appeared to be taking care of the house and children.

Russ DeLuna gestured for her to have a seat on a dark green

sofa. "Drink?" he asked, lifting his glass. "Iced herbal tea. Peach. Good."

She declined. He sat on an oversized easy chair. The little girl crawled onto his lap and sat, thumb in mouth, watching Billie. "How can I help you?" he asked.

She explained Penny's disappearance, her parents' need to find her, and asked for anything that might provide a lead.

"She's a nice kid," he said. "A little shy at first, but only with me. Great with my two. Sometimes she'd ask me about what I did—I'm a writer, when possible. I'm afraid she thought I was a romantic figure—the artist in the garret. Instead of the househusband in the garage with the dishes still to wash."

He was indeed attractive, radiating warmth and acceptance. Billie wondered if Penny's crush could have been on him. Was his car yellow? Too good to be true, an interior voice warned. Some instinctive malleability instantly accommodated the other's tempo and temperature. Dangerous for an unhappy adolescent. "The garage?" she asked.

"There's a room over it that I use when possible, as when somebody like Penny is around to watch the kids. I'm working on a novel, but I freelance articles, too. Generally, I'd hire Penny only when I had an actual sale and a deadline. Given the situation, we didn't spend a lot of that time talking. Now and then, once the kids were asleep, she'd come up to the studio to say good-bye before she left, and we'd talk awhile." He shook his head. "Can't remember about what, however. Probably about what I was working on, that sort of thing."

But enough about me, let's talk about my novel, Billie thought. Charming, but shouldn't a novelist be more observant? A father notice more about the baby-sitter's psyche? And that room above the garage, the romantic garret. Danger and more danger.

"Your work sounds like it'd be really interesting," he said. "You like it?"

"Most of the time." Better be hypocritical than admit to being such a rank novice that she didn't yet know if she liked the work. "How did you find Penny?" she asked.

"She found me. Answer to a madman's prayer. She left a flyer in the mailbox. Said she had references, was an honor student. She seemed worth the try. After all, I was right there, up in the studio. I could monitor her the first few times."

"Did she talk about school? About her plans?"

Another head-shake. "Sorry. She couldn't do homework while she was here. She left when they were asleep. She told me once that she, too, wanted to write someday. But it didn't sound like a burning ambition."

It sounded more like adulation. Emulation. This good-looking, obviously loving man who had to be a little starved for company, whose wife was never home. . . .

Was she imagining Penny's emotions or her own?

"Once, I finished an article while she was sitting and that night, we did hang out awhile. The article had been about adolescent sex— safe or none or whatever. She asked to read it. Her comments were pretty mature for a high-school senior."

He had gone over the line. Billie felt queasy at the image of this charming grown man and Penny discussing the sexual habits of her age group. "She didn't talk about her own social life, did she?" she asked.

"I certainly wouldn't have encouraged it. It was weird enough having her discuss the theoretical habits of her age group. She didn't seem uncomfortable about that, but I was!"

Maybe he wasn't too good to be true. Maybe he was an actual nice guy. Which would mean there were such beings. The thought made her inexplicably sad. Or perhaps explicably, but she didn't want to look at that right now. "I wondered if you ever saw anybody pick her up, particularly a young man driving a yellow hearse."

"A hearse?" He shook his head. "Our arrangement was that she'd come over, get through the awful late-afternoon hours, feed the kids dinner, get them ready for bed, read to them. I'd come in and kiss Molly good night——"

"Paolo, too," the little girl said in a piping voice.

"Paolo, too," he said, ruffling her hair. "That's her brother, the live wire over there." He gestured toward the playpen. "Then once they were asleep——"

"And my Bepsy, too," the little girl said.

He nodded. "Bepsy, too. That's Molly's teddy bear and best friend and she gets kissed, too. And I'd turn on the intercom and go back to work and Penny'd go home. Mostly by bus or her bike. Bed-time here is early."

"Did your wife ever meet Penny? Talk to her?"

He deliberated for a while, his daughter studying his face the en-tire time. Then he shook his head. "I don't think their paths crossed. Sorry."

So was Billie. She tried to think of what she'd learned. Surely there was a nugget of information there, but if there was, she couldn't detect it.

Sally O'Neall answered the door with a tissue in one hand and wel-comed Billie with the desperate joy of a woman who'd been talking to children for too long. "Stayed home today. Feel like shit," she said. "I won't breathe at you, I promise. Come in, if you can stand chaos." Her children, a boy of around three and a girl who looked eight were mashing ground beef and mashed potatoes on their plates, ask-ing, "Do I have to eat it all?" with whiny regularity, and when their mother's back was turned, transferring the unwanted edibles to a dog who sat below the table.

Sally's counter held several open containers——of tissues, jumbo-sized graham crackers, plastic-wrapped sliced bread, open, peanut butter jar, and bottle of brandy. Theirs and hers. There was also a fan of unopened mail, most of which had the glassine windows of bills. Dishes and pans soaked in the sink.

"I am not generally quite this much of a slob," she said. "But then, I am not generally here all day. Join me?" she asked Billie as she poured brandy. "Helps the coughing, I swear. Breaks something up. Maybe consciousness."

"Thanks, but—"

"Not on the job, eh?" Sally said, producing a small thrill of professionalism in Billie's solar plexus.

"But as soon as I get home," Billie said. Not necessarily true, but kinship established. I'm sure as hell not going to quarrel with whatever gets you through the days.

"Good going," Sally told her children. The girl was pale and hostile-looking, her features thick and her expression sour, a face and a stage that only a mother could love. "You did a great job and nearly cleaned your plates." She offered them a special treat—watching a video. The girl, of course, sneered at the choice, then gave in sullenly. Maybe she was getting her teens over early.

"The dog's obese," Sally said when the children were upstairs. She settled into an easy chair in the cluttered living room. "I should banish her to the yard during meals, but I figure they aren't starving to death and it gives them pleasure to think they're putting one over on me. Anyway, I have to confess something. You're my first grown-up all day, or I would have told you right away that I don't think I can help. I don't know much about Penny. I mean, I checked references and all. She's a sweet-enough girl, and smart, too. And good with the kids. I told her I thought she should consider teaching young ones. She has a special talent. If you'd see her with her little brother, you'd know what I mean. She had to bring him along one time, and I was touched by their relationship. Mine never stop bickering.

"But there was something sad about her, too. Some . . . wistfulness. I'd look at her and actually feel it, catch the sadness, if that doesn't sound too ridiculous."

"She never gave you a clue as to why?"

Sally shook her head. "I feel really bad about it now. Maybe there was something I should have asked. I . . . If I say I'm hanging on by the skin of my fingernails, that doesn't justify it, but maybe explains it. I don't want to sound whiny, just honest, okay? I didn't want one more set of problems—or one more kid. And she seemed needy as hell, ripe to latch on to any sympathetic soul. Oh, God, I sound like a creep!"

How wide could anyone throw the net of concern? Did Sally, too, wake up near dawn in a sweat, worrying what would happen if she slowed down to take a breath?

"I feel incredibly guilty now that she's run away. I knew something wasn't right." Sally put her juice glass of brandy on the end table. "I didn't mean to become a person who'd let a girl go under for the third time because it was easier."

"Don't take it on yourself. She didn't tell anybody anything, and your plate's already overfull. But here's an easy one—how did she get home after sitting for you?"

Sally smiled. "Mostly, she rode her bike over and back, or walked. We don't live that far and I wasn't hiring her to go out dancing or on a date. The men are not exactly lined up out there for me, the kids and the dog. Besides, I'm too tired and too broke. I always feel like a pariah saying that in Marin. End of the rainbow, wealthiest county in the galaxy, or whatever. I feel like the Ancient Mariner—water, water everywhere and not a drop to drink. Only it's money, money everywhere . . . except in my house."

"Trust me, I understand." There were a lot more people like them than anyone wanted to admit. The men who waited for jobs along the freeway exit. The leftovers from divorces.

"I hired Penny about five times in as many months when I thought I'd go crazy if I couldn't be by myself for a few hours." She held up her right hand and ticked off fingers. "Once, I went to an afternoon movie. Once, to a masseuse—a birthday gift from the women I work with. Once, I hiked on Mount Tam, once I sat on a bench at the transportation center where the bus lines stop. All I wanted to do was watch other people need to get somewhere while I didn't. And once I drove up to Napa, then turned around and drove back. And there you have it—my social life. Except for forays into court, trying to get my husband to pay his share of their support. I think Penny was here one time while I did that, too."

"Listen," Billie said. "I really do understand."

"So I'm sorry," Sally said. "For you, too. In any case, I'm useless."

"Nobody picked her up after she was here, then. No boyfriends mentioned?"

Sally shook her head. Upstairs, the video provided a steady background of screams and metallic crashes. At least, Billie hoped it was on tape, and not live.

Not too long after, Billie made her farewells. She liked this woman, knew they could be friends if either had a spare minute or emotion. Billie left her card. "Call me if you think of anything," she said. "And good luck. See you, I hope."

Not quite a Sam Spade interview, but what the hell. Maybe the next would be different.

The Feldspars had found a replacement for the missing Penelope Redmond, a prudent girl who refused to open the door to Billie, but spoke briskly and with finality through the intercom. And all she would offer was, "Go away."

Only one more on the list. Billie thought about how bad things came in threes. Catastrophes. Strikes. Information-challenged interviews. She'd had four. Did that mean she was on to her second disastrous set of three?

"Please," she said prayerfully, and left it at that.

Fourteen

She'd saved the least promising for last. Sunny Marshall lived next door to the Redmonds, too close for Penny to keep secrets there, and too close for the mystery man to have driven Penny home after a job.

Billie retrieved the *Independent Journal* from where the paperboy had tossed it and carried it to the front door as a pass.

"Come in," Sunny said after Billie had identified herself.

Billie was surprised to feel an unpleasant sense of familiarity. Where had they crossed paths before?

Or was it only her imagination? Sunny, who could not have been friendlier or more at ease, showed no sign of recognition. She led Billie to the back of the house, the kitchen, explaining that her children were "at the trough" and she hoped Billie would understand.

I don't like her, Billie thought. Beyond that, nothing was forthcoming.

Sunny Marshall's house looked designed and furnished for elegant comfort. It was twice the size of its next-door neighbor, the Redmonds and with more lavish materials—what looked like rich and long-gone virgin redwood, windows etched with peacocks, French doors leading to deep porches, plump, pillowy sofas and chairs in glowing colors. A dream house, if Billie allowed even her dreams to wander this far from possibility.

The kitchen was—because of her name?—sunshine yellow. It was also filled with the noise of two-year-old twin boys, and an older child—four, Sunny said—plus high-pitched squeals and shouts issuing from a TV built into the wall. The counters were clear except for a vase of daisies. Out of season, but real, Billie verified by a quick and surreptitious touch.

"Sophia said you might stop by," Sunny said. "I'm making coffee; care for any? Peet's Decaf Sumatra."

"Thanks, but I'm fine." Billie wondered if male PIs were offered libations at each stop.

"Harley's at a fund-raiser," Sunny said. "People think he only works two, three hours because that's all they hear him on the radio, but aside from all the preparation for the show itself, there are all these charitable and civic events the station expects him to attend. I try to go along, but since Penny's gone, I'm having a hard time finding somebody willing to put up with these monsters"—she smiled indulgently at her children as she said the word—"at the cranky time of day. Somebody as good as Penny was."

Her laugh was a silver-gold sound, and again Billie felt the shiver of dislike, of familiarity that had bred contempt. "I wanted children just as soon as I was married, and I got my wish—but I forgot to say I expected them one by one. Three under four terrifies even the agency sitters. Takes a strong teen—who needs money—to tackle my gang."

Billie smiled tolerant acknowledgment of sitters and babies and anything else. "Your husband has a radio show?" she asked. Harley Marshall. Billie couldn't place the name, not that she was a connoisseur of the airwaves, and definitely not of DJs.

"I must sound arrogant!" Sunny put her hand to her mouth. "As if everybody should know that! Truth is, nobody uses his name. He's called the Talkman."

"Oh, of course." That's right. They'd found him. His real name. But there was no justice on earth, if this was the lair and refuge of the expansive-voiced, narrow-minded Talkman.

Sunny invited Billie to join them, the twins in their high chairs, the four-year-old in a booster seat and herself at the white kitchen table to which she brought a tray carrying her cup, a china coffeepot, a small pitcher of milk, a sugar bowl, a white ceramic oblong that held artificial sweetner, two yellow-and-white homespun napkins, and a second cup: "In case you change your mind," she said.

The twins, busy twining strands of spaghetti into their mouths and hair, stared at the novelty of her. Their faces were splotched with tomato sauce, making them look like disaster victims. Their older sibling—Billie could not tell if the androgynous figure with the bangs was female or male—stared at the TV and swung its foot, kicking the table with each bump. Cups rattled, but Sunny said only, "What would you like to know?" And that was directed at Billie.

"Anything that might help me find her. What she was interested in lately, who she saw, hung around with. Whatever seemed unusual, or that didn't fit what you knew of her." She waited to once again be told that the lady of the house hadn't noticed much of anything, ever, let alone that which might be unusual.

Sunny shrugged. "She didn't confide in me much. You know how kids are about anybody with three kids. I'm just the old married lady next door." She laughed, showing beautiful even teeth, radiating a joyful self-confidence that came only to those who were adored since birth. Why would she be with Talkman, unless his sexist messages were a lucrative persona, nothing more. And why Billie's lingering sense that she knew this likable woman and didn't like her?

"I was part of Penny's college fund and not much more," Sunny added, "which is how it should be, don't you think? Teenagers can't waste time noticing adults or they'd never get there themselves. She was fond of the children, though, and that's what mattered."

"Did you think she'd changed lately?"

"In what way?"

"Did she seem depressed? Withdrawn? Worried about something?"

Sunny leaned back in her chair and smiled. "Not at all."

Perky people don't recognize angst when they fall over it. Billie should have known she'd answer that way.

"Penny's an even-tempered girl," Sunny said. "That's what makes her wonderful with my boys. I'm not saying she doesn't have mood swings. What teenager doesn't? But I actually thought she was happier lately."

"Why's that?"

"Well, she didn't tell me this outright, mind you, but I think she had a crush. At long last. She was too much of a loner before, if you ask me. And this one wasn't one of those woe-is-me things." She waved her hand, as if to shoo away the very idea of such negative emotions.

"This is recently?"

Sunny nodded. "I think one reason she didn't date much was because her parents didn't let her be a kid. Off the record, they behaved as if Wesley were her responsibility. It's to my advantage, because she's so good with kids, but I don't know how good it was for Penny. She's such a serious girl. All she used to think about was her schoolwork, and I'm not saying it's good to let your studies slide, but all of a sudden, she didn't seem as intense about it, which seems to me healthier. She stopped arriving here with ten textbooks and lined tablets asking if she could use the computer. After the boys were asleep, she'd watch TV, relax a little instead."

Billie was less than convinced that Penny's changed interests signaled happiness. Her symptoms sounded more like lethargy, an inability to focus or concentrate, closer to clinical depression than lovesickness. But such interpretations wouldn't be in Sunny's smiley-faced data bank.

"Love does that to people, you know?" Sunny said. "Always did it to me at her age! Oh, how Mom complained about that vacant air, the daydreaming."

"Did she talk about the object of her affection? Mention his name?" With difficulty, Billie kept her voice low. Otherwise it was apt to escalate into a begging, desperate shriek. *Please,* you *have* to know his *name!*

" 'Fraid not. All of this is speculation. It's not as if she said anything. Only one time when she was here, for some reason, I was looking out the front window when she left, and I realized she wasn't walking home. It registered on my memory because it was weird. I mean she lives directly behind that hedge, but there she was, waiting out front, and a car pulled up." She allowed a momentary combination of distaste and confusion to play across her features before she continued. "I say a car, but not a normal one. It was grotesquely large and old. And," she tapped a nail against the wall. "This color." She shook her head. "It's a nice color for a kitchen, I think, but a car?"

"Penny ever mention this driver's name? A name?"

Sunny looked downhearted. "I don't think so. As if I of all people would be against romance! And why else not talk about him? Golly, she knew about my whirlwind courtship. I knew Harley for two months—ten weeks, to be precise—when we married. I happen to think if you know it's right, you know it's right."

She poured herself more coffee, looked inquiringly at Billie, then sipped before she spoke. "She asked me whether I believed in love at first sight, and I said I did. I *do,* 'cause it happened to me. I was working at the station when Harley came to check it out. One look and I was a goner. He moved here from Vegas six weeks later, and we were married a month after that." She rolled her eyes. "My mother nearly had a fit! Making a genuine wedding in that timespan." She smiled at Billie, sharing her happiness.

Billie smiled back.

"I hope I wasn't a bad influence," Sunny said. "Gadzooks, I wasn't giving *advice!* Heaven's sake, I immediately became pregnant, with Jory there. I hope she doesn't adopt that idea, too!"

Billie wrote out notes while she thought of her ex-husband's immediate, irresistible chemistry, and how wrong that powerful sense of "right" could be. "Then the name Stewart doesn't ring any bells?" she asked.

Sunny shook her head. Her smartly cut hair was a strawberry-blonde that did not, but should, exist in nature. It blended with her surroundings, finding its place in her household spectrum between the yellow walls and the polished copper of the hanging pots.

"I mentioned the mysterious chauffeur when she came to sit the next time." Sunny reached over to one of her sons who was at-tempting to fill a nostril with compressed bread.

"And what did she say?"

"Not much, but she smiled. That's why I was sure she liked the driver. And then she showed me this heart she was wearing which to me means he gave it to her. Why else would she follow up mention of the driver by showing it to me?" All the time she spoke, she fussed with her boys, cleaning the bread-stuffer's face, spooning spaghetti into another's mouth, grabbing a cup of milk before it tipped over.

"Plus," she continued as she mopped milk droplets that had made it over the rim, "another reason I thought she must be in love because the thing she was wearing wasn't really . . . it was sweet, of course. A heart with a design etched in it. But to tell the truth, it was worn. Some of the plating was worn off. Kind of an odd treasure, so I thought it had to have sentimental meaning, because it certainly wasn't valuable. I fussed over it, of course. Wanted her to feel good about it, about this secret love of hers. I told her about a similar heart I had and how I'd loved it. Of course, mine was personal—it had my initials. Hers just had a design, and that worn spot.

Penny's family isn't rich, but she's grown up with nice things so I think its importance to Penny was as a token of somebody's love. The only value it could have would be *emotional.*"

Finished with the children's toilettes for the moment, Sunny now smoothed the *I.J.* on the table in front of her, pressing it flat as she spoke to and watched Billie and her sons. Billie watched the unconscious motions, wishing she had some of that instinctive tidiness hardwired in her own brain.

"Do I sound like I'm making fun of Penny's charm?" Sunny's expression darkened. She looked overly concerned. "I don't mean to."

"No," Billie said. "I understand what you're trying to say. Not at all."

Sunny pursed her lips, still visibly irritated with herself. "I was a lucky child. I grew up with more than my share and sometimes I think—I've tried not to be like my mother that way, but I sounded like her just now."

So she was a rich girl. Billie could less and less understand the match with Talkman. But Billie completely understood the mother Sunny was trying not to emulate. She'd had one, herself, a million years ago when wisdom was confused with knowing the price tag, if not the value, of the world's goods. Of course, with the divorce, her mother's form of intelligence was as worthless as the paste imitations she'd scorned. With the divorce, she stopped trying to know much, except where the next comforting drink was.

"The amount she cared about that thing was all out of proportion to its actual value is my point."

Billie nodded.

"Wait a minute—*Lucas,*" Sunny said. "That was it, or Luke. The driver's name. It just came back to me. First name, I think, so not George Lucas, of course." Her rich-girl's silvery laugh filled the room again. "And now I remember—it was because of the car. Because I'd mentioned it. She said Lucas was good with mechanical things. That he'd restored it all by himself—although why anyone would want to, I surely can't say."

Without warning, one of the twins hurled his plate to the floor. "Ryan!" Sunny said, with reproof but no anger. Life amused her. She stood up, retrieved a sponge and cleaned his mess. "Can you believe this is how he signifies being finished? What is our visitor going to think of this family's table manners?" she asked the baby.

Lucas somebody. Or somebody Lucas. Good with mechanical things. That narrowed the field to the merely impossible.

Then who was the Stewart she'd talked to Wesley about? Were they the same? Lucas Stewart? Stewart Lucas? Or maybe she was involved with several males.

Sunny washed the boys' faces, sponged off the high-chair trays and plunked an oatmeal cookie in front of each.

Billie looked at the now-flattened bottom half of the *I.J.'s* front page. SUPERVISOR PUSHES DRIVE FOR LIGHT-RAIL SYSTEM. HIGH-TECH ATTEMPT TO SOLVE MYSTERY OF MEADOW MOTHER AND CHILD.

She hated thinking about the people in the meadow. First, the lost child and all the anxiety it provoked, then its presumed mother, and then, awareness that not a squawk or rustle had followed their disappearance. So easy to see just how it could happen that nobody noticed or missed them. Look at what was happening with Penny. People were halfhearted—and then, only when prodded.

Sunny resettled in her chair at the table. In the background, the anchor listed this year's Oscar nominations, then listed supposedly surefire nominees who had been slighted—just in case they hadn't noticed the slight and didn't already feel sufficiently rotten. Sunny sighed. "Where were we?"

"Lucas. Good with mechanical things."

"Oh, right. She said he was a model-builder, or started out as one. Or did it along with something else, I'm not sure. Sometimes, with the kids around, I get so scattered . . . but I remember the model-building because I thought she meant tiny trains or cars or balsa-wood airplanes. And she laughed! You know that teenage laugh that just shrivels you?—the one that means you're so out of it you're laughable? She said his models were for the movies, for special effects. Spaceships, monsters, robots, airplanes—little things we see on-screen as enormous. They do a lot of it with computers now, though. Still and all, I had no idea there was such a job. It seems so peculiar."

"Did she say where he does this?"

Sunny shook her head again. "Don't think so. At least, I don't recall."

"Did she by any chance mention ILM? Industrial Light and Magic? The special-effects house. George Lucas's place."

"I honestly don't know." Sunny wrinkled her brow, pondering, then shook her head.

"Do you think he was local?"

Again Sunny considered this, her perfect upper teeth biting on her perfect lower lip. "I think so, because . . . well . . . guess I don't know that, either. She didn't say."

He had to be, that was all there was to it. It made sense. Besides, the universe owed Billie a break. He had to be local and work at ILM. Billie stood up. "You've been really helpful."

"You're being kind. I'm sorry I didn't pay closer attention." She, too, stood. The twins howled and the older boy put his hands to his ears. It was a wonder Sunny Marshall could keep track of her own name, let alone her baby-sitter's crushes.

"Honestly. I'm more hopeful of finding her now, thanks to you."

"I do hope so." Sunny's expression clouded. "I'm finding it really hard without her."

"One thing," Billie said when she was near the door. "I keep having the sense we've met before." She didn't mention the heavy negativity that came with the feeling. "Have we?"

Sunny looked wide-eyed and apologetic. "Gee, I . . . I'm sure I'd remember if we had."

But they had. Billie was sure. And something bad was a part of it.

"I know what it must be," Sunny said. "Bet you were at one of Harley's fund-raisers, and I was there, too. Bet that was it."

Not in this lifetime, Billie thought. Not even if I could afford charity banquets. "Bet you're right," Billie said. "And I'll bet that happens to you all the time." She was starting to sound like Sunny Marshall. "Well, thanks again."

The twins continued to howl as Billie let herself out the door.

Once in her car, Billie allowed herself a second of elation. She had a name—two names—and that of his likely employer. She had a chance, finally, to find him and through him, Penny.

And then reality returned. ILM was fortified and impenetrable, its hatches battened against curiosity-seekers. The place might as well be making actual interplanetary weaponry for its degree of paranoia and security. Billie knew this for personal fact, having tried for employment there before coming to Emma. She'd called their job line and found the commercial division needed a production assistant, and figured that "assisting" somebody had to mean they'd explain the job. Therefore, she could do it.

That was then, pre-Emma, when she still believed she was a quick study and could conquer or fake pretty much anything.

But she hadn't been given the chance to bluff her way through. She'd inflated her résumé and pretended an urgency—she was being relocated if she couldn't find a new position that could keep her here—and still and all, she never got so much as an interview.

The receptionist let it drop that three hundred people had applied for that minor-league job, including people with a great deal of experience who wanted out of Hollywood and up into the promised land at the end of the rainbow. She strongly suggested that Billie fold her tents and fade away.

Billie's choice of new career was determined by the fact that ILM's talent pool was Olympic-sized, and Emma's consisted of a tiny puddle near the drain.

And now Billie, in an ironic twist she didn't appreciate had to storm the fortress in order to do her alternate job. Why couldn't Luke work at Safeway? Or Nordstrom?

Oh, God, she suddenly thought—please let this be for real. Please don't let it turn out to be a joke. Don't let the reason her Luke wouldn't work at Safeway be that he's really, truly Luke Skywalker.

Fifteen

It was a good morning, clear and bright, and he sat in bed savoring it, not sure what set this day of his vacation apart, made it different and better than those that preceded it, but something did. The weather? So clear and bright after so much rain. But the day before had been clear as well and he hadn't felt this quiet elation, this sense of peace.

Then he realized what it was: Penny wasn't with him. Probably because he'd slept late, but even so, it was unusual of her to be this considerate, or to face his housemates on her own. Maybe she was finally feeling more relaxed and less paranoid around them. He stretched and contemplated the day. It looked good for a hike, or even the beach. Didn't seem to be any fog, although it wasn't always easy to guess what was happening on the coast from here in the valley.

He wondered if he'd take her along. Wondered if he wanted to, if he had to, if he'd entered some unarticulated whither-thou-goest covenant with the girl. She seemed to think so, was constantly looking as if a moment's separation was a betrayal. He couldn't imagine how their tiny history had been so completely rewritten.

Like the way she insisted on calling him Luke. He didn't mind all that much, but the others did. They kept their mundane lives separate. They even complained that if she absolutely had to use it, he was Lucan, not Luke. The fact that she didn't like the authentic, period name made her all the more suspect. Or maybe they'd resent anything she said. He couldn't pick his way through his mixed feelings about her, and the stew of affection, resentment, confusion, impatience, and worry was forever simmering.

Penny was like the strays he used to bring home, annoying the hell out of his mother and proving her right, time after time—he loved the idea of the dog and hated the unending responsibility. The Kestrel, Morgana, was just the right amount of responsibility. He built her a mews and covered the window at night so great horned owls couldn't come devour her. He showed her a little attention and fed her a mouse a day and she was satisfied.

This time, Penny had trailed him home, and he couldn't stand the responsibility. Hadn't signed on for it. He couldn't wait until she realized it was time to go home, deal with her life and finish high school. It had better be soon.

And then, no girls. He never thought he'd yearn for celibacy, for estrangement from the entire other sex, but the prospect beckoned, clean and uncomplicated.

He stretched and dawdled, looking out the window at the glorious midmorning and at Mr. Oliver's tidy garden, deliberately fenced-off from the jungly tangle of the rental unit's yard. Oliver's flowering cherry tree had burst into purple-pink blossoms overnight, dark limbs full of bell-shaped petals amazing against a backdrop of greens brightened by the recent rains.

He wanted Mr. Oliver's orderly yard and life. He wanted to worry about tiny problems—thrips and mites and aphids. He wanted to talk to plants and never once have the plant talk back. Maybe he'd aim for it today—plant something, lots of things, so there'd be color all year outside his window.

Except he knew he wouldn't really do it, wouldn't see it through the seasons and the grunt work. He wasn't like Mr. Oliver, not sufficiently attentive or careful and would probably let everything go to seed. He was a procrastinator. Look how he was delaying the downstairs reunion with Penny. She was sure to be pissed. As soon as she arrived with her unanticipated set of assumptions, he'd backed off. Except that night she came up and into his bed. Big mistake. But only that once. That twice. Talk about paying for your sins.

He'd thought to give her a brief time away from sour and oppressive parents. From being a teenager, a high-school senior with all the extra pressures of that year when your entire future bears down at you top speed. That was all, breathing space. God knows he wasn't ready for another relationship, especially not with an hysteric. If he ever dated again, he'd look for an emotionless cow of a girl. He was sick to death of histrionics and had been even before Penny Redmond appeared.

Penny's overdramatic denunciations of her life and family were juvenile, but she felt everything so passionately; she was so needy. He knew firsthand that families could be unbearable. The difference was that he had a better sense of self-preservation than she did. He hadn't chucked high school and run away. He'd taken his time and their money until he finished college—they worried about how it would look to their friends if they refused to send him on to higher education, and he cynically played on that—so that when he left, he had the means to be independent and the break was clean and final.

But maybe the day he met Penny, when she'd stopped to admire his car outside the yogurt store, maybe that day he hadn't felt completely independent. With Yvonne ranting to everybody about how he'd destroyed her life, maybe he'd been ripe for being admired. Pathetic, but probably true, because for the life of him, he couldn't figure how else he'd gotten into this mess.

And then Penny, suddenly seductive, acting as if his offer of refuge translated into a request that she come live with him and be his love, not merely share space. She treated his insistence that he wanted instead to protect her, give her a little time, as if he were insulting her.

He felt sorry for her parents, if this was the way she handled whatever she didn't like.

And last night was the worst, the dispute about the goddamned gold heart. Such a stupid thing. He knew she was right. The thing was a worn out piece of costume jewelry, worth nothing, even as evidence. But it was the principle of the thing, his stubbornness about her stubbornness. They were a really bad combo.

Later, when they were alone in his room, she'd cried that everybody treated her like an infant, with him as prime offender. It was all a jumble to her and a mess to him. Her fault. His.

You'd think she'd move out if life here was unbearable. That's what she'd done about her real home. No such luck.

She had noplace to go. He knew that, but it only made matters worse.

He pulled a sweatshirt and jeans on, uncovered the kestrel and promised her a delicious mouse, then used the bathroom, where somebody had left globs of spit-out toothpaste in the sink again. He stared at the gelled dribbles. They weren't dirt, hair, or scum. Toothpaste didn't interfere with anything and shouldn't annoy him. But it did. It was one more way in which what he wanted, needed, and deserved wasn't allowed him.

He heard himself with horror. When had he become this testy asshole? Maybe he was this way about everything, including Penny. He'd try harder. After all, he was older, out of college, employed, and she was none of those things. He went downstairs filled with benign resolve.

He didn't see her, or anybody. Gary and Toto had left hours ago for their jobs, and since Alicia wasn't in her office, she was probably out with a client. He peeked around the corner, to the enclosed porch where Kathryn sat peering intently at a screen. It was her machine, and when she occupied that space, her office as well, but otherwise—which was most of the time—the entire household could use the room and the computer. Those times that Kathryn worked at home, she was wrapped in a virtual Do Not Disturb sign and she was not to be considered here at all.

Back in the kitchen, he took a mouse out of the freezer, putting it on a paper towel to defrost. Even that made him think of Penny with irritation. Sleeping in a room with a creature who tore up and ate little mammals upset her. The speed with which Morgana devoured her mouse disgusted Penny. The fact that most times, Morgana left the mouse's nose uneaten revolted her. When he bought crickets as a special treat for the bird, Penny shuddered and gagged. But none of this made her go to the living room couch.

Penny insisted she could love the bird, if only it didn't have to eat. Typical of her logic.

He made coffee and oatmeal and luxuriated in the absence of people. It was how it should be with only the finches on the live oak breaking the silence.

Maybe Penny had been pulled outside by the lure of Oliver's tree or the chippering yellow-bellied birds. Or she'd gone to "his" spot up and around the hill. She'd loved it when he'd shown it to her, a deep-set channel, now a fast-moving stream lined with redwoods and ferns. On such a day, it would be magic to sit in its dappled shadows.

He glanced at the front page of the *Chronicle*. Nothing much and nothing at all about the skeletons. Good. He wished he'd never poked that stick in the dirt. All it really meant was that Toto's uncle, who'd let them use his pasture, was furious. He'd been hassled by the police and had his field chopped up and made hazardous for his cows. The normally placid dairy farmer had banned them for life.

He finished breakfast and thought about going to the beach, taking advantage of this weather before it dissolved into more rain. The water would be way too cold, but hearing and seeing it, reading, maybe running the beach sounded like a full vacation packed into a day.

He'd leave now, while Penny was gone.

He added his dishes to the collection in the sink, took the pitiable mouse corpse upstairs with him, and, after he put on a sweater as padding, fed her on his fist. There, in a matter of two, three minutes, he'd made the creature happy. She didn't scream protests about his going off without her as he changed into bathing trunks under his jeans, and prepared to leave. He was going to stick to birds from now on.

Back around sundown, his note said. He could almost taste the clean sea air, hear the silence broken only by the waves, the muffled human noises if, indeed, anybody else was around, the seagulls and the sea lions who floated near shore, people-watching, and he felt muscles from neck to ankles unclench.

Outside, he took a deep breath of the fragrant air, but almost instantly felt it whoosh out of him. He looked again at the empty gravel drive, the spot closest to the garage where he'd left it. He'd left his car there—so that he wouldn't block anybody, so nobody would need to wake him up with a request for either his presence or his keys because the car had to be moved.

Good thinking, except it was gone. As were all the others', except Kathryn's, so it wasn't as if somebody's car had broken down and his had been used in the emergency.

Too bad about never interrupting Kathryn. He stormed in and stood by her computer while she waved him away with one hand. Finally when pages flipped out of the printer, she looked up. "What?" she asked.

"My car. It's not out there."

She blinked, readjusting from appointments and contracts to him. "She took it."

"She? Who?"

"Who the hell you think? Your cookie."

"Penny?"

Kathryn shrugged and pulled off her glasses to rub her eyes. "You didn't give the okay?" She put her glasses back on and looked at her printer. "Guess not."

The room, Kathryn, the computer—everything dissolved into blank emptiness. She'd moved in on his life and taken it over, every bit of it, without asking, without permission, without basic human decency. "Where was she going?" he asked, his voice unfamiliar and hoarse. "Where did she take it?"

Kathryn looked back from the stream of papers coming out of the printer and regarded him quizzically. "How would I know? She said she had things to take care of and that she'd be back in a while. She had your keys. I thought for sure you knew." She shrugged. "That was two hours ago."

"Okay," he said. "Okay. She went to the police, about the heart she found."

"Doubt it." Kathryn stood up, checked the time and pulled a sweater off a peg on the wall. Despite her comfortable natural padding, she was always chilly and everybody had stopped making fun of her about it. "Unless she had some kind of conversion experience. Last night she was crazed about not doing anything in person with the police, or was I delusional? Did I fantasize that incredibly boring and infantile performance?"

"Then to those ladies she baby-sat for?" He knew he was being ridiculous.

Kathryn shrugged again. "Did you write her *script?*" She rolled her eyes. "The girl can't make up her own words and say what's obvious." She looked at her watch and gathered the newly printed pages, put a clip around them and slipped them into a leather briefcase that was the most elegant item in Kathryn's mundane wardrobe.

When she created her garb, however, she went crazy with orna-ments. "Listen," she said, "I have to go. I'm supposed to have this at the office in half an hour."

He still felt literally stunned, as if Kathryn had thwacked him with the news. He nodded, and moved away, signaling that he wouldn't hassle her anymore. And then he remembered. "Wait—I bet I know where she went, and you—your office is in Sausalito, isn't it?"

"No," she said. "They moved it last night."

"I mean—could I have a lift? You can drop me off on Bridgeway, anywhere."

Kathryn sighed, nodded, and gathered up her papers before turning off the printer. "I don't know when I'm coming home. There's a meeting—"

"Doesn't matter, don't worry. If I don't find my car, I'll get home on my own. Buses and stuff." Whatever happened, she'd already ru-ined his goddamned day.

"Then I'll see you in a couple years, the way the buses run, but it's your call."

"I'll take the lift." He didn't know, couldn't tell if it would relieve or enrage him to see his big yellow hearse parked where he now sus-pected it would be.

Sixteen

Billie sat in her car, drinking Styrofoam coffee while considering the innocuous, anonymous building across the street. It didn't look like a fortress, but as she studied it, she felt like the heroes of the fairy tales she read Jesse. Gender issues aside, the king had ordered her to cut through that iron mountain with her piece of straw or die. She had to get far enough in to find Lucas' address—if he in fact worked here. If he hadn't been lying to Penny, or hadn't been from out of town, building his models in L.A. or elsewhere, up here sightseeing or visiting. And if Luke or Lucas— or Stewart—was his name.

Quests were thrilling in stories; in the day-to-day, they were a royal pain.

She allowed herself a second to appreciate the clear blue air of this winter morning, tossed her empty coffee container into the litter can and nodded. Time to go. Big day ahead. Find girl, close case, accept applause.

She smoothed her tunic sweater over her tights, tightened the laces of her boots, applied fresh lipstick and fluffed her hair as much as it would cooperate, touched each silver earring for good luck, and soldiered forth, across the street and into the reception area.

The keeper of the gate behind the desk was not the same young woman Billie had confronted during her job search, but of the same vintage and basic design. The last had been a dark blonde beauty. This one had black hair and smoky features. Both past and present were politely disdainful of outsiders. "Yes?" she asked. "Can I help you?"

Billie took another deep breath, curling the muscles of her shoulders and back into her "silly, dithering blonde me" persona. She giggled, softly, nervously. "This is going to sound really dumb. Embarrassing, too."

The receptionist apparently didn't waste energy on verbal or facial responses.

"Don't laugh, but like, I was at a party last week, and I met this guy. And we hit it off right away . . . except I got a little bombed, you see—that's the really embarrassing part." She gestured overly much, pointing at herself, hanging her head, doing the dork. "I told him my entire life story, about being robbed and all—I won't bore you with that, but it had happened in the City the night before. But I would never have said anything if I hadn't had too much to drink. Which I only did because I was still freaked when I got there. But the thing was, he was nice. I mean, really, and not in like a jerky or dull way. That isn't what I mean. I mean decent, and kind and, oh, nice. You don't meet a whole lot of guys like that." Come on, she mentally telegraphed. Look as if you comprehend, as if you've been there, too. What's happened to sisterhood?

The receptionist watched with infinite patience and not a trace of any other emotion.

"I— We—oh, got a little . . . Anyway, when I wasn't fit to drive myself home, I wound up sleeping in his car, plus he loaned me money. He wrote his name and address on a slip of paper, said I could return the money whenever, and now my parents sent me some, so I could repay him and I really want to, but I can't find that slip of paper anywhere, and I'm afraid he'll think of me as a total jerk, a rip-off artist, so I was hoping you'd help. I mean, you know how they say nice guys finish last and all? I don't want him to think that."

The receptionist allowed two micromuscles in her forehead to contract into a slight frown. "Why here?" she asked. "I don't understand. Why come to me?"

"Didn't I say?" Billie closed her eyes and tilted her face to the ceiling. "Now I'm even *more* embarrassed! I must sound like a complete idiot!" She certainly hoped so. "He told me he worked here. That part I remember, because we talked about special effects, the different kinds of things you do. You know. So that's the one thing I remember, and it wasn't written on that paper. Oh, and his name. Lucas."

The receptionist shook her head.

Billie bit at her bottom lip. "Or it could be Luke. It could be a first or last name—and I don't mean George Lucas. It wasn't him. I know that much." She waited for a smile, something, then gave up.

"I think he's the only Lucas we've got," the receptionist finally said. "And he's not based in this building, anyway."

"It might have been his first name. How about Stewart?"

"Lucas Stewart? Luke Stewart?" She shook her head again.

"Are you positive? I'll bet both his names were on that piece of paper. Damn!"

The receptionist sat back down at her computer keys, watching the screen. Then she shook her head.

"Then what if it's the other way—Stewart Lucas?" Billie asked.

"Like I said . . ."

"Right."

"I think maybe you've been had," the receptionist said. "A lot of people want to work here, people who love movies, special effects or just computer graphics, and maybe this fellow took it one step too far. To impress you, probably." Her bland expression managed to signal the end of this consultation.

Time to do a Puffball. Billie thought about her white kitten, a Christmas gift when she was seven. Puffball had gotten out of the house in mid-January and been killed by the neighbor's dog.

Her eyes welled immediately. Pure reflex now, Pavlovian. Cry! The director would say. Faster! Your heart is broken! She'd worked on it until the first syllable, the barest mental whisper of "puff" activated her tear ducts.

"Listen, don't cry." The receptionist stood up and came around the desk. She was shorter than Billie, narrower, and looked made of a substance lighter than air. It was possible that she herself was a special effect. "He conned you, gave you false info when you were vulnerable. Bet he realized all along that meant he couldn't get his money back. And doesn't really deserve it. The name on that paper was probably fake along with everything else, so he wasn't nearly as nice as you thought. And don't be ashamed. It happens to all of us."

God bless sisterhood. "But he said—" The phone rang. Damn. Just as her performance was winning over the audience. "I can't believe he lied. Oh, this is awful—I'm leaving tomorrow. Going home for a while and I wanted this off my conscience." The receptionist started back to her desk to answer the phone. "You sure there's absolutely no Stewart Lucas or Lucas Stewart?" Billie persisted. "Or maybe Luke as a nickname for something else altogether? He's cute, brown hair, about six feet, and he drives a hearse."

"Hearse?" The receptionist leaned over her desk, lifted the receiver and held up one finger, signaling Billie to wait. She politely routed the call, then replaced the receiver and turned back. "You said his car—"

"An old hearse painted a shimmery yellow. A good place to sleep, even if it wasn't for my eternal rest yet."

The receptionist almost smiled at her lame joke. "Well," she said, "I guess there could be two six-foot tall cute young guys with brown hair who drive cars like that, but there is a guy who works here who rebuilt one of those and drives it. It's older than he is."

170

"Yes—he said he'd had to redo it from the street up."

"But his name's not Luke or Stewart, it's Stephen Tassio, so I don't know . . ."

"It has to be the same person because I know he didn't lie. Stephen . . . you think I could have mixed up Stewart with that?"

The receptionist nodded. "Stephen's a good guy, all right. A little weird, but in nice ways. The party you went to—was it one of those Middle Ages things?"

"No. Everybody was pretty young. I think maybe I was the oldest person there, and I'm twenty-five." The receptionist didn't blink. Maybe Billie actually did look younger than she was, maybe people weren't just flattering her.

"Not middle-aged. Middle Ages. Medieval stuff. He likes to dress up in fake armor or something and be a knight. There's a bunch of them who go out and hold tournaments or jousts, whatever you call it. He even has this bird—a hawk or something—who lives with him, like the knights had. Of course he got his bird through a rescue society. It'd been shot or something and couldn't be in the wild anymore. But the Middle Ages bit, it's a whole thing, he says. People involved in it all over the world."

"What's it called?" Billie asked, trying not to slobber in her eagerness.

The receptionist shook her head. "I thought maybe you were part of it, too."

"I don't know if we even have such a thing in Indiana." She pretended to pull herself back to the issue at hand. "Anyway, now that we know who he is, could you let him know I'm here? My name's Audrey. Audrey Miller."

God bless that blank-faced high-school classmate. Maybe whenever she needed a name and an empty shell of personality to fill, she'd be Audrey, whose four-footed clients weren't likely to notice. But the truth was, unless Audrey had really changed, even spaniels probably forgot her immediately after they were returned home.

"Tell him the girl from the party. The one who was robbed. This is great. I feel so much better."

The receptionist nodded and pushed buttons for an extension. Then a crease reappeared between her eyes as she listened to a message. Someday it'd become permanent, ruining the carved appearance of her face. "I forgot. He's not here," she said. "You want to leave the money in an envelope with me?"

"I'd rather . . . When will he be back in? I could go take care of a few errands. . . ."

"He's taken two weeks off. Probably camping somewhere. He likes doing that when he isn't—jousting or something. You want his voicemail?"

"No, it won't do any—I'm leaving for Indiana tomorrow. I could give him my folks' number and ask him to leave a message as to where I can mail the . . ." She enjoyed thinking aloud as Audrey. Audrey wasn't quick-witted, and her sluggish thought process bought Billie breathing space to think on her own. "But wait—I would just hate for my parents to find out about the mugging—they hate that I moved to 'crazy California,' as they call it. That would about push them over the hump, and until I get established . . . well, until I get a real job—I'm a fabric designer—they kind of subsidize me. Only partly, but . . . you know?" Stephen Tassio, she repeated to herself. Even if we're at an impasse, that was something. How common a name could that be? She'd find him. Why'd he take off these particular weeks? Pray that it wasn't so he could drive across the country with the girl. Do not let him be only a courier, delivery service for the real Luke or Stewart, waiting for her far away.

"Could you give me his number instead? Or his address?—I'll mail it directly to him with a note."

The receptionist looked sympathetic, but shook her head. "I'm sorry. I'm not allowed to do that ever, at all, but in this case especially. Stephen left strict, strict rules that nobody is to be given his phone number or address. And in fact, I don't even have them. He moved because of this situation he's in, and he lives with friends, and I don't know their names or where they are."

"What about mail? Or if you need him suddenly?"

"He has a post-office box in San Rafael. And a beeper when he's not on vacation."

"That's odd," Billie whispered. "That doesn't fit the guy I met or the one you described. Do you think he's involved in something criminal? Running from the law?"

The receptionist smiled weakly and shook her head. "Hardly. He's—Don't repeat this, okay? Don't tell him I told you when you see him, but he's being harassed."

"Meaning?"

"Stalked, except he thinks that's too humiliating, not a guy thing, to even say the word about an ex-girlfriend. A crazy ex-girlfriend. She used to wait across the street there, scream at him, cry, until we called the police on her. He wouldn't. Too un-macho, I guess. He said she'd calm down, get over it. Meantime, he's hiding. In fact, I'll bet he's not anywhere around here because the ex would expect that."

Hiding, Billie wondered, or enjoying a honeymoon with Penelope Redmond?

Okay, then. She had a name. Neither of the names she thought she was after, but all the same, this was progress.

It was suspiciously easy. There, in the phone book in the kiosk around the corner from ILM was a listing for Stephen Tassio. Name and address in Larkspur. If what the receptionist said was true, it had to be his former residence, but maybe if she dialed it, the computerized operator, not knowing about stalkers and paranoia, would give forth the new number.

Instead, voice mail picked up, stating the obvious, that she'd reached the number she'd dialed.

What if Stephen Tassio hadn't moved at all? Maybe that was a ruse, to get the possessed girl off his case. Or what if the receptionist was a whole lot more devious than she'd seemed?—what if she considered Billie—even pathetic Audrey—as the possible stalker? Everybody lied. That's what Emma said.

She could just imagine Emma's acidic comments if she set off on an obscure hunt for the man without checking the obvious first.

She wrote down the address and number and returned to her car.

The Tassios' overinflated plantation house looked misplaced and out-of-scale in a neighborhood of large but relaxed shingled homes that blended into their landscape. To get there, Billie had driven up a road that curved abruptly to one side so as not to disturb an ancient tree. But this house was pure arrogance and made no attempt to be compatible with its surrounds. Stephen Tassio's home, or former home, or the home in which he currently or previously rented a room—whatever this was—belonged in a different sensibility. Enormous columns guarded a front door large enough to admit the King's guards, ceremonial high hats, the horses they were riding, and the carriage they pulled.

The man who answered her ring was dwarfed by the lintel high above him. You're a small and mortal thing while I am a majestic monument to myself, the doorway's mouth seemed to proclaim. Behind him, Billie saw gilded mirrorwork and a marble floor. What royal guests did these people anticipate in the charmingly sleepy town of Larkspur?

"I'm looking for Stephen Tassio," Billie said. "I'm—"

"Then your wish—and mine, too—has been granted, doll." His smile was more than half leer. "You found him."

In his fifties, she thought. Probably nice-enough-looking man before he sagged. He was pillow-soft and sloping. Even his hair was feathery, too fine and sparse to assume a shape. Couldn't be the man Penny ran away with, whose car was older than he was. "You— you're Stephen Tassio?"

174

"Have been all my life."

Then maybe Stephen wasn't Penny's Luke or Wesley's Stewart, after all. But the receptionist had said his car was older than he was. "And you drive a yellow hearse?"

His smile and all its component parts faded. "What's he done now?" he said. "I'm Stephen Senior. You're looking for Junior. Why do you care what he drives? Was he in a collision?"

If he thought that might be the reason for her call, why didn't he ask if his son was injured?

"Who is it?" a sharp-edged voice called out.

Stephen Senior ignored the sound.

"He hasn't done anything," Billie said. "Nothing's wrong. We have a mutual friend I'm trying to reach. I lost her address and I think she's staying with him awhile. That's all."

The owner of the voice appeared behind the senior Tassio. She looked as razor-edged as she'd sounded. "What's going on?" she demanded. "We don't accept door-to-door solicitors. We have a notice posted, so it's illegal to come here."

"She's not—"

"I'm looking for—"

"—selling anything," Senior said.

"Why didn't you say so?"

"Look, Marie . . ."

"What does she want, then? Is she a visitor?"

He considered this, then nodded. "More or less."

"Then why haven't you invited her in? Show a little common decency!"

This seemed a practiced routine the woman had to complete before she did what she was furious with her husband for not having already done. This was the machinery that primed them for the next step.

Senior sighed, then gestured to Billie to enter.

Perhaps she shouldn't judge on first impressions, but even if the couple had been less abrasive, their door and entry-hall decor were enough to convince her that she couldn't like them. She thought of Stephen in a job that never required clothing more dressy than a flannel shirt, driving a thirty-year-old hearse, and she approved. This was a family whose best hope would be a misfit.

"This is lovely," she lied. "You certainly have a beautiful home." Billie liked this part of her job—seeing the stages people erected for their personal dramas. This one was a still life. Embalmed shrine to success. A property statement, not a home.

Mrs. Tassio's nod was in acknowledgment of the praise her home deserved as she directed Billie and her husband into a room of watercolored silks, fragile side tables, embroidered runners, and gilded accessories.

The sofas and chairs were so far apart, interaction below a scream would be difficult. The coffee table was distant enough from the sofa so as to make retrieving an actual cup from it hazardous, liable to spill and stain a pink-and-cream rug, too delicate to endure the pressure of shoes. Guests would socialize here only because they had to, not because they wanted to. You couldn't live in this living room.

She paused at a small table filled with silver-framed photos, one of which was of a smiling young man in cap and gown. "Your son?" she asked Mr. Tassio. He nodded.

Junior was nice-looking. Open-faced, inviting. She wondered if he always looked that way, or if graduation's promised freedom from these people was what had lit his face.

Billie sat gingerly, refusing the offer of a beverage. "And you are?" Mrs. Tassio asked. "I never caught your name." She shot an accusatory glance at her husband.

"Billie August." No need for Audrey here. She told the truth, at least partially. She explained that she was looking for a female friend of Stephen's who had inherited money but didn't know about it.

"Another girl, then." His mother sealed her mouth so tightly she had no lips, only lines radiating from where they had been. Girls, then, were bad. Stephen's girls were bad.

"Truth is," Senior said, "Stephen's close-mouthed about his whereabouts lately. He hasn't lived here in a while."

"Only right after college," his mother said. "While he was job-hunting, but it didn't work out. Not at all. Stephen himself, well, that might have worked, but there were all these girls, a parade of them, and his friends. Strange people."

"Who, Marie?" Senior asked. "Who was strange?"

"Remember Alicia Malone?"

Her husband nodded and smiled. "Pretty child," he said. "I always liked her."

Mrs. Tassio sniffed. "After high school she became weird and then she infected Stephen. He was normal till then. She's the one dragged him in with her crowd. People who think it's still the Middle Ages, or should be. Pretend to be lords and ladies. Thanks to her, he arrived here with a wild bird. Filthy thing that sat on his wrist, on a leather band. It ate mice. My freezer was filled with them." She shook her head. Her hair was salt-and-pepper, pulled back into a twist. Attractive on anybody else, as would have been her black turtleneck and slacks, but the style only emphasized the steeliness of her temperament.

Billie had a moment's pleasure imagining Stephen's hawk defecating digested mouse upon this living room.

"Last time we knew his whereabouts it was with this girl Yvonne," his father said.

Mrs. Tassio inhaled loudly, then let the air escape in a ragged exhale. "I'm glad that one's over," she said. "She was not . . . You could tell how far downhill he was sliding if he was with her. She was different. Not . . . educated. Not refined. Cheap, if you understand what I'm saying. And after they broke up, she had the nerve to come here and accuse us of causing the rupture because we didn't approve of her! What a piece of work! There's no law says I have to let whatever my son picks up—mangy friends who don't own a decent suit, a hawk, or Yvonne—into my house. A woman's home is her castle, too."

"Then you don't have his new address or phone number?"

"I wouldn't have known he'd moved if that . . . person hadn't come here and carried on that way. Stephen is not your ideal son. He lacks social niceties, like telling his parents where he lives, calling sometimes, even visiting. Without the bird."

"Did Stephen ever mention Penelope Redmond?"

"You might be getting the idea that Stephen mentions very little to us, Miss August," Senior said. "You'd be correct in that."

"Is this Penelope the girl who's inherited something?" his wife asked.

Billie nodded.

"At least his taste in women has improved since Yvonne."

An interesting judgment since the only information she'd been given was that imaginary money floated on her imaginary horizon.

"Then I thank you for your time and consideration." Billie stood up. "Please let me know if you do hear from Stephen. It's important that I notify Penelope." She handed them one of her cards, the one that simply said, *Investigator*.

It was interesting what you gleaned while searching for something else altogether. Peel back the fronts of those tidy homes and see how they've organized their lives, how closely they resemble their facades and landscapes. Learn a lot.

What she hadn't learned, however, was the only thing she'd been hired to find out. Where was Penelope Redmond?

Seventeen

Penny crouched behind a fan of green leaves at the far end of the dock. The end of the walkway was edged by potted cymbidiums, all heavy with about-to-burst buds. From here, she had a clear view of an entire line of houseboats including the small one three down. The one where her father was when he should have been at the office or the store. "Just Kidding," he called his company. A good name because it was obviously a joke, nothing he had to pay attention to.

Penny sat quietly, knees to her chin, a baseball cap on her head with its visor tilted down. She watched a woman come out of a boat and unlock a shopping cart from her front wall. Then she went back in and reemerged with bulging trash bags. When the cart was full, she wheeled it toward the parking lot.

Penny didn't try to hide. Nobody would notice her or if they did, she'd be taken for a kid playing hooky. Which, actually, she was.

Arthur was also playing, not hooky, but around. She knew what it was costing her—literally and figuratively, as her English teacher would have said—to have him give these strangers champagne and tiny violins and new sofas while Penny saved for the tuition he wouldn't pay, the prom dress he wouldn't buy, and her mother did his books, took care of his office, helped in the store. He traveled so much, was on the road so often, her mother said, the least she could do is take care of the scutwork. Penny was no longer sure that he was ever on the road, except for the freeway to Sausalito.

The car with its JUS KIDN vanity plate was already in the lot when she got there. She could wait. Whenever he came out, she was confronting him, letting him know he couldn't get away with this any longer. She'd threaten to tell his boss at the store, the manufacturers who thought he worked for them.

In return for silence, she'd make him promise that he wouldn't hit Wesley or her mother anymore, that he'd give them more money. Pay her college. And, of course, he'd have to stop doing this. She watched a pelican skim over the bay, its wings inches from the glassy surface mirroring its flight. A noise interrupted—two large men in blue jumpsuits wheeling a dolly with only blue quilted cloths draped over it. They entered the little houseboat.

A few minutes later, they emerged with three sections of a black leather sofa. No relationship to the green velvet she'd seen moved in. The woman must have multiple personalities.

On their next trip, the men carried a stiff-looking white sofa with pale wooden legs and framework. It looked like the Barishes' furniture, which they always referred to as being Louis the something. Half the time she sat for them it was because they were "going antiquing." Their kids weren't allowed in the living room.

Her mother was always talking about what "went with" their house, what the "look" of the place was supposed to be. She thought her mother went overboard with "the look" thing, but still, she had a point, and what kind of "look" went with green velvet, then a black leather sectional, then a Louis? What kind of person changed her mind every few days? The houseboat was small, perhaps two rooms on deck and one or two bedrooms below, where windows showed above the water line. It couldn't house two living rooms, or a den or family room plus a living room, plus two bedrooms, one for the little violinist.

180

She stood up and briskly walked back to the parking lot. Maybe they found change sexy, a turn-on. But it was certainly not economical, and Arthur was dead set against renting. God, one time her mother had wanted to rent folding chairs when they were having a camp reunion for Wesley and Arthur had blown up. "Renting furniture is pissing money away. Skip the middleman and burn my cash right now instead. Save time." The campers had sat on the floor to eat their sandwiches. Her mother tried to make it seem on purpose, called it an "indoor picnic."

Now look at the hypocrite. Unless, maybe the woman was paying for this, and Arthur just happened to visit during sofa-shifts.

The movers wheeled their dolly back to the parking lot. The mistress was changing more than sofas. Out with a brass lamp with a black leather shade, out with a massive planked coffee table. In with ruffled shades—one of the men carried them while the other wheeled a round of glass, a gilded base, and two clear-glass lamps.

Penny seated herself in front of a piling and waited for more, watching a woman take a baby out of its car seat. She was glad she didn't sit for anybody here. Too scary, and she didn't have much confidence in water herself. She'd drown trying to stop a drowning.

Odd to choose a houseboat when you had a baby, but the whole colony was a little apart from normal. A mix of suits, artists, leftover hippies, and whoever was quietly growing cymbidiums at the end of the dock. Kids at school said drugs were run in the waters that filled the spaces between Sausalito, Tiburon, and Mill Valley.

The men loaded the dolly with a gold-and-white-painted headboard and night table, plus two gilded, pouffy-shaded lamps. And they took out a large boxed set she couldn't identify until one of them called to the other, who was still in the truck, "Don't forget the canopy. I have the rest of the four-poster."

She might vomit, imagining Arthur naked below the canopy. Why were they switching beds? Had they already worn one out? How long had this setup been going on?

181

The men wheeled an empty dolly back and got into the truck. Penny listened to the warning beeps as it backed out of its space. Something nagged at her, something separate from the things she already knew about, a kind of "What's wrong with this picture?" sense. She thought back, tried to think this through, but her mind skipped and wandered.

She decided to wait for Arthur in the parking lot. It was more comfortable, with the piling as a backrest, and it was his only way out—unless he rowed off, which he wouldn't. She rested her head on her knees as she again tried to figure out what the new thing was that bothered her about the moving people, and felt the shadow rather than saw anyone. Her heart rate doubled even before she lifted her head. She hadn't seen him—he'd seen her.

But it wasn't Arthur looming above her. "Luke!" she said. "What are you doing here?" She scrambled to her feet.

"A better question would be what you're doing here. Or, more precisely, what is my car doing here?" His voice had a whole new sound, as if he'd wrapped a worn-out blanket of calm over spikes and crags of anger.

"You were asleep and this was important. I thought—"

"It's two in the afternoon!" He was furious. No mistaking it now.

"I . . . didn't realize. I was watching. Luke, men came and—"

"And stop calling me that."

"That's who you are to me. That's who you were when I met you."

"No, I was Stephen, the guy with the weird car, remember? It wasn't until you invited yourself to one of our—"

"You told me to come. You did!"

He shrugged. "Whatever. I didn't think it mattered, the Lucan the Steward business, but I changed my mind. It's—it's a symptom. You never want to live in the twentieth century. You want to live in The Principality of the Mists all the time. You love make-believe so much you're ruining my life!"

She stood and took off her cap in some instinctive humbling motion, then had no idea of what to do except brace herself. This felt like an earthquake, at least inside of her.

"My name's Stephen. And you had no right to take my car. You're taking *everything.*"

"I'm sorry. Really, honestly. I didn't think it'd matter. You were sound asleep, and we didn't have any plans—"

"Maybe we didn't, but I did! And that isn't the point. You've got everything screwed-up. For starters, why the hell did you come here? What game are you playing?"

"Not a game, and you know. About my father."

"So he's having an affair. People do. My father has them nonstop. So they're creeps, but it's not the end of the world and it doesn't have anything to do with you."

"I told you—he treats us, all of us, like—"

He brushed aside her words and walked away, then turned back. "You know what? I don't give a shit about your father. My family's fucked, too. Everybody's is, but people don't have to screw up their own lives because of it. When are you going to get your diploma? How are you going to get a decent job if you don't? How are you going to live? Off me? That isn't a plan, Penny. That isn't what I meant."

He made everything wrong, turned it inside out and upside down. Maybe if he knew more about how weird things were at the houseboat, he'd see this wasn't ordinary, this demanded attention. "Luke—Stephen, these men came and changed the furniture. Three times since I first came here. Three times that I saw, let alone when I wasn't here. New sofa and bed and lamps and coffee table—"

"Get this straight—I don't care. Everybody's crazy their own way—what I care about is getting *my* shit together."

"So do I, that's why I came here."

"Not this! You can't straighten out your father."

"Stepfather."

"If he's playing around, then he is. Tell your mother, let them work it through."

"I did."

"And?"

"She . . . didn't believe me." She didn't want to say more. It bothered her even thinking about how her mother had reacted.

He shook his head and waved her entire family off. "I want to straighten *us* out. Now."

"M-meaning what?" She could barely get the words out and when she did, they hurt her throat. Nothing was crooked or in need of work between them. He was her one ally on earth. She heard a high, thin scream like a dental drill in a faraway part of her skull, coming closer.

He seemed reluctant to speak, then he sighed. "Maybe if we talk it through, calmly, you'll see. There've been misunderstandings right from the start, beginning with what you thought I was offering you, what you thought I meant. Nobody's fault—just wires crossed."

He was kicking her out—turning back on the promises he'd made so she could get away from the screaming and hitting and lying and her father's woman and other life.

He was a liar like everybody else. The high voice moved closer, through the center of her brain. It aimed for her face, found its target and plunged through her eyes like needles. "You're making me leave, aren't you?"

He shifted his weight, looked uncomfortable. She was right, then, no matter what he'd say.

"It isn't that, not exactly. And not like today or anything. Listen, this is no place for a real talk. Can I have my car keys?"

"What are you going to say? Where am I going to go if you—"

"Don't get hysterical. That's one of your problems, acting as if everything's so tragic, so dramatic."

"This is! I can't go home! He's—They're—" Her mind flooded

with images of them, of him, of her mother pretending to be crippled so she could get money and get away from him, but she never would—not even if she collected a million dollars because she wanted that house, the furniture that all "went."

She suddenly realized what had been wrong at the houseboat. "They didn't switch anything else," she said out loud. "There couldn't be a house where the rest of the stuff went with all those different sofas. But nothing else went. No chairs, even."

"What are you, a reporter for *Architectural Digest*? Stop changing the subject. I'm not throwing you out and I'm not saying you have to go home. There must be other solutions. But for as long as you stay with us—"

With us. Not with him. With us. She didn't matter to him, not in any special way.

"—it'll work better if you get a few things straight about, well, about how the place works. What's appropriate and what isn't."

Sounded like he was training a puppy. Like she'd been messing up, spoiling his life.

"Like last night, about your necklace. Such a stupid racket, and you know, the rest of the house isn't real excited to have a runaway there, so the least you could do is not . . . take over. And since you eventually agreed, couldn't it have been sooner?"

"What do you mean, take over the house? I agreed not to do that?"

"No." He sounded exhausted, as if he wanted her to know she was wearing him out and she hadn't done anything, except borrow a car he wasn't using.

"I'm sorry about the car, really. I will never, ever, take it again. Unless you tell me to. Is that what you meant I had agreed to? Because I can't remember, but I'll never forget again. I thought I'd have it back before you woke up. I'm sorry."

"I'm not talking about the car. I meant all that squabbling and hysteria before you agreed to make the phone call and notify the police. It could have been so easy—couldn't we skip the fireworks from now on? Everybody would be happier."

They all were against her. She hated them. Hated him. Why should she do anything he wanted?

"You're immature. Compared to us, I mean. I'm not blaming you—it isn't your fault. You're normal, that's all. You're eighteen, haven't been through much. But it makes life really—"

"I've been through plenty! I'm not a baby, the way you make me sound! I made a fuss because I understand more than you do. You're all manipulating me, pushing me around. Whatever's comfortable for all of you is what's right, and screw me!" The scream drilling through her skull hit a well of tears and she blinked and brushed hard against her eyes. "I'm not doing any of it. I'm not calling the Marshalls. They'd never understand in a million years why I left and—"

"Isn't that where you were this morning?"

"I never said I'd do it on my own. You were supposed to write out what I'd say. Besides, none of you care if my entire life is ruined by it!"

"You think you're grown up, but that's the most childish— You won't take care of messy things, loose ends. You don't do what you say you will."

"All you want is peace and quiet. That's not adult—that's dead! More time for the crossword puzzle or the computer, and to hell with everybody else!"

He took her arm and held it. "Calm down," he said, acting like a jailer. "Okay, fine. I'll go tell them. You can wait in the car. They won't see you, it'll be done, and then we'll stop at the police, or you'll call—or I will, and then we're going to have lunch and a reality check. You get that? You're a spoiled little girl, no matter what you think. All you want is what you want, when you want it. Now get in the car. The day's ruined, anyway."

186

"My stepfather—I want to see him. I want him to know there's no more secrets."

"Are you crazy? Didn't you run away from them? And you think I'm going to stand around here like a kidnapper? Like I'm responsible for your running away? Get in the car and give me the charm."

She got into the hearse, but clutched her necklace.

"I'll give it back, but I want them to remember what I'm talking about, think about where they got theirs what they know about them, and call the police."

"This is too stupid," she muttered, handing it over. But if she cooperated, got this over with, she could use a lunch. Her stomach growled. And maybe when he wasn't so hungry, he'd look at her in that kind, loving way again, and go back to being Lucan the Steward, then she could be Gwyneth for as long as life itself.

"Which one should I go to first?" he asked. "Where are they?"

"They? Who?"

"The two women who had hearts like yours."

She'd forgotten she'd said that. She'd made up that there was a second one, added on only to shut them up and make the hearts seem even more common. But what was the made-up name? And why did she have to do this at all? There'd been thousands of girls with heart-shaped pendants, and if she didn't happen to know all of them, did that make them less common?

She couldn't remember what she'd said. Instead, she thought of somebody who worked all day, who was never going to be around. "I'd see Mrs. DeLuca first," she said. "She's in San Anselmo."

"DeLuca? I thought Matterson. Or Masterson. Like in 'It matters some' is what I thought last night when you said it."

"Well, you thought wrong." He must be testing her. She didn't remember giving him any specific name.

He shrugged and started the car.

"It's out of the way," she said. "San Anselmo. You should skip it, or go some other—"

"It'll be fine." He was so wrapped up in his little adventure, he didn't even care. But maybe it was okay. Maybe they could go home straight from there, skip the Marshalls. Maybe they could get back to where they'd started.

"Life is so much easier on everybody," he said, "when you handle things instead of whining about them."

She closed her eyes so she couldn't see him way up on the pedestal where he'd placed himself. She wanted to slap him, drag him back to real life, scream at him. But she controlled herself, an act of great maturity, if only he were mature enough to notice.

Eighteen

Billie's car was aimed toward the office where she hoped to find Stephen Tassio. Not in the flesh, but in the computer. That group the receptionist had mentioned—his mother had sneeringly referred to it, too, hadn't she?—the medieval thing. Maybe there was a way to find him through that. If, indeed, people who were in love with the Middle Ages were able to balance that alongside the artifacts of cyberspace.

The fleeting thought of the senior Tassios made her shoulders slump as if the couple had settled on her like twin gargoyles. How could they care so little about their son? What happened during a life to cause such estrangement? Between Penny Redmond and her parents, too. She rolled her head to ease the strain in her neck.

Odd that she would even ask, given that she knew the answer anyway, from personal experience. She had next to no contact with her own parents in the hope that the farther the distance, the less sharp the pain would be. And it was in fact a partial cure. She believed in running away from some problems. What else was a divorce? Distance made the heart grow calmer.

Had the Tassios ever felt about Stephen, Sophia Redmond about Penny, the way she did about Jesse, the linchpin of her life?

She hadn't seen her son in what felt like too long and then for only brief and insignificant moments. A kiss and a glimpse of a sleep-swollen face and footed pajamas in the morning, and then, when? She had promised to be home to tuck him in and hadn't made it. All she'd gotten to do was turn off the light he'd insisted be kept lit pending her arrival.

Maybe that's how estrangements of the Tassio and Redmond kind began. Maybe parents didn't have to do anything directly to shut off communication. Not being there might suffice.

She glanced at her watch. Nursery school was over and Ivan didn't have class today or tonight, so no extended day for Jesse. A quick stop home wouldn't hurt. She lived so close anyway, a matter of five or six blocks. No big thing. While she ran around in search of Stephen, she didn't want Jesse becoming the shoemaker's child.

Touch base, that was all, then back to the office for a spell on the computer. She could work as late as she needed. While she U-turned to head home, one stay of the guilt-corset loosened. Not the one about Cameron re-kidnapping Jesse. Not the one about not being able to provide the niceties, let alone luxuries for her son. Not the one about needing to keep her son from his father. Not the one about the way the house wasn't kept up, or the one about whether Ivan really paid enough attention, or the one about the junk food too often served up or the dozens of other undone or half-done items that squeezed her rib cage smaller than Scarlett's so that day or night, she could barely catch her breath.

"Mommy!" Jesse said, with enough surprised delight to break her heart and a running knee-tackle that nearly knocked her over. He seemed able to leap from sitting cross-legged to a full sprint. Maybe he had a future in sports. "Mommy! Ivan—Mommy's here!" He clung to her knees in his baby-monkey pose, which she found—and the monkey knew she found—irresistible.

And where was Ivan? All she could see was Jesse, plus her semi-nice brown sofa, the usual droppings on the puke-green carpet that had come with the house and that she couldn't afford to replace.

Jesse's trains and trucks, two of her half-read *New Yorkers*, an unruly stack of sheet music, a bowl with a dozen Cheerios, and a half-empty glass of juice.

"Hey, mister!" She lifted her son, although a new solidity to his three-year-old flesh and density to his bones made it harder to arc him out of gravity's pull. "You're getting enormous! Mind if I plant one on you?"

He wrinkled his nose and squirmed, laughing the whole time. A few weeks ago, he had entered a tough-guy phase—swaggering, bragging, and declaring that there would be no more kissing, but either he'd forgotten, or he was allowing her to break the new rules on this special occasion.

Ivan walked in from the kitchen. His welcoming smile was mildly concerned.

"Mommy's here. She'll make us dinner and read to me and I'll—"

"Wish I could stay, Jess, but I have to get back to work."

Jesse looked as if he were deciding whether to have a tantrum or not at this news.

Ivan, on the other hand, looked relieved. Trouble hadn't brought her home at this unexpected hour.

She wondered if he paid enough attention to the boy. His course load was packed, and his workload compounded as he studied in a language that was still new to him. She knew he was the best deal possible for her, maybe the only one—where else would she find a barter system nanny? It was pointless to be annoyed that the TV blared a mindless cartoon while Ivan did his classwork in the kitchen.

"Tell me about your day," she said to Jesse, postponing a Serious Talk with Ivan for the evanescent Time twins—Some Other and When I Have. "What did you do in school?"

"I made bubbles, and painted, and we made juice from the inside of oranges, not a can! Vanessa brought in this machine that smushes them and juice comes out! I did it, too!"

Bad California mommy, whose kid was dazzled by juice coming out of fruit, not packaging. "Was it good?" she asked.

He nodded, gravely, his eyes wide. "Could we get one of those machines?"

She couldn't remember if a wedding-gift juicer was packed up somewhere in the house. "I'll try," she said. "Know what? Right now, I have time for a story if you'd like. Or we could play piano and sing, or——"

The doorbell rang. Then, much too quickly, rang again.

Ivan, raised to worry about anything the least out of the ordinary, glanced at Billie. "Expecting anybody?" he asked.

She shook her head.

The bell rang a third time. Either an emergency or the kind of person she didn't want to know. Billie put her son down, close to Ivan, and went to answer it.

"Where is he?" a thin, wild-eyed woman asked before the door was half open. "I know he's here." She flicked an errant strand of dark hair off her narrow face. "I thought you'd be at the beach, at *our* place maybe, but then I saw you go here."

"I have no idea what you're talking about." Behind her, Billie heard Ivan tell Jesse to stay on the sofa, then he moved closer to her. She'd forgive his preoccupations as long as he was alert when it mattered. "Who are you?"

"I'm the one you think you've replaced. I'm the cast-off."

"Ivan?" Billie asked. "Is this a friend of yours?"

He moved still closer, all six feet three inches of him. He had a broad and smiling face and wasn't particularly muscular, but the size of him alone was a comfort. "Who are you?" he asked, his accent thickening with each syllable. "What you want here?"

"Who's he?" the woman asked Billie, as if they were confidantes. "What's he doing here?"

"Listen carefully," Billie said. "I'm calling the police unless you either make your point or get out of here."

The woman stood straighter. Billie realized she was quite young. Only the tension pulling her every muscle made her look indefinable but ancient. "Like you don't know that I'm Yvonne," she said. "Stephen's Yvonne. I know he's with you. I saw you at ILM. I saw you at his parents'. I want to see him. I have the right to see him!" She put her hands up, palms toward Billie. "Look, I'm clean. No weapons. I only want to talk. He has to talk to me!" She leaned closer. "*Stephen!*" she screamed into the house. "*Stephen!*"

"Make her go away," Jesse whimpered from inside the living room.

"Where is he? Is he already at the beach? You meeting him there?"

"This'll take a minute." Billie pushed forward over Ivan's protests, closing the front door behind her. Her internal organs pulsed with the understanding that this woman, the one who was said to be stalking Stephen Tassio, had stalked her. Observed her through the day—and she hadn't noticed. She was unable to believe her own stupidity. She was unfit for her job, might as well hand in her resignation. Blind, oblivious—here she'd been mentally castigating Ivan for being preoccupied—when she'd led an insane woman to her home, to her child. And what had prompted Yvonne to make it clear that she wasn't armed at the moment. Was she usually?

"He's mine," Yvonne said, her voice a cat's, if cats could speak. "He's mine."

Billie felt dumbfounded, but that wouldn't do any good. She thought of Emma, tried to be Emma, to bulk up, add years and solidity. "Go away," she said in a low but steady voice. "I'm talking forever. I'm taking out a restraining order against you, you understand?" She had no idea if such small provocation would get her one, but maybe Yvonne didn't know, either. "If you show your face in this neighborhood again, if you ever once come close to my house, to my child, my baby-sitter—you will be arrested. Do you understand?"

Yvonne burst into tears. "But I love him! He's mine! It was his parents—they put a wedge between us, they poisoned his mind. I can make him understand. Give me the chance, a few minutes. You don't need him—you've got that one." She waved at the house. "I can't live without him. He has to see that, has to understand."

Or? This kind of sick passion, possessiveness, was too often a preface to a headline-making event. All the "If I can't have you nobody can" murders. Because, of course, they love the corpse so much.

And then Yvonne changed tacks, anger replacing desperation. "He owes me," she said. "Owes me big, and he'd better pay up. I never finished college because of him. Palimony. A lawyer said I had a case. He can't go spending his money on somebody like you. He owes me!"

"He isn't here," Billie said. "I've never met him. I'm looking for him because maybe he knows what became of a runaway. I haven't found him, either. I don't have an address or a phone number or anything. Go away."

"He'll ruin you, the way he ruined me. It's all a game with him, like his imaginary world thing, his *Society* people—that's all he cares about." Her hand's gesture seemed to brush away the imaginary thing. "Not any kind of society people I ever heard of. 'Creative,' they called themselves. Their name. 'Creative . . .' " She shrugged. "Some shit. Can't remember what they were creative at. "Creative Assassins. Right. A lot of crap about lords and ladies in the meadow. Hell, get a grip, look around—this look like a castle? The fake names—like he's suddenly, really, Lucan the Steward. Like he's tight with King Arthur."

Lucan. The Steward. Luke Stewart. Billie felt a schizy split of rage and terror at her intruder, and excitement about seeing the hunt more clearly. "I don't know him, never met him, and you'd better get out of here and stay away from us."

Yvonne made Billie think of a vibrating wire. Even stock-still, waves of energy, tension, and near hysteria jostled the air around her. "I'll get out," she finally said in a growl. "But don't think it's over. I'm not through with this. Never will be. True love is forever. I won't be through with Stephen until one or both of us are in our graves."

Billie watched the madwoman make her way to and then into her car, a dark hatchback that looked victimized by inattention. *You will stay away. You will never again frighten my son. You will . . .*

She reentered her home, slamming the door, the image and fear that persisted behind her. "How about I read you a story before I have to head back out?" she asked Jesse.

He beamed and nodded. As long as the people in his personal drama, even the reduced cast he'd been scripted, stuck to their assigned roles, stayed in character—even if he knew they were only acting—all was right with his world.

They were the opposite of estranged. They were intertwined pieces of the whole—as long as she played her role, that of protector. Jesse was simply too young and trusting to comprehend that she had led the snake home to Eden. She was glad her son didn't hear the hint of a tremor in her voice as she began, for the hundredth time, his current favorite, *The Velveteen Rabbit,* the story of the toy who loved his boy, who was saved from disaster on the discard pile. The story of Jesse, who, she feared, remembered being taken and not returned.

She had to make sure and keep his story the same as the rabbit's, complete with happy ending. And the happy endings had to happen every day, with every new installment.

She refused to allow her voice to shake. Instead, playing for the second balcony, she read:

" 'There was once a velveteen rabbit, and in the beginning he was really splendid. . . .' "

Nineteen

Number twenty-seven, she had said. Brown-shingled. Second or third on the left. She was paranoid, made everything more difficult than it had to be, insisting that he park where she couldn't be seen, around the corner.

What was it about him that attracted normal-seeming girls who then went bonkers? Yvonne hadn't seemed crazy at the start— would he have lived with someone who did? He found girls with the seeds of craziness, but what did he do to make that seed bloom and grow to blue-ribbon size?

He pressed the doorbell of number twenty-seven, waited, then repeated the process.

Maybe they were around back. There were obviously children, if Penny sat for them. Maybe there was more of a play area behind the house, because out front, there was almost none. He walked up the narrow cement drive that led to a shingled single-car garage, and saw a plot of mostly dirt behind the house. A wooden climbing gizmo, two beach chairs, and a sandbox with a rain-filled cover over it. No Mrs. DeLuca, no DeLuca kids.

And whatever energy had driven him from his home this morning to Sausalito, to here, was suddenly and completely dissipated. What the hell was he doing? And why? Who cared? He'd been so furious with her—still was—that he was proving a meaningless point by hammering it into the ground.

Probably all he wanted was to be important, be the guy whose wits had broken an old, unsolved case. Maybe his ego was just that pathetic. He wandered back toward the street. The hell with it. They'd go home to San Geronimo and make a plan—not about the stupid pendant, but about her future. Which had to take place away from him.

"Thanks again for accepting that package," a light voice said as he emerged from between the houses. "They insist on delivering them the one hour I have to—"

"Hey!" a male voice said. "What are you—?" Stephen looked over to where a middle-aged woman stood holding open the front door of her house for a guy in a maroon sweatshirt. The guy who was shouting at Stephen, coming his way, double-time. "You looking for somebody?" He'd seen too many Clint Eastwood movies, acting like Stephen was here to blow up the neighborhood.

"I'm looking for Mrs. DeLuca," Stephen managed.

"She's not there."

"Yeah, I . . . I thought maybe she was out back."

"No."

"Okay," Stephen said. "I'll try some other—"

"What about?" the man asked.

"About?"

"What do you want to see her about?"

"Nothing important. A question."

"You selling something?"

Stephen shook his head again and backed off a step. A lunatic vigilante with nothing to guard against. But he had only himself to blame. He should have dropped the issue way sooner. He attempted a half-nod, the sort of thing that signaled leave-taking when there was no relationship whatsoever.

The man looked at the shingled house, then at Stephen. "You want to leave a message? Your name? What this is about?"

Stephen shook his head. "Thanks, but no." He repeated his sociable, impersonal half-nod and walked by the man, toward the corner.

And realized the man had gone inside the shingled house. He lived there. That's why he was so worried to see Stephen prowl around it. He lived there, so he must know Penny. He'd go back— he was here, after all. Anyway, he wanted to establish that he wasn't some kind of neighborhood creep.

The man in the maroon sweatshirt answered the bell and looked annoyed by the sight of him. "Kids are napping," he said, interrupting Stephen's attempt to introduce himself. "Could you keep it down?"

"Yessir. Just wanted to say sorry if I worried you. I didn't realize this was your house. I'm here on behalf of Penny Redmond. You know her, right? I believe she baby-sat for your wife."

"Is Penny okay? Do you know where she is?"

Jesus. Why was the guy so eager? How did he even know she was gone? It had only been a few days. "This is actually about a gold heart she found. Apparently, your wife has, or had, one that looked like it."

"And? I don't get this yet, and I'm more concerned about where Penny is."

Stephen was getting a really bad feeling from this, like DeLuca and Penny . . . Maybe he was one of her many secrets.

"And how does she know my wife, let alone my wife's jewelry collection?"

"Penny? Because she sat for—"

"*Me.* Penny sat for me when I was on deadline. I'm a writer."

He said it belligerently, as if Stephen had asked him what he was doing home in the middle of the day. Maybe too many people did.

Mr. DeLuca checked that the door was unlocked, closed it behind him and stood warily on the top step, arms folded over his chest.

Stephen tried to speak softly and clearly and to make his point, even though he could barely remember it. "Look, Mr. DeLuca, if I— Could I maybe just show it to you and you can tell me if she had or has something like it? See, Penny says the design is really common, that lots of girls had them. That's all we're trying to establish here."

"Man, you're not making sense. It's not like Penny to get worked-up about whether something's too common or not. What have you done to her? And you forgot to say your name, too."

"Stephen Tassio." He should have said *Mr.* Tassio to the asshole. He held out the pendant and chain. "Is this familiar-looking?"

DeLuca seemed ready to fit a butterfly net to Stephen's head.

"She found it in a field in West Marin. Near where they found those bodies. I say she should take it to the police, that maybe it's important. She says it's so ordinary it can't mean anything. That's all I'm trying to find out. She says your wife had one like it. Either your wife showed hers to Penny or told her about it. So did somebody else she sat for. If that's so, then probably she's right and I should get off her case. And I don't want to be like a jerk with the police, if every girl really had one . . ."

DeLuca looked at Penny's trinket, then at Stephen. "I have no idea. You could have taken it out of Betty's jewelry box this morning and I still wouldn't know, except she wouldn't wear it now. It's not power dressing. But she wasn't as conservative when we were undergrads." He shrugged and looked at it again. "And she wasn't in a sorority, either. Against her principals to join anything back then. So maybe. Times and taste in jewelry change, so she probably had one if she said so. Although when Penny would have met Betty . . ."

There was something creepy about the guy. Why shouldn't Penny know his wife? Was she buried in the cellar? Or was Penny *his,* as if he owned her?

"What color car do you drive?" DeLuca asked abruptly.

"Yellow, why?"

He looked at Stephen, then put a hand on the doorknob. Interview over. "You want to give me your number? So I can ask Betty about that thing?"

Stephen didn't want to, but he'd look like more of a phony if he refused, so he wrote it on the back of his business card.

"Listen," DeLuca said as he pocketed the card, "If you know where she is . . . do everybody a favor and make sure she gets home. Soon."

"I'm trying, sir," Stephen said.

"Good, then," DeLuca said. He grabbed the edge of the door, ready to close it.

"One question," Stephen said. "Why did you mention sororities?"

DeLuca took the charm back and pointed at the tracery. "The Greek letters here. I just assumed they were the name of a sorority."

"Vux? You mean that?"

DeLuca shook his head. From inside the house, Stephen heard a sharp wail. "Not Vux. It's Greek."

"Greek? It doesn't look like——"

"Greek script. Three letters."

"Do you know which——"

"Gamma Mu Chi," DeLuca said with a shrug. The wail intensified. "And now, you can hear, I assume, that if there's nothing further——"

"No, sir. Thanks for——"

DeLuca nodded and closed the door behind him.

Stephen heard the lock turn. That had been humiliating, and stupid. Time to go home.

She was sitting in his car, pouting. "What took so long?" were the first words out of her mouth. Like she didn't know where he'd been, or why. "Can we get some food now?" was the second question. She didn't even ask what he'd found out.

Something that had softened inside him solidified again. He was not going to be bossed around by yet another crazy woman. Maybe Penny was right about the jewelry being common—but he was right about finding it out. He drove to her old neighborhood.

"For God's sake, don't park near my house," she snapped. "You want my mother to see me? And don't park where the Marshalls can see, either. It's not like everybody doesn't know I left in this car, or are you turning me in?"

He kept his voice calm, the way animal trainers did with wild things. "I want this over with, Penny." Somehow, he realized, he'd come to equate getting this heart thing settled with getting Penny herself settled. Which was to say—out of his life. "You said Sunny Marshall—that's her name, right?—had one like it."

"So what? She was a rich girl, my mother says. She probably had everything." She slumped down into the seat. "I'm hungry," she whined.

"Answer me this," he said. How come you can waste your life snooping after your dad when what he's doing is wrong, but not criminal, but you can't spare a minute to maybe provide information about a double murder?"

She crossed her arms over her midriff and slumped lower in the car.

"And what was it with you and DeLuca?" he asked. "He's a real creep. Arrogant asshole." Knew Greek and acted like everybody should.

"Creep? He's nice. And smart. Like, *wise*."

And Stephen heard a familiar sound, a tone inside her voice that she'd used on him, when he was her hero. So what had DeLuca been, and for how long, and what happened between them?

"Could you at least leave the radio on this time?" she said.

"No." He opened his door. "I'll keep the keys to myself, thanks."

She closed her eyes and moved even lower in the seat. "My

mother is going to recognize the hearse and call the police. Then you'll be happy, right?"

"I can't see your house from here, which means she can't see me. She's in a wheelchair, for God's sake, what is she going to do? Leap up screaming, 'I'm healed'? Admit she's faking it? Why don't you think about what you're going to do about your life instead of worrying about hers. Why don't you consider changing your mind and going home to work things through?"

He didn't look back as he walked up the three steps onto the Marshall's porch. Even from around the corner, Penny's eyes bore into his back. He could feel her hair's red tendrils reach for him. Forget R&R, vacations. He couldn't wait to get back to work—even if Yvonne decided to once again lurk in the parking lot every damned morning. At work, difficult projects were doable. Creating new worlds was easier than dealing with women.

He studied the large house. Its yellow was almost the same as his car's—with thin lines of emerald green and turquoise banding the froufrou designs. The porch was filled with white wicker furniture with plump turquoise pillows. Really nice, he thought. And this is what Penny found obnoxious.

A woman with red-gold hair responded to his ring, a baby perched on her hip. She smiled at him, as if she expected strangers to be pleasant.

Pretty. The word registered and reverberated.

Gorgeous. Even though she was older than he was, a mother. *Gorgeous.*

"This is going to sound weird, I know," he began after he'd told her his name. "But I'm a friend of Penny Redmond's, and I understand—"

"Penny?" She clutched her baby closer, as if maybe the fat-legged infant would hear Penny's name and be inspired to run away herself. Or himself. "Do you know where she is? Her parents are worried sick. Awful thing to do to your mother when she's already in a wheelchair." Then she looked at him for real this time. "But that's not why you've come here, is it?"

Smart, too. "No, ma'am."

She studied him, then moved her head toward the innards of the house. "Come on in," she said. "But let's not make too much noise. My husband's trying to work and these babies are cooperating for just this minute." She waved him in with her free hand. He heard a cry from a back room. Sunny sighed and shook her head, but didn't look angry, or as if she ever could be angry. The baby on her hip scrunched its face and sobbed, too.

"Doesn't have a clue what's bothering his twin, but he'll cry all the same. Or maybe they do have a special ESP. Anyway, let me go relieve my husband, who will never get a single thing done, don't I know, while he's with the kids."

She didn't say whether Stephen should follow her, but he wanted to. Wanted to be near this shining, calm, and happy person. Waiting in the hallway seemed stupid, anyway, like a delivery boy, so he walked a few paces behind, toward a kitchen bright with the same yellows, whites, green, and turquoise as the house's exterior. Sunny's name seemed also her favorite color.

A thin man in running shorts sat at the kitchen table, a legal pad and ballpoint pen in front of him and a yowling baby in a high chair next to him. The man looked up with obvious relief as his wife entered.

"Can't get much done, can you?" she said. "Maybe you should talk to the Shriners about how it is to try and work around children. Go take your run and clear your head."

Talkman nodded wearily, then noticed Stephen. "And who might this be?" he asked.

Stephen marveled that the voice, rich and creamy—"words of white chocolate," somebody had said—was the same in a kitchen as over the air. He'd somehow assumed the sound was electronically enhanced. It coated each syllable and made a phrase such as, "And who might this be?" sound fraught with meaning.

"Stephen Tassio, sir, but Mrs. Marshall told me you were working and I don't mean to interrupt."

"He's Penny Redmond's friend," Sunny said. Both babies had stopped crying upon sight of each other. Another child was on the floor, coloring on an oversized paper. He—or she—stared at Stephen, a red crayon held immobile.

Talkman lifted an eyebrow as if waiting for more. For what?

"But I'm not here about her," Stephen said. "Except indirectly. I'll only take a minute of your time, I promise, but I'm here because of something Penny mentioned, and I thought you could help about it. Mrs. Marshall, actually. About telling the police. You might have additional information you or I could give them."

"The police?" Talkman looked puzzled and mildly amused. "Why? About what?"

"Coffee?" Sunny Marshall asked brightly. "It's fresh. Peet's, too—the best beans in the world."

Stephen wondered if Sunny was her real name, or, if not, when she'd been given the nickname. At what point in her life had she become herself? At what point would he? Penny's resentment of this woman made him still angrier with her.

"Sit down, Stephen, why don't you?" Talkman said. "If you can stand the ruckus. Two-year-olds are actually robotic aliens. Their brain cells are way less developed than their motors, and the possibilities are terrifying. And when you get two two-year-olds and a four-year-old big brother, it's the domestic equivalent of a nuclear disaster. On the other hand, so far you aren't making particularly good sense yourself."

Stephen pulled out a bright green chair with a matching cushion and seated himself where somebody—Sunny, of course—had been reading an article about air-conditioning. He liked being where she had been. Envied the man across from him. Talkman seemed too unkempt for her. Too . . . unimpressive. And the things he said on the air—the jokes he made about women—they infuriated Kathryn and Alicia, but both those women had weak senses of humor. It was obvious that the man liked women—look at the one he'd chosen. "I need to say that I really enjoy your show, sir," Stephen lied, knowing that if he hadn't said it, he'd feel like an asshole, and would somehow be insulting Sunny. He smiled, needed to verify that he knew what he was talking about. " 'When I was a lad in Nevada . . .' " he began, trying and failing to get the lush tone of the man across from him. "I like the anecdotes, the things you remember."

"Yes, well, thanks. It's better'n diggin' ditches, I always say. Push that stuff aside. Sunny'll read it later. Or we'll forget about air-conditioning. A thousand years, Marin didn't need air-conditioning—now . . . this global warming or what? We'll camp out at the beach all summer instead. That's more fun, anyway."

Stephen grinned. "I'm hoping to do that today. I'm on vacation from work and this weather . . ." Why the hell was he babbling this way in front of her? He had to get a grip on and stop sounding like an idiot!

"In February." Sunny stood behind the center island, leaning on it. "I grew up in the Midwest, and I still can't get over February being like this. Even if it's only for a day or two between storms. And to be so lucky as to have a beach a few minutes away, as if it's all set up for whenever we need it!" She smiled again, then sipped her coffee. "Meantime, tell us what brought you here."

How to say it without involving Penny? He'd meant to think this through in advance and would have, if Penny weren't so damned irrational. "About two months ago, Penny found a heart-shaped charm, a pendant—a thing you'd wear on a chain in a field, near where the police found those skeletons. Did you read about them?" He waited until both of them nodded. "Anyway, it wasn't all that special, but she liked it." He remembered that he had it with him. Where was his brain? "Wait—here it is." He pulled it from his pocket and put it on the table.

Talkman looked at it, then at Stephen without saying anything. He didn't seem impressed or overly interested, but then Stephen hadn't reached the point yet.

"Her lavaliere," Sunny said. "She wore it here, talked about it." She nodded. "I just told a detective about it. Well, we talked more about the person who I suspect *gave* it to her than about it." She smiled knowingly at Stephen, twinkling—the laugh she was controlling showing in her eyes.

She'd been talking about him? She'd thought the heart had been a gift from him?

"The police were here?" Talkman asked.

She shook her head, and her hair bounced in the light. "A private investigator trying to find Penny." She looked at Stephen with what she probably thought was a stern expression, but it was charming. "You obviously know where she is if you have the necklace, so you get her back home, young man. Her mother's worried sick."

Stephen nodded, but he wanted to get away from the lecture that seemed to be readying itself and back to the topic.

Talkman lifted the charm, turned it over, then shrugged and handed it back. "What about this?" he asked.

Sunny's eyes were wide and a small smile stayed on her face as she waited for Stephen's answer.

"What I wondered— Well, now that it turns out those people—the skeletons—were murdered and the police are trying to find stuff out, I wondered whether you remembered anything about the one you had that could help the police. We thought it was just a design, then we thought it said 'Vux,' but turns out, it's Greek. Script, not print. Maybe a sorority thing." He sounded lamer with each word.

"My sorority—most sororities I knew of—had pins, not any-thing like that," Sunny said. "And they had those nice blocky let-ters." She smiled again. "I'm not much help, am I. But does this mean you really didn't give it to Penny?"

Stephen shook his head. "Found it." All he wanted was to find a dignified, nonhumiliating way out of here. A way that wouldn't erase that light in Sunny Marshall's eyes, wouldn't make her realize what an ass Stephen Tassio was.

"Why didn't Penny come here herself if that question's so im-portant to her?"

"Actually—"

"I'm sure she was nervous, with her parents so close," Sunny said. "Although that isn't to say I approve. Not at all. Things can be worked out. Have to be. Running away doesn't solve anything."

The twins, each in a high chair, smeared apple sauce over the trays and onto their faces, crooning and giggling as they drew swirls and runnels. He felt a peculiar stab of pain and loss seeing that no-body shouted at them to stop, or rushed to douse them, take away the mess.

These were tolerant people. Honesty was the way to go. "To tell the truth," he said, "I was the one who pushed about it, and now it seems pretty dim of me. Penny thought it was ridiculous to try and track it. She said those hearts were common."

Sunny nodded. "Mine was a Sweet Sixteen favor, I think."

"I apologize, sir. I watch too much TV. Trying to be a good citi-zen, but I probably sound like a jerk."

Talkman smiled and shrugged. "I can understand. We all want to be heroes."

He was humoring dumb Stephen Tassio who wanted to be a Hardy Boy. "It seemed worth pursuing," Stephen murmured. "I'm not sure why, anymore."

"Well," Talkman said, lifting the chain and heart again, "since this doesn't indicate your taste in jewelry, let me say that it's a pretty poor piece. Look—the plating's so thin it's all but gone over here. Man to man, here's my advice."

His white-chocolate voice was getting into it, becoming even lower and more majestically rich. You had to listen to that voice, really hear it. "Buy your girlfriend something newer and better and chuck that."

"Harley!" Sunny said. "He never said he was Penny's boyfriend—did you? Are you?"

Stephen shook his head. If they only knew how unfriendly he felt toward her. And how stupid. He'd done this out of anger. Out of disgust with her lies and evasions, with how she did and didn't spend her time. He'd done this to prove something to her, and instead he'd made a fool of himself in front of these two incredible people.

"Hey—how'd you know that thing was near the skeletons?" Harley looked at Stephen appraisingly, then he grinned. "You found the skeletons, didn't you? You're being modest. Paper never said who or how, as I recall. No wonder you're involved in it—you *were* a hero—don't need to become one. A modest hero. Very nice."

"No, sir," Stephen said. "Not exactly. I didn't find them both. Just the first one. Part of it. And not just me." He knew he shouldn't have said that the second the words were out.

"Penny, you mean," Sunny said. "Is that how she found the heart?"

Stephen shrugged acknowledgment. "Kind of." He looked from one Marshall to the other. "So do you think it's worth turning the heart over to the police?"

Talkman smiled. " 'A man's gotta do what a man's gotta do.' Whatever you think is right."

Translation, Stephen thought: Go ahead, be as oafish with the police as you were here. Stephen would have blushed if he ever did. He nodded, stood, scooped up Penny's lavaliere, and apologized for wasting time.

"I'll bet you're that boy she went away with," Sunny said, looking as if she'd discovered gold. "Her boyfriend. The one the detective's looking for. Otherwise, how'd you know what's going on with her now? You're the boy with the yellow hearse, aren't you? I'm so glad you've turned out to be such a nice person."

Stephen didn't know how to react. Why was a detective tracking him?

"You're the one," Sunny said.

"I get the distinct impression you are making the young man uncomfortable, Sun. Glad to have met you, though, Stephen," Talkman said. "And good luck."

Get a life, he probably meant to add. Get a life and stop playing games.

"One thing," Sunny said. "Whatever your plans are—first, please, tell Penny to come home and work things out. Please?"

"I'll try. I really will," Stephen said. "There's nothing I want more than that."

Twenty

They weren't exactly panic attacks. If they were, Billie told herself, she couldn't objectively evaluate them this way. But even after reading Jesse every word of *The Velveteen Rabbit* and going over the events of his day again, and knowing that Ivan would check all locks and call 911 the second he heard anything suspicious, and even after starting a healthy, balanced dinner for Jesse—which should have alerted her son to the fact that things were nothing like normal—she still felt sudden "what if" churns of emotions on the way back to work.

Good thing the office was so close, counting parking, because even that amount of time stretched to include flashbacks—history she not only saw, but felt, as if new—things she had buried clawing again on her nerve ends. Jesse kidnapped. Her mother's drunk see-saws from rage to silent depression. The repeated shocks of relocation, all the lost alliances and sense of security. Her father's abrupt departure one afternoon while his kids were in school and his wife at the club, all signs of him—clothing, sports equipment, and books—removed without so much as a note. "I hate scenes," he later said. "You know there would have been one." He considered that both explanation and defense.

Bad surprises and danger. Always. She'd vowed to never, ever, let her life, her parenting, be that way.

By the time she'd reached the office and parked across the street, she was ready to admit she wasn't up to the needs of the job. Part of what she loved about the very title of "private investigator" was its intimation that competency was a given. You knew something or could find it out. But you needed more than a job description and title to be competent, and Billie wasn't going to make the grade unless she was more careful, more observant, more aware of occupational hazards.

She entered the small, marble-tiled elevator lobby of the old building, but took the stairs—they were at least dependable—and continued, nonstop, with her mea culpas.

She had to behave like an investigator. Starting now. Better late than . . .

She pushed open the glass-and-wood door of Howe Investigations.

Zack looked up from his computer. His left cheek bulged.

"Malt balls now?" Billie asked.

"That took deductive skill." It sounded more like *"Ba tooga didug-div skih."* He gestured to the crystal bowl, filled to overflowing with the dark candies as he crunched and chewed.

"How the hell do you answer the phone sounding like that?"

He swallowed. "Emma wants to see you."

"About?"

Zack shrugged. "She's on the phone, but I'm to buzz her when you called in. Beeper not working, is that it?"

"I—" Sweet Jesus, where the hell was the thing? She'd forgotten all about it. She dug into her pocketbook and found it trying valiantly to reach her, silently vibrating against her wallet, calendar, and tissue container. She looked at it, saw the office number, and bit at her bottom lip while she exhaled in exasperation through her nose. "It didn't fit who I was saying I was. . . ." At dawn, at ILM when she was sheepish Audrey Miller. What about the hours since then? "I forgot all about it."

Zack shrugged. "You've only had it a few days. I've seen a couple or three newcomers in this office. It's like learning to drive. They remember to turn on the signal, but not how to also check out the new lane before zooming into it. Or if they remember that, they forget about not slowing down then. Or if— You get the idea, right? Don't be too hard on yourself."

"You've been here two years and something," she said. "How many new ones did you observe?"

"Seven of you guys. She isn't great at keeping associates."

Even less good at it than Billie had imagined. An apprentice had to put in six thousand hours at slave wages, which translated into one hundred fifty weeks if the newcomer worked eight-hour days, five day a week. Three years, give or take, but in two and a half years, seven people like her had walked in and out of this office. Her own odds of enduring felt shaky.

"Don't listen to statistics," Zack said. "Numbers lie. I can think of two who were here at the same time and then together, decided to become Chippendale dancers instead. Male stripping pays better than this. Another one developed an ulcer—"

"Because of her?" Billie whispered.

He shrugged. "Who can say? Anyway, he moved to Pennsylvania." He popped another malt ball into his mouth while he did further calculations. When it was swallowed, he continued. "Dobson worked here the whole time. Left right before you appeared, from what I can see on the records. So we're up to four of the seven—and you're one of them, so it was just two who said, in essence or in fact, 'Life is too short to spend another minute working for her,' and slammed the door. She fired one of them for incompetence and he became a security guard and the other one—that one was kind of mutual, like a divorce, that one moved to Mexico, from what I hear. You don't look like a quitter—are you?"

"Stay tuned. This is where I'll find that out." Billie walked toward her cubicle and told him he could let Emma know she was here. She was working on a computer search on the net. That sounded pleasing and professional and might mitigate her other offenses.

What had Yvonne said—"Society for Creative Assassins"?

Life wasn't overgenerous when your best lead was a madwoman. She was sure Stephen Tassio wasn't an assassin, but given that she had no good alternatives, she'd look for an organized society of assassins, at least until she was summoned by Emma and fired.

She hit the keys lightly, afraid, she knew, of offending the peevish brains inside the machine. She envisioned byte-sized but testy spirits, sneering at her ineptitude and gaffes. The Internet was incomprehensible. She didn't understand how there could be an infinitely-expanding anything. It hurt to think about it, the way it had hurt as a child to think about infinity itself, about what was just beyond it, outside it.

Instead, she tiptoed on the keyboard and searched for the Society for Creative Assassins. An interesting concept. The Assassin Elite. No tawdry gunshots or garroting. Instead, something inventive and new that required imagination. Like perhaps boring somebody to death. Taking someone out via a defective bungee cord on a jump. . . .

For God's sake! Eight thousand three hundred and sixty documents under *assassins!* What was going on in this world?

Her fingers tiptoed toward the entries. And found video games. Role-playing games. Nothing about actually murdering someone for gain. She wasn't sure if it was a relief or a further irritation.

She tried to narrow the field by typing in the entire title Yvonne had said—Society for Creative Assassins—and now the machine told her there were one million three hundred eighty-one thousand, seven hundred and . . . This was incredible. Terrifying! She scrolled down and found odd entries whose connection to assassinations was vague at best. Entries about cremation. Gilbert and Sullivan. A science fair. Training Latin American militaries—at least that bore some relationship. Apparently, anything that contained the words *Society* or *Creative* or *Assassin* qualified.

But surely Stephen Tassio wasn't involved in any of them, and none of them required medieval garb and titles.

The next entry was: *Society for Creative Anachronism.* Subtitle: *Living in the Current Middle Ages.*

Of course.

For a long time, she sat reading and learning. There were formal guides, explanations for newcomers. She was intrigued by the world these people had created, but frustrated as well, because there seemed no way in these files to find Stephen Tassio. Or Lucan the Steward. Only the world in which they sometimes dwelled.

She clicked onward, moving around until she found a map of the U.S. divided into segments. Kingdoms, they were called. She clicked on the Bay Area, part of the Western Kingdom, The Principality of Mists, for a close-up. Then she tapped in her zip code, looking for nearby groups, and there it was, in Novato.

She felt as if she were getting closer to Stephen himself. She could go to a meeting of the Novato group, could meet Stephen—if he wasn't afraid to go where Yvonne might find him—without arousing suspicion.

But when? What month? What year? Her spirits deflated again.

She found mention of the "Rialto" newsgroup, a site where members talked online to one another about SCA issues, and, feeling like an outer-space explorer, she headed there with great hope.

The addresses of the message-senders were sometimes cryptic, based on their SCA names, but then—her pulse did the equivalent of a bloodhound's alert sniff—often their "mundane" twentieth-century name was in parentheses next to it.

"Stephen Tassio," she murmured as she searched. "Put in a message. Say something. Yvonne can't get you on here."

But she couldn't find a *Stephen Tassio, S. Tassio, Stephen, Steve T.* . . .

Anything. He was the strong and silent type of knight. Not even a Luke. A Lucan. A Steward. Who would have thought a computer could provide such a wild and emotional roller-coaster ride?

The messages were in the order received, not alphabetized. There was a good chance she'd missed him. She scrolled the list again.

Marcia, Louis, Miranda, Andy, Brooke, Esmeralda, Susan, Alicia, Anne . . .

She had the feeling of having missed something, and scrolled up. But there was no Stephen anybody. No *S*.

Zack knocked on her door and simultaneously opened it. "Emma'd like you to come into her office," he said with a grin. "Now." He headed for the copy machine.

"This is the neatest thing," she said, pointing at the computer. "You can't believe what you can—"

"Please," he said with a dismissive wave. "I would have never be-friended you if I'd suspected you'd turn into a Net zombie. I've lost more perfectly good people when they entered that machine, and mutated." He turned his back and set the pages for duplication.

She whispered a promise to return, and took a series of deep breaths. She would fight for this job if Emma were as displeased as she might have a right to be. Or maybe this meeting was to be their first mentor-apprentice session. Maybe Emma would tell her the sort of insider thing she'd expected to hear and learn all along.

With a final deep breath and five strides across the reception area, she tapped Emma's door and entered, ready for the worst.

Sophia Redmond sat across from the desk. She turned when the door opened, and Billie had to work to control a gasp. The woman's face was patched with deep purple. Her bottom lip looked as if it had split and was only now beginning to heal.

"Fell," Sophia said before Billie managed greetings. "Looks worse than it is."

Emma waved Billie into the other chair.

"What have you found out?" Sophia asked.

"Mrs. Redmond phoned several times today," Emma said in a voice bleached of all emotion. "She feels this matter is rather urgent. We tried to reach you."

Billie willed the heat rising in her to stay away from her cheeks, to keep itself hidden. "I'm sorry," she said. "I didn't realize my pager wasn't working correctly until a few minutes ago. It's fine now, but . . ." She worked at looking repentant, humble, sorrowful.

"Where is my daughter?" Sophia asked.

Emma leaned back in her chair, waiting, taking no responsibility for her associate's incompetence.

"We're making good headway," Billie said. Accent on the "we." "I now know the name of the young man she left with—the one with the hearse. And I know where he works and some of his special interests. Unfortunately, he's on vacation right now, he lives with other people and everything's in their names, his parents do not know his address or current phone number which he's keeping secret because of an ex-girlfriend who's harrassing him, making life unpleasant. But I'm on the track of a group he belongs to." That sounded like much more than it was. Maybe Sophia Redmond wouldn't realize it was nothing. That it had all been about Stephen Tassio with whom Penny might or might not have remained. Sophia's daughter was as far away and invisible as ever. "I realize every minute must feel endless to you," Billie said, "but it has only been a few days, and I expect to find her very soon."

Sophia stood up and walked to the window. What was wrong with that picture?

Emma followed Billie's sight line and smiled wryly.

"Mrs. Redmond," Billie said, "you were in a wheelchair last time I saw you. This is very . . . exciting. You look quite comfortable walking."

"My words precisely," Emma said.

Sophia turned, looked down at her legs, then at Billie. "It's partly why I'm here." She pointed to her swollen cheek, the black eye, the lip. "I . . . didn't tell the truth."

Which time did she mean?

"I wasn't . . . I could always walk. The man's becoming— He's vicious. He always had a short fuse. But he's worse. I thought if I could collect disability money, you know, and a settlement from the city, I could afford to leave him. Even if I had to stay in a wheelchair forever. When Penny's father walked out, I was so poor, and with a child . . ."

Tell me about it, Billie thought. And, she suspected, Emma was having precisely the same thought with the same inflection. Sophia's voice dripped self-pity. She obviously thought her story was unique.

"Arthur would never let me take Wesley away. That's his son. His. If I left, I'd have nothing. And how would I find another husband at this age? I'm doomed."

"He hits you, and you said it's getting worse. This is very bad," Billie said. "Very dangerous. Go to a shelter. Get away."

"I can't. You don't understand. You're young."

Billie knew it was no use if it wasn't Sophia's idea. Time to move on. "What happened to your disability claim?"

Sophia shrugged. "Just my luck. Somebody took movies of me when . . . Well . . . I was moving around. Ruined my whole chance."

Billie, eyes wide, glanced at Emma, who actually came close to a smile.

The damned tape had worked, then. Obviously the insurance company caught something she hadn't. Incredible! So she wasn't the screw-up queen yet. Not completely.

"The point is, I don't want her to come home," Sophia said.

"Penny? Not return? But you hired us to—"

Sophia shook her head. "He's worse than ever, and I think, if she comes home—he's so angry with her now, so very angry. I'm afraid he let me hire you because he wants her where he could do her harm. They had some kind of face-off, accusations were made, but see, he always was unfair to her because she wasn't his. If she comes home, I'm afraid he'll hurt her. Maybe worse."

"But," Billie said, "she's still in high school. What will she—"

"I have no other options."

Nor did Penny now, thanks to her.

"Especially now that there's no hope of the disability, I have no earning capacity." Her phrase sounded practiced and she seemed resigned to, even welcoming of, the role of victim. And she didn't seem to wonder who else might be injured by her passivity.

"Penny," Billie said. "If she shouldn't come home, where should she go?"

"This boy? Maybe she could stay with him until she's on her own. It's not ideal, but whose life is? Certainly not mine. All I ever wanted was to live like a normal, ordinary person, and look what's happened. One bad thing after another."

"But it's February. In four short months she could graduate, have her diploma. You don't want her on the street, do you?"

"Of course she doesn't want her daughter on the streets," Emma said. "Mrs. Redmond suggests that Penny remain where she's gone. Win-win. They can both have what they want." Emma flashed Billie warning glance. Parent-child workshops were not one of the services they provided. Then she turned to Sophia Redmond. "Or are you saying you want to end the investigation?" she asked.

"Oh, no. Don't stop. Arthur—he wants to find her, too, for bad reasons, but he'll pay. You have to find her. Just don't tell him. Let me know she's safe, and tell her to call me, please. I can explain everything. She has to understand how we . . . how everything got so bad. Will you?"

Billie nodded.

"And when you call me, don't say if you found her. Don't say where she is. Just say you're ready to report, and I'll come here. Arthur . . ."

Billie nodded again.

"She has to understand," Sophia repeated.

That was fine with Billie. If only she herself understood.

Twenty-one

Despite his embarrassment at having been an idiot there, Stephen left the Marshall's house smiling. Sunny was the right name for her. He was amazed how his mood had improved since he'd rung her bell. Good thing Penny had made him park halfway to the next neighborhood. He wouldn't want her to see the grin he felt forming and reforming on his face. She'd be too eager to make fun of it because she'd understand it. All the same, Penny could take lessons from that woman. Should. It wasn't just that Sunny was beautiful, which she was. She was good as well, she had a way of making you feel special. She was . . .

He heard his thoughts and laughed at himself. A crush like a kid in junior high. A crush on a happily married mother of three. Great going.

Whatever. He'd met Sunny Marshall and now he knew what he wanted for himself, what he would look for from now on. A healthy, sunny woman, the opposite of the unhappy, clinging types he attracted.

He speeded his pace, past the Redmonds', toward the corner. There was still time for sunset on the beach. He'd check out of the San Geronimo house for a few days, be by himself. Penny would understand, or she wouldn't. His life didn't have to be revised just because a teenager misunderstood it.

When he turned the corner, he saw the hearse gleaming in the afternoon sun and felt a jolt of relief. He hadn't fully trusted it to be where he left it. Things seldom were with Penny Redmond.

He loved the car's size and color, a slick wash like transparent layers of sunshine laid one upon the other, with mother-of-pearl as the adhesive. What a buy it had been. He couldn't figure why people were so squeamish about its former function, but maybe if they weren't, the retired cars would sell for what they were worth, and he wouldn't have been able to own one. He opened the door.

She wasn't there. No note, no sign of her.

He slammed the door and looked around. Nothing. Nobody. He wheeled and kicked the tree at the curb. Where the hell would she go? She, who was afraid to let the car be visible from her parents' house. She who said she had nowhere else to go but his house, his room, his bed, his life.

He took five slow, deep breaths because he'd been told it was a technique that helped regain perspective. Maybe he was jumping to conclusions. What if while she had sat here she thought things through and decided—as he himself had suggested—to make peace with her parents? Maybe something had finally clicked in her brain, like common sense.

That had to be it because it was the only possibility. There was nowhere else to go in the middle of a residential neighborhood.

He locked the car, pocketed his keys, and walked back toward the Redmonds'. To make it official, discuss dropping off her stuff tomorrow. He felt his leg-irons being unlocked, and he walked briskly, lightly, back to the white Victorian.

A scowling man with a thin, old-fashioned moustache answered the door. So her father was home from the houseboat already. Stephen had imagined him larger, less slickly dapper, more contemporary. This man looked out of place. The moustache didn't go with the beer bottle in his hand, and his posture and expression made Stephen think this wasn't the man's first drink of the day. "Ah," the man said with a nod. "Finally. I've been waiting."

Just like Penny to assume he'd figure out where she was and stop by. To think she could do whatever she pleased, be as irresponsible as the urge of the moment, and leave tracking-down, retrieving, and mopping-up to others. He followed her father into a large room, all flowery patterns and flounces. He didn't know what it was about the place, but it made him nervous. Trying too hard, maybe. Reminded him of his parents' house, only fussier.

"Hot as hell, isn't it?" the man said. "Weather freaky as hell lately. Must be that El Niño shit. Shouldn't be this hot in February. Whole world's falling apart." He sounded slightly muzzy.

Stephen nodded agreement although he found the temperature perfect.

"You must like it, though," Mr. Redmond said.

"Yes, sure do." What was going on? How could he get to the point and get away—and where was Penny hiding herself? "I'm heading for the beach from here, I like it so much."

The man stared at him blankly. "Stinson," Stephen said to fill the silence. "Or maybe Limantour, at Point Reyes." Where the hell was she?

"What are we talking about? It's back here," the man said, and Stephen followed him into an old-fashioned kitchen. "What do you think?" His gruff voice and attitude didn't go with his appearance, either.

"It's a very nice kitchen. . . ."

"What the hell you talking about? Or is your mind still at that beach you're so eager to get to? You said we could talk."

"I'm sorry, sir. Talk about what?"

"The job. The stain on the wall, the flooring—the whole thing. Upstairs bath is fixed now. No more leak—but the estimate you gave my wife is ridiculous." He peered at Stephen intently. "Isn't that why you're here?"

"I don't think so."

"Water damage? You're the contractor, aren't you? We talked this morning. You said you'd come over and we'd talk."

"No, sir, I—"

"Then who the hell are you, barging into my house under false pretenses?"

"You asked me in, Mr. Redmond. You are Mr. Redmond, aren't you?"

Arthur Redmond squinted at Stephen. "Damn," he said. "Then who are you and what did you want?"

"I wanted to speak with Penny."

"Ha!" The sound was mirthless. "Go ahead, then! If you can find her. And if you do, tell her to give us a call, too. Hasn't been seen in these parts for some time. Ran off with a lunatic. Why do you want her? Who are you?" He drained the can of beer, and in one smoothly practiced move, tossed it into a lined trash can, opened the refrigerator, and took another out. He didn't offer Stephen one.

"I—I'm a friend," Stephen said. "I thought— Are you sure she isn't here?"

"You think I'm hiding her? Lying? You want to search the house?" He laughed his hard bark again, then said, "Go ahead. Look for little Penny. Maybe you're right, maybe I misplaced her and she's under the couch, or in the fridge. I'd ask the wife, but she's never home now that she isn't crippled anymore."

"Excuse me?"

"You aren't married, are you?"

"No, sir. No."

"Good for you. Trust me—it's nothing but trouble. Women are impossible to start out with and then they go rancid with age. Happens fast, too. And their kids make it worse. Especially kids that aren't yours. Penny didn't have any friends except the crazy who abducted her, so who are you?" He peered at Stephen with the overbright intensity of the slightly drunk. "Do I know you?"

The room was warm, but Stephen felt a chill, as if the refrigerator door were still open. "I'm sorry for the misunderstanding, sir. Sorry to have interrupted you."

"What did you want with her?"

Stephen shook his head and went back into the flouncy room, then to the hallway and the front door, and all the while, Arthur Redmond followed him, his belligerent questions piling upon each other.

"Are you the one? Did she run away from you, too, now? Are you the one?"

By the time he reached the front door, Arthur Redmond was shouting answers as well as questions. "Yeah, you must be. That's the only thing that'd make sense."

"It isn't the way you think, sir."

"How do you know what I think? And where is she?"

"I don't know. That's why I came here."

"I was right—she ran away from you, too. Did she say she was coming here? After everything she's done. She said things to me, about me. Spied on me."

"Thanks for your time," Stephen called out over his shoulder as he left the house, the porch, the front of the Redmonds' house.

"I'm still talking to you!" Arthur shouted out the door. "Where the hell you think you're going?"

Not until he was five doors down and could no longer hear Arthur Redmond did he feel able to breathe freely. The suffocation was a feeling his parents too often inspired with their eternal war, and when he'd been a child he'd thought he would be strangled by the poisonous strings of words that ensnared him. But at least his parents battled at a lower decibel level than Arthur Redmond's.

Penny's mother wasn't pretending to be crippled anymore. She wouldn't go to jail for fraud the way Penny feared. He wondered what had made her stop the pretense.

He was so absorbed by his thoughts he almost tripped over a scrawny boy standing still in the middle of the sidewalk. "Sorry!"

"You were in my house," the boy said. "I saw." His arms were like skewers inserted in the knob of his elbow, and the backpack he dragged looked more substantial than he did. Stephen got the feeling that confronting him cost the boy a great deal of courage. "Who are you? Is my mother okay?"

"Who are you?" Stephen asked. "Who is your mother?"

"Wesley Redmond." The boy's hair was brown and straight and looked like it was cut at home. Stephen wondered how much taunting he got from his well-coifed classmates.

"Penny's brother?"

A wispy cowlick accentuated the boy's nod. "You own the hearse?" he asked back. "You're the one? The Stewart?"

"Do you know where she is?"

Wesley nodded again. "She saw the schoolbus and waited for me and we went for a walk. When we got back to the hearse, it was locked up. You went to my house?"

"I thought she might be there."

"My dad sounded really mad. I could hear him from here."

"He thought I was somebody else."

"My mom okay?" Wesley asked.

"She wasn't there." How sad that he had to keep asking that question, that the accustomed images and possibilities in his brain required that question.

"Is Penny ever coming home? Does she tell you? She wouldn't tell me."

"I don't think she knows yet. For what it's worth, I think she should."

"It's way worse since you took her away," the boy said. "I told her that, and I shouldn't have, because now she'll never want to come back. Could I live with you, too? She said it's a big house."

"What else did she say about it?"

"That there are these other people, too, in San Geronimo. I've never been there, but she said there weren't pavements, like here. That there were horses around, and a place with a stream and redwoods. She said nobody carried on about the house the way our . . . That you had a bird that lived in your bedroom and a big kitchen where everybody hangs out and the other people lived there together for a longer time than you did, and this man next door has a garden that . . ."

Stephen stopped listening. She had ruined his sanctuary. He'd have to move again. Look how freely the boy was relating everything he'd learned, and he'd learned too many details that could too easily migrate from this boy to his parents, to somebody else—and to Yvonne, who frankly scared the shit out of him. San Geronimo was tiny, small enough for her to track each street and watch each drive. For all he knew, she was watching now, watching Wesley Redmond, who'd give her all the information she could use.

"She said she was going to get a job and then I could live with her and we'd go to court, she said, and they'd understand. She'd take care of me."

"Ah, kid." Stephen looked at the boy and tried not to notice the bright moisture filming his eyes. Another victim, he heard himself think—but whose? His?

"Since you took her away," he'd said, making Stephen the demon.

"Ah, kid," Stephen repeated. "It'll work out. You'll see." He patted the boy's skinny shoulder, then turned and walked back to the car. He could feel the eyes on his back, the silent plea to be seen, noticed, saved.

But Stephen's "saving others" days were on hold. He was disconnecting the Penny Redmond distress line.

She was by the hearse, trying to look invisible in her old neighborhood. He didn't want to see her that way—vulnerable and quietly anxious. He had no room for anybody else's problems right now.

"Get in," he said, after he'd unlocked the doors. "I'm going to the police—"

"Why?"

"Because. Because if I don't, it'll nag at me. Because those are Greek letters on it, not a design and they could stand for something. A Greek word, or a name, maybe." *Because if I don't, I won't be totally, irrevocably through with you.*

"I'll never get the lavaliere back from them."

"Of course you will, once the case is solved."

"Like it ever will be. A thing that old."

Of course she wouldn't get it back, but who cared? He felt her eyes on the side of his face, burning, like losing her amulet was the worse thing in the world. And he didn't care.

"After that, I'm taking you to the house and I'm cutting out for a few days. I need to think before I go crazy. I need to be alone."

She looked stupefied, as if this idea were incomprehensible, beyond the sphere of the imaginable. "Don't make me be there without you," she said. "I don't want to be alone with them. I—"

"This isn't about you," he said as he drove. "This is about me. I have to think and you should do the same. It's not right to tell your brother you're going to take care of him—"

"You saw Wesley?"

"—when you don't know how to take care of yourself. It's not right to tell him where you are, where I am, or that he'll come there, too. And your father is furious about your snooping."

"You talked to him?"

"I didn't know where you were—I thought maybe you were making peace with your family. But he figured out who I was, and he is royally pissed with you. I don't blame him anymore."

"Oh, Luke!"

He didn't want to try the five-breath technique. He didn't want to be calm. "He said something about your spying on him."

"That was from before."

"Who cares? The result's the same. You really need to think of what you're going to do from now on—and so do I."

Tears ran down her face, out her nose. He didn't care. She cried, head in hands, all the way to, and even, he presumed, while he was in the police station. And when he returned to the car.

He wanted out, but he didn't want to be cruel. "I didn't mean to make you so sad," he said. Then his shoulders slumped. "I care about you. I did. I still do, I guess. But I can't take care of you, Penny. It's too big a job and I'm barely taking care of myself. I can't handle your problems and you don't want to handle them yourself. I wanted to give you a safe place while you needed it, that's all. Not a permanent address. Can't you understand?"

"But it doesn't have to be permanent. As long as we're okay, the two of us, then as soon as I figure out what to do—"

"Call me when you do." He had nothing more to say. He was tired of words.

She broke the silence within two blocks. "Somebody's following you," she said.

"For God's sake!" He pulled over, his heart racing. Yvonne. God help him, she was everywhere, spreading like a stain. He'd never be rid of her. Or of Penny. They'd be his barnacles, rock-hard growths attached to his flesh.

But he saw nothing peculiar in the traffic stream as it passed him. "Which car?" he asked. "Where?"

"Now I can't tell, with us being stopped and all."

"What kind of car?"

"I don't know. Dark."

"Black?"

"Maybe. But you know how those dark colors all look. . . ."

He took a deep breath. No time for all five. He wasn't going to let her terrify him, make him stupid. He took one more breath and, after a final look outside, behind his car and even ahead, seeing nothing out of the ordinary, he turned the ignition key. The girl needed psychiatric help.

"I saw it," she said. "I'm not making it up. This car was just sitting over there across the way until you came out of the police staton, then it pulled off."

"Cars do that. They pull off," he said.

She rode sulkily. "You'll see." She turned to look out the back window every few minutes. "There," she said once, "there it is again."

His heart bumped and stalled before he paused for a reality check. There'd been nothing the last time, there was nothing he could see in his rearview mirror this time. "That so?" he asked wearily. "Can you tell what kind of car it is this time?"

"I can't see the back where the name'd be."

"The color?"

"Black, maybe?"

"Are you sure it's the same car as before? Where would it have gone when I stopped?"

"It could have passed, then waited somewhere. I saw that in a movie."

"Do you see it right now, Penny?"

"Well, now I'm not so . . ." The certainty drained from her voice.

"Lots of cars are dark."

"Yours isn't. It makes you such an easy target. So conspicuous. I know it's cool and it was cheap but even so it must be real easy for whoever that is to tail you."

"Or you," he said. "Ever think of that? You're the one who's missing." And that used up his last reserve of Penny-energy. He was too tired of her to open his mouth and say another word.

Twenty-two

The meeting was over. Sophia Redmond had left the office with a bruised face and two working legs, and Emma's mind reverted to a due diligence investigation. She had to make a phone call before it got too late in St. Louis. The prospective VP of Finance's official background had potholes big enough for him to fall into and disappear. The lawyers who hired her wanted verification immediately and she wanted that particular set of lawyers to be dazzled by her work.

The outer door closed. Sophia was gone, then. Odd, sad, unlikable woman.

Emma couldn't remember the number, and she sat down and rooted around her in-box, dimly aware Billie was still standing there. Waiting, but for what? Had they made some confusing arrangement? Was there further business? She looked up at her green associate. "Coffee?" she asked, getting up to refill her cup. "There's an extra mug."

"No thanks," Billie said.

A shame that a missing teen had to be the first assignment for somebody this insecure. Adolescents were a bitch to find. Old enough to fend poorly for themselves, but too young to be plugged in to the system where an investigator could sniff them out. Penny

Redmond was connected only to school and family, and if she chose to sever those ties, she could disappear. Any teen could. No bank account, no telephone, no electric bill, no property owned, no credit history, no nothing to keep them from evaporating into the nether-world of like-minded souls. And too often, when they were finally found, it was via a headline—the teenage corpse by the road where she'd hitchhiked—or a police statistic—a hooker, or a junkie.

Sophia Redmond's request that her runaway daughter *not* come home gave Emma a sense that long ago, a bad end might have been built in for that girl.

Billie cleared her throat. "The tape," she said.

"Ah, that."

"The insurance company accepted it. Felt they had a case."

"Seems so." Emma glanced at the clock. Three-oh-six. Five-oh-six in St. Louis.

Billie waited.

Emma felt her mouth purse. Then she sighed, with resigned ex-asperation. Okay. If she was going to let Billie believe her scrambled cinema verité had done the trick, then she might as well go all the way, massage the girl's ego, much as it went against Emma's grain to waste energy and breath on employees' emotions. On anybody's, her daughter would have said. And in fact, had.

But then, Caroline couldn't understand how weak you'd become if you were praised for inferior work. The world did not run on good intentions. Caroline didn't see that she and her brother functioned differently and that, not parental preference, was the basis of his success. Caroline, who made an art of sibling rivalry, was convinced that Nathaniel was and always had been the favorite, and that had doomed her to a bleak existence, made revenge her life's work and survived on a diet of bile and resentment. An annual Christmas letter and photo so Emma could track her grandchildren's development, and that was that. But Emma couldn't criticize any other style or philosophy of mothering after she herself had failed so miserably.

Which had nothing to do with Billie August, who stood there, twirling a ballpoint pen. "Could I ask your opinion about what I'm doing with the search so far?"

Emma considered the possibility that she was as much of a shit as her daughter said. What did it cost to give a little? If she was secretly saving Billie's ass (and her own, to be honest), why not go all the way? "First I want to congratulate you," she said. "They're sending us another case today."

There. She'd said it and lightning hadn't struck. She lied a thousand different ways every day. What did it hurt to add one more?

Billie beamed. "I can't believe it," she said, demonstrating common sense. "I thought I had totally screwed it up. Which doesn't mean I'll ever play it as close to the line again. I mean, I was lucky this time, but I won't count on that in the future, I promise."

"Now," Emma said, "you wanted a sounding board about Penny Redmond? I heard what you told Sophia. Anything else?"

Lots of words that added up to nothing, far as Emma could tell. But she'd proceeded logically. Interviewed friends, neighbors, the presumed boyfriend's employers—or at least the receptionist at his place of employment. "We could probably do more about that, now that we know his name," Emma said at that point.

Billie looked surprised, then nodded. Emma recognized the look of total absorption—she'd been so intently looking ahead to what the next step was that she hadn't realized she had additional knowledge now, that if it seemed warranted, she could circle back, find out more.

Maybe. The guy was deliberately and successfully hiding.

Billie was talking about this group he belonged to. He lived with other people—had more or less fled to them when his ex got crazy. And since the Creative Anachronism folk appeared to form the basis of his social life, it followed that he was most likely living with fellow members. . . .

It sounded like a logic syllogism. If this is true, then the girl had taken her fancy education too seriously. Life wasn't logical and people were anything but.

". . . good probability he lives with them," Billie continued. "I was online when you called me in. The group has a website. I found out where the local groups are, and that there's a big event this weekend—Presidents' weekend—in Arizona. I got all excited until I realized he probably won't go, not if he's hiding from this stalker, this . . . Yvonne." She stopped abruptly upon saying the woman's name.

"What?" Emma asked. "Something?"

"She . . . It's just that I did something incredibly stupid before I came in."

Aha. The real reason for staying behind. The true agenda.

"I stopped home for a few minutes, and she—this Yvonne—had followed me and it freaked me out. My home, after all. My kid! She thought—still thinks—I'm Stephen's new lover. She didn't exactly threaten me, but all the same, she was threatening."

Billie had been an actress. She dramatized things. Made for interesting stories, but not calls to action. "It's bluster," Emma said. "You don't have what she wants and you aren't preventing access to him, either. If this woman isn't completely over the edge, she'll lose interest in you. You'll see."

"I hope you're right. I can't stop thinking about her—about me, too, my capabilities. If I couldn't spot somebody following me, then—"

"Okay," Emma interrupted. "You'll be more observant from now on. Back to your question. You seem on track with Penny Redmond. See what you can get from the Net. You might want to think about the hearse, too." There. The experienced pro offers up an angle. Never say that Emma wasn't teaching her hire. "There might be hearse-lover groups online."

"The one I found only listed cars for sale. Not helpful."

She'd already thought of it. "In that case, since we're billing that pathetic woman by the hour to find her daughter, what say we cut the chat?"

Billie stood up instantly, nodded and left.

You could waste your life blathering. Now to try St. Louis. Who knew, maybe human-resource people also worked late now and then.

She couldn't figure that woman out. Offered to share her foul coffee, gave an attaboy, then behaved like she was being attacked if you tried to thank her. Billie had to remember that this wasn't her life, it was her job. Get on with it and try not to become an Emma, measuring life in billable minutes and nothing more.

Back to the Society for Creative Anachronism. She was actually eager, excited by the possibilities and by the imaginary world itself. She understood the appeal of retreating into the world as it should be, not as it was or is. The Middle Ages would not be her first choice—but if somebody wanted to recreate New York or Paris in the 1920s, she'd consider a divided life.

She returned to where she'd been, remembering that nagging and now-frightening sense that she wasn't paying enough attention to something. A name had pricked her brain, but which one, and why? She'd have to go through everything all over again, wait and see if the warning tingle reoccurred.

"Where are you, Stephen?" she asked the machine. She failed to get the tingle, to get anything, including information. She couldn't access the list of upcoming events or local members, but it probably didn't matter. Stephen Tassio's name wasn't going to be on an online discussion group or a list of members. He was hiding. She returned to the discussion group. If nothing else, it was a way of learning more about them.

They discussed just about everything: the construction of armor, pros and cons of outsiders at events, what sort of medieval twist to give one's speech ("forsooth" was declared an embarrassingly primitive gaffe)—even whether bunny rabbit was, would have been, or could be, medievally kosher. There were countless responses to each question, including the one concerning the hapless rabbits. She read one letter after another, checking each e-mail address, since even though they sent greetings and signed off with their SCA names, their "mundane" names were often part of their address, or put in parentheses after it.

She moved quickly, scrolling back to see if she'd missed anything interesting, returning to the master list for the same reason, saying the mundane names out loud and flooding with adrenaline when she heard herself say, "Stephen," but she'd mispronounced a Stepan, and that was his medieval name. "John, Laurel, Mary." None felt significant—nothing triggered a particular response. What had? And why couldn't she find it, feel it, again?

The building's heat acted as a sedative. She switched to full names to keep herself awake and slightly more challenged. Last stop before the damned hearses, she told herself. And why would he go online to talk about a car he already had if he wasn't online here?

"Jane Heller, Sam Browne, R. Tannenbaum, no Stephen Tassio, no Stephen T., no S. Tassio . . . DeeDee Stanley, Alicia Malone, Douglas Newber—" She'd just said something she should have listened to . . . She scrolled back again, said every last name and this time, she paused at Alicia Malone. Alicia. That was the name she'd seen elsewhere, too. Not the most common name, and she'd heard it. Somebody had said it in the last few days, and pray to God it hadn't been Ivan when they'd had a glass of wine late the night before. Ivan's romantic complexities were too often the subject matter during a time that was supposedly reserved for reviewing how her household was doing. According to Ivan, his life was seldom going well, and it was endlessly complicated, because of his adoration of and overenthusiasm for the opposite sex.

One of his girls had been a Tawny, she was sure. And the other complication, a Brittany. "Very American," he'd thought.

So who was Alicia? It wasn't as if Billie's life was a long waltz between friends and gossip and lots of names, so Alicia had to be part of the search for Penny.

She opened her notebook and held her breath. Please have written it down. Alicia couldn't have been all that important or she'd remember something more than the sound of her name, but please let her have documented it.

And there it was, a fit. Mrs. Tassio going on about Stephen's dreadful friends. And one, the Malone girl, who'd seemed quite lovely until she pulled him into her weird group and approved of his getting that bird. And Mr. Tassio, murmuring, half to himself, that he'd always been fond of Alicia.

Billie felt like Lewis and Clark. Both of them. She'd found something in this new world, even if she didn't yet know what it was or meant.

She went out to the reception area and borrowed Zack's phone book. "Malone," she whispered. "Be listed." It would be so unusual as to be heretical, but there were miracles.

And there was her first occupationally-based one. "San Geronimo Valley Financial Services" listed Alicia Malone but only a phone number. Still, it was something. She kissed the white pages and grabbed the phone.

The message said that the office was closed and Alicia Malone out of town until after President's Day. Billie left a message, anyway. "Damn," she muttered as she hung up. But Emma probably knew some way to get the address that went with the number. Billie could at least find the office, be ready on Tuesday after the long weekend.

The weekend seemed very long indeed when thought of that way.

The outer door opened and Yvonne, looking as if she'd lost weight in the last two hours, barged in. "Ha!" she said, pointing at Billie. "That's what I figured!"

"Jesus Christ!" Billie said. "I told you—"

"Can I help?" Zack asked Yvonne in a tone that would have deterred anyone normal.

Yvonne ignored him. "You're a detective," she said, her finger still aimed at Billie. "At first, I thought you came here because you were hiring one. That you were looking for him, too. I waited. I can be patient." She nodded several times in agreement with herself. "You have no idea how patient I can be."

"Yvonne," Billie began.

"You know this woman?" Zack asked. "Is she a client?"

"This is Yvonne. I don't know her last name. She's looking for her former boyfriend on her own, not as a client."

"Not former." Yvonne wagged a finger back and forth, chastising them. "We're for keeps. He's been forced to—"

"She hasn't hired you?" Zack asked.

Billie shook her head.

"I want to," Yvonne said. "Now that I know you weren't here to hire somebody, you're here to be hired yourself!" She giggled, then abruptly grew serious again. "That's what I want to do." She finally let her hand fall into normal position. No more finger-pointing. A step forward.

No way in hell Billie could knowingly work for a lunatic, provide a stalker with information—assuming she could get any. Even Emma Howe, with all her rules about not inflicting your own morality on clients' issues—even she wouldn't put an innocent in danger for a few bucks.

"I'm really sorry," Billie said, "but I couldn't do that. I'm too booked. I couldn't."

Yvonne flashed a look at Zack, as if he might be prompting Billie to lie, then she looked back at Billie, and then to the closed glass-paned door. "Who else is here?" she demanded. "Somebody here better not be too busy for me. I have my rights, I'm a citizen. Everybody treats me like horseshit." The woman zoomed from rage to heartbreak without missing a beat.

Yvonne's eyes overflowed, and she brushed at them as she spoke. "You don't realize—this is the anniversary of our last time together. Two months ago today, in the rain, we went to Stinson, our special place." Her voice had grown dreamy, heavy, as if drugged as she sank into her tale. "We'd been there before. The bartender owns a house and sometimes he rents out the guest room to special friends. Stephen took me there. Everywhere—Mendocino, camping in the Trinity Alps, Big Sur—Point Reyes a lot. . . ."

"Listen, I appreciate your interest, but—"

"It was storming, but we put on our slickers and went on the beach. The ocean was wild, the rain—he took my hand, held it. I thought he was going to ask me to marry him, that's what I thought!" Like a badly played violin, her voice grew ever higher, thinner and piercing.

"Thought he would *marry* me and instead he'd been pressured into getting rid of me." She pressed her palms against her solar plexus. "It hurt him, but he had to do it. His parents forced him. Exactly two months ago today."

Billie nodded acknowledgment.

"Can I help you?" Emma's voice was strong and level as she stood in the open door of her office. Billie had no idea how long she'd been watching. She was carrying her briefcase. "Is there a problem?"

"I—she—I want to hire her but she's refusing! She doesn't like me—the Tassios poisoned her against me. I have money—oh, not enough for his kind, for his family, for his mother, but enough for you! I have to find him! Isn't that your job? I'll die if I don't find him soon. He ruined my life—I never finished college because of him. He owes me."

"I'm sorry, but perhaps we could discuss this another time?"

Emma moved toward the wild-eyed woman. Zack stood, too, looking temporarily benign, permanently large and powerful. "Right now is not a good time for us and you look as if perhaps you should think this through first, decide if you truly want to—"

"You're brushing me off, too? You're *detectives*! What kind of game is this? 'Come back some other time'—who are you kidding? The time is today. *Today*. The anniversary of our last time together and I'm bleeding inside and all I ask is a little help."

"Ah, Emma, this is Yvonne. . . . She's looking for Stephen Tassio?"

Emma's right eyebrow rose almost imperceptibly.

Yvonne spoke right through Billie's words. "You were with his parents, you were at his work—you're after Stephen, too, but you don't know him the way I do. I could help you. I know where he must be. Last chance—will you or won't you?"

Emma took a deep breath. "Won't. Will not. Clear enough? Now, our business here is over." Billie, Emma, and Zack advanced like a V-shaped weapon aimed at Yvonne.

"I won't forget this!" Yvonne screamed as she backed out the door. "Don't think I will!" Her voice shook and dimmed as she walked down each stair, but she never stopped talking. "I don't need you, never did—I just wanted to make it easier, give you a chance, too—but now . . . whatever happens—it's your fault!"

Emma looked taller than usual, muscles on alert. "Not good," she said. "She's hell-bent on proving something today. She could kill herself, kill him, or kill an innocent bystander."

She meant Penny. The most likely innocent bystander. Billie felt her pulse in her throat. "She has no idea where he is, that's why she followed me all day. Process of elimination, but now, she's going to the beach, I bet. All that talk about their last rendezvous."

"If he's anywhere near it, he's both a fool and god-awful easy to ID in a hearse."

"He wouldn't go back to the same place with his new girl, would he? Even if it's his buddy's place?"

"We don't know him. Don't know if he gives the place special significance, and she's crazy," Emma said. "Yvonne's seeing patterns where there aren't any. There's no point calling the police about a skinny girl who's angry, but that doesn't mean she isn't big trouble. I'm really worried about Penny. She's in the way. In Yvonne's way. Hurry—maybe we can still see her, follow her."

As they raced down the stairs, Billie thought hard, willed herself back to her front door, at Yvonne's car parked across the street. God knows, she'd stared at it long enough, remaining on her doorstep, watching until there was no trace of the madwoman. "A little wagon," she said. "Black, maybe. I don't know what make. Sorry."

"Maybe a straight line isn't the fastest way this time," Emma said. "Maybe following an unknown car driven by an unstable woman to an unsure destination is how we'll actually find Penny Redmond." She glanced at Billie. "Alive. Maybe. If we hurry."

Twenty-three

Penny sat at the top of the stairs, too furious to go into "their" bedroom where the only roommate she had left was the scowling, brown-eyed hawk. She couldn't believe Stephen could dump her and leave her and go off to the beach alone. As if she were nothing more than a chore he couldn't wait to finish.

He hadn't even asked her to feed Morgana, like she wasn't grown-up or responsible enough to trust. Not that she wanted to touch a frozen rodent, or get near the creature whose look always struck fear in her, as if it really was from the Middle Ages, looking out from behind eyes that had hated what they'd seen for seven centuries.

But all the same, she wasn't a baby, incompetent, unreliable, irresponsible—and she wasn't to be treated like one.

And now what was she supposed to do? They didn't want her here, but she had nowhere else to go. No money. And Stephen didn't care. All he'd said was, "Go back to school. Get control of your life so you can do what you want to." Easy for him to say, but impossible to do. But that was his complete conversation, except for, "You are not my permanent responsibility. I wanted to bail you out, not make you my foster child."

She closed her eyes, still mortified by the memory of those words. His voice had been flat. A robot's.

Now he was gone, off with his sleeping bag and camping gear. He hadn't even told her where he was headed. And here she was, at the top of the staircase, listening to the rest of them, like a kid eaves-dropping on the grown-ups' party. Somebody—Alicia maybe, she was the one who sounded like an opera singer when she got loud—said "With *her!*" in a way that made Penny know they were talking about her. About her staying here while Stephen wasn't because three of them were leaving for the long weekend. Some big deal event in Phoenix, something called Estrella. A tourney, she thought. Big-time, between two kingdoms. Camping out for two nights, and Kathryn, Alicia, and Toto were going, trying to talk Gary into com-ing, too, even though he thought he was getting the flu. Their excited voices tried to sell him the idea.

And then a low murmur and back to the *her.* Why were they so concerned? What did it hurt if she stayed in Stephen's room?

She should kill herself. Solve everybody's problems at once. Then they'd all feel sorry about how they'd treated her, and they'd deserve to.

The phone rang—only once before it was answered by some-body speaking too softly for her to hear. She moved down, step by step, in a crouch, minimizing if not eliminating the staircase creaks.

"Kathryn Meyers here." She sounded very official, businesslike. Nothing like the vamp she was around Stephen.

Whoever was on the other line must have done some talking, be-cause she just kept going "uh-huh," to show she was listening, until finally she said, "He isn't here right now. Could I take a message?"

Then the call was about Stephen. But what could have needed verification?

"I see. Well, I don't really know. Maybe Point Rcyes. But he said to leave messages at a place in Stinson. Here's the number."

Kathryn knew where he was. He'd told her. Told everybody except Penny. Left them a way he could be reached, left Penny in the dark, like she was the same as his insane ex-girlfriend. She wanted to cry—and to kick somebody at the same time. She wanted to hurt all of them, all at once, for how much they were hurting her.

"What are you doing?" Toto, usually silent and smiling, looked up the stairs. "Eavesdropping?" He seemed incredulous, like nobody he'd ever known would do such a thing.

"Sitting here, that's all."

Still looking in shock, he went back into the living room, where the phone and everybody else was. Then Alicia appeared at the foot of the stairs. "There's no use pretending you weren't there the whole time. Come down and let's work things out."

Penny had the sense of being called into a courtroom with a small jury ready to send her to the gallows.

"Come on, Penny." Alicia sounded tired.

She hadn't realized she wasn't moving. Her brain and body weren't working together anymore. "I'm—" *Sorry* had almost emerged from her mouth, but it would have been a lie and she swallowed it. This wasn't something she was doing to them, this was something they'd done to her.

"I know you're disappointed," Alicia said. "But don't act like a stubborn child. Come downstairs and talk it out."

She wondered if they had any idea of how many times they used "child" or "baby" or "infant" when they spoke to her, if they realized what a constant insult it was. But she went downstairs.

"So you heard us," Kathryn said when she came in. "Heard the phone call."

"I— It was an accident, but—you weren't supposed to do that. I mean isn't that the whole thing, keeping it a secret?"

Kathryn looked bored and disgusted. "It was the police, all right?"

"How do you know? Anybody could pretend to be the police, all they have to do is find you, or whoever's listed in this house." They weren't only mean, they were stupid.

Kathryn sat down on the green armchair. Its side was yellow where the sun had baked it. Rolled-up sleeping bags and bulging duffles were piled near the fireplace. They probably had all kinds of medieval gear in there—eating bowls and garb along with modern inventions like toilet paper. Penny considered it hypocritical to live in both centuries at the same time.

"It was not Yvonne," Kathryn said as if each word was a boulder she had to hoist. "I can tell Yvonne from the police. And why do I have to explain anything to you? You're the one he didn't want to have that number. How much did you hear?"

Penny tilted her chin up, and looked into the distance. She'd heard everything, but she wasn't on trial and she didn't have to answer.

"If we don't get on the road soon, we might as well not go," Toto said. "We won't get there until it's half over at this rate. You coming, after all, Gar?"

The scarecrow shook his head. "Feel like hell, man. Just want to sleep."

"If Gary changes his mind and goes, you'll be here all alone," Alicia said, but not like she cared. "Will you be okay?"

If she was so concerned, she could ask her to go along. It wasn't like they didn't know she was interested, and she could have faked a costume out of tablecloths or pieces from the fabric store. They could have included her, but that idea had never occurred to them.

"I get it," she said. "You're afraid I'll steal the silver." A joke, but nobody laughed. There was nothing in the house worth taking, except the computers, and she wasn't a thief in the first place. "Or I'll have a keg party, or play with matches and set the place on fire. Why do you treat me like I'm a disease?"

246

"Did you— How much did you hear of the telephone call?" Kathryn asked again.

"Kath, that isn't important. Can we get on with the packing?" Toto said.

Penny said nothing. Let them worry about whatever they imagined. That she'd stalk him the way Yvonne was. That she'd tell Yvonne where he could be reached. Whatever they were afraid of, let them keep the fear. They let her keep hers.

"Okay, listen, that isn't the point, anyway." Alicia's mouth was tight, as if holding in something, but she kept talking, looking like a stranger. "You might as well know now. The thing is, Stephen isn't coming back."

"Not coming back when?"

"Ever." Alicia's face was all downward curving lines. "He felt too strung-out to face a scene with you, so he's waiting till later to tell you on the phone."

"What do you mean, later?" Penny felt like a kid on the schoolyard, spinning until she was sick. She could see only a blur where they were, mouths speaking an unknown tongue. "When is 'later'?"

"Who knows? Whenever. That's not the point."

"Where is he going? Where has he gone?"

"I'm not talking about a side trip like this weekend. He's moving out. He is not going to live here anymore. He doesn't feel safe here and it's gotten too . . . I know you understand, even if you're pretending you don't. He's gone. History."

"Without . . ." She couldn't finish that in front of them. Without telling her? What had happened to his code of honor, to the idea of living chivalrously in the way the Middle Ages tried to be? "I don't believe you. He's not like that. You're lying, taking advantage of me while he's at the beach."

"Ah," Alicia said. "You heard everything, didn't you? But the point is, we're going to need a new housemate because we need the rent money, so you have to find another place. Soon. After this week-end, we'd like to start cleaning up."

Toto, looking relieved, as if someone had just lifted Penny off his back, stood up and waved good-bye. "More packing to do," he said softly.

"The bird," she heard herself say, of all stupid things. She didn't even like the hawk, but it was so much Stephen's. "He would never leave Morgana."

"We'll get the bird to him when he has a new address, which won't be for a few days at least."

They had excluded her while they plotted against her. Even Stephen. She had a sharp pain in her center, the way, she was sure, it feels when your her heart breaks. "What do you want me to do?" she said, hating that her voice trembled, that she couldn't look di-rectly at them because they'd see she was crying. She sat, head bowed, and heard shuffling feet, a soft "okay," and thought she might now be alone, so she looked up.

Alicia hadn't gone. They had silently chosen her to handle things because they all thought she was good at things like this. When she spoke, her voice was soft. A "real Mommy" voice, Wesley would call it, because he divided their mother into the "real" and the "mean" and only the soft, considerate version counted with him as "real Mommy." She blinked even harder, thinking of him.

"Go home, Penny," Alicia said gently. "Finish school. Give your-self a break."

"I can't. I can't stand it there."

"At school?"

"No. Home."

"Did they do something bad to you?"

"Yes. No. Not the way you probably mean. Maybe. He hits us and my mom. It's awful."

"If you're being abused there are agencies that will help you, and there's the police. They'll stop him."

Penny shook her head. "I can't do that. If they take him away, then how will my mother live? Or Wesley?" She shook her head again. "I can't get rid of one bad thing and make another bad thing happen. I had to leave—and I have to figure out how to make Wesley safe now, too."

Alicia was silent for a while. "Well, then," she eventually said, "what you want is to find out where you really belong. You know it isn't here." Penny had to strain to hear past the growing roar in her ears. "I'm sorry for what you thought Stephen was offering and what he really was, but that's how it is. You have to pay more attention to real life."

A fine thing to say for a woman going off to live in the Dark Ages. Penny silently stared at her own fingers.

"We're going to Arizona," Alicia said. "It's an annual war—well, you know. Stephen isn't joining us, in case that's what you're thinking. He's too nervous about being in such an obvious place." She sighed. "We've gone the last few years, so Yvonne would expect him there. Anyway, we have to get on the road. Why don't you take the long weekend—all of it—to give this some thought? It'll be quiet here, and maybe that'll be good. You know, helpful."

And all Penny could do was nod, and then, because she couldn't really agree, because the downward movement of the nod dumped her onto the hard surface of the nothing ahead, she heard herself say it again, even though it annoyed Alicia. Annoyed everybody, and she didn't know why. It was an honest question and she needed an answer. "What am I supposed to do?"

Alicia's tone changed. "Anything," she said sharply. "Anything except look dazed and made of stone. Do *something*. Grow up. Decide where you want to be down the road, then think of what you need to do to get there. What *do* you want, Penny? You only talk about what you don't want." She exhaled loudly, like somebody fresh out of patience. "I have to finish packing." The voice that was always so controlled that Penny thought she was a serenity phony was now sharp-edged and mean. Alicia's real self, finally out, but only for Penny. Only for the scapegoat.

"If you decide to leave before we get back, don't forget to feed the bird first and lock up. You can put the key under the back-door mat." She turned and shook her head and put her hands out, palms up, conceding to a horrible but inescapable fate. "If it will help you find a place, or whatever you need, use my car. The key's on the table there. Just be sure it's back before I am. Gas tank at the level you find it, too, please."

Penny started to thank her, but she was gone, as they all would be soon, as Stephen already was.

And now Penny was supposed to do something. Whatever it was that would get her where she wanted to be. She stayed on the flowered sofa and wondered where that was and what she'd have to do. It felt like having her brain roll into a brick wall until it split open. But even so, it was less painful than thinking about what Stephen had done to her.

Twenty-four

There weren't many cars making the trek to the coast at this hour of a late February afternoon when fog dripped down the crevasses of the mountain, boding low visibility on the ocean side. It had been so beautiful inland, earlier. Hot, even.

Billie half wished for the bumper-to-bumper traffic of a sunny weekend day. It would be something to talk about, at least. The silence in the car was strained, and since Emma made no attempt to turn on her radio and provide alternative sound-cushioning, Billie didn't suggest it, either.

Forget small talk. They'd exhausted the potentials of the foggy tendrils. They'd speculated on just how bad it'd be on the beaches, commented on the microclimates of Marin and how amazingly different one area could be from another, talked about the need to dress in layers, said how nice it was that at least it didn't snow—except on such rare occasions they made headlines—although the torrential rains could be horrifying enough. Not to mention, they mentioned, the summer fires that would be the end result of all the rain-encouraged vegetation. And then, having explored the farthest limits of local weather-talk, they lapsed into uncomfortable silence.

Normal people would have said something to the effect of, "How's it going?" But Emma wasn't the norm.

Billie decided it was out of bounds to ask Emma what she was working on, how things were going for her. Emma set boundaries without saying a word.

The car smelled of stale cigarettes although Emma didn't smoke. The front seat's upholstery apparently had been used as an auxiliary ashtray and dump. And the backseat was no better. It looked clawed by something gone berserk and was strewn with bags, duffels, and empty styrofoam cups.

The scenery dissolved and reshaped itself as they drove out Sir Francis Drake, beyond San Anselmo's antique shops to Fairfax, a town clinging to as much of the sixties as it could, back farther in time to the central valley where the conveniences and abominations of civilization were less visible, houses nestled in clusters off-road and out of sight. Woodacre, San Geronimo, Forest Knolls. She and Cameron had looked, but hadn't found anything there when they were house-hunting, and she liked the mix of old and neglected, and brand-new and stunning homes, the privacy and yet the close-ness of houses running up the hills or nestled at their base. She liked horses in front yards, the tiny library and post offices and the pleas-ant oddness of pure unspoiled country, with a city still only minutes away. And a golf course straddling the highway.

She understood why Stephen Tassio would have felt safe there when he needed to disappear.

"This might be where Stephen lives," she said. "I found two mes-sages on the Internet that mentioned the area, and one was from a woman named Alicia Malone—that's her real name, what they call her 'mundane' name. But there was only an office number. No ad-dress.

Emma nodded. "Give me the number. If we don't find Penny tonight, I'll make a call. Guy owes me a favor. But who is she?"

"Stephen's mother said she was the one who lured him into the group, so it seems too much to be a coincidence."

"You think the girl's with him still?"

The girl. She kept making her secondary. It was for the sake of Penny that they were on this chase, but it was Stephen, not Penny she felt close to. She knew his parents, the receptionist at his place of work, his crazed ex, and as little as each had provided, it was more than Penny's people seemed to feel or know. Billie had a rough idea of his life, interests, what made him unique, while Penny remained a shadow figure.

She'd all but forgotten her, and not for the first time. Penny Redmond, the girl nobody knew. How lonely she had to be. "I can't imagine where else she'd go." Billie felt an ache as the adolescent took up residence in her brain.

"Assuming we reach Stephen in time, Penny will either be with him, or he can probably tell us where she is. We can deliver her mother's message and we're out of there. Then it's up to the girl to contact her mother or not."

There was an angry, hurt undertone to Emma's words, as if she had a stake in which option Penny would take.

"I hope she makes contact," Billie said. "That mother's falling apart."

Emma shrugged. "Either way, it won't be our problem anymore."

Her voice had returned to its normal level of impatience as the conversation once again dragged to a halt. There were just so many trees and grasses one could study through the windshield. "Did you get the message about the woman who called?" Billie asked after an awkward pause. "Miriam, with the blood in her trash can?" Cocktail-party chatter without the cocktails. This was too hard.

"It's sad," Emma said. "The woman is losing her mind piece-meal. She was once the smartest woman I knew." She sighed heavily. "She was a rebel when I met her. Way ahead of her time liberating herself, if anybody still uses that term. In fact, speaking of time, if we have any on the way back, would you mind if I—well, it would be both of us, of course—detoured to her house? She lives in Mill Valley, on Mount Tam. If we take Panoramic Highway back instead of this road, she wouldn't be more than a minute or so out of the way, and maybe I can calm her down."

Whatever minutes they spent detouring or soothing Miriam's fears were minutes lost with Jesse, but this was as close to collegial as Emma had ever been. "No problem," Billie said.

"Funny what life does to you," Emma murmured. "Or not funny at all."

They passed the small valley towns and headed toward the sea, through Samuel P. Taylor park, a place Billie considered close to holy. Like stained-glass windows, the late-afternoon sun broke through the redwoods making green prism into gold, lime, emerald, and dark mossy shadow, landing on ground carpeted with rust-and-maroon redwood needles. This was the tapestry and geography of peace, a place of solace, serenity and insight—if only she could find time for contemplative solitude.

They were not necessarily following Yvonne's dark hatchback. They had seen a car like it on Fourth Street when they left the office, but had not caught up with it, and then had lost it as it raced down Sir Francis Drake, and their hope that the police would stop the speeding car and ease everyone's worries was not realized. Now, there were only occasional glimpses of the little wagon as it sped around the twists and turns of the roadbed. They had seemed on a logical course of action when they raced out of the office. Now, on this verdant country road, Billie felt as if she'd left the clear sense of urgency back at the office.

They reached Olema, the T-junction with Highway One, and Emma idled indecisively. "You think he went—she went . . . which direction?"

Billie shook her head. "It seems irrational for him to return to the scene of his and Yvonne's last time together. Or does it even register for him that way? Maybe it's just his friend's place to him, so I can't tell. But I kept hearing how much he loved camping. Point

Reyes, maybe? It's so large, so many campgrounds, the odds would be against her finding him."

"Which is to say, who the hell knows?" Emma shrugged and turned to the right, toward the National Seashore. They reached the visitors' center and went in to ask a few questions.

The last time Billie had been out here had been with Jesse. They'd stood directly on the infamous San Andreas Fault and she'd showed him the fencing that the 1906 earthquake had yanked in two, relocating the pieces several feet apart. Explained about the odd Point Reyes peninsula which geologically belonged in Monterey, but had moved north on its own and was continuing up toward Alaska. Of course, he didn't understand. Nor did she. But she felt it was sufficiently amazing to bear repetition.

And before that, she remembered driving here alone a month before Jesse was born because she thought a long walk on Limantour Beach would clarify her thinking about the future of her marriage. She could still picture herself, enormous in a blue denim tent of a dress, walking barefoot on the hard sand, hemline drenched by surprise waves. She could still hear the chorus of seabird colonies in the surf and those in the ponds and estuaries a few yards inland, the pelicans flying in formation above all of it. She had looked to the timeless elements around her for answers, but had gotten none. Days later, two teenage boys wrongly thought they'd snuffed out a campfire, and the Mount Vision inferno roared through the park, consuming an acre every five seconds at its worst, more than twelve thousand acres before it was contained. Shortly after Jesse was born, she'd put him in a sling and gone to see the spectral grayness leading down to the ocean, and had taken it as a belated but sufficient answer.

As her next visit had been when she was heartened by the multitude of tiny bishop pines sprouting under their burned progenitors. Their seeds had required blazing temperatures to be released. The land was restoring itself, starting over. She thought, perhaps, that she was beginning to catch on, that if she kept returning, this place would keep teaching her.

The ranger was shaking her head, looking patiently amused by the idea of anyone's getting a legal campsite at this hour. "They've been reserved for a long time now," she said. "You know that myth—or maybe it's real—that it's always hot and pretty on Presidents' Day weekend. We're booked even now, before the weekend starts. 'Specially because of this break in the weather. We keep some slots open, but people were lined up for them when we opened this morning." She shook her head again. "If your friend didn't have a reservation, he isn't here."

"Illegally, then?" Billie asked.

The ranger shrugged. "I always tell 'em it's a whole lot cheaper getting a room around here than paying the fine."

Back in the car, they followed an increasingly dusky, then dark Highway One along a shore spotted with weathered homes and country-style restaurants until they approached Stephen's other seaside haven, the single downtown street of Stinson Beach. "Maybe we were wrong," Emma said.

We. Emma's first "we." Billie savored the word and moment.

"But let's look for 'their place,' " Emma said. "Maybe leave a warning for him. Meanwhile, he's probably warm at home while we chase around."

There was actual camaraderie in the line, companionship and ease. Billie felt the frozen wasteland between them melt at its edges. Only the smallest of puddles, but a warming trend, at least.

She scanned the few options at the sleepy beach town. A bookstore, cafe, a market—and a shingled house with a small sign, half-hearted, reading, The Bar. "Their place, maybe?" Billie said.

Emma pointed. Halfway hidden by the building, the dark hood of a car. But it wasn't Yvonne's. When they parked and inspected it, it turned out to be missing its front tires.

The house was tiny, the "bar" almost a dollhouse-sized affair, albeit fully stocked. Two men sat at a small pedestal table near the window, playing chess and drinking dark beer. The man behind the bar had been on a tall stool, reading. He closed his book and stood up as Emma and Billie entered. "Welcome," he said. "Help you?"

Billie was acutely thirsty and ready to appreciate anything wet. She also thought buying something was fair trade for information, but most of all, she felt she should follow Emma's lead.

"I'll have a beer," Emma said. "What's on tap?" She glanced at Billie, who nodded and said, "Make it two." Beer wasn't her favorite, but there it was. She wanted to belong, and suddenly, wine seemed potentially effete, coffee too abstemious, soda immature.

She had to stop thinking this way, as if she were preparing to play a role, as if she were always deciding what this character Billie would do in a situation. But she accepted her beer and sat down on one of the five stools in front of the bar, as did Emma, and waited for a cue from her employer.

"Stevie here yet?" Emma asked.

The bartender tilted his head, then shook it. "Who?"

"Stevie Tassio."

"Stevie?"

Emma laughed and her features reacted as if she'd put a softener over them. "I'm the boy's aunt and this here's his cousin, my sister's child, and I guess Stevie's too grown-up for that nickname now, is that it? Stephen, I mean."

"You're relatives?"

Billie nodded and smiled. "Aunt Emma and cousin Billie Jo. From near Ukiah. He mentioned us, then?" she asked brightly.

The bartender shook his head again. "Did he know you were coming out?"

"Oh, yes. We're meeting here. I admit I get things jumbled if I don't write them down, and I didn't. But he said a house with the word 'Bar' outside. Ther isn't another one, is there?" Emma the Stern had blurred her edges and become a flustered, worried generic woman of a certain age.

"Is Stevie—I mean Stephen—still with that dark-haired girl with the fancy name?" Billie asked. "Something foreign, although, of course, she wasn't."

"Yvonne?" the bartender asked, and when Billie nodded and said, "Yes!" he shook his head anew. "Broke up a while back."

"What a pity! I thought we were about to be invited to a wedding," Emma said.

"Maybe there's somebody new," Billie said, poking Emma with her elbow.

The bartender shrugged. "Wouldn't know. He didn't say."

"Well, now, I'll ask him myself—what else is the point of meddling relatives, right?" Emma laughed at her own weak joke. "So— where is my bachelor nephew?"

"Left a while ago. He didn't say anything about meeting anybody. We touched base, that's all."

"He left? Why would he be out this way if he wasn't meeting us? He's too young to be as forgetful as I am! Or did he have a hot date, is that it?"

"Didn't say. He was alone when he was here. See, I'm kind of voice mail for people passing through. People leave him messages here. He comes by to check."

Alone, Billie thought. Then Penny was where? Had this search been in the wrong direction from the start? Penny wasn't with him. She might never have been, and she could be anywhere on earth.

"Aha! Maybe he did have a date," Emma said.

The bartender shrugged. He seemed more pragmatic than romantic. "Or something came up, change of plans. There were messages. Two. No, wait—one hung up. Didn't leave her name, although I have my suspicions."

Her. Crazy Yvonne probably, behaving less impulsively and more thoughtfully than they had. She'd called to find out if Stephen was there, had verified his presence, and hadn't wasted gas and more important, time at Point Reyes.

"And the other phone call? Some kind of emergency?" Emma asked after downing the last of her beer.

The bartender shrugged. "Doubt it. He was here when that call came, too, and he took it. All's I know it was a man who said something like I should tell him it's about jewelry. That doesn't sound like an emergency to me."

Emma glanced at Billie, who shook her head. Jewelry?

The bartender wiped at an imaginary speck on the small bar. Billie wondered how he filled his days. "I think . . ." he began. "Don't be offended—but I think he's got a whole lot on his mind these days, and I think he just plain forgot about your date. I'm real sorry. He will be, too."

"Oh, dear. This is a . . . I'm not sure what we . . ." Emma, anything but the "oh, dear" type, dissolved herself into pure confusion. "Young man, could we leave a message for when he checks in with you?"

"Could be awhile," the man said. "Days, even."

"Understood, but will you leave word that Aunt Emma and Billie Jo were by as planned, and now I guess we'll head back to Ukiah. Beat the storm."

"There won't be a storm. Presidents' Day is coming up." The bartender grinned. "Always nice that weekend."

Emma nodded. "Fine, but tell him to give us a ring. He knows the number. Unless he's forgotten that, too!" And with an incredulous, politely upset little-old-lady laugh, she was up and off the stool, walking to the door with a slight hesitation, residual bewilderment in her stride.

"You're good," Billie said when they were outside. "Did you ever act? Onstage, I mean?"

Emma looked sideways and up at her sharply, as if grossly offended. "Of course not!" she snapped as she unlocked her car door. "So what do we know? Apparently Yvonne didn't come here, maybe just made that call to find out if Stephen was here. He's not camping and there's no threat, and Penny Redmond is not with him, unless she was outside waiting in the car, but what sense would that make? No reason for us to hang around. Is there?"

What the hell did Emma have against acting onstage?

"We'll go down Panoramic and take a jog by poor Miriam's, and still get home early, okay?"

Like her approval mattered. "Fine," Billie said. By all means take the longer, harder, foggier, more dangerous route so we can waste time with a loony.

"Two birds," Emma said, even though one of their birds had flown the coop. Miriam's trash can hardly seemed worth the time.

Somewhere off the road that wound over and down the mountain were spectacular vistas of deep valleys, lush vegetation, waterfalls in this rainy season, and always, wildlife. But none of that was visible in the combination of night and the ever-increasing white swirls. Emma said nothing but sat straight and at the ready behind the wheel. The narrow road twisted and the headlights of oncoming cars flashed onto trees a second before the cars themselves appeared. "We all love this, don't we?" Emma muttered. "The near-wild at our back door. Nature's splendors left unspoiled. But every so often, don't you secretly wish they'd pave the damned mountain or put a freeway ramp over it or a tunnel through it so getting to the beach would be easier? Not that I've ever said it out loud before, for fear of being reported to the tree-huggers."

Billie allowed herself a small laugh of acknowledgment, but she swallowed the end of it as she saw flashing lights and a cluster of cars directly ahead. "Roadblock."

Emma had seen it in time and was braking. "Accident." She exhaled dramatically, loudly, out of exasperation with the delay, or sympathy for the unlucky driver who hadn't seen the next curve.

The other stuck drivers had turned off their ignitions and were milling around the scene, dark shadows in the fog. "Ghouls," Emma said. Then she leaned closer to the windshield and tilted her head, squinting. "I know that guy." She gestured to where three highway patrolmen stood. "Excuse me a sec."

So much for ghoulishness, Billie thought. The scene through the windshield was like a surrealistic silent film. Everything in motion and nothing clear-edged through the veil of fog. Drivers, hugging themselves in the chill, relieved it wasn't them this time. A tow truck raising an oversized crane, its back aimed toward rescue in the brush. An ambulance, motor idling, exhaust rising and joining the gauzy air. A fire truck. The Highway Patrol's motorcycles. And all lit by overbright lamps braced against trees and on car hoods, their light bouncing back from the wild dark beyond the slender paved ribbon.

This could last forever, Billie thought, wondering if they should attempt a U-turn on the narrow and congested mountain road, then backtrack to Sir Francis Drake. Couldn't stop at Miriam's, then, but who cared? Miriam's fears were imaginary. Billie's were real. Penny Redmond was still missing. Crazy Yvonne was still hellbent on proving something awful.

The fruitless search was exhausting Billie's small fund of optimism. Even when and if they found Penny, nothing would be improved, given that her mother didn't want her back. What was the point of all this? If, in fact, the girl was safer away from home, then her runaway instincts were correct and self-preserving. Why beat the bushes for her?

And how could her mother jeopardize both her children—give Penny up and remain in an environment that endangered her skinny-necked little boy?

It was chilly in the car and she wasn't dressed for it. Out at the side of the road, near the chrome-yellow tow truck, which huffed and heaved as it tried to raise the fallen car, Emma talked to a tall, potbellied man, showing more animation than Billie had ever seen from her. Hands pointing toward the tow truck, nods, head-shakes and finally, after what seemed an eternity, a handshake and return to the car. She looked straight ahead, through the windshield and her voice was tight. "Very bad news."

"The driver's dead?" It was and wasn't a question. If they had recovered the body and there was any sign of life at all, there would be paramedics working frantically and the ambulance would not be idling. "I didn't realize they had reached the car yet."

"It's just off the road. Didn't fall far at all. Climbers were able to get down to it, to the body."

Billie swallowed hard and shook her head. What was there to say of the waste of life? It happened too often and too easily—too many drinks, too much velocity, too little belief in the laws of physics. Stupid and sad.

The tow truck inched forward. Billie couldn't imagine how, with the limited space in front of it, it could haul up an entire car.

Emma cleared her throat and turned so that she was almost looking at Billie, as if she'd intended to, but couldn't at the last moment. "The driver was murdered."

Billie stared at her in the dark. The pupils of her eyes caught some of the white of the lights outside, made Emma look feral. But also very sad. Very human.

"Beaten around the head with something hard, like a baseball bat. The killer obviously expected the car to fall all the way down, maybe to burn, and in either case, the head wounds would be written off to the crash. But a gigantic tree stopped the fall, caught and held the car. It's immediately off the road, nose-down." She grew silent, but Billie knew it was only a pause.

She didn't want to hear the rest. She already felt it aching in her marrow. No need for the finality of words, the confirmation. He was so vividly alive in her mind.

The yellow truck heaved and grunted and exhaled steam and the back of the fallen car slowly rose until it was visible over the road's edge. It looked like no normal car. There was no softly curved bulge of trunk under a rear window.

A hearse the color of sunshine. A horribly apt choice for Stephen Tassio's last ride.

Twenty-five

They sat in silence for what felt a long time, watching the continued efforts of men and vehicles to rescue the car and restore the road, even if they could perform neither service for the driver.

Emma sat lost in thoughts of the sudden curves from life to death. She never thought about any young man's death without putting her own son's face on the victim. The habit was a ridiculous form of self-important hysteria. But she was never without a sore awareness in her solar plexus of her son's vulnerability. Maybe every mother was. She'd never asked anybody else. She glanced over at Billie, then decided against starting now, and thought instead about Stephen Tassio.

Who was he that someone should waylay him, as seemed the case, murder him and disappear? It had to have been done within seconds. The road wasn't busy this evening, but it was nonetheless one of only a handful of arteries from the ocean side of Marin, and never deserted for long. Precisely how long before she and Billie arrived at the bar had he left? Were the two phone calls related to this?

They'd had the right impulse, she and Billie, but their good intentions had only paved the road to hell. They hadn't found or stopped Yvonne, and now Stephen Tassio was dead and she couldn't help but wonder whether that was cause-and-effect.

Who had Stephen Tassio been besides a ticket away from home for Penny Redmond?

And, most of all, *what was the point?* It was a question she asked more and more often, and she was still waiting for the smallest whisper of an answer. It wasn't as if she confronted senseless death on any regular basis. Aside from half of Nathaniel's world in the plague years. But what was the point of any of it, of the sweat and time and brainpower to supposedly "solve" things? The effort put food on Emma's table, but what good did it ultimately do? What had she or the lawyers she worked with, or the police or anybody ever truly "solved"?

The scene outside the car was alien and disorienting. Shadows cast by the white-hot lights were misplaced, as if a small sun had fallen to earth, textures unnaturally combined—misty swirls and fronds and bark against the chromed and lacquered surfaces of equipment, the deep silence of the mountain broken by low voices and the metal-on-metal cries of the machinery.

She heard her own jagged sigh with surprise. As did Billie, obviously. The girl, whose profile had been still as sculpture, turned sharply, her mouth slightly open.

She is surprised that I have human feelings. The thought produced a bristling pang at the base of Emma's skull. Neither the sensation, the resultant pain, nor the accusation behind it was new. It had been cultivated and maintained by Caroline's nonstop insistence that she was Emma's victim, the daughter of a woman lacking normal emotions.

And all because Emma was not the hugging, kissing, pat-on-the-back kind. She was the pay the bills and put-shoes-on-the-feet kind, but that didn't suffice, and just because she didn't constantly announce to the world the inner workings of her psyche . . .

She realized how far into the muck of self-pity she'd sunk. "Up to my neck in dreck," her friend Janine used to say, and although it wasn't Emma's lingo, she'd understood it immediately.

Emma yanked her attention and thoughts back to present reality. Billie was beside her, not Caroline. Billie was the one who'd been surprised that Emma had feelings, or, at least, had the same she herself had. Annoying, but not impossible to understand.

Emma had to get it through her skull that Billie also had a set of feelings. She had to see her without the lens of baseless resentment—because she was young, because she was beautiful, because she merely had to exist in order to produce smiles of welcome, because she was not nearly as tired as Emma was.

And she had probably never before had a close encounter with violent death.

She moved her hand six inches to the right so that it covered, softly, Billie's. The younger woman's mouth half opened again, but she didn't pull her hand back.

"It's rough. Every time." Emma patted Billie's perfect, unlined and un-sunspotted, patrician hand. She would work at getting over those flares of rage at nature.

"He . . ." Billie breathed in and out, shook her head.

Goddamn, she's going to want to talk about it, Emma thought. Why do people say that actions speak louder than words if they then go on to insist on tons and tons of words. Inside other people, unsaid words apparently piled up, festered and inflicted pain. But why dump them on decent people?

Outside, the yellow tow truck moved into reverse with steel screams and warning beeps and the hearse, looking like a wounded behemoth, heaved back on the roadbed. People applauded and two drivers honked their horns either in a salute to the skilled rescue efforts or in impatience to get on with their commutes.

Billie sat still, her mouth tense. Damn. Emma knew how to get people to talk, pull out their feelings. She just didn't like to use the techniques outside of billable hours. "Poor guy," Emma said, and that pretty much covered it.

Unless you were Billie. "Nobody had a bad word to say about him," she began. "He sounded generous, kind. Almost as if the person I made up for the ILM receptionist was who he really was. She wasn't surprised that he'd have given me money and a place to sleep. Maybe in person I'd think he was nerdy. All that computer stuff, I don't know. But I bet he was interesting. So young, too. And his fantasy life, that other world he was a part of. A nice Middle Ages, a world with codes of honor."

Eulogy for a stranger, Emma thought, but this wasn't information she wanted. She didn't want to know who Stephen Tassio had been, didn't want to hear how Billie's pain would shape her description and her tone. Didn't want Stephen, who was irretrievably dead, becoming three-dimensional now.

"The only negative words were his mother's, about the quality of his associates. He didn't check Dunn and Bradstreet before he showed affection. Played at being a falconer, loved the world that almost was, the ideal world of six hundred years ago. The people who should have sheltered him, loved him unconditionally, or even conditionally . . . It doesn't seem surprising that he was attracted to a dream world of sorts, to a new family of other dreamers. People entirely unlike those . . . his . . ." She shook her head again, tendrils of hair like blonde fog in the light of the distant lamps. "I don't get it, how people treat their children. . . . I wonder what his mother will feel when the police come to her house. Grief? Irreparable loss? Or—since she'd written him off as an embarrassment already—relief?"

Again there was silence, but this silence was soft-edged, wrapped around them, not sitting between them.

"And who would have—could have—done that to him? How? Didn't anybody see the attack?"

"It wouldn't take long," Emma said. "If he was the kind of person you said, he'd have stopped if somebody seemed in trouble. And then what? A minute?—two? He'd be taken completely by surprise." She sighed. "Yvonne," she said softly.

"It's horrible that everything special about a human being can be killed that quickly. That finally," Billie whispered. "We're designed badly, aren't we? We'd take a machine back to the store if it were that fragile." Then she looked at Emma as if seeing her clearly for the first time in a long while. "I'm sorry. I sound like a fool. Unprofessional. No detachment. I'm sorry."

Emma felt her hand muscles contract, willed her palm and fingers to stay in place, to not go crazy and overdo it, for Christ's sake, but she was overruled and once again she softly patted Billie's hand. "Don't be sorry," she said. There were probably other touchy feely words a goddamned role model might say, but enough was enough.

"I had changed my mind, but maybe we should make that other stop, after all. Lighten up. Remember that life goes on." Not that Miriam was precisely comic relief, or even Emma's definition of "life." She was another variation of the theme of loss, another tragedy, but this one orchestrated by nature, whose cruelties were not considered criminal outrages. Not even considered abberations, more was the pity. To Emma, violent death had come to seem less frightening than the nonviolent, piece-by-piece variety.

Billie's smile was tremulous. "The case of the bloody trash can?"

"Unless— It is later than we'd expected. Did you have plans?"

"Jesse's asleep by now, so no, I don't." Billie looked out the windshield again. "It's frustrating to watch this and do nothing. I know there's nothing to do—the police are in charge. They'll notify, and clean up messy ends and look for the person with the baseball bat or tree limb or whatever it was."

"And P.I.s are not allowed to be involved in an active, ongoing homicide investigation," Emma said. "Except in the movies and on TV."

Billie nodded. "I read the book you gave me."

"I told them about Yvonne," Emma said. "The phone calls. The woman who hung up. The man he talked to."

Billie nodded again, but this time, with reluctance, as if begrudging the words she was about to say. "I hate to say this, but I was thinking about Penny Redmond, too. It could have been . . . He came out here alone. If she was with him, but they were having problems . . . Of course, we don't know if she was *ever* with him. If he was the guy driving the car when she left. Or somebody who borrowed it that day."

"I mentioned Penny as well. The situation. Had to explain why we knew about the dead boy, little as it is we know."

"Maybe it was somebody else altogether, somebody who had nothing to do with his romantic life, or Penny's running away. That other message. And even Arthur Redmond. He's such an angry man, if he knew who the boy who took Penny away was . . . But of course, he didn't. Neither did I. I didn't know Stephen. I have nothing to offer."

She was getting a taste of the futility. The "What's the point?" would gnaw at her, but not for a while yet. "What the hell," Emma said. "Let's go solve a mystery."

Miriam lived on the flats of Mill Valley, or at least on the semi-rounded, on the gentle slopes approaching Mount Tam; and unlike her neighbors farther up the road who often as not were cantilevered, half-perched on stilts that clutched the steep mountainside, she had a level yard edged by what appeared to be a wall of ivy. Even in the dark, the love expended on the plot of ground was obvious as she toured her visitors through her garden en route to the "scene of the crime."

Miriam waved toward the vertical ivy. "I would show you where I saw the blood next door, but we'll have to go around because of that thing. I hate it, hate having a fence. I try to cover it with vines, but it still looms like a prison wall. But at least the deer can't get in, and I can have my roses. They just love roses. And this . . . It's a . . . this . . . this, um . . . thing? Before the fence, I thought it was a bush because it never had the chance to grow!"

Miriam was diminutive and dimpled. Her dark eyes were lively, although now and then, as when she'd tried to remember the word "tree," her conversation halted and her eyes turned puzzled and worried. Two seconds later, they were again as bright and intense as ever. Emma listened to Miriam intently explain each bit of flora. She wanted to punish—or hide from—nature whenever she saw Miriam, which is why she tried to avoid seeing her. Coming here had been a decision to be brave, which was easier with somebody else along.

Emma's own yard was an unkempt mess, and had been forever. Back when she had small children and toys littering ground hard-packed from ball games and the pressure of sand boxes, she'd incorrectly believed she'd become a gardener someday. Back then and through till now, her only garden knowledge was to warn her children to not to go near the shiny green-and-scarlet poison oak and not to eat the blossoming pink-and-white oleanders, a deadly plant even the deer didn't touch. Emma's total botanical knowledge.

Her children had made it to adulthood, which meant they were at least as smart and self-protective as the dim-witted deer.

Miriam waved her flashlight to a new spot, passing over without comment a bulky green trash can on wheels. "See this flower?" she asked, the beam revealing blue petals, closed against the night. "One of my favorites, a . . . It's a . . . oh . . ."

Miriam had been trained as a botanist, that was who she was under all the layers of roles: housewife, mother, and widow. It was unbearable watching her core shred like worn silk.

We don't get to keep a thing, Emma thought. And if we do, we surely don't get to choose what it should be. "Is that the trash can?" She pointed in the direction of the enormous green plastic tub she'd seen.

"What? Oh, no." Miriam chuckled, as if the idea were laughable. "That's for prunings and clippings, for the green collection. They compost the stuff. So do I, but not the bigger limbs."

"Then where is your trashcan, Mir?"

"Where it should be. Outside the fence, in the enclosure dear Charlie built us. Why?"

Emma smiled to hide the fear Miriam's degeneration caused her. "You asked me—"

"I'm glad you reminded me because tomorrow's trash day and I would have forgotten. I have to clean the cat's box."

"Maybe we should take a look at it," Emma said.

"The cat box? Why on earth?"

Emma wished she could shake her, rattle things back into place. "The trash can," she said gently. "The one you called me about."

Miriam nodded. The flat dark look fluttered over her face, a split second of acknowledgment and mourning. "Yes. Good. Although I've washed it down, of course."

"Of course," Emma said.

"It would have smelled. Attracted rodents."

"Lovely garden, and thanks for showing it to us," Billie said.

She'd been silent except for politenesses since they arrived. She hadn't yet let go of the scene on the mountain, Emma realized. But some instinct pulled Billie back when etiquette was required. She wore white gloves in her soul and probably sent thank-you notes to everyone she interviewed.

Emma remembered that she wasn't going to think those stupidly resentful thoughts anymore. Except, of course, when she forgot to remember.

The trash can sat inside its latticed enclosure, the doors of which were slightly open. "I leave them that way. It's easier for the trash men," Miriam explained. "They work so hard, poor dears. Besides, Charlie was a craftsman, do you see? I don't want them bumping his woodworking here."

"Anything unusual in it this time?" Emma asked her old friend.

"I didn't look. I took out the trash an hour or so ago, and it was already dark. It was in the morning that I saw the blood that time." She looked near tears. "Do you think I'm a cracked old lady?"

"Of course not," Emma said. "Why would we both be here otherwise? I might visit, but my associate wouldn't. We're here investigating for you, dear."

"Because you see, all I could think was what if something horrible is going on and nobody makes a fuss?"

"Of course." Emma felt as if she might drown under a tsunami of exhaustion. Coming here had not been the best of ideas this particular evening. She was too tired to be tolerant of what was happening to Miriam. Too tired to check whether it was gaining on her as well.

"Jeffrey Dahmer's neighbors didn't do anything," Miriam went on. "And look what happened there! All those dead boys!"

"You're right." Each word was an effort. She couldn't remember being this tired before in her entire life. She put her hand on the lid, for what reason, she couldn't have said. There was nothing there, if there ever had been, but this looked as if she cared, as if she were behaving professionally. Or as if she were performing a faith healing for a trash can. Emma lifted the lid.

Miriam's attention wandered, and she waved to a man in a gray sweatsuit at the end of the street. "My neighbor," she said. "Man never sits still."

"Is he hiking now with that backpack? It's dark." Emma inspected the underside of the trash-can lid. Nothing.

"A perpetual-motion machine," Miriam said. "He hikes and bikes and runs or swims laps in his pool—well, swims in summer—or goes camping, and his wife's just as bad. Exhausts me to watch, and makes me angry, too. They don't use a single one of those muscles on their garden, which is a disgrace. I don't know why people like that want a house. They're never in it, except to watch TV too loudly, and they don't care about it."

"Want to flash that light this way?" Emma asked Miriam, who obliged.

Nothing except two bags of trash, one in paper and the other in a tied-shut white plastic bag with a Safeway logo, the sort the market used for potentially leaky or sweaty goods. Miriam disapproved—of all excess packaging. She carried string bags to the market and used them as much as possible.

"If I'm stuck with plastic things," Miriam once had said, "I use them for the cat's poop. Can't put poop in the compost, you know."

That part of Miriam was still intact. She always had the least-used trash can Emma had ever seen, and discussed it, because it galled her to have to pay the same collection fee as "the trashmakers," she called them. She was as hyperclean about her natural environment as she was about her garden and her dwelling. Recycling, buying without excess wrappers—the proof was in the can. Emma had done her share of pawing through people's trash, looking for receipts, bills, and bank statements. Had she needed to investigate Miriam, she'd have come up with zilch. Miriam used the backs of mail for memo paper. She reused aluminum foil, used the curbside recycling for cans and bottles and newspapers. She used fabric napkins and towels, and composted all vegetable matter the city didn't collect in the green cans. The obsession with world-cleanliness was so ingrained, it was going to take a very long time for the forces erasing her mind to reach that portion.

"Kitty," Miriam said. "Have to clean her litter."

"I think you already did, dear," Emma said, pointing at the Safeway bag.

Miriam looked into the can and sighed. Then her attention

turned again to her neighbor, now at the far corner. "What's he doing?" she asked.

Down the street the man in sweats stood with a trash-can lid in his hand. "Cheating the system," Emma said. "You pay for pickups, don't you?"

Miriam nodded.

"I bet he doesn't. He uses other people's cans, and he left some meat in yours."

"They are wasteful people," Miriam acknowledged. "And meat-eaters."

"Let's go inside," Emma said. "I'm chilly."

"But the stain on their deck," Billie said softly. "Should we . . . ?"

"They dropped something and didn't clean up after it," Emma whispered. "We aren't a housecleaning service. Dirtiness is none of our business."

Miriam stood in place, looking as if there were something she wanted to remember, but couldn't.

"Weren't we going to have tea?" Emma asked.

"Was that what I was forgetting?"

Billie still gazed at the horizon. "I think . . ." she murmured.

"—that we should go inside, drink a cup of tea and get on the road." Emma enunciated each word. She was dealing with two brain-numbed women.

Miriam turned toward the house, paused, shrugged, and then took a step or two.

The neighbor appeared, waved and nodded at them before entering his house.

"I remember. There was a stain on his deck," Miriam said.

"We'd be trespassing," Emma said. "Besides, it's dark. We couldn't see. I'll stop by again."

She walked Miriam to the door, which is when she realized that Billie, still in her trance, hadn't budged. "Billie?"

"Two minutes," she said. "I want to check something."

Emma shrugged and went into Miriam's fussy but immaculate living room. She and her old friend sipped tea and reminisced about long-gone husbands and departed friends. Miriam was losing the present, but still had a hold on the past. The conversation didn't lift Emma's mood. She needed to be home with a beer, a bad TV show, and a nearby bed. An empty one. No energy for even a quiet night with George. She remembered—he had his meeting. Good. She was ready to make her farewells, but where the hell was Billie?

As if on cue, the apprentice appeared. "I have something of an update," Billie said. "On the case."

"What case?" Emma asked.

"The one we came here to solve."

"But we did already." Well, *they* hadn't done squat. Billie had stood there in cloud-cuckoo land and Emma had done the deducting, but why split hairs and look bad to Miriam?

"Except," Billie said, "I was bothered by the shot Miriam heard and the stains—in your can, Miriam, and the neighbor's deck. And his backpack tonight. So first I walked around the front of his house. He does have trash collection. His can is pulled out of the enclosure, waiting for pickup, so there went that theory."

"Maybe he only pays for one and needs two," Emma said.

"They are so wasteful," Miriam said.

"Perhaps," Billie murmured. "But I had this different idea, so I went across the street, now that he was home, and checked out the can we'd seen him at."

The girl was milking this for all it was worth. Emma should have never hired a prima donna. *"And?"*

"And . . . I found a . . . a body part in plastic wrap."

Miriam put her hand on her heart. "Oh, my—"

"A head," Billie said.

"Oh my god!" Miriam looked about to pass out.

Sweet Jesus—she finds a head and nonchalantly—a *head!*

"But not a human head. A deer's. A young buck."

Emma stared at her, then at Miriam, then back at Billie. Then she laughed. "You have a criminal next door," she told Miriam. "A Marin criminal."

"I'm sorry," Miriam said. "I don't understand."

"You know it's illegal to kill deer in Marin, don't you? Even during hunting season. Pretty much every inch of this county is off-limits. Basically, it's an absolute, total no-no. Frowned upon the way, say, grand larceny or embezzlement is not frowned upon."

"And that young man, you think he—"

"I do indeed. I think one too many deer visited him—"

"But he never planted anything. He had no garden to ruin. Not a single flower."

"I think I saw remnants of weed," Billie said.

"That's what I meant. Just weeds!"

"Marijuana," Billie said. "Deer love it."

"Venison is tasty," Emma added. "And there it was, a visiting venison on the hoof. That was the shot you heard, and then he must have panicked. Good venison—but what to do about it? Is his pool drained by any chance?"

"I don't know. The cover was on. That stretchy kind that hooks over metal things."

"Bet it is. Bet that's where he did his butchering. Now his freezer's full, but he still has the problem of disposing of the inedible parts without going to jail. So he doesn't do it all at once, and he surely doesn't do it in his own trash can. Each week, he leaves a souvenir in a different can, or maybe a few cans after people put them out for collection. For all we know, he does this all year round, finding new neighborhoods for the body parts each time."

"What should I do?" Miriam asked. "It's a crime."

Who really cared? Didn't want him to do it again because shooting a gun in a residential neighborhood is insane, but who really cared if this man or the next speeding car on the freeway thinned the herd? The wildcats, their natural predators, were all but gone. So Miriam's neighbor got to eat venison instead of the turkey vultures. Was it worth jail time?

"You should ask him when he's going to have you over for dinner," Emma said. "For venison. Ask with a smile. That'd let him know that you're not hostile or a threat, but that you know, so he'd better not do it again."

"I can't do that," Miriam said.

"All right, but why?" She was afraid of forgetting what she was to do, Emma thought.

"I don't eat meat," Miriam said.

Emma and Billie merely nodded.

The Last of the Mohicans does Marin. Emma envisioned his wife nagging Deerslayer because Bambi's head and antlers took up too much room in their freezer. No space left for the frozen yogurt and vodka.

They left Miriam debating what course of action she wanted to take. It was good, Emma thought, to be reminded that the ludicrous was also part of the big picture.

Billie sat silently in the car, her hands crossed on her lap. Ever that proper miss, Emma thought, but she looked like perfect hell, hair gone straggly and face as lined as one that young could be.

"Penny Redmond," she murmured. "All this and we still don't . . . The police. They'll be able to get his address, right? To notify . . . Oh, God. I should—"

"It's an open homicide now," Emma said. "You'd be interfering, or seeming to. Instead, go home and get a night's sleep, why don't you? Leave it till morning."

Billie looked over with naked gratitude. And something else. The damned girl was always waiting. Expecting. "Good work about the deer." Emma's voice sounded rusty. She cleared her throat. "Very clever."

"Thanks."

"There's something on the desk might be fun for you," Emma said. "Sexual-harassment case. You'd be perfect for it. Soon as we find Penny or give it up."

Billie smiled and nodded.

I'm not stroking her, or whatever they call it, Emma reassured herself.

"Miriam's was fun," Billie said. "Figuring it out, I mean."

Emma's turn to nod. It had been. Small antidote for a dead end and a dead young man, but small didn't mean nonexistent. You took what you could get. Maybe that was the point.

Twenty-six

The honks made Penny realize she had done it again—slowed to a near stop on Sir Francis Drake during the morning rush hour. All those people hurrying toward the City, the ferry stop, the bus depot.

Another honk. All those people angry at her, but her foot was too tired to press any harder. Last time people honked because she was speeding or weaving—something. She couldn't help whatever it was.

He was dead. She couldn't believe it.

No. She could. She had been afraid of that. She had seen that somebody was following them, warned him, and he had made fun of her.

But all the same, dead? *Murdered?*

The policeman said "suspicion of foul play," not an accident. He'd been looking for Alicia because the phone number Stephen had given the police was listed as Alicia Malone's. Penny explained that she lived there, too. Gave her name. It was hard saying even that because as soon as she saw the cop, she knew it was something bad—her brain exploded. Maybe she nodded. Anyway, the policeman took that as a yes.

The policeman said . . .

More honks. She pulled into the slowest lane and tried to concentrate but it was too hard, too noisy inside and outside. She couldn't attach, move with them. She was no longer connected to anything—not to people, if Stephen was gone. Not to gravity or inertia. Her car—Alicia's car—would do whatever it wanted. She wasn't connected to it, either.

And when she had calmed down enough to speak to the cop, all she could think of was Yvonne, and she told him about her but she didn't know her last name. Didn't know where she worked, what she did.

She felt bad now that she'd said it because after a while she knew it hadn't been Yvonne. She wanted him back, so why would she kill him? Besides, Stephen wouldn't have stopped his car—not even Stephen—if he saw Yvonne's car or Yvonne.

She thought Gary had slept through the whole cop thing, but then he came down and said he'd heard. He was more rumpled and wild-haired than ever, and he looked as if he'd been crying, but said it was his cold. Later she heard him snoring. Asleep and snoring as if nothing had happened while she paced and cried and couldn't even close her eyes so that they got gritty and hurt, but still stayed open and all the while she felt scissors snip the air around her, till she hovered above earth—thin, two-dimensional, arms out, holding nothing.

Near dawn, from her point in space, she'd been able, finally, to connect the scraps and see what must have happened. And what she saw wasn't Yvonne at all.

She saw Arthur. Stephen had visited him. Until then, Arthur hadn't known who Stephen was, not for sure, probably not at all. And because of Yvonne, nobody could have found Stephen unless he showed his face on purpose, said his name, let Arthur Redmond know him and about him. She'd warned him about her stepfather's temper, which was worse than ever now that he was afraid of her—

afraid because she knew about his other woman. He was going to lose his slave-wife and slave-kids because of Penny.

Arthur had expected her to be in that car with Stephen. She was supposed to be dead, too, now. It all made shudderingly-clear sense.

That's what this was about, that was its meaning. Penny had to set things right, make it up to Stephen. Tell the world the truth. There was always a reason why things happened and now she saw this one clearly. As clear as the picture that would be worth the thousand words nobody listened to or believed. Stephen was dead and she might as well be, unless she made things right. If it was dangerous, then it was still right that she face that danger.

Stephen had died for her, because of her, because of their connection. She had to be worthy of him. In his world of knights and ladies, ladies fought too, and all lived by the code of honor. She could, too.

She packed Stephen's camera, a notebook. Everything. She didn't have much, but what was the point of leaving it here, with only Morgana left to care, if birds cared about anything. Maybe she'd come back and maybe not. This way, she had her freedom, her choices to make. She'd get Alicia's car back to her somehow, or leave a message about where Alicia could pick it up. So what if she'd be angry about the car's being somewhere else. So what?

She heard a long honk, like a scream, saw the wide-eyed horror on the face of the driver of a car veering away from her. She clutched the wheel of Alicia's car and tried to remember about not pressing too hard on the pedal, but she couldn't concentrate on things like that when so much else was on her mind. So much that was so much more important.

Billie could have used five more hours' sleep. Could have used a night in which Jesse did not have a bad dream—that brought her son to her bedside. His thumb was in his mouth as he stared her into opening her eyes. This was serious. He'd almost completely given up the thumb. "What?" she'd whispered. "What's wrong?"

By then he was beside her on the bed. "Do I have a skeleton inside me?" he asked.

Two A.M. and her son was into Human Anatomy. It would be amusing, maybe, if she weren't exhausted. "Yes," she said. "It holds you up and mine holds me up." She yawned. Wasn't going to ask why and hear the long, digressive explanation. Was not.

He stared at her, his thumb back in his mouth.

She gave up. "Why do you want to know that in the middle of the night?" she whispered.

He looked down, then at her. "How would it get outside me, like that baby's?"

"What ba——" Oh. The skeletons in the cow pasture. "Well, when you . . ." No. That wasn't going to set his mind at ease. Couldn't do the "When you grow very, very old" routine with a baby involved.

"His mommy, too," Jesse said mournfully. "Hers was on the outside, too."

"And it frightened you, didn't it?" She'd told Ivan about limiting and monitoring Jesse's TV. The news, pumped and primed only for the worst of humanity, was definitely off-limits. She lifted her son and carried him back to his room where she sat on the side of his bed while he neared sleep again. As if she'd answered anything, except by existing. By being there for him, evasive as she'd been.

"But Mom?" he murmured a few seconds after she thought he was asleep. "Ivan said it was because they were dead. That's how their skeletons got on the outside because the outside they had disappeared. Is that true?"

She might evade, but she'd taken a vow long ago to never lie to him. "Yes," she whispered back. "There was a terrible accident a very, very long time ago, before you were even born." Not exactly a lie. Maybe it had been an accident. At least, an accidental meeting with the wrong person.

Another silent spell and she was sure he was asleep, and then his eyelashes fluttered. "But Mom?" His voice was hollowly urgent. "What if it happened to us?"

No theology, no metaphysics, no philosophy was going to work here. Vow or not, major lie was called for. The lie of saying you were in control of anything important. She stroked his dark honey hair. "It won't, Jesse love," she crooned. "It simply won't. That's a promise. No bad accidents for us. No bad things. I will keep us safe. That's my job. Yours is to rest now so you'll grow big and strong."

Night Fears put aside, he slept. Billie stayed wide-eyed till dawn.

In the morning, he was all activity and smiles and they were back to trivial household concerns— he had no idea where his shoes were, or how the Cheerios box got under the sofa pillows.

Meanwhile, Ivan was making ominous murmurs about his mother's health, about how worried he was, which was nothing compared to how worried Billie was going to be if he intended any long-term relocation to his mom's north-country bedside. Billie couldn't bring herself to ask him about it out loud, to sound as hard-hearted and selfish as she knew her priorities were. In theory, she had the backup student-sitters, but the idea of the phone calls and arrangements, the juggling of their schedules—semesters had changed and who knew if they were all compatible anymore?—gave her a case of the vapors, whatever *they* might be.

At least the search for Penny Redmond was about to be con-cluded or abandoned. Emma had called someone she knew and found out that Alicia Malone's business address was that of a private home as well. The house, please God, where Stephen had lived and who would—please God still more—have had Penny living with him. And still there today. And given those givens, Billie would de-liver Sophia's message, write up the report, and that would be that.

Or it would not please fate to provide any of it, in which case, that would still be that.

Alicia Malone's house was off Creamery Road, built on the side of the street that sloped down. It looked as if it might fill like a measuring cup in a good rain, although it was set up from the ground, with lattice separating the first floor from its foundation. A causeway for the runoff, she supposed. The pale blue house had the look of something quickly constructed for transient use.

She walked down the three front steps and rang the bell, noting the peeling paint around the window frames, the yard filled with plumes of pampas grass, the indestructible scourge of organized gardens, and she felt a perverse fondness for the place and whoever lived in it.

The man who answered her ring and question said his name was Gary. He looked in his late twenties, about her own age, and was extremely tall, gangly, and unkempt. His hair, his sweats, his oversized beard, were in harmony with the yard outside. His nose was red and his eyes bleary, and she reminded herself that this was a house of mourning as she explained that she was here to see Penny Redmond.

His shaggy eyebrows raised, and he invited her in. "You could leave a message. She isn't here." His voice was hoarse and nasal. "I've got this bitch of a cold. Everybody else is gone."

The room was full of listing or sagging pieces with crocheted Afghans and Indian fabric throws covering arms and backs, and all colors faded or muddled. The coffee table was buried under sloping piles of magazines and books. Predictable rental unit furnishings, except for the computer and a strange arrangement of leather and metal in a corner.

"My armor," Gary said, following her glance. "I was getting it ready. Thought I was going to Arizona with the others this weekend. There's a war there."

"Excuse me?"

"Every year this time. A battle, a feast. In fun," he said. "We're part of a group that, well, we . . ." He blew his nose, to buy time, she thought. ". . . re-create the Middle Ages. The way they should have been. I felt too sick to go. I thought I'd work on the armor this weekend, but I haven't had the energy. Or heart."

"Because of Stephen?" she asked softly.

His shoulder twitched in a shrug. "I meant because of the cold."

She adjusted her emotional expectations and wondered how little he cared about Stephen or his fate. Had he stayed back because of the sniffles or because he had a plan to use against an enemy? The war in Arizona sacrificed to the war at home. . . .

"I won't take much of your time," she said. "I'm interested in finding Penny Redmond."

His noncommittal palms-up gesture fit all the other people she'd spoken to who didn't know and didn't mind not knowing, Penny Redmond. "She lives here," he said. "But I don't know where she is."

"Is she due back soon, or at all?"

He shrugged. "Don't know. I never could make sense of her, and she was going to have to leave anyway, and that was before Stephen—"

Billie nodded. "My condolences to all of you. It must be awful, losing a good friend, especially through violence, somebody you live with."

Gary looked as if he were considering her words, then he nodded.

"But about Penny."

His shrugs were a tic, a universal response, no matter the comment. "What about her?"

"Do you know where she might have gone? When did she leave?"

"Not long ago. She didn't say where. Look, maybe you don't know this, but Stephen was moving somewhere else, too. Because of her. Getting away from her. The girl is bad news. She ruined everything here, or he did, bringing her here."

Billie looked at the man's bloodshot eyes, at the overflowing basket of wadded tissues next to the computer, and still thought he might be faking the illness. He obviously bore a deep resentment against Stephen Tassio.

"She looked weird when she took off," Gary said. "Acted weird, too, although it's hard to tell with a girl like her. Took Alicia's car. Said she had permission, and frankly, I don't want to get involved when I already feel like shit. Last time she borrowed a car, it was Stephen's, and he went ballistic. He loves that . . . loved that car," he finished softly. Then he coughed, cleared his throat and drank water out of a glass that had been sitting atop a pile of newspapers.

"Do you know where she went that other time?"

He nodded. "Because Kathy told me she dropped Stephen—when he went after her—at the houseboats. Plus later, before he left, Stephen had this gigantic fight about it with Penny. They fought a lot, about everything, but this time it was about how she was always going there, asking for trouble. He mentioned Issaquah Dock. I couldn't help but hear."

"Do you have any idea why she went there? And more than once?"

He shrugged again. "Nope. She's weird. Doesn't have to have reasons. Nobody likes her. Not even Stephen did after a while. It's not just that she's a kid, it's that she's a baby, and they aren't the same thing. She only thinks about herself, only wants somebody to take care of her. Stephen had truly bad luck with women, probably because he was always out to rescue somebody. A kind of one-man Save the Children." He didn't smile when he said it. He looked, instead, mournful.

"But about her coming back?" Billie asked softly.

He started, then let go of a shrug. "We told her she had to move out. For one thing, Stephen wasn't coming back except to pick up and move his things. Especially the bird. Jeez—I forgot to feed her." He grew silent and Billie felt she was watching him program in feeding the bird. "We had to tell her," he then continued. "Damn, that was awful. I understand why he did it that way, but all the same. But the thing is, even if anybody liked her, which nobody did, she couldn't pay rent—she never once tried to pull her weight—and we need somebody who can. The rest of the people are gone for this weekend. In Arizona. That's why Alicia's car was here. Maybe she said the kid could take it, to look for apartments. I don't know. Not that I'm saying Penny killed Stephen, but she was definitely a millstone and they had an ugly parting. And the thing is, she could have taken Alicia's car yesterday, too. And she knew where he was. She eavesdropped."

"But you were here. You'd know if she left."

"Too out-of-it with this cold to notice."

"And this morning? She didn't let you know . . . ?"

"She was angry because I slept after we got the news last night." He shook his head in weary dismay. "Like sleeping meant I didn't care about Stephen. Like she didn't notice I was sick as a dog."

"How did you find out about Stephen?" Billie asked.

"The cops. I heard them, but I was upstairs. I asked Penny how they knew Stephen's address. He was trying so hard to keep it secret. She said it was because of the heart. This thing she wears on a chain with like 'VUX' written on it. They fought about that, too."

Hadn't the bartender said a call was about jewelry? "Why would the police know the address because of a necklace?"

"Because she found it in the field where they found the skeletons. Stephen found the first skeleton because they were looking to see if there was more stuff around. Stephen told the police about it after they found the second skeleton and he left ways to contact him. That's how they knew."

"Okay, so the police came, talked to Penny, and then what?" Her mind swirled with information that sat on its surface like oil spills.

"She went nuts. Said she was going to take care of everything, and it didn't matter that we were throwing her out."

"Did she take her things?" What felt like years ago, Billie had seen the redheaded girl drag a suitcase out of her house. Had Penny Redmond simply run away again?

This shrug was definitive. "Frankly, I make it a rule to notice as little about her as I can. Especially when she's the world's sole authority on feeling bad, angry about everything. Like the police called and Alicia gave them the number at the beach where Stephen takes messages, and Penny overheard it and threw another fit. Like we were telling a killer about him. Like Stephen wasn't our friend way before he was hers."

The police. The jewelry call at the beach could have been the police. So much for that lead. "Could I look around her room, see if she left anything?"

Another shrug, which Billie took as permission.

"First door on your right at the top of the stairs," Gary said.

The room managed to be both cluttered and abandoned-looking, the mattress on the floor, its bedding crumpled and tossed to one side, the top of the dresser littered with pieces of a broken coffeecup, paper scraps, stubs, a comb, pennies, the flat carpet speckled with the unknown, and still, a sense that nothing lived here.

Except for a small brown-and-gray hawk on a perch, scowling at her. She backed up a step despite its shackled leg. "Don't mind me," she muttered as she poked through the leavings on the dresser, unfolding papers that contained nothing of interest, opening drawers still crammed with male attire, then two drawers, empty except for a lone sock and a rumpled pair of underpants. She checked the closet and the bathroom, and found nothing to which she could ascribe significance. No sign of empty medicine-cabinet space where her things might have been. No sign of her except the two empty drawers.

He'd never given her a great deal of space. It seemed obvious that it was to be a temporary living arrangement, and, from the sounds of it, an unpleasant one on both sides.

And Penny had known how to reach him, how to make that phone call. He'd abandoned her and she'd found out where he was.

And had access to a car. Damn it all to hell. She didn't want to think in that direction. Yvonne had killed Stephen. It was the only logical possibility.

Time, then, to get on with it, to head for the houseboats. Penny probably had a friend there, a new escape hatch. All this effort to tell a runaway to stay away.

She took a deep breath and waved farewell to the little hawk, hoping Stephen's former housemates would take care of the bird. When she glanced at it, its dark eyes no longer looked angry nor did it seem as menacing. It looked hunched, small and trapped. She shuddered and closed the door behind her.

Twenty-seven

She didn't need them. She didn't need San Geronimo. She could stay with a friend—somebody who wouldn't—or whose parents wouldn't—tell where she was.

No. She couldn't trust anybody that much. She wouldn't stay with anybody. She'd stay outside.

It wasn't as if she'd freeze to death, and it hadn't rained for days. People lived under the freeway. Or maybe there was a shelter.

No. She'd stay right here on the docks, find a place to hide and sleep overnight while the film was developed.

No. She'd find a one-hour place for the film and go directly to her mother today with proof of what he was doing.

Proof positive. There it would be, the seeing-is-believing thing, right in front of her eyes, his mistress and him, the kid he bought the violin for, the way he spent their money and blamed them for needing food or college application fees. The way he hit her mother, pushed her around, terrified Wesley. With photos, let her mother try to say Penny made things up, exaggerated, didn't understand, or just plain lied. Let her try to defend taking his shit and letting him dump on her children.

And then, she'd call the police and tell them that Arthur had killed Stephen Tassio.

And when they took him away, she'd sleep in her own bed and be freer than running away could ever make her.

Penny moved slowly, checking the parking lot to be sure Arthur's car was there, then slowly progressing down the slatted walkway, wishing the woman's houseboat were closer in, wishing for places to hide, but there was only the boardwalk winding through. No side alleys, except the gangplanks leading into each houseboat. How was she supposed to get the shot, the proof?

She clutched her paper bag feeling clever for making herself look like she belonged there, someone bringing home the groceries. Plus, it was something to put in front of her face, to hide behind if Arthur suddenly appeared.

She'd taken the bag from under the sink and the cabbage that stuck out of it from the refrigerator of the San Geronimo house. The cabbage was already on its way to becoming slime and nobody would miss it. She'd stuffed the bottom of the bag with a sweater Stephen hadn't taken, the one Morgana liked to sit on. It still smelled of him, and maybe of her, or had, before the cabbage got to it. She'd put his camera in the bag as well. He didn't need it anymore, and she thought there might be a photo of her inside, maybe one of the two of them.

But she wasn't going to think about Stephen anymore. He was dead. He would have come back to her, she knew, but now he couldn't and all she could do was avenge his death.

Her head felt like static, like blurs and spots. She wrinkled her brow, stopped walking and felt lost even though there was only one way and that was ahead. She couldn't remember anymore what the photo of Arthur and the Other Woman, that photo she was going to take had to do with catching Stephen's killer. Light-headed and fearful, she felt determination and clear vision bleed out of her.

Then she remembered her mother needed proof she didn't have to stand by her husband. And remembered that Arthur was afraid she was going to tell about the other woman. Had been all along, since before she ran away, and had thought Stephen knew, too. Thought she'd be with Stephen last night and that he'd get them both. So if she trapped Arthur with her camera, exposed his secret like his worst fear, it'd be evidence for the murder, too. She'd get him for everything at once.

She could tell the police she'd had the photos earlier. That Stephen had actually shown them to Arthur to try and force him to leave the house in San Rafael. And forced to the wall that way— Arthur struck back. It could have been true if she'd thought of it sooner.

She walked forward with confidence, invincible, carrying the forces of right in her shopping bag. The little houseboat was quiet, its curtains drawn and a warm light issuing from within. Her body temperature rose at the thought, however quickly squelched, of what was going on inside.

She reminded herself of the need to stay calm.

A wave of vertigo hit. She'd forgotten something of vital importance. Lots of things. Like how she'd photograph through curtains. Like even if she found an opening, how she was going to take a clear photo without a flash. Without alerting them to her presence. Without being caught because if they did come after her, where could she go? There were sharks in the Bay. That's why people hadn't escaped from Alcatraz, and she didn't like water in the first place.

She tried to think of Stephen, think like him. Would he have said to give it up? Or would he have said to be brave, to grow up, to *do* something—*anything* except whine or feel sorry for herself? *Get control of your life,* he'd said over and over. This was what he'd meant, and she tiptoed on, toward the pastry-box square of boat.

There was no getting access to the front of it. She knew that from earlier trips. But there was the catwalk on the side and maybe at the back, the part that faced Richardson Bay's openness—nothing but birds wheeling overhead, and a dilapidated, anchor-out "pirate" boat using the Bay illegally, as homestead and toilet. The rear of the houseboat, the view of water and anchor-outs and Tiburon across Richardson Bay—he wouldn't block that with a curtain, would he? If he did, why live on the water at all? The day was clear, all fog burned off, and maybe there'd be enough light back there so that she didn't need a flash, could do her work without alerting him.

She took a deep breath, looked left and right, put down the shopping bag, shoved the camera into the waistband of her jeans, and climbed onto the narrow catwalk that rimmed the boat. Pressure rose in her throat, what felt like air bubbles popped in her brain. She wasn't good with the idea of falling into the icy Bay.

She had to be brave, she told herself with each creeping sideways step. Had to risk something. Had to *do* something, Stephen said.

She stepped as lightly as she could, on tiptoes, sideways, knowing that the anchor-out or the neighbors could see her, call out or call the police, ruin everything. This no longer seemed a foolproof or wonderful idea, but she had nowhere else to go, no other option.

Slowly she made her way to the back of the small houseboat. She thought she heard voices inside, but they were muffled and distant.

And finally she was at the end of the walk, and with one careful, deep step, down onto a small floating deck with two padded, bird-stained chaise lounges positioned for drinks at sunset, she thought bitterly, the water staining red and yellow, Arthur and the bitch cooing.

All this as she turned, eager and at the same time reluctant to see if these windows were also covered.

They were not. In fact, French doors covering the entire back of the boat were open. She crouched, half hidden by a large palm in a redwood tub, and peered around. Sunshine, intensified as it bounced off the Bay, poured through the open doors onto a polished wood floor, an oriental carpet and a carton with a stack of Styrofoam cups and what looked like trash all around it.

And nothing more she could see. Puzzled, still crouching, she edged forward, tilting her head so as to see further.

The sofa was angled with its back to the front door and it was yet again new—a old-fashioned burgundy one. High-backed brocade. A table with curved legs, a lamp with a fringed shade, the arm and foot of an upholstered chair—random pieces at odd angles. You couldn't read or talk or put things on the tables the way they were. One painting of clouds and angels—hokey, even she knew that—on the otherwise empty walls. What kind of house was this? New furniture all the time, but not enough to make a room, and none of it set so you could use it.

There was nothing else in the room except a wing chair. She edged over until she could see it.

Which was when she saw much more. The shadow of some-body just out of sight. A strange light, not the lamp's, shining on the chair and its people. A male voice, its owner also out of her line of vision, "That's it, now, again! Come on, give it more!" He sounded like the coach at school. Or a director.

And the man on the chair, his head back, his suit—his shirt and tie and suit jacket—and his knees—knees, not trousers. Bare knees, naked legs splayed, and between them, a little girl, kneeling, her back to Penny. A really little girl, she thought, her heart racing wildly at the wrongness of the scene. A little girl with a bow in her hair, a white blouse and dark plaid skirt—a school uniform and kneesocks—old-fashioned, like the sofa—a very little girl kneeling in front of the man whose eyes were closed, his mouth half open . . .

And Arthur's voice saying, "Again!" and Arthur himself, his back to Penny but no mistaking his voice or abrupt gestures. Arthur di-recting them. And the oddly placed light, the shadow that remained at an angle despite Arthur's movements—Arthur the director and the shadow, a photographer.

She wondered if they also shouted at the little girl to play the vi-olin. Or had that been for another little actress? She wanted to cry.

She had imagined another woman, but this was so much worse.

The camera. She raised it and, holding her breath, pushed.

The flash went off. When had she set it? Or it was automatic—but for whatever reason, the flash went off and Penny sensed rather than heard a pause inside. She tried to fold into herself, but she was too slow, her feet nailed to the deck, her brain swelling until it squeezed off all signals. She moved one half-asleep foot behind her—and fell, onto her rear.

The little girl stopped her hideous movements and half turned, her head tilted as if listening for a signal.

Perhaps because she didn't know what to do next. No further directions filled the sliver of silence. The narrow figure turned until Arthur Redmond, his facial muscles moving from confusion to shock to rage, stared at his stepdaughter and raised his hand, pointing, as if gathering and urging on his troops, shouting, his protests joined by the man on the chair. But it was only Arthur whom she heard shout, "I'll kill you!" Only Arthur she saw as she stood, heavy-limbed, and felt the heat of his purple-faced fury as he lunged toward her.

Twenty-eight

Issaquah Dock. She passed blue-awning shops — a deli, a wash-and dry, a bike shop—the necessities of life, and entered the parking lot in search of a greenish Ford, Gary had said. Not new. He didn't know any more than that. Sorry. His gangly body had listed toward the computer while they'd spoken.

He was another reason she was glad she had no life. Another eligible male she was delighted to have skipped.

What was the allure of houseboats to Penny Redmond? If she had indeed returned here, then it was the third time that even oblivious Gary knew about.

She didn't ponder this for long. Penny Redmond's motives were obscure, some muddle of adolescent conflicts not worth the analysis. All Billie wanted was to find the girl and move on, but every time she'd thought this was about to happen, the conclusion wiggled free of her grasp.

Three "greenish" Fords were on the lot. One a custom and horrifying lime convertible, one a silvery aqua, and one she'd call evergreen. Nobody was on the lot or at the entry to the dock, so she started walking. Worse came to worst, she wouldn't see anything out there and would come back to the lot to wait for the girl. Catch a few rays meantime.

The houseboaters were either intensely industrious and off to work, or intensely sluggish, lolling out of sight. In either case, the walkway was deserted and silent, except for soft creaks as it moved, the slaps of water against pilings, the soft music of wind chimes and the occasional outraged shriek of a seagull. What a pleasant way this was to live, with escape always possible. A sort of committed non-commitment with the promise that you could literally cut loose and take off, you and your house, if you needed to.

Although, in truth, most looked permanently settled on concrete berths. And the fantastic towering and unbalanced shapes of some made travel in them unlikely. But the idea remained appealing.

Not a sign of anyone the entire dock's length. Where was Penny Redmond and how was Billie supposed to find out? She leaned against a wooden railing lined with potted cymbidiums, tight young buds in clusters, wishing her mind were as fertile as the plant.

A door opened. Hope rose.

A man exited. Hope faded.

He looked her way.

She knew that thirties moustache. Arthur Redmond moved sideways on the walkway, looked back at the house, tilting as if to see around it.

Why would Penny have come here? Why would Arthur? Was he tracking her, too?

The open door ejected yet another Redmond, but not Penny. Sophia raced out and pushed at Arthur, who lifted his hand without looking at her and slapped her face, his attention elsewhere.

"Leave her alone!" Sophia screamed. "Don't you dare touch her!"

"You crazy?" Arthur still didn't look in the direction of his wife.

"I told you!" Sophia moaned. "I told you she knew!" Then, her voice at a high, painful-sounding pitch, she screamed at the house. "Run away! Run away!"

And as Sophia screamed, Billie saw a figure in shorts—hair like flame in the sunshine—creep around the side of the houseboat away from Arthur and Sophia. Nearest to Billie. The girl held on to the house, one splayed hand grasping the siding until the next hand pressed flat against another portion. She walked in tight sidesteps on a small ledge that ran the length of the boat, pressing herself against the siding, as if to blend into it, become invisible.

Billie's muscles tensed to move toward the girl, catch her and run with her, all of which, of course, was impossible. She was afraid to even utter a sound until she knew why Penny was hiding and Sophia screaming.

On the other hand, the assignment had obviously resolved itself. The family was together again, albeit peculiarly. Or was the runaway once again trying to escape? If so, there was no chance of that this time. Her parents might not be the wisest or brightest folk, but if they'd stop quarreling, surely even they would remember that the houseboat had two sides.

"I told you!"

"You told her!"

"I'll kill her!"

"A camera! Why else——"

No neighbors popped heads out of houses. Billie would have thought there would have been more of a sense of community here, but maybe they were calling the police or Sheriff's Office or whoever patrolled this part of the county.

All in an instant, Penny made it to the front of the house, her face contorted as she raced onto and down the tiny front stairways and away from her parents, who ceased fire when she appeared. Arthur made toward the walkway. Sophia blocked his way, screaming, "Run!" to her daughter until stoop-shouldered Arthur pushed at her with both hands and she fell against the guard rail as he moved on. "Run!" she screamed again.

And Penny did——away from him, toward Billie who watched in confusion from the end of the dock, a dead end. "Wrong way! Turn around——the other way——run!" she shouted, the bystander sud-

denly part of the action, encouraging what she'd been hired to pre-
vent.

Sophia lumbered to her feet, heading after her daughter.

Lemmings. There might as well have been a gigantic No
Exit/Final Exit sign at this end. Her peripheral vision caught something else happening at the house and she glanced its way to see
three people leaving—two men, one in jeans, carrying a large video-
cam, one wearing a suit and holding the hand of a young girl in a
school uniform. They made their way briskly off the dock, toward
the parking lot, and despite the screams and scrabbling of the people with whom they'd just been, they never looked back.

Penny shouted, "Stop those people!" Sophia glanced their way
without interest and turned again toward her daughter. "I can explain!" she shouted, but Penny waved her mother off as if she were
foul matter.

And Arthur exploded into words and motion. "Goddamn it!" he
shouted at no one in particular. "You . . ." It was impossible to tell
who he meant, and it was irrelevant because much more to the moment, in a blur of motion, he pulled something from his pocket.

It couldn't be, Billie thought. It would be insane—way, way
over the edge, but it was, and as clichéd, as stupid as the action appeared, he raised the gun and aimed at his daughter.

Sophia, screaming and puffing, ran, zigzagging in her own
clumsy fashion from one edge of the walkway to the other, like a
football player on a tricky play.

"Get out of there!" Arthur shouted, leaning left, then right.

Sophia's bulky body blocked her husband's clear view until she
stood between him and her daughter.

Billie looked at Penny. "Jump!" she said. "Jump now!"

"I'm afraid," Penny said.

"You have to!" Billie was going to have to as well. In a second. If
he was crazy enough to shoot that thing.

302

"Get out of my way!" Arthur shouted at his wife. "You were in this together!"

Billie screamed. "Call the police! Call the police! Nine-one-one! Anybody—everybody! Somebody!" Her phone was in her glove compartment, but there were at least six houses that could hear her—surely somebody was at home in one of them. This wasn't a damned bedroom suburb, this was Sausalito's houseboat colony—there had to be an artist, a computer genius, a trust baby, a cantankerous retiree . . . somebody had to be home. Somebody had to hear her.

"You!" Arthur bellowed. "The goddamned girl snoop—what the hell are you . . . ? *We* hired you—you were supposed to . . ." He grew silent, then his skin darkened. "You found her, then, didn't you? And switched sides." He waved the gun in the direction of his cowering stepdaughter, who looked at Billie in confusion. "You brought her here, you bitch." he shouted at his daughter. "A detective! Goddamned detective to spy on your own family—to ruin me!"

"Jump!" Billie shouted, although the girl was within a hand's reach.

"Sharks," Penny whimpered. "Or I'll drown."

"It's shallow here. No sharks. Jump!"

"I'm afr—"

"Jump! Get behind a boat and hide!"

The girl looked at her with wide, crazed eyes, looked at her stepfather and mother, and climbed the wooden railing.

Arthur bellowed and raised the gun just as Penny was on the top rail, her head and shoulders vulnerable above her mother's silhouette.

Sophia screamed, "Don't shoot her!"

Penny jumped and screamed.

Arthur pulled the trigger.

Sophia gasped and crumpled onto the planks.

Arthur looked down at her, then back at the end rail. His step-daughter was no longer visible.

Billie was. Very. Her outlines ached, she felt them so acutely. An accidental visitor, she wanted to say. Not part of whatever this is. But Arthur, looking again at his wife, who lay motionless, a dark stain edging her midriff, seemed no longer to notice Billie.

Billie's mind turned over the controls to her muscles. Her legs and arms reached out, forward, and she sprinted, top speed—before he snapped back, before he synthesized what he'd already done—forward into Arthur. And then used the only self-defense technique she really knew—the knee. Up, hard. Arthur's grunt sounded as if it emptied out all the air in his lungs. He doubled over. She grabbed at his hand, dug nails into his palm, felt the split second his hold loosened, and yanked away the gun.

And then she backed off, stunned, looking at her hand, as if someone else had forced the gun into her grip then forgotten to say what to do next.

But she had seen movies. You pointed it. You cocked the thing on top and pulled the trigger. Or you didn't have to cock it, you simply pulled. If thugs could figure it out, so, surely, could she. The thing was to look as if she knew, look as if she'd won marksmanship medals. The thing of everything seemed to be to pretend competence. She held up the pistol and pointed it at him. "Don't think about moving except where I tell you to," she said. "I have a phone in the parking lot. I'm going to use it. Walk in front of me and do not try anything stupid." That sounded right. As long as he hadn't left home with only one bullet in his gun this morning. Even if he had—as long as he didn't remember.

Apparently, he either hadn't or didn't. He seemed cowed, stuck in a mix of furious disbelief and shock.

And with each duo of boats they passed, she shouted again. "Call nine-one-one—somebody's shot!" She shouted it twice each time, herding Arthur.

"What did you think you were doing?" Billie asked between shouts. "Shooting your wife? Maybe your daughter? With an eyewitness here? Were you going to kill all of us—me, too? Did you think nobody would figure that out? How stupid can you be, Arthur, and for what? What is *wrong* with you?"

She enjoyed venting spleen. Easy, too, when pointing a gun. Easy to be the tormenter. The bully. Everything she hated. Horribly, guiltily, pleasurable, too. Burns the adrenaline, perhaps, blocks the physical memory of the fear.

They didn't need to go the distance. She heard sirens. Thank you, whoever had called. A sense of community—or fear—lived on. Then there they were, two men in blue, guns in their hands, followed by paramedics, running.

"Drop it!" the police shouted at Billie. "Drop it right now!"

"Okay, sure, but I'm not the—"

"Drop it, lady!"

"She killed my wife!" Arthur shouted. "About to kill me, too! Thank God you're here!"

"His wife's hurt—shot—bleeding—out there," Billie said to the paramedics, who set off, top speed, around her. She put the gun down on the boardwalk, afraid to literally "drop it" the way they said because guns went off accidentally all the time in movies, her only firearms text.

She tried for a beguiling, ingenue smile. "That's his gun," she said. With her prints all over it. "Officers, you surely don't believe I was the one who—"

They looked as if they surely did, until one of them, having taken his good time about it, spoke. "We'll decide that, but the first caller said it was a man waving the gun. Big ruckus, the caller said. Another caller said a man shot somebody. You want to explain that?" he asked Arthur.

"There's a girl in the water," Billie said. "Hiding. Maybe hurt. She's behind a houseboat. Can I— Can somebody get her back up

305

here? She'd explain everything." She sincerely hoped there was some truth in that.

Arthur's mouth curled downward sourly.

"Freeze her toes off," the blond policeman muttered. He glanced at his partner, who nodded, and he moved past Billie.

"Her name is Penny!" Billie called after him. "I don't know if she'll trust you. Even in uniform." Billie turned to the remaining cop. "She's pretty freaked-out. Could I— Could we all get back there?"

The paramedics looked up from Sophia as Billie, the second policeman, and Arthur approached. "She's alive," they said. "Bleeding pretty bad, but alive." They stood and lifted the gurney.

"Want to leave a blanket?" the dark cop said. "A girl's coming out of the water."

The medics left a packet, a silvery thermal blanket folded inside, the sort that earthquake kits supplied, and then they were off with the pallet between them. Billie heard a reassuring moan from Sophia, her eyes still closed, as they moved out of sight.

"Penny!" Billie called out. "It's okay—it's over—the police are here. Come out. Come back up."

By the time they were at the end of the walkway, Penny was being helped back up over the wooden railings by the blond policeman. She winced as she touched her foot to the ground. "I hurt it," she said. "When I jumped."

"I said it was shallow," Billie said.

"You didn't say *that* shallow."

"Low tide," one of the cops said.

"I could probably have gotten off the houseboat that way. Instead of coming back to the dock," Penny said. "Could I have walked across to Tiburon?"

Both cops shrugged. "Varies with the tide. Be chilly."

"Your mother's alive," Billie said, although Penny hadn't asked.

306

"I guess I'm glad." The girl was wet only to her waist, which was still enough to leave her shivering. She looked at Billie. "She knew. My mother knew about this."

The silvery blanket was wrapped around her. Billie stood, unsure what the girl had meant or of what to do now. It seemed less than necessary to pass on her mother's message not to return home. This job was over.

"You keep your mouth shut," Arthur Redmond told his step-daughter. "You just shut up with your lies that nobody would believe anyway. You just keep your lying mouth—"

"That's enough," the blond cop said. He looked at Billie. "This more than a domestic call?"

Penny stared at her stepfather and spoke as if half-asleep. "He wanted to kill me," she said, "not my mother. But she"—she gestured toward Billie—"told me to jump. Otherwise, I wouldn't have, and he'd have killed me."

Arthur glared at his stepdaughter. "Everybody knows you lie—"

"I said enough!" The sound and its intimations were powerful. It comforted Billie to see the dark side of the police force of postcard-pretty Sausalito, to know it existed. Once you knew Arthurs existed, you needed to know the other, too. The cop handcuffed the musta-chioed man and read him his rights.

Meanwhile, Penny was gazing at the blond policeman with much too much adolescent admiration and reverence, even given the sit-uation. Another dangerous curve ahead if she wasn't careful.

"I had a camera." Penny took a deep breath. "I took a picture."

Arthur snorted and pointedly looked at Penny's empty hands, first the left, then the right.

She stood straighter. "I left it on the catwalk. It will show you what it's all about. Not that I knew until today."

Arthur, who had been contemplating the graining of the walk-way's planks, looked up sharply.

"I thought you were having an affair," Penny said. "I thought that was disgusting enough."

Arthur stared, all bravado gone.

"Sounds like you've been very clever." The blond policeman smiled at her.

A camera? Would somebody tell Billie for what? Or was this what Emma had warned about?—her job was finished, even if she was left not knowing what, if anything, any of this had meant.

"It's about . . ." Penny looked at Arthur with revulsion. "It's about dirty movies. Probably lots of them. With a kid. Or kids. I thought it was about another woman. A mistress." Her eyes flicked over Arthur once again, then lowered, as did her voice. "And my mother was part of it," she added.

"She tried to save your life," Billie said. "She stood in front of a gun."

"We should get you to the hospital now, and for a formal state-ment," the dark cop said. "Tend to that ankle."

Penny nodded, but she stayed in place. "One more thing. He killed my boyfriend. He killed Stephen Tassio up on the mountain last night."

Billie inhaled sharply, and felt a stab of fresh grief.

"You're crazy!" Arthur said. "I don't know what you're—"

"I warned you—" the policeman said.

"Stephen went to see him yesterday, and he thought Stephen knew about this. He thought I knew, too, but I didn't, and neither did Stephen, but he thought we did. So he followed him—probably thought both of us would be in that car, and killed him."

"This is a— You can't listen to her, she's a—"

"You'll have your chance to speak," the dark policeman said. "Whyn't you go along with Officer Dunlap there and get your chance to tell your story, and how about you, miss . . ."

"August. Billie August. I'm with Howe Investigations."

"Emma, eh?" The men exchanged a cryptic look. Billie didn't ask for an explanation. Nor did they, of her.

"We'll get you an ambulance, young woman," the blond policeman said.

Penny looked crestfallen. "Couldn't you drive me?" she asked. "I don't need an ambulance. It's twisted or something, that's all."

He raised his eyebrows. "Afraid not. Maybe . . ." He looked at Billie, who silently sighed and nodded. That, for certain, would be the end of it.

"Could you drive this young lady to the emergency room at Marin General? I'll meet you there after I check out that catwalk for the camera."

It sounded like the reasonable plan, even though it was obvious Penny, shivering and in pain, would have preferred waiting for her hero. But the two awkward sets of people—handcuffed Arthur and his captor, and limping Penny and Billie, who reminded herself that the emergency room at Marin General would absolutely be the end of this—moved along. She wished it felt more like moving forward.

Twenty-nine

Billie hovered while sitting still. Technically an impossibility, but Emma felt the blonde's propellers whir as she leaned forward, her eyes on the report she'd completed, her antennae waving wildly, seeking approval. The girl sent up a dust cloud of anxiety every time she entered a room.

But she wasn't a dummy. Her report was well done. The fancy schools had taught her how to write a coherent sentence, which is more than could be said of most of Emma's transient help. Plus, to Emma's great surprise, it was short. To the point, with nothing irrelevant or tangential added in. "So the runaway ran back," Emma said. "Returned herself."

Billie flashed a look of wary alarm. Did she think Emma's remark meant she hadn't done her job? Jesus, but this girl should be on medication. Had to watch every damned word with her.

"Wish she really had gone home," Billie said. "She'd have saved me the need to make a statement and, most likely, to testify in the criminal case. And she could have saved Sophia a bucket of blood."

"Screwed-up families. . . ." Emma patted the report. "What now?"

"Me? Whatever you say—I thought that harassment thing? I was going to pose as a new hire, or have you changed your—"

"I meant with them. The Redmonds. The parts that don't get on a report."

"Oh."

Billie looked worried again. The girl needed a muscle relaxant, a stiff drink, or good sex.

"Arthur's out of business," Billie said, "of course. Sophia's got a messed-up set of kidneys. A 'Be careful what you ask for' story. She's going to be on disability legitimately. What she wanted was the cash to live without Arthur and he provided it by shooting her. She told Penny she'd cooperate with the police. Which means she'll cut a deal. She said he—more honestly, they—made 'designer' films. Repping kids' clothing didn't pay the Marin mortgage and lifestyle, and Just Kidding was mostly a front for the movie biz. These were one-of-a-kind films and not for sale—except to the man who 'scripted' his private fantasy. Sophia insisted it was akin to having one's portrait painted. A privately commissioned work of art, not pornography."

Emma snorted. "Right. The art of pandering and child endangerment and sexual abuse and prostitution." She shook her head and sighed. Too much of the genius of mankind went into justifying its stupidities. "They'll bilk us," Emma said. "I can hear Sophia whining about poverty even now. We'll sic Zack on them, but even so . . ."

Billie looked offended, as if Emma had said something off-color. Little Miss Ingenue, blue-green eyes all innocent. As if she didn't have a mortgage, bills to pay. "Money matters," Emma said. "Ethics and adventure and righting wrongs is well and good, but you still have to pay for the gas in your car and the food you eat."

Billie nodded.

She'd show she had nonmaterialistic human concerns, too, annoying as it was to feel the need to do so. "So . . . the kid, this Penny, you think she can she do the job? Run a house and take care of her brother?"

Billie shrugged. "She's eighteen. Old enough. I told her I'd check in with them. Gave them my number to call if there was any problem."

Emma raised both eyebrows but said nothing. Did Billie honestly consider becoming a surrogate mother was what was meant by not getting over-involved?

"A formality," Billie said after a moment. "They won't call me. When I drove them home, their neighbor came over and invited them to dinner and said she'd keep an eye out for them. Although with three kids under four, it's hard to believe she has a lot of free time. But in case of emergency, she's right there."

"Who's that?" Emma looked at Billie's notes. "Oh, right. The lad from Nevada."

"His wife."

Emma cleared her throat. "They have any lead on the people who were in the houseboat?"

"Depends how good a photographer Penny turns out to be. She only had one chance." Billie brushed at the air dismissively. "I know I don't need to, and I don't know if pure curiosity is a good or bad thing, but I wish I knew more, like how the operation worked."

"Well, somebody's going to be hired to investigate that for the trial . . . but not us," Emma said with a smile.

"If there's a trial. One fast photo is all the evidence so far. That, and a long spell of furniture rentals. Who'll be able to verify that the child in the photo—assuming you can see her at all—is really a child? It doesn't sound as if this is going to have a tidy ending."

"Nothing does." Emma said. "This couldn't. The Tassios are going to have to limp on. The Redmond kids. . . . Nothing real is tidy."

Billie was silent for a moment. "How did the Redmonds find those awful men? "There must have been lots, because Penny saw a different sofa go into the house every time she was there, and surely there were times she wasn't around. And the children, for God's sake—where did they find them? Where were their parents while this was going on? What happens to them now? Or do I even want to know?"

Emma liked shapely stories as much as the next person, but that wasn't how it worked. "Your report's fine," she said, ending their tête à tête. Time was money, whether or not Billie-girl could bear the idea. They'd already lost the day before while Billie chauffeured Penny to the hospital, to the borrowed car, to the house in San Geronimo, to the bus stop for her brother, and then home. She was going to bill the Redmonds for every cent of it—and fat chance of collecting any. So it was charity work, and now they needed hard currency before they became a charity case themselves. She lifted the thin file folder with the basics of the sexual-harassment suit they'd discussed.

"Meanwhile, you want me to go online?" Billie asked. "Dig more about Glenda the Good or anything?"

"Not right now."

"So that's it, then?"

"Something else?" Emma asked in a voice that wasn't eager for anything, she hoped.

"Not really." This time, Billie made it halfway to the door, then turned. "Look—this wasn't on the report. I know you think I go on and on, or babble . . ."

Like she was doing right now.

"I wanted my report to be really tight, but the thing is—Penny accused Arthur of killing Stephen Tassio. I know that isn't our business, but it bothers me. Even if he thought Stephen and Penny knew about the porno business. Why only Stephen? He wouldn't be any safer with only one of them gone. I don't know if the police are taking her accusation seriously—there's enough real stuff there before they even would get to murder, but—"

"Whoa! Arthur Redmond?"

"That's what Penny told the police. Arthur isn't charged or anything yet, but—"

Stephen's college yearbook photo had been on the front pages of the *I.J.* and the *San Francisco Chronicle*. Handsome young man, he'd been. "He didn't do it," Emma said. "Couldn't have."

Billie's head pulled back a fraction and she stood waiting, mute as a startled sheep. Sometimes Emma got the sense the woman was actually afraid of her, although it was a complete mystery why anybody would fear a plainspoken, hardworking, middle-aged woman—her benefactor, in fact, who showed Billie every courtesy and concern.

"I happen to know that Arthur Redmond was at a Bay Boosters meeting that night. Started with drinks at five P.M., right before we reached Stinson, and didn't end till ten or so. By which time, Stephen was long dead. So when and how could Arthur Redmond have done it?"

Emma could almost see through Billie's skull to one of her redeeming traits—her curiosity—as it did battle with the sheep cowering under that milky skin.

"How do you—"

"Know?" Emma asked crisply. Damn. No need to have snapped back so quickly. Her personal life was personal. Shouldn't have taken the bait in the first place. Had to show off, be She Who Knows. "Because," she said, ". . . A friend was there. He told me."

Billie turned on her blue-green stare again, and Emma began to suspect that it was a device she consciously used, a mask. That she played on people's assumptions. People exactly like Emma. The woman might be more interesting than suspected. Behind that neutral mask, Billie was raising eyebrows, asking what the story was, Toots. She was finding it difficult to imagine that Emma regularly ascertained where Arthur Redmond had been of an evening. In lieu of that, and given that the two of them hadn't returned from Miriam's until late, and even then, Emma hadn't been rushed or worried—this friend who knew must be a very special friend indeed. The sort you can contact at any time. Or the sort who is waiting at home when you return. Or vice versa. Very interesting.

She watched Billie's poker face, masking racing gears and wheels that popped with the shock of Old Lady Emma's having a male friend she saw late at night. . . . Was it possible? Could it be that Emma the over-the-hill hag had a lover?

Go ahead, deduce, deduce. Don't waste all that tuition spent on your logic courses. Detect. But she'd help, too. "The group has a tradition," Emma said. "They insult each other as a way of bonding. You know, the how ugly so-and-so or his sport jacket is, how bad his golf game is, that kind of thing. I don't get it, but neither do I have the time, energy, or inclination to analyze what makes men tick. The group, at least the money it raises, does good things for the county, and the jokes are one of the ways they raise cash—they pay for the privilege of insults. The reason I know was that the night we were at Stinson, Redmond's joke managed to offend those rhino-hides, and that takes a lot. He was so gross that even those whose race, sexual preference, country of origin, and income level weren't insulted were turned off. That's the only reason he was mentioned." She folded her hands.

"So who . . . ? I don't like to think this way, but Penny had a car that night—Alicia's—and she knew where Stephen was, and she'd been dumped. Of course, Yvonne . . ."

Emma scowled. "Of course Yvonne. But the police get paid to speculate about that," she said. "We don't." Far as she was concerned, this conversation was over, and if that was as far as she was concerned, then that was as far as it was going.

Billie started to shape a word. Emma suspected the word was *but*. Then apparently she decided against speech and merely nodded.

The *but* hung in the small office like a hard-edged modern sculpture.

"Well," Emma said cheerfully. "Good going on this one but I hope the next one's a little less physical."

BUT!

"We'll read about it in the papers," she said.

"Thanks—about my report and all," Billie said before making her exit, leaving Emma a souvenir, the two-ton *BUT!* hovering above her head. Emma stared at the window. The sky was slating over again to the point where she stood up and turned on the overhead lights. Presidents' weekend, too. So much for the myth of its balmy weather. And too bad about Billie. Bright, but she had the marks of not lasting. She'd get all entangled in the *what if*'s and *what then*'s, be discouraged by reality, and then she'd quit.

Emma wondered how long it would be before she had to advertise again. She might start a small pool with Zack and George on that.

Thirty

Billie sat at her desk, rereading the file and rechecking the clock, always surprised at how little time had passed. Finally she pushed the file away from her. There was nothing to hold her here. Two hours deferred out of the required six thousand weren't going to matter, so maybe she should go home, catch up on domesticity.

She wished she could have talked more about Stephen Tassio's possible killers, but that was a wish for Emma to revise her personality. Speculation didn't produce revenue, but the dead boy could, and *should* be given a moment's consideration. A moment's mourning, a moment's concern. Emma's overreaction was an insult.

Nor had Emma needed to act as if Billie intended to adopt the Redmond children just because she showed some humanity. They had been dealt enough insults by adults who should have been caring for them. She didn't need to add more. For God's sake, they were kids. It takes a village and all that. Why didn't Emma understand? She had kids of her own, but maybe she had wrecked their lives a long time ago.

Wesley and Penny had looked like characters in a fairy tale when Billie left them—the orphaned brother and sister, holding hands, Wesley nearly quaking with concern. And even though they weren't

in a dark wood, or under a witch's spell, they were sure as hell abandoned and had been for a long time. It was just that upscale subur-
banites did it with more panache.

She was exceedingly tired of Emma's narrow range of emotions,
and not ready to believe that a refusal to have feelings—aside from
fierce ones—was a bottom-line requirement for this job. Surely
somewhere in the field there was a more entertaining and humane
PI. And if not—if the entire profession was comprised of fire-
breathing bullies—Billie wanted to know now, before she dug in any
more deeply.

She looked at the computer almost wistfully. Stephen Tassio and
his misty kingdom were now lost inside it. She tidied her notes from
Emma's single attempt to train her. She had notes on the databases,
the CD-ROMs, the online services—the "dossiers" they'd prepared
for Audrey Miller, Talkman, and herself. She nearly tossed the lot of
them, then reconsidered. No matter where she worked, she'd need
information on begging the computer to yield up its innards.

She put the pages in a neat pile, then separated each "case" and
put them side by side so that the tabletop beside the computer
looked businesslike, as if serious sleuthing had been going on in this
room.

Maybe the next assignment wouldn't veer so close to the bone.
No children involved in the harassment thing. No rotten parents.
Perhaps, no automatic Emma—or Billie—buttons to be pushed.

She looked again at the slim file. A Mr. Barton Davies, CEO of
a company that made "tourist souvenir items"—key rings featuring
cable cars, tiny red Golden Gate bridges, Alcatraz T-shirts and mugs,
little hearts that had been left in "Don't call it Frisco." Buxom plastic girls whose breasts read "two of the hills of San Francisco."

The business was doing well. Not so, thirty-eight-year-old Mr.
Davies, one of the two principal owners, married and the father of
three. A quality-control supervisor had been let go four months ago.
Three months and three weeks ago, the former employee's lawyer

had notified Mr. Davies that the discharged worker was bringing suit, claiming her career had been destroyed by Mr. D's amatory advances which she'd virtuously put in check. He had, on various occasions, fondled, patted, propositioned, and threatened. She'd refused. He'd retaliated. Or so her suit claimed.

The defense lawyer, an old friend of Emma's, wanted the skinny on the accuser, one Tina Bright, twenty-six, divorced and childless. Wanted whatever damaging information would weaken Ms. Bright's stance as the irate madonna. Unfortunately, Mr. D was known to be a letch, but he insisted on his innocence this time.

This job sounded infinitely more enjoyable than tracking a sulky, mixed-up teen. Now Billie could work with maladjusted adults.

What should she wear? Would Emma think a question about what people who worked in a tchotchke factory wore would demonstrate ignorance or a lack of imagination? Billie felt a flare of anger — at herself for the dithers and at Emma for creating a climate that gave her the dithers.

She decided to hang it up for the week. Might as well be with Jesse during a portion of daylight hours. Make a real dinner and give Ivan bonus free time.

She pulled her bag off the back of the chair and half stood up, but reconsidered. The weekend that so beckoned her must look excruciatingly long to Penny Redmond. Maybe a call before she left. Nobody, meaning Emma, would know and Billie, upon hearing that all was as well as could be expected, could selfishly enjoy her own weekend.

Penny sounded tired.

"Thought I'd check in and see if everything's all right," Billie said.

"Guess so."

"Last night went all right?"

She could almost hear the teenager shrug. "Wesley freaked. About Mom and the shooting and all. And the cops were here, looking for evidence, and that didn't help. But it's all right. I stayed in his top bunk and that calmed him down, and when he went to school today, he seemed mostly okay."

"Did you go to school?"

Long silence. "It's just that . . . it's going to be a hassle, my missing so much. Tuesday, after the long weekend, I'll go. I kind of . . . Today, it's Friday, anyway, and with all the other things, you know?"

Billie murmured assent. It had been an incredible blow to the head—her boyfriend killed, her father a corrupt criminal who attempted to kill her and her mother—all in twenty-four hours. She must be reeling.

"The thing is . . . ?" Penny left it an open question.

"Yes?"

"Wesley should be home by now, but he isn't. I went looking for him, but I couldn't find him." The idea didn't sound complete, but Penny left more heavy air in her wake.

"And you're worried," Billie said.

A deep breath. "Like I should have been at the bus stop maybe, even though he'd hate it if I treated him like a baby."

"Does he have friends he visits after school?"

"He's not allowed to just go off and . . ." She seemed to remember that those who allowed or disallowed were not around. "He knows I'd worry."

Billie thought of the knobby-jointed boy's profound attachment to his sister. Disappearing did not sound like the little she knew of Wesley, and Penny obviously agreed.

"I mean he's not that late," Penny said, "but all the same. . . ."

Billie glanced at the doorway, making sure the prison matron wasn't around to observe what she was about to do. The door was clear, with only Zack outside at his desk. "I'm just leaving the office," Billie said. "Would you want me to stop off at your house? Help you figure this out?"

"I'd like that," Penny said. "I don't know why I'm so jumpy, but

I'd feel a lot better if he'd come home." She sounded younger and less sure of herself by the second.

"Give me time to clean up here and take care of a few things," Billie said. "And try not to worry." When she hung up, she considered what she might have meant by saying she'd help Penny figure out where Wesley was, given that she hadn't exactly proven herself a bloodhound in finding Penny herself.

Emma was right. She should back off and leave this to whatever community Penny already had, the people who knew her, knew Wesley, like the next-door neighbor. Sunny. The pretty woman with the gorgeous life. The one who'd stirred up negative sensations, a sense of having been insulted by her. Snubbed. Treated shabbily.

And then an image, like a flashcard behind her eyes. Outside a nursery school, near Billie's home, maybe four months earlier. She saw the blonde woman holding the hand of her four-year-old as they entered the building. Billie had been on her way to work at the mall, frantically assembling herself as she walked to the bus stop—her car was in the shop. She was going to be late, was going to be further in debt because of the car; her morning coffee burned at her stomach walls, her son had been having a tantrum she had to will over to Ivan, she'd felt raggedy and badly put together, and the day had barely begun. And there was this woman in a tennis outfit, the tiny skirt barely covering perfect legs, and on the wrist of the hand holding the child's, a bracelet set with diamonds that caught the morning light. And then the woman laughed, a silver-gold sound that was echoed by her child as they entered the excellent preschool that Billie was never going to be able to afford for her son.

The sight had burned itself into her retinas, stopped her dead on the pavement as if it was a physical blow.

That privileged woman with the world's options laid out like a buffet had been Sunny Marshall Billie now realized. Or perhaps not. But the image, the envy, the aversion and sorrow had been directed at someone close enough to who and what Sunny was, and Billie still felt its long-lasting half-life, even when the actual woman had been nothing but warm and pleasant. It was interesting and troubling to think about what this meant about her powers of judgment. Maybe of anybody's.

"Am I interrupting?"

Billie stifled her automatic apologies—for thinking, for breathing—and waved Emma in.

Emma entered, then stood in front of Billie's desk, declining an offer to sit down. "I'll be just a minute. Wanted to tell you . . . Well, the *I.J.* came, and—you didn't have your radio on, did you?"

What kind of question was that? She seldom did. The one day she had, Emma had been upset by the program, even though Billie was oblivious to it. She hated being forced to look up at the woman. She was tempted to stand up herself, be taller than Emma again, have the other woman crane her neck. But she didn't want to be thought of as jumping to attention, so she passed.

"Well, then," Emma said. "This should interest you."

She wasn't carrying the paper she'd mentioned.

"Maybe provide you with that conclusion you crave. 'Closure,' they call it, don't they? And everybody aches for it to happen to everything."

So she'd come into Billie's office to make sure she ended the week with a put-down.

"Me, too," Emma said. "This one's different."

Say what? Billie had to clamp her jaw shut in order not to let it drop. Emma was confessing to caring about something?

"And I did meet her."

"Her?"

"Yvonne."

"They got her." Good. As good as such a sorry story could be. "It's over, then."

"But not the way you'd expect." Emma looked around, then decided to sit down in the straight-backed chair and be eye-to-eye.

Almost as if she'd been nervous about doing it until she tested the waters. But that was impossible. Emma was as sensitive as a bulldozer.

"She's dead."

"Oh God." Billie's blood thickened and grew heavy in her veins. "What's going on?" she whispered. Death after death. "Who— What happened to her?"

Emma shook her head. "She killed herself. Early this morning, or late last night. She committed suicide—and here's the worst of it—she shot herself on the Tassios' front doorstep. She was there when Mr. T went to get the morning paper."

Billie said nothing, just let herself be possessed of the image of Yvonne's rage and ultimate revenge against the people she believed had ruined her life. The image of Stephen Senior already burdened by news of his son's death, already dreading the morning paper with Stephen's face on the front page, opening his oversized door and finding the dead girl in a pool of blood. Of Mrs. Tassio, the impeccable, the immovable. It had been a horrible but inspired ending to Yvonne's life. Death as a weapon.

"No note, no nothing, although she had a photograph of Stephen under her. The police aren't making any statements or accusations yet, but it seems fairly obvious. She'd spun all the way out of control, destroyed him and then herself. And managed a pretty dramatic number on his parents, too."

Billie sat in stunned silence, her mind filled with the image of that self-important doorway and its desecration. Then she abruptly thought of her own front door and the same madwoman standing there the day of Stephen's murder, and a valve inside her system clamped down so violently she nearly blacked out. When she breathed, the sound was jagged.

"It's over now," Emma said softly, and Billie had the odd sensation that she understood, had made the mental leap along with Billie. "For real. Our estimate of her wasn't far off the mark. Too bad.

Too bad about the boy. Too bad about both of them." She smacked her palms on her thighs. A very final, finished-with-it sound, and then she stood up. "It's Friday, Billie. We've got our ending now, that closure, so go home and do whatever it is that makes you forget about people like that."

Billie couldn't remember why she'd had such a hate on for Emma a few minutes back. She stood up, too, and nodded. "Thanks," she said. "I guess . . . I guess that was good news."

"Not really," Emma said. "But then, you didn't ask for good news. You only asked for a conclusion."

"Then that's what I'll settle for."

"Always take what you can get," Emma said. "Then at least you have something. Like long weekends. Go now. Enjoy yours."

"I will," Billie said. "I may actually get home before it rains. . . ." She glanced at the darkening windows. "Almost. And then I'm going to bed just as early as Jesse does and going no farther than my own backyard until Tuesday. I'll be at the factory at eight A.M."

"Speaking of which—when you're there, stay in touch with the office. Say you wear the beeper for your kid, you know. And don't forget to check it this time, okay? Don't get so absorbed making gewgaws you forget why you're there."

Well, God forbid they should part on a completely equitable note. But Emma had said to take what she could get. "I'll remember, boss," Billie said. "I'll try real hard."

Thirty-one

Billie approached the Redmonds' deep porch. The flowers in the clay pots were in need of water, and behind them, the house looked closed and silent. Perhaps Wesley had surfaced and the two of them were watching TV in a back room.

She rang the bell. Someday, she wanted a housey house like this. One that was part of the collective unconscious. Spacious rooms of benign orderliness. A cared-for garden. Wise papa on one side of the fire, benevolent mama on the other. Cheery family pets.

That the current occupants didn't fit the wholesome bill wasn't the house's fault. While she waited, the phantom Billie floated through its rooms, phantom-lived the life she'd once envisioned. Two artists in a rambling house. A passle of children—all adorable, artistic and precocious. Cam's sense of color providing surprises on the walls, rooms full of crafts from the world over gathered on back-packing treks with the entire clan and adapted to their use in ingenious ways. Music as a constant.

That's what she'd imagined. Cam, too, for a while. That was a nice time, while they had the same delusions.

She rang again.

Artistic, they'd said when they found their house, ready for their creative input. It had been the only one in Marin they could afford, and that, barely. For which she owed Cam a debt of gratitude. He was the one who wanted to buy, not rent, and nowadays, with her neighborhood gentrifying at warp speed, she couldn't have touched her tiny quarters, her only material asset. Rooms that were odd-shaped and cramped, awkwardly arranged. No central heat. It had been built as an unheated bungalow for San Franciscans escaping to sunny Marin from the city's summer fogs. Billie and Cam had felt sorry for its homely self and adopted it, thinking it would be temporary. Turned out they were talking about their marriage, not their house.

She rang one more time, half turning away as she heard the bell sound again through its rooms. Where was Penny? Wouldn't even a ditsy teenager leave a note? Billie hadn't been delayed that long by news of Yvonne's suicide, but maybe Penny had decided she wasn't coming.

Billie retreated down the steps. She made one tour around the house, just in case. Around the side, the narrow hedged run between the house and its neighbor. To the back, a long, sloping expanse of green ending in a rectangular plot as wide as the grounds, filled with spiny, bare bushes.

A rose garden. Had he promised her one?

But no Redmonds. A garden shack, a small stoop, and back stairs, then around to the side facing the Marshalls with a garage—one car, it looked, the way we lived then. Attached to the house. Sophia the earnest homemaker had even put crisscross curtains at its rear window, but through them, Billie saw the dark blue Lexus she'd helped Penny retrieve at the dock, its JUS KIDN vanity plate a sick joke.

Wherever Penny had gone was within walking distance.

And that was it.

She was only two steps closer to the curb before she knew that wasn't going to be it at all. Something was out of kilter and she was supposed to have learned from Yvonne to pay attention to signals.

This one wasn't even subtle. There should be a note or there should be Penny Redmond.

Maybe she'd gone next door. Sunny's kitchen was inviting. It was worth one last check. If she wasn't there, that would definitely be it.

She crossed the driveway, admiring an emerald Jaguar in the driveway. It looked newly washed and waxed. And even if it was Sunny's second car, for when she was child-free, Billie wasn't going to allow that frisson of revulsion. Of envy, really. It was all a crapshoot, and Billie couldn't go around resenting others' good fortune.

A man in a navy-and-white warm-up suit answered her ring. He had to be the Talkman, the lord of this manor, but Billie was surprised. She'd imagined him coarse-featured and burly—the sort of barely civilized brute called "a guy's guy." Potbellied or overmuscled. But he had a runner's lean look, and his features were bland, perhaps, but finely shaped. It annoyed her that he didn't fit her stereotype, although she had no idea from what pieces she'd put together her prefabricated image.

"Sorry to bother you," she said. "I'm looking for Penny Redmond."

"Oh, well, then. You've got the wrong address. She's one over." He pointed toward the Redmond's house.

"I know. But she doesn't seem to be there, and I thought maybe she was visiting at your house. I've met your wife, and she seemed close with the girl. I know she offered to help now that Penny's parents are . . ."

"Sunny's at some god-awful kiddie birthday party. Nobody else is home. No." He shook his head to make his message clear. He was obviously used to saying everything several times so his dimwitted audience could get it.

"Did she come over at all?"

"Penny? Uh-uh." He also shook his head, in case "uh-uh" was too difficult a concept.

"Do you know if her brother got home?"

"Wesley? Didn't know he wasn't there."

He seemed ordinary enough, except for the voice that sounded plumped with sweet liquid, like a cordial-stuffed chocolate. But the rest of him was nothing special one way or the other. Certainly he wasn't the foaming-at-the-mouth idiot she had pictured. Dull, even, this not-at-all-a-lad from Nevada. Was his boistrous, hundred-percent-on-air persona a lucrative act, nothing more? They said comics were often silent depressives offstage. Maybe that was also true of overly opinionated radio hosts.

Yet Sunny had fallen in love at first sight, she'd said. Billie couldn't decide with the sight of what. Maybe women like Sunny needed low-key mates, to keep the jollity balance on keel. And a whole lot of people associated a dull seriousness with significance and wisdom.

He looked mildly anxious. "I was just going for a run," he said. "Before the sky falls."

"Okay, then," Billie said. "Thanks. Tell Sunny hello from Billie." She waved and headed across and down yet again. Seldom did one find such a richness of porches in a day. Or a year. "And if you see Penny, tell her to give me a call."

"Uh-huh," he said with no enthusiasm. He stood in the open doorway, watching her retreat. Maybe he was on something. Downers. His wife left and he sneaked 'ludes.

And why was she wasting a minute speculating about him? She so quickly became involved in other people's love stories, analyzing where they'd gone right and she hadn't, searching for the big secret.

Well, the big secret was there was no accounting for taste. Sunny had been a genuine golden-girl catch. Complete with the gold. She'd settled for too little, could have and should have done better.

Which was rich—the divorced, penniless woman deciding the contented, stable one had made a mistake. Still, they'd been married only five years. After five years of her own marriage, Billie had still been pretending that all was bliss. Time would tell.

What was it about time, the idea of it, that bothered her?

She shook her head. It didn't rattle the errant thought back into place. She headed for her car.

Time, her mind said. Time.

Marches on. Waits for no man. Is money.

Time to go home and forget about this just as Penny Redmond has forgotten about you. Be grateful. End of story. She had to think about what she needed to stop for on the way home, not time.

And tide. After time. Flies. To wash our clothes, wash our clothes, wash our . . .

Time out.

It'd be Jesse and Billie alone tonight. Great. She'd rent some merry animated romp with no darkness to it, and make popcorn and they'd get in their jammies and watch. That was what it was all about. And that was enough.

It took forever to find a parking space near VideoDroid. Everybody and his sister and whining child was in the store looking to have their minds taken off the week they'd just completed.

She picked an innocuous movie about a basset hound, although she thought Jesse had already seen it. But that'd be all right. When he liked something, he liked it, and saw nothing odd about viewing it again. He had no problems with commitment. Security, not novelty, was the spice of his life. Probably grow up to be as dull as old Talkman himself.

Once in the car, she put the tape on the seat beside her and felt it bump against her cellular phone. She'd forgotten to turn it on again, not that it mattered. Billie had become conscientious about the pager. The phone was hers, for emergencies and reaching other people's pagers.

She aimed the car toward home. Friday night and Ivan would be off to a new romantic adventure. The boy did not learn from experience. Or maybe his Slavic soul, even transplanted to California, required its share of agonies.

But his heartbreak-seeking apparatus complicated her life, too, when Ivan slipped into Chekhovian darknesses and needed to talk. She reminded herself that things would ease with time. In roughly a year and a half, Jess would be five and ready for kindergarten, paid for by the state, not her. Less child care, less expense. Present chaos was not permanent. Just give it time.

Time again, still nagging.

Plus, she thought, when Jesse turned five, she'd be close to full PI status, if not already there, and greatly enriched earnings. More cash, less expense. Bliss city.

When you are five, my son . . .

Five. *That* was what was wrong. That's what it was about time. The length of time Sunny had been Mrs. Marshall. Because in those files she'd been arranging this afternoon, in that original play-search of Talkman, there'd been a pre–San Francisco wife.

She remembered and felt a fluttering excitement fill her. They hadn't found divorce proceedings in the Nevada records. She'd thought that perhaps he'd divorced in California, but now she knew he'd come to San Francisco from Nevada five years ago and married Sunny five years ago—that whirlwind courtship of two months— and their oldest child was just over four. So when had there been time to discard wife number one?

The question, pushed to the center of her consciousness, seemed important. But almost instantly, it was flipped sideways by the sight of a dark car crossing the intersection she faced, license plate JUS KIDN.

What the hell game was that girl playing? Hiding from her, then tooling out seconds after Billie left?

Drop it, an Emma-inspired voice barked into her ear. The girl's a screw-up. Don't get involved. You did what you promised. Your role in that family's life is over. You've got your own family.

But what if Penny wasn't playing games, but still searching for Wesley? Had been doing so around the neighborhood while Billie searched for her.

What if they'd crossed wires and missed each other by seconds—which seemed obvious—and Billie's nonappearance had sent Penny on some wild-goose chase? What if . . . ?

Billie flipped on her right-turn signal, and once again—but absolutely for the last time, she promised the nagging Emma-voice—went after Penny Redmond.

Thirty-two

Emma zipped her bulging briefcase and grimaced at being in thrall to force of habit. No way she was going to work tonight. George was bringing takeout. It was her favorite time when they could talk over the week in leisurely fashion, take as long as they they needed. For anything. You reached an age, and time seemed the only true luxury.

Besides, she felt stale and tired and there was no rush to the papers stuffed in the canvas case.

Which only underlined the complete lack of any need to take a bit of this home, but she couldn't resist and she didn't want to be "cured" of this problem, either. Would cost a fortune and years of boredom lying on a couch to find out she was indulging a pathological insecurity. Something her mother had done to her a thousand years ago. And then—so what? What would be better for the knowledge? Still, she felt a bit of an ass, and an obsessive compulsive one at that.

"Goofing off already?" Zack asked. "Oh, 'scuse me—I meant *taking* off."

"I am, and so should you. Get a life."

He looked at his watch. "It's seven and a half minutes before five. I'd be ripping you off, cheating you."

She picked a crumpled ball of paper out of his wastebasket and tossed it at his head. "And have a good weekend," she said. "Give my son my not overbearing, but very real love, okay? And tell him not to work so hard."

"Will do. And he will send back precisely the same and equally fervent wishes that I will deliver Tuesday morning. You'll lock up, then?" he asked, and when she nodded, he saluted her and was gone.

The phones rang. Both lines. Simultaneously.

She was tempted to let the service pick up, tell them the office was closed. But then, of course, they'd page her and it would prolong the agony. She sat down at Zack's desk and tried to remember how to avoid disconnecting anybody. "Yes?" she said after she'd pressed the first line, asked it to hold and pressed the second.

"This is Emma Howe agency?"

"More or less," she said. "Who is this?"

"Ivan."

Terse. Accented. Sense of urgency. Had the Cold War started up again, the Evil Empire resurfaced without her noticing it?

"I am nanny."

Damnation. A basso profundo Mary Poppins. So it was about Billie, wasn't it? Had to be. She had a college student tending her child, living with her, but she hadn't said the gender. His voice seemed to be resonating through a tall, burly body. Echoes of Rasputin, maybe. An in-house Russian giant. Young. She wondered what the real relationship was between Billie and this man. "She isn't here. Left a while back."

"A while? How much while?"

"An hour, I'd guess." "Can you hold a second?" Emma fumbled with the hold button while he muttered darkly about having to leave house now, this instant. "Yes?" she asked the second caller.

"Is this Billie August? Is this the Howe agency? I'm looking for a Ms. Billie August?"

Emma was suddenly sick of Billie's very name. Why all these

people calling at five P.M. on a Friday? "This is Emma Howe," she said. "Ms. August isn't here at the moment." Maybe she could fix up this high-pitched girlie-girl with Ivan. Between them they'd produce children with voices in the normal range.

"I'm calling for Mr. Bradford Davies?" She made it another question, as if Emma should agree with her, tell her she was on the right track. "Mr. Davies, is with—"

"I'm familiar with Mr. Davies," Emma said.

"Yes. Of course. And we're expecting Ms. August Tuesday morning, after the holiday weekend—?" She paused, leaving her question that was not a question dangling.

"Yes?" Emma prompted back. The exchange felt like a stupid game that would never end.

"There's been an unexpected change of plans? Mr. Davies would like Ms. August to wait until further notice instead? Could you let her know? We're sorry for whatever inconvenience this may cause your—"

"I'll let her know. Thanks." Emma switched to the other line.

"This very bad!" Ivan was saying on his line. She got the impression that he'd been speaking nonstop while he was on hold. "You know where is she?"

"She told me she was going home. Maybe she stopped to buy groceries. When she does come in, would you tell her there's been a change of plans and she's to come to the office, not the factory, on Tuesday?"

"We do not need groceries."

Her blood pressure rose. Why should Emma have an iota of interest in whether or not Billie needed to stock the larder, or in the domestic arrangements of her new hire? Neither item was supposed to intrude on this office. "Well," she said, "that's the best I can come up with. I'm sure she'll be back any minute. . . ." Why bother? Why reassure this stranger about a situation she knew nothing about?

"If you find anything, you call me, please yes?"

That kid of Billie's was going to speak an interesting variation on the mother tongue by the time he entered school.

"I have evening appointment," Ivan said. "Important arrangement."

"Sure." Emma would bet the ranch the important arrangement had to do with realigning his testosterone. She hung up. So where the hell was Billie? She'd distinctly said she was going home to hide out for the entire weekend. Made a point of it. Besides, if she knew her baby-sitter needed out by five, she should respect that.

Or maybe that nervous chatter's function had been to create static, noise to cover up—poorly—a lie. About what? A somebody still more appealing than Ivan sounded—a TGIF quickie en route? At least that would show a little . . . a little something.

She stood, deeded the phones to the answering service and frowned at the need to delay her weekend's start in order to get the message—Davies', not Ivan's—to Billie. She suspected the postponement meant he'd opted for a quick and silencing payoff that would dissolve the job before it began, which thought did not brighten her mood.

She looked into Billie's cubicle as if it would yield clues to its occupant's missing-in-action status, but all she saw were three files lined up on her desk. Three? She'd only been on the one case. She looked at them, puzzled, then laughed. Faux files. The imaginary dossiers they'd drawn up. The girl was pathetic.

And as if the word *pathetic* triggered recognition, she realized where it was Billie must have snuck off to, why she'd lied. Emma didn't know whether to laugh or cry. Billie hadn't gone to a lover— not even to the supermarket. She'd been afraid to admit she was going to Penny Redmond, to try—futilely—to make up for the insults life had handed the girl and her brother.

Well, then . . . what was the number there?

She picked up the one actual file, ruffled its pages and shook her head in amused despair. A puzzlement, that Billie. So intent and intense—look at her notes. So afraid she'd miss something important that she recorded everything to the point of tediousness. Did anybody have to know when Penny Redmond last baby-sat for some woman named Sally? She wasn't *missing,* didn't need a "last seen" or worse, "last baby-sat at." Or that she showed Sunny Marshall some necklace thing—a heart with 'VUX' written on it. And next to that, in the margin, three arrows pointing at the heart. One said: *GREEK.* The second: *Jewelry call?* And the third: *SCRIPT.*

VUX?

But in the end, she'd found the girl, which was what mattered. Not in the expected manner, not without mess and bloodshed—but that wasn't Billie's fault.

She tried the Redmonds, but got only their voice mail, Arthur sounding oily. She hung up, put the folder back in its precise formation with its make-believe kin and dialed Billie's cellular.

"The mobile number you are calling is not currently in operation or it is out of a—" Emma slammed down the receiver. She wasn't out of range—hadn't driven into the High Sierras. She was in San Rafael playing idiot Samaritan and her phone was off, damn her!

She took a deep breath. Okay. She'd page her and wait. If Billie didn't call back, and quickly, then there'd be a phone call to her later on—one that connected—to suggest that she find someone else to drive insane.

She'd give it ten minutes. Not one second more. The girl was eating into her weekend. Enough was enough.

She dialed the pager and began her countdown. And wondered why she'd never seen Greek letters that looked like they could spell. 'VUX.' She looked at the notes again, *"Script,"* she said. "She wasn't talking about a script, was she?" She made a phone call on the second line. "Reference desk, please," she said.

Billie felt in a frantic trance. She kept the dark blue car in sight, although shortly after she'd turned the corner and begun to follow it, she'd realized that Penny was not its driver. The head she saw behind the wheel was close-cropped. Adult male. If it weren't for the license plate, she'd had given up the pursuit as a mistake.

It had taken two or three blocks more before she was able to find a position in a lane beside his, from which she could see more of his face.

Harley Marshall. The Talkman. He'd said he was going for a run.

She was worried at first that he'd see her—then not worried at all. Who cared? She wanted—would—demand an explanation. What logical reason could he have for driving the Redmonds' car? She'd seen the Jaguar, for God's sake. She'd seen this car in the Redmonds' garage. And where were the children?

He couldn't be going to retrieve them because they couldn't have gotten anywhere far on their own. Wouldn't have even if they could.

She thought about calling the police, but didn't know what she'd be reporting. I see the wrong person driving a car, Officer. Where, they might well ask, was the crime in a neighbor's borrowing wheels?

Then Emma. She needed to talk to Emma even if Emma ranted and raved and screeched about this. She reached with her right hand for her phone and turned it on, dialing the office number in a series of frantic stabs while she kept her sights on the dark blue car.

The exchange answered, promised they'd be in touch with Emma. "Say it's an emergency!" She wondered if it was one even as the words came out. But the service meant that Emma had gone for the day, maybe for the weekend. Who knew when she'd decide to call in for messages? And it wasn't going to do any good to insist this was an emergency—Emma had pretty much told the service that everybody considers their need an emergency, and weekends, particularly Friday evenings, were sacrosanct. People who might really need her knew to tell the service to beep her.

She could do that. She kept forgetting about the thing. Nobody used it to reach her, anyway. But she had it. Thank God. She reached for the phone again, and punched in Emma's pager's number.

And froze. What was the number for her to return? What was Billie's cellular phone number? She glanced down, turned the phone over, examined it even though she knew the number was not on it. She'd barely ever used it, never had to tell anybody its number, and it had plain and simply fallen out of her mind. There was a way to bring it up, buttons to punch, but what were they?

Had she written it down anywhere? How could so much depend on such a stupid thing?

She needed to pull over, think this through, make her mind work the way it was supposed to, the way it usually did, but then the blue car might get away altogether. Thank God for Friday-night commute congestion. He couldn't move too quickly, which was lucky for her—

Her pager buzzed. She nearly wept with relief.

Emma stood tapping her foot, waiting. Finally she sat down at Billie's pitiably neat and insignificant desk. There wasn't anything worth snooping through in here, only those files she kept as souvenirs. Maybe she was afraid of forgetting what was available on the computer. Emma flipped open the one about the dog-groomer. There, next to the notes, in the careful hand, underlined, was the CD-ROM source. That must be why she was clinging to them. She opened the one about the radio fellow. Excessive notes again. Everything. What a worrier. Did she realize that in a few weeks, this would all be second nature to her? Look at this: *elim. 'Illogical' poss—e.g., a Marshall b. '35 too old, one b. '92, too young, lvs. Harley.* Why write that down?

Reg.vote Rep. in Nev. (prob would be in Ca., too?) Mar. Rec. on disk e.g., Harley m. Genia Ann Christophe, 1989 (so

track thru maiden name, too?) L. V. No div. Rec. Maybe CA—
by County.

Those rich-kid schools of hers had taught her that more is better. Jeez, but they'd forgotten to say that thoroughness was different
from clutter. The real, the necessary, and irrelevant junk all tossed
in there together.

She looked at her watch. Six more minutes. Her eyes wandered
back up the page filled with the small, tidy script. Genia wasn't the
current Mrs. M, was she? She opened the Redmond file and found
it, as, of course, she knew she would. Sunny. Genia's nickname? Except—here it was. Married five years, three children (boys), aged
four and two-year-old twins. *Love at first sight"*—she even wrote
that. Emma shook her head. The girl's mind was an open pit—ready
to receive whatever was thrown in. Trash, treasure, dead bodies . . .
Genia Christophe. She looked at her notes on her call to the library.
Genia. Gamma, that looks like a "v" when written. Christophe. Chi,
that looks like an "x" and Mu, for Marshall, in the middle like a
proper monogram. Mu, that's written like a "u." *VUX.*

Four minutes. Might as well use them. She looked at Billie's
meticulous entry about Genia Christophe, looked at the length of
Harley's marriage. Considered looking under Marin County for a divorce record for the first Mrs. M, but decided not to waste the time.
Nevada was where they'd lived. Nevada was the place for "quickie"
divorces, not California, where property had to be divided and all
manner of mess delay, and conflict occurred. Why move to the difficult state to split?

Then she changed her mind. She would use the data bank after
all. Not, however, for divorces. It was births, not dissolutions, she
was after, and more's the pity.

Thirty-three

Billie pulled the beeper off her belt and held it in a shaky right hand while she drove. The blue car headed down congested Second Street, onto San Pedro Road, then stopped, caught in traffic. Every commuter had suddenly craved food, and the lines into the full parking lots around Trader Joe's and Whole Foods resulted in standstill chaos. The better to read the beeper, then.

And the number to call was—her own damned home! Disappointed anger was immediately replaced by panic. Ivan wouldn't page her except in an emergency. She pictured Jesse—then stopped, willing the awful images away as she punched in her number on her phone and held her breath until she heard Ivan's "Yes? Hello?"

"What's wrong? What—"

"Why you aren't here? Your boss says you were coming home. I told you, I am sorry to inconvenience but Robin, the girl from my history class—"

"Ivan, stop talking, this is—"

"You understand she is waiting right now. I tell her I would be—"

"*IVAN!*" He putted to a stop. "I'm sorry—honestly, but something happened on the way home and would you *please* call the office, right now, this instant—no, call Emma's cellular. This is an emergency—tell her to call my phone. Tell I didn't use my beeper because I can't remember my phone number, but she has it in the office. No—don't tell her that—*you* have it, repeat it to her." Why hadn't she thought of him? Her mind was all flying trash. "Pray God she hasn't left."

"I just talk to her. Something for you about Tuesday and a factory—"

"Ivan—now! I'm in big trouble!" That would do it—an external threat trumped romance. "I'm in danger!"

A lie was excusable. Telling him she was in a state of confusion, experiencing possibly baseless and definitely inexplicable anxiety wouldn't activate his rescuer fantasies.

"I come there," he immediately said.

"No! Call Emma—you watch Jesse, and I promise to be home as soon as I can. But I'm afraid—I'm afraid something awful is going to happen to two other children if you don't make the call. Tell her that—tell her that Harley Marshall is driving the Redmonds' car. You have that?"

"Harley? Like big American bike?"

"Never mind! Harley and the Redmond kids are missing. Now! Okay? You have her number—it's on the refrigerator, see it? Okay? Call it. I have to concentrate on driving. Got it? Harley—Redmonds. I'm hanging up."

She drove on. What had prompted those words about the Redmond children? Had she even consciously thought that before she'd heard herself say it?

But they were missing—she kept looking in vain for a head, an arm, any sign that they, too, were in the car, being chauffeured. Penny's mop of red hair would surely show—unless she was tied up, or down, or stashed somewhere. All those scenarios were dreadful.

If the kids were in the car now, where had they been when she was at their door and wandering around the grounds? And, why should Harley's being with or near or somehow involved with those children feel ominous?

Because he said he was going for a run before the sky fell.

Maybe he simply had changed his mind.

After all, the two families were close. Sunny had been the one who had the only real information about Stephen, who monitored Penny's moods and new romance, who'd shown her how to use makeup and talked to her about love at first sight, who underplayed her privileged upbringing and standards by being kind about the inferior quality of Penny's "lavaliere."

That same worthless trinket that Gary said Penny and Stephen had quarreled about. A love gift from Stephen, Sunny had thought, but Penny had found it in a field in West Marin during one of Stephen's medieval outings. The field where the bodies were found. The quarrel with Stephen was about going to the police.

And at Stinson—the phone call for Stephen. That message about jewelry.

Stephen. People shifted, relationships changed, and old meanings were blown up and around. The incomprehensible began to make sense, and if she'd thought confusion was bad, this—this almost-knowing, being this close to seeing what did make sense and why—was much worse.

Her phone rang. "Emma?" she said. "Don't holler at me—" Goddamnit, why say that? Why admit . . . "This could sound crazy, but I don't know what I should do. I went to the Redmonds and they weren't there, then I saw—"

"Tell me where you are!" Emma snapped. "I'm on the way to my car now—keep talking. If we get cut off, I'll call back."

Emma was on her way? This was almost as staggering as the speculations that had made her light-headed.

"I called the police but we need some kind of location—where are you? Where is he?"

"I'm afraid that maybe he already—that they aren't—"

"You talk too much. Where the hell are you?"

She told her, heard silence in return and, with no other options, drove on. Even by the time she inched beyond the shopping center and the high school and traffic thinned continuously as commuters turned off San Pedro Road for the side streets that led home, there was still no sign of Emma's blue-gray Toyota and her phone's speaker was silent, except for occasional static.

Billie had never felt more alone.

The phone suddenly snapped out a question. "You still on San Pedro?"

"Emma?"

"Who the hell else would it be? You on San Pedro? About where?"

"Just past the tennis club. It's starting to rain. Where are you?"

"Around, okay? And I know it's raining. Do your best. This is like two-car surveillance. I'm ahead of you. Took all the side streets I could. So you just had another lesson, all right? Listen, I'm hanging up to give the police our location. I think he's headed to China Camp. Big, loose, empty park this time of night, this time of year. Cops'll come around the back way, be there when he arrives."

"They believed you, then. I was afraid they'd think this was a ridiculous . . ." She let the question dribble off as she felt, then heard, Emma's heavy silence. That Emma would not be believed was ridiculous.

"He had a daughter," Emma said. "Amelia. Born six years two months ago. Now hang up and keep him in sight. Be right back."

A baby girl. No-fuss divorce. He meets a beautiful rich girl on his interview and that's that. Who'd ever know? The wife thinks she's making a move. He pulls off the road in ranch country and boom—they no longer exist. He drives on and starts a new life. The Nevada people figure a divorce in California, and vice versa, and so it goes. Lost contact. Divorce is like that. See my new kids?

Penny finds the heart. Tells Sunny, who maybe tells Harley about

Penny's romance, the heart. And Penny becomes a link to the past. But why Wesley? Simply by being tight with his own sister? By being the innocent bystander. *Both* kids were innocent bystanders.

She pictured the police coming around the peninsula from its other side, arriving at China Camp before Harley, dousing their lights and waiting in the dark, and it calmed her. But all the same— why hadn't Emma called back? How was she supposed to tell her what was going on?—how much harder it had become to distinguish the dark blue car from its fellow travelers as it melted into the wet night sky? A set of taillights seen between swipes of the window wipers was all. She had to get closer.

Was Emma having trouble reaching the police? Had they not believed her?—had that all been bluster? Where *was* she, and— Jesus Christ! They weren't even near China Camp—weren't at the end of the road yet, weren't around the turn and— Was that him? Were those his lights turning right?

And Emma miles ahead, unaware nothing was approaching her anymore?

Billie veered right as well, without knowing where she was headed—looked at the street sign and could not read it at this speed and without light, but dialed anyway.

"Yeah?" Emma's voice said. "Okay, you're back. Good. What idiot cut us off? Now I'm—"

Emma couldn't be speaking to Billie. Her voice had no contempt, no anger at having its directions disobeyed, and the idiot mentioned was a third party, not her.

"Emma, he—"

"Billie? What are you—? I got cut off from the— How the hell can I get through to them if—"

"He isn't going to China Camp! He turned off already—to the right where the road splits. I'm behind him, but I swear to God I have no idea—"

"The quarry," Emma said. "Or McNear's. Or the brickyard."

" '*Or*'?" How far apart were they? How would the police pick one? How could anybody get anywhere in time, then?

"I have to get that dispatcher. Just—keep him at bay. Delay. Protect yourself. I'll be there. The cops'll be there."

Where? Either-or? Fine. Right. Delay. Protect self. Save world. "*How?*" Billie wailed.

"That's my name," Emma said, and hung up.

Thirty-four

It became a blur of determination, of rain, of wind that made the landscape shiver. Of fear and dislocation, the terrible sense of being locked in a nightmare. Traffic thinned— she could make out his taillights, could follow more discreetly. But that in no way lessened her terror.

Where were the police? She tried to tell herself that this was all going to turn out to be a case of error. Innocent mistake—hers. Harley Marshall would have good reason for driving the Redmonds' car. She would apologize.

Except here they were on a Friday evening on a deserted road in the dark, heading toward a brickyard or a quarry. How to write that off as innocent?

And how had she become a part of this parade? The noise of the wind and rain made her yearn for home, her son, the place where she belonged. Instead, she was lost and sliding toward worse, and all she'd wanted was to understand—never, ever, to play superhero. She didn't have what it took—would never have auditioned for the role.

Jesse, Jesse, she repeated like a mantra. *I'm so sorry.*

She decided that she'd turn back as soon as she knew precisely where Marshall was headed. She'd call the information in to Emma and let the officials take over, and with that decision, she felt enormous relief. She'd be safe. Jesse would be safe. She'd get her bearings back. Now, although she could place herself as approaching the tip of San Rafael and the Bay, she had the sense of being nowhere, off the map.

The growing noise and press of the wind against the sides of the car, the tilts and slides of the green landscape, the rain that clouded the windshield dislocated her further. She stayed as far back as she could, let the occasional other car pass her, and tried to look as if she were not following him.

They passed the entry to a business. Brickyard, she saw. One option down. She felt an irrational surge of hope. If he wasn't going to the brickyard, maybe he wasn't going anywhere frightening. Wasn't doing anything less than honorable, the idiot voice inside her piped again. This was all a mistake, a misunderstanding.

And then JUS KIDN swerved to the right and accelerated. She couldn't make out a sign, if there was one, and cautiously followed up a wide drive. The blue car skidded to a halt and careened in a violent U-turn, heading directly toward and then past her. Now she could see dimly, black on black, the silhouettes of enormous machines against the sky. She was outside the quarry. He'd tried to head into the quarry. She could see the heavy chain-link fencing that had caused his U-turn change of heart. There was no good reason for him to have tried to go there at this hour, to have expected the doors to be open, allowing . . . what?

By the time she was back on the road, there was only the twink, then disappearance, of a solo set of taillights.

I will turn back as soon as I know, she reassured herself again. I will do what's right, tell Emma, then leave.

She followed the lights. McNear's it was, unless he surprised them again. She'd been there with Jesse last summer. Sunlight flooded each remembered image, made them painfully beautiful and jeopardized. The pretty beach on Rafael Bay. The fishing pier lined with seagulls watching the waters. Volleyball courts, picnic tables. A large swimming pool. A sense of being on a pinprick of land in a world of water.

She looked behind her before turning in—no lights, no sirens, no Emma, no anyone. They were on another road, would have to backtrack to get around the expanse of China Camp's trails. Marin needed more asphalt, direct lines instead of all these protected open spaces. But there must be a fire trail, some secret back passage for the law to take. For times like this.

The dark around her thickened. And then, again remembering that summer day with Jesse, she felt a surge of excitement. This was a park with a gatehouse, an entry fee—a ranger. He'd call for help. He'd *be* help.

Except he wasn't there. The little house stood empty and a sign nearby suggested an honor system of payment until the park closed at seven P.M. Maybe then somebody would return to check on things, although tonight, maybe not. Not even desperate teens were willing to be blown around and doused for the sake of illegally drinking a beer.

What was he doing in there? Where were the children?

Images of two new graves on the shallow strip of beach flashed across the dark windshield. Stephen Tassio's face, that she'd never seen alive and animated. She'd been too late for him. Trailing too slowly.

Harley must have killed Stephen. Harley was a killer. The phone call—the man about the jewelry. He'd known that Stephen was involved. Penny had told her about the visits, the battle about the pendant.

Poor, poor Stephen. If that was what happened, then poor Stephen. The innocent middleman. Trapped by the fluke of finding a glittery piece of costume jewelry somebody else thought endangered him. Or of befriending a troubled girl.

Poor, dead Stephen.

There couldn't be any more murders to protect earlier murders. Not on her watch.

She dialed Emma. *"The mobile number you are calling—"*

Don't panic. Don't despair. Had to mean that Emma was around the corner, that the quarry blocked the signal. Didn't mean anything—the troops were approaching.

While down on the beach . . .

Move faster. No more lost children. No more small skeletons. No more Stephen Tassios. She put the car in gear and drove forward, only her parking lights on. She could run him over, use the car as her weapon. Or not—she'd simply see what was happening—be able to tell the police when they arrived, speed things up and avoid confusion. The thing was to go forward.

Her pulse beat hard in her throat and ears—she could hear it, as if she'd just run miles.

And then it was smothered under a hard, shattering explosion. Glass. In the woods. Under her tire. Beer bottle. Soda bottle. Some bottle. She felt the tire sag, the car tilt and drag lumpily.

Stranded in the rainy woods with a killer.

And they were still there, on the beach, with time against them no matter her problems. She had her feet, her wits. If she stayed paralyzed in her car, which was her impulse, she was a sitting target. His last victim had been in a car. She refused to be the next.

Use the brain, it's all you have.

She left her car, clutching her raincoat tight. It wasn't sufficiently warm or waterproof and the wind entered between each thread. She trotted down the path toward the parking lot, slowly, trying not to slide on wet leaves, mentally mapping the landscape ahead, based on the one Sunday she'd visited with Jesse. She had forgotten how long and winding the road into the park was—doubly so on foot. How many eucalyptus trees lined it, creaking and moaning in the storm.

They broke in high winds, she knew. Too brittle. Burned, too. Too oily. They seemed out of a horror film, echoing the protest she felt, threatening to crack as she ran and slipped between them on the endless path, as they reached for her, blowing and contorting into nightmare shapes.

Finally she rounded a curve and was on the parking lot that faced the open Bay. Far off, the San Rafael–Richmond Bridge, the East Bay refineries.

But here, no sign of life. No adult, no children—no car on the parking lot. As if they'd blown into nothingness. Lifted off and taken out to sea. Or never existed in the first place.

She ran to the left toward the beach, her breath a harsh sob, her wet hair stuck to her face.

No one. She went closer to be certain—the dark wet made vision nearly impossible. They weren't there. They weren't anywhere.

She ran up the small rise to the swimming pool, afraid she'd see the children facedown in it. And he'd be gone—out a secret exit he knew. Out for a run all the way home. *"Got caught in the storm,"* he'd say.

Of course, people would say the Redmond kids had broken in for an illegal swim. Too bad about those kids.

But the pool, inside its high, locked fence, was deserted.

No one was on the long fishing pier. Not even the seagulls.

She walked back to the parking lot and stood sniffling, stymied until she realized she was ignoring the other side of the lot. Beyond the volleyball court, beyond the picnic tables, beyond the portable toilets. She and Jesse had never gone in that direction and, in fact, few did. It wasn't scenic or inviting. She wasn't even sure it was officially part of the park, because the place dwindled from manicured hillocks and walkways into unsculptured nature and then, the look of a small dump, where rocks, cement and old boards were tossed haphazardly. No beach, just a stony, difficult edge to the land. This side bordered the quarry which lay behind the low, littered rise. She could make out the tops of the towering machinery from this side, too, and a fence on the little hill, with KEEP OUT signs.

As her eyes scanned the dark corner, she saw a still-darker bulk against the rise. She reflexively ran toward it. Had he left the car, left them dead inside? Wet as it was, the hair on the back of her neck rose.

No one was in it, at least in the seats, and the trunk was open. She stared at that. Spacious enough to hold somebody. Definitely Wesley. And if Penny were in the backseat . . .

No one was in it now. She listened, but heard nothing except the endless rustle of the buffeted leaves, the moan of the wind, the smack of rain. Nothing. And there was nothing else and nowhere else to look. She stood defeated.

Then realized there was a somewhere else. So obvious that she'd missed it. The enormous expanse of water bordering this tip of land. She looked again at the quarry fencing, wondered that he'd parked so close to it, and trailed it over the crest of the small hill down toward the water, where it extended as a barrier about twenty feet out. Not far enough, she thought. Tempting for kids who could too easily take the dare to get around it.

And now she saw them, and his plan. They were all no more than shadows. She moved closer as silently as possible. This was probably a substitute plan for when the quarry had proven impregnable. Anything to play to the idea that the Redmond kids had gotten themselves into fatal trouble. People would *tsk* over it, shake heads in sorrow—that Penny Redmond was certainly a bad influence, encouraging her little brother to go into the water on a night like that. She had seemed so responsible when she baby-sat, but something must have snapped. Ran away, then this. Maybe because of the stepfather. Just thank God she stayed sane while she was with my kids!

But while she heard those future voices, Billie crept toward the shadow people and finally made out the rocky edge of the land.

354

She saw only two of them at first. Harley carried Wesley into the shallows, along the gate. Billie saw the torn and twisted spots in the fencing—the marks of other would-be intruders. It was too easy, too much a setup to wedge their bodies in the preexisting holes. As if he'd found a custom-designed murder site. And it would be totally believable that the storm-encouraged tides had driven them there, wedged and trapped them.

Wesley's head dropped onto Harley's shoulder. He looked like an overgrown child being taken up to bed.

He'd drugged them. They'd have properly water-filled lungs when found. The rain was a lucky break for him, gave an unexpected sharp edge to their supposed prank, made it more believable that only tragedy could be its result.

She stood above them, watching Harley's careful slow steps. He had the boy in both hands, which meant he was unarmed, for the moment. They were as equal combatants as they ever would be. She squatted and searched the ground until she found a fist-sized stone. And then another.

"Stop!" she screamed as loudly as she could. "Stop that right now!"

It took awhile for her bellow to register in the surrounding din, but Harley looked up at her with no sign of comprehension. "Everybody knows!" she screamed. "The police know. There's no point—put him down!"

She saw Penny now, below her, sitting propped against the low rise. Her hands looked bound and she stared at Billie with a drugged, dull-eyed lack of interest. "You shouldn't be doing this," Harley said, and even through the rain, his voice was rich and convincing.

"Put him down!" she screamed again. And if he did? Then what? Then Harley could use his hands. She'd be worse off.

Then . . . then she'd have another idea. Their car, maybe. Tie Harley up. Leave him. "Put him down!" she screamed again, and to her amazement, he did.

And started toward her, reaching into his pocket. She saw it then, the glint of metal in his hand. He had a knife.

She had a rock. She raised her arm and aimed. He was a perfect target, directly below her and so resolutely enraged he barely reacted to her arm in motion. Barely reacted at all until the rock hit his midsection, the knife flew out of his hand, and he fell with a shout.

She scrabbled down the short hill, sliding and tripping, toward the children. But his hand grabbed her ankle, pulled her sideways, down. . . .

Not a big-enough, hard-enough rock. Not enough.

"You're dead," he snarled. He held on to her while he twisted. Looking for the knife, but it wasn't near enough, and it was too hard seeing anything clearly and he was too winded to be completely mobile and dangerous. Yet.

She had a minute and another rock. All he had was her ankle.

She kicked at his hand with her other foot, kicked as hard as she could, hoped to hear breaking bones, but settled for a momentary loosening of his fingers. And she scrabbled to her feet, digging into her raincoat pocket at the same time until she stood, looming above him as he tried without success to get his footing again.

This one to the head. No squeamishness. Not thrown. Pounded. This was the end of of the line. Whoever she'd once been, she wasn't anymore. She was going to kill.

She raised the arm.

And felt it pulled down from behind as a voice said, "Don't move. I have a gun aimed at your head."

Harley Marshall, who'd been halfway to sitting again, looked up and over, then silently lay down flat on his back. Obedient man.

"Your radio show stinks, too," Emma said. "This is a pretty extreme way to get you off the air, but whatever works."

Billie hadn't heard the car, hadn't heard her. "Emma," she whispered. "Emma, I thought—"

"Why don't you untie the kids?" Emma asked her. Then she spoke into her phone. "The side next to the quarry. Down by the water," she told someone.

"What happened to everybody, where were the—"

"Bad accident on North San Pedro. Fatality and injuries. They had to stop, call for help. I came as soon as I could."

"God, I can't thank you enough, I was so—"

"The kids, Billie."

Billie felt the flash of resentment, and then she looked at Emma, her steel hair flat and dripping onto her face, the gun aimed at Harley, who looked bizarre on his weedy patch of earth, lying like a sunbather in a storm. And Billie smiled, nodded, and went to untie Penny Redmond. And as she did, she saw headlights, heard voices, and was glad of the rain so no one could tell that she'd burst into tears of relief.

"You did it, then," Emma said. The police had taken Harley to the lockup, Penny and Wesley for observation. Harley had practically tortured Penny to try and find out who else knew about the heart and its engraving. Triple-A had towed Billie's car and Emma was driving Billie home.

"I didn't do it," Billie said. "You did. Kind of like 'Superperson.' You appeared out of nowhere and descended upon us in the nick of time."

"I had a more efficient weapon, that's all. But I saw what you were doing. You were going to smash his skull. Kill him."

"And you'd consider that a loss to mankind?"

"I'd consider it a mess. A PI is not supposed to be—"

"—involved in an active homicide case," Billie continued in a singsong voice for her employer.

"—the *perpetrator* of a homicide case."

"That rule wasn't in the book you gave me."

"It didn't say you couldn't murder people?"

Billie shook her head. She was drenched and exhausted and filthy. And in a state of quiet joy.

"Ach," Emma said. "That's the problem with book learning. Leaves things out. That's why the excellent on-the-job training I provide is so important."

"So this was another goddamned learning experience," Billie said.

"Sure as hell."

"Then these hours—they count, right? Against my six thousand."

"I didn't tell you to go chasing after a car."

Billie leaned back in her seat. Of course she was going to count them. Of course Emma was going to behave as if she'd somehow robbed her via those two—make it three—extra hours. But as that still left Billie with five thousand nine hundred and twenty-seven more hours to go, and probably just as many head-to-head arguments with this difficult, admirable woman, why waste breath now? Just because, in its own bizarre fashion, their test of wills, battle to the death, was enjoyable? At least it seemed so right now.

Not a perfectly happy ending. There were too many casualties. But Emma had said to be contented with a just plain ending. And Emma, it turns out, was sometimes right.

And that was good enough.